Praise for *The Gir*

"Father-and-daughter authors Ted and Rachelle Dekker deliver a suspenseful story of light and hope in the midst of a dark and fearful world in their first joint writing adventure, *The Girl behind the Red Rope*."

BookPage

"The Dekkers have conjured a propulsive end-of-the-world saga that doubles as a provocative examination of religious obedience and faith."

Publishers Weekly

"The powerful metaphors woven into this eerie tale are meant to be savored, but the book's suspenseful plot drives the story forward at a racing pace, making this a riveting novel that will long haunt readers."

Booklist, starred review

"*The Girl behind the Red Rope* ramps up the stakes with each new page and catapults readers into an intense, action-packed ride through the most treacherous world of all."

Family Fiction

"A gripping story that had me examining myself, holding my breath, and guessing to the end."

Interviews & Reviews

"*The Girl behind the Red Rope* is a deep read. One that shows how easily human beings can be deceived and betrayed. . . . Overall, it was a great tale. I recommend it to all."

Urban Lit Magazine

BOOKS BY RACHELLE DEKKER AND TED DEKKER

The Girl behind the Red Rope

NINE

RACHELLE DEKKER

R
Revell
a division of Baker Publishing Group
Grand Rapids, Michigan

© 2020 by Blue Monkey, Inc.

Published by Revell
a division of Baker Publishing Group
PO Box 6287, Grand Rapids, MI 49516-6287
www.revellbooks.com

Printed in the United States of America

Library of Congress Cataloging-in-Publication Data
Names: Dekker, Rachelle, author.
Title: Nine / Rachelle Dekker.
Description: Grand Rapids, Michigan : Revell, a division of Baker Publishing
    Group, [2020]
Identifiers: LCCN 2020008338 | ISBN 9780800735968 (paperback) | ISBN
    9780800738693 (hardcover)
Classification: LCC PS3604.E378 N56 2020 | DDC 813/.6—dc23
LC record available at https://lccn.loc.gov/2020008338

The author is represented by The Fedd Agency, Inc.

This book is a work of fiction. Names, characters, places, and incidents are the product of the author's imagination or are used fictitiously. Any resemblance to actual events, locales, or persons, living or dead, is coincidental.

20 21 22 23 24 25 26   7 6 5 4 3 2 1

PART ONE

There will come a time when you believe everything
is finished. That will be the beginning.

Louis L'Amour

ONE

OLIVIA'S LUNGS BURNED as short bursts of air escaped her mouth. Her pulse pounded violently inside her head and for a moment blocked out everything but the vibrations of her feet slamming against the forest floor. But as quickly as the world had gone, it came rushing back in, and she wasn't alone. Lucy was behind her, and the group of armed mercenaries was closing in.

A dozen, maybe more, had descended upon the small motel. They'd come from all sides, clothed in black and armed to the teeth. She and Lucy had narrowly escaped out the fire exit and into the thick of the forest. The trees were a godsend but difficult to navigate. And they were two against many. The odds weren't in their favor.

Olivia listened for the buzzing of radio static, the hustle of approaching boots, but it was hard to hear through her heavy breathing and panicked inner voice. They were supposed to have more time. She thought they'd be one step ahead. She had under-estimated them, a mistake she couldn't afford.

She heard rustling a few yards to her left and changed course. Pockets of moving lights dotted the darkness as their pursuers' flashlights bobbed. They were closing in.

She looked back at Lucy. "Stay close," Olivia said. The girl did, following only a couple of steps behind. Lucy could easily outrun her, but she was faithful to do exactly as Olivia directed. Always so obedient. Always so consistent. Even as a child, Lucy had been Olivia's favorite.

She pushed any thought of the past from her mind. She couldn't get distracted. Saving Lucy needed her entire focus. The past was behind them, and only what lay ahead mattered.

Through the light of the piercing moon, Olivia could see the ground sloping down. She charged for it, picking up speed, Lucy right behind. They plunged down the side of the small ravine, ankle deep in fallen leaves, an icy chill nipping at Olivia's cheeks.

When the slope met flat ground, she lost her footing and stumbled, narrowly avoiding spilling onto her face. She paused only for a heartbeat, then ran west. She knew where the moon was and used its position to guide her. Their salvation was west.

Lucy was close enough that Olivia could hear her steady breathing. Not rapid and broken like Olivia's. The forty years that separated them played a part in why. But only part.

They hadn't put but a couple of yards between them and the steep slope when the flashing lights crested the edge. The trained hunters were too fast for them to outrun. Olivia needed a different strategy. Her mind tumbled across potential solutions, landing on only one that gave Lucy a chance for escape. They needed a moment of cover.

Olivia searched the darkness, looking for a space. Collections of thick pine bushes scattered throughout the forest would have to do. She raced toward a large grouping, ignoring the ache in her knees. She maneuvered around and slid to a stop behind the prickly thicket.

Lucy pulled up behind her. "We shouldn't stop," she said.

Olivia placed a finger over Lucy's lips and pulled her closer, dropping to a squat and guiding Lucy to do the same. They didn't have much time. Olivia listened through the life of the forest, through her own violent pulse. For this to work she'd have to move quickly.

"I need you to stay here," Olivia said.

Lucy's eyes flashed with concern and confusion. "No—"

"Listen to me," Olivia said, her tone hushed. "I'm slowing you down. They'll catch up. You have to wait here. Let me pull them away, then continue west, as fast as you can, until Texas, like we talked about."

"No, I want to stay with you," Lucy said, her voice small with fear.

Olivia's heart broke. She wanted nothing more than to hold Lucy close, save her from all that had happened and all that would come. Save her from the trouble she herself had created for the girl, a miserable mistake that would never be forgiven. Yet there, crouched in the darkness, Lucy's bright blue eyes pleading with her for sanctuary, Olivia thought maybe, if she could save Lucy, just maybe she could save her own soul.

She brushed back Lucy's fiery hair, placed her palms on either side of the girl's face, and forced soft words through her rising emotions. "This is the only way, my sweet girl."

"But I don't know anything but you! I can't remember," Lucy said. Tears gathered in her eyes and shimmered in the starlit night.

"I know. I took your memories for your own protection. I know that's hard to understand, but you have to trust me, Lucy. Do you trust me?"

"I do."

"Good girl. Then do what I say now. Run west, to Corpus Christi, yes?"

"Yes."

"Find Summer Wallace—she's a friend of mine. Tell her Ollie sent you to find the robin. It's very important."

Lucy nodded.

"You can trust her. She'll help you. You must find her."

"Please come with me," Lucy said. A tear slipped down her cheek and Olivia wiped it away.

"Remember what I told you. You are the key, Lucy. I gave you a weapon that will keep you alive, but it also puts a target on your back. I wish there had been another way . . ." Olivia swallowed hard against the sorrow threatening to overtake her. "Everything I ever did was for you. Even if it was misguided."

Muffled voices drifted toward them on the breeze. Olivia peered through the small gaps in the pine bushes and saw the distant flashlights approaching. They were out of time. She reached for the pistol tucked in the back of her jeans and turned to Lucy.

A final look at the young girl's soft face. A face she'd come to love more than any she'd ever known. Without children of her own, Lucy had occupied that place in her heart, been her reason and purpose. Goodbye was harder than she'd imagined. The thought of never seeing this face again would break her if she sat here any longer.

"Wait until I pull them away, no matter what you hear. Do you understand?" Olivia asked.

"Yes."

"Then run. Don't stop until you're safe. Find Summer. Be careful who you trust."

"When will I see you?" Lucy asked.

The truth was too hard, so Olivia forced a small smile. "I'll find you. I promise." She softly placed her hand around the back of Lucy's neck and pulled her forward. She kissed the girl's forehead, unable to control the wells of tears that gathered in her eyes. So she hid her face, dropped her lips close to Lucy's ear, and whispered, "I love you, sweet girl."

With that Olivia took off east. She pumped her legs hard and fast. She ignored the aching of her joints and the overwhelming sadness that was yanking at her heart. The farther she rushed away from Lucy, the colder the world grew. Twenty, then thirty, nearly forty yards she estimated before she slowed to a stop. Without second-guessing her choice, Olivia aimed the pistol skyward and yanked the trigger.

The weapon felt like it exploded in her palm, the impact of the single shot cascading down her arm. The sound of the bullet cracked against the silent night, and within a couple seconds she saw the distant lights. She sent another shot and heard approaching radio commands. Olivia waited a final breath—she wanted to make sure she had drawn them—and then with as much confidence as she had, she ran.

The more noise she made, the better. She wanted them all to rush her, to leave a clean, open path for Lucy. She knew what drawing them would mean for her, but she pushed through the fear and ran.

Dodging trees, trying to keep her footing firm, she struggled to take painful breaths. They approached quickly, from all sides. Moving as if with one mind, they emerged from the trees two and three at a time, the moon giving enough light to trace their shapes. She was surrounded.

She came to a full stop and raised her firearm. It was illogical, yet still she turned in a circle. She couldn't possibly aim at all of them. But they weren't firing at her. They approached carefully, weapons pointed directly toward her, triggers untouched.

They wanted her alive. Otherwise she'd already be dead.

"Dr. Rivener, put down the weapon," one of the masked soldiers commanded. A voice she recognized well.

Olivia ignored his request.

"Where's the girl? It'll be easier on everyone if you just tell us," he said.

When Olivia's silence continued, the speaker nodded to the agent to his right, and he signaled to several others.

"She couldn't have gotten far," one said, and the group before her trimmed from a dozen to half as groups split off to search for Lucy.

Olivia had never been much for belief, but in that moment, she prayed to God that Lucy had done exactly as she'd asked.

"Dr. Rivener, lower the gun," the team leader spoke again. "We don't want anyone to get hurt." He was taking slow steps toward her.

"Then don't do this," Olivia replied. "Please, Seeley, you don't have to do this."

The masked man stopped and after a beat of silence lowered his weapon. His men inched forward, their guns still trained on her, and he raised a hand to reassure them. They froze, and he pulled back his dark mask.

Starlight softly lit his face. Olivia knew his square jaw, sharp nose, dark eyes. Strong and symmetrical features that Olivia had always found handsome. The helmet hid his thick black hair.

They'd been teammates. Colleagues. Now they stood as enemies on either side of a war that would change them forever.

Seeley held her eyes for a long moment before speaking. "You know I have to take you in." His voice was kind though his words were deadly.

"This isn't right," Olivia said. "You're a good man. You know this isn't right."

"We have orders."

"Forget orders. You know her. She's just a child."

"Don't be naïve, Olivia," Seeley said. "You forget what we were trying to do here."

"What we were trying to do was wrong. It cost us everything."

"It doesn't have to. Lower your weapon. Come in willingly. Hammon is reasonable, and you are an incredible asset."

"Now who's being naïve?"

Another moment of silence passed between them, then he glanced left to another soldier. "Take her."

Olivia took a step backward, gun still raised, as she tried to control the fear causing her fingers to tremble. "You can't kill her, Seeley. I've made sure of it. She's the only one who knows where the information's hidden."

The soldiers all paused. Seeley stared at her as his men waited for orders.

"We both know what's at risk if anyone gets hold of that information," Olivia said. "To the Grantham Project, to all those involved, to the country. Kill her and the whole world will know what we did."

She pictured Lucy one last time. Again she found herself praying redemption was real as she took a breath and resolved her end.

Seeley took a step forward, putting the pieces together a moment too late. He opened his mouth to instruct, maybe even to intervene, but Olivia had already pulled the trigger on her weapon. Once, twice, three times, as bullets exploded from the gun's barrel and into the soldiers.

They responded in kind. Two bullets sank deep in Olivia's gut, then a third and fourth in her chest and shoulder. Her final moment was encased in agony as she collapsed to the forest floor and her world went dark.

TWO

"ORDER UP," A husky male voice barked out the small serving window from his place behind the grill.

Zoe pushed herself away from the long counter where she'd been perched and turned to grab the warm plate that sat on the metal shelf. "You leave off the tomatoes?" she asked as she glanced at the burger and fries that occupied the plate.

"Did you tell me to?" the cook asked.

"Yes, Pete, I told you to," she replied.

"If you told me, then I did it. I listen." Pete shot her a playful wink and turned back to the greasy grill that sizzled with raw meat and frying bacon. Zoe lifted the edge of the top bun with a clean knife and saw a large slice of tomato tucked below the layer of iceberg lettuce. She huffed.

She looked up at Pete, who glanced back at her and gave a shrug. "Must not have told me."

Zoe rolled her eyes, carefully pulled the tomato free, and tossed it in the trash can behind her. "You do stellar work as always," she mocked. Pete replied with a chuckle, not bothering to give her another glance.

She walked around the edge of the long counter that divided

the single-level diner and toward the last booth on the right. It was occupied by a single gentleman, Lawrence Peters, fondly referred to as Lou, who was a regular patron of Eat at Joe's, the less-than-average dining establishment where Zoe had been employed for the last eight months.

She approached the table with a smile and slid the plate in front of the graying man. His face and hands were permanently stained with grime from twenty-five years of working in coal mines on the outskirts of Sherman, Texas.

"Here you go, Lou," Zoe said. "I made sure there weren't any tomatoes."

Lou glanced up at her, his brown eyes filled with genuine kindness, a quality few people had. He had a way of making a person feel like family with a simple smile. "Thanks, doll," he said. "You tell Joe I said he should give you a raise."

Zoe laughed at the thought and shook her head. Joe Brunski, the owner, would rather chop off an arm than pay a penny over what the law required. Zoe was pretty sure the man was constantly scouring paperwork in the back office for a loophole to pay them less, or better yet, not at all.

"If you need anything, you let me know, Lou," she said and headed back to her usual spot behind the counter. The place was small, eight booths in all, four on either side of the front door. A loud bell clanged with the comings and goings of bodies. A long, thin counter with ten barstools stood opposite the booths, and a small walkway cut the diner in half. When Zoe and Jessie Mack, the only other waitress, were both working, they had to turn sideways to maneuver around one another.

The kitchen was barely big enough for two people, which suited Pete just fine. He preferred to work alone. There were two single bathrooms for paying customers only. Even though Eat at Joe's sat along US Highway 75 and saw passing travelers, Joe would have none of it. He could sniff out a freeloader like a bloodhound.

"You have to pay to play," he'd always say. Which didn't make complete sense, but very little of Joe and the way he ran the diner made complete sense.

The bell over the door dinged, and Jessie walked through, an unfolded newspaper held over her hair. "Man, it's really coming down out there."

"Forecast called for rain," Zoe said.

"Did it? I don't remember seeing that, and I checked. I always check," she said, folding the wet paper and tossing it in the trash. "You know I cleaned out my car this weekend? Piece of crap, not sure why. It's a piece of junk, so who cares if it looks and smells like junk? Well, I guess I care since I spent my only day off cleaning it out."

Zoe geared up for a Jessie spill, a phrase Pete had coined to describe the rate at which Jessie could talk once she got started.

"I know I checked because I washed my hair yesterday, and if I had known it was going to rain I would have waited. Rain and Texas hair never mingle well, my mother would say. So, I'm sure I checked." Jessie tossed her bag and coat under the counter and dipped to use the reflective surface of a napkin box to check her hair. "Anyways, as I was saying, I cleaned out my car this weekend and I had an umbrella in there, and I thought to myself, I haven't used this in months so it's just cluttering up my back seat for no good reason. And then two days later it rains like this?"

She straightened and looked Zoe dead in the eye. "You would think I could catch a break. I mean, don't I deserve a bit of peace for once? After the radiator troubles with my piece-of-crap car and the water leak in my shower—I swear if that fat, idiotic super of mine blows off my bathroom leak one more time—and you know,

I'm pretty sure there are rats in the walls as well. I really have to move. I know I say that all the time, but this time I mean it."

Zoe smirked and tuned out the ramblings of the frantic waitress, as she often did. She glanced out the large square windows into the pouring rain. It had been dark for a couple of hours now. It wouldn't be long before they got some daylight back, as the winter turned to spring and the sun stayed out to warm the cold earth.

This was her first Texas winter, and the worst part was the way the people complained about the cold, even though it wasn't that cold to begin with. It had been a relief to escape the horrid heat of summer, and Zoe wasn't sure she would survive another sweltering heat. But she'd made a commitment to herself that she'd stay put for a while this time. Melting summers and all.

And Sherman wasn't so bad. It was quiet, friendly, and relatively private. People didn't mind leaving you to yourself, which was arguably the only requirement for Zoe when picking a place to stay awhile. That and a Taco Bell. One of the only reliable things in Zoe's life was the soft taco. It never really changed.

"I priced out the new complex going in over off Peach Street," Jessie continued, "but there is no way I can afford that working here. Not unless I got a roommate, and I'd rather sleep outside in this rain."

"You could live across the street at the motel," Pete piped up from the kitchen, "like little Zoe here. Then you could stop complainin' about your car and your terrible apartment, because you'd be free of both."

"I'd rather be homeless," Jessie said, then shot an apologetic glance at Zoe. "No offense, honey, but that place is just depressing."

"No offense taken. It works for me," Zoe said.

Jessie nodded, a familiar look flashing behind her eyes. A look Zoe dreaded. Curiosity.

"Why are you still there? I mean, there's plenty of places in town. Seems strange to still be squatting at that dingy motel," Jessie said.

"Like I said, it works for me," Zoe replied, "and it doesn't have rats in the walls."

Pete chuckled and Jessie cut her eyes at Zoe's snark. "Whatever you say, but it isn't normal for a young, single cutie like yourself to be stowed up alone in a travelers' motel. Oh, the trouble I got into when I was twenty-four and ten pounds lighter. I mean, how are you going to meet people?"

"Who says she wants to meet people?" Pete questioned.

"Everybody wants somebody," Jessie shot back, then to Zoe: "I mean, right?"

Zoe didn't really want to have this conversation anymore. She didn't like the places this kind of inquiry could take them.

The bell over the door rang again and two men, both unfamiliar, walked in. Probably semitruck drivers. They saw a handful of those, as the large gas station next door often serviced semis.

Zoe glanced at Jessie. "Your turn."

"And another mindless shift begins," Jessie scoffed in a whisper. Then to the two drivers she cooed, "Hey there, fellas, sit wherever you'd like, and I'll be right with you."

Zoe rolled her eyes and grinned. The bell rang again. She glanced over her shoulder and saw a girl, couldn't be older than seventeen, standing in the open doorway, drenched from the rain. She was breathing heavily, her eyes wide with surprise as she took in her surroundings.

"That one's all you," Jessie said under her breath as she approached Zoe from behind.

Great, Zoe thought. She walked around the end of the bar toward the strange girl. "Booth or barstool?" she asked.

The girl snapped her eyes toward Zoe and dropped her hand from the diner door. The pneumatic hinge slowly pulled the glass door shut. The expression on the girl's face was like a startled deer, innocent and terrified.

As Zoe took a step toward her, the girl's body tensed. Zoe took a step back herself, suddenly uncertain what the girl might do.

"You alright?" she asked.

The girl looked in all directions, then brushed beads of water away from her face. Zoe yanked a handful of napkins out of a holder and extended them to her. The teen glanced down at the offering and slowly accepted. She wiped her face clean and dried her hands.

"Better?" Zoe asked.

The girl nodded. "Yes."

"You wanna table?"

She looked at the row of booths to her right and then pointed to the first one. "This one?"

"Sure," Zoe replied.

The girl moved quickly, sliding into the left side of the booth. Her movements were rigid, fast, like all her nerve endings were wired, and she barely sat fully in her seat. Zoe grabbed a menu from the bar and placed it on the table in front of her.

"What's this?" the girl asked.

Zoe just looked at her for a second, waiting for her to say she was kidding. But she didn't. She just sat there staring up at Zoe, waiting for an answer.

"The menu," Zoe said.

"What do I do with it?"

Again, Zoe paused for the punch line. Nothing.

"You order food from it," she said. "Have you never used a menu before?" She still expected the girl to look up, laugh, and say, "Of course I have. Who hasn't used a menu?"

But instead the girl took hold of the single plastic sheet and studied it with fascination. "I can have anything?" she asked with wonder.

She looked up at Zoe, a childlike sparkle overcoming the fear that had been there earlier. It made Zoe uncomfortable and unsure of how to respond. The girl returned her gaze to the menu. Zoe wasn't sure what the girl had taken, but it was pretty clear she was on something.

"Maybe you should just start with some water," she suggested.

"Yes," the girl replied. "That would be good." She smiled up at her, and Zoe nodded. She turned and walked back behind the counter to get a glass of water.

Pete leaned his head through the pickup window and shot Zoe a sly grin. "Ask her to share whatever it is she's taking," he said.

Zoe ignored him and returned to the table. She set the glass down. The girl had moved to the dessert menu that advertised the latest options, and she held it out so Zoe could see.

"Is this good?" the girl said, pointing at the new strawberry swirl milkshake. "Can I have it?"

"It's pretty average for a milkshake, if you like strawberry," Zoe said.

The girl glanced at the picture again, then beamed at Zoe. "Yes, I would like this."

Zoe paused, placed a hand on the booth, and leaned forward. "Can you pay for that?"

The girl's eyes shifted curiously, and she looked at Zoe as if she spoke a foreign language. Zoe tried to control her fading patience and slid into the booth across from the strung-out girl.

"Listen, no judgment—I don't care what you do with your time—but you probably shouldn't be here right now," Zoe started.

The girl's smile washed cold, and she shrank back into the booth.

Terror regained control of her body. "Is it not safe here?" she asked, her voice low.

She locked eyes with Zoe, and Zoe could feel her desperation. Her bright blue eyes begged for help, the kind of help needed by a child seeking refuge. It struck something deep inside Zoe's stomach that caused her to question the assumptions she had started making.

"Are you in trouble?" she asked.

The girl's eyes flicked back and forth, then back to Zoe. "I have to be careful who I trust."

The words resonated with Zoe. She herself lived by them. The girl's tone was frail and honest. Her eyes weren't red. Her hands were steady, her skin clear, her voice open. Nothing said "strung out" except for her strange lack of awareness. The kind you would expect from a child. An innocence shone in the corners of her eyes and asked to be sheltered.

"Can I call someone for you? Family, or a friend?" Zoe asked.

Hope sparkled in the girl's eyes. "Yes. Summer Wallace."

"Okay, do you know her number?"

The hope died out. "No."

"Do you know her address? We can look her up—"

"She lives in Corpus Christi."

"The city?"

Again, a wave of joy fell over the girl's face. "You know it?"

"I know where it is," Zoe said.

"Can you take me?" The girl leaned forward excitedly. "I have to get there as soon as possible."

"You can't go right now. It's hundreds of miles from here."

Like a switch being flipped back and forth, the girl's expression changed again. From hope to fear. Wonder to despair. "It's that far?"

"Do you not know where you are?" Zoe asked, suddenly much more worried than she'd been before. Something was clearly wrong with this girl. Maybe she shouldn't have intervened. Yet something pulled at the strings of her heart, and she couldn't make herself stand up and walk away.

The girl shook her head, her eyes misty and on the verge of tears, and Zoe longed to comfort her. She gave a warm smile, hoping to make the teen feel more secure. "You never told me your name."

"Lucy," the girl answered.

"Just Lucy?" Zoe asked.

"Just Lucy."

"Cool, like Beyoncé."

"What's a Beyoncé?"

Zoe gave an awkward laugh, then realized once again she wasn't kidding. Who was this girl?

"Hey, are you hungry?" she asked. "Let me get you something to eat. My treat."

Lucy gave a sheepish shrug and then a tiny corner smile. "Okay."

"Fries and a strawberry swirl milkshake coming up," Zoe said.

Lucy's smile grew, and Zoe felt a warmth that she hadn't experienced in a long time circle inside her chest. The way Lucy smiled made her think about her little brother, the way he used to glance up at her when she shared her watermelon with him. But that memory was tinged with pain, and the warmth turned cold as she shut the memory back inside the box with the rest of her past.

"After you eat, we can talk more, and maybe I can help you," Zoe said. "Would that be okay?"

Lucy drilled Zoe with an intense stare, and Zoe felt the penetration of it in her gut.

"Can I trust you?" Lucy asked. Like a child would, wanting to be saved but remembering not to trust strangers.

The question nearly took Zoe's breath away. Maybe she should have felt warier of the peculiar teenager, should have been more reserved with her own trust, but all she could see was a fragile girl who needed protection from the cruelty of the world. The way Zoe and her little brother had needed protection. Protection they'd never received. How different her path would have been had someone come along and sheltered her from the diabolical nature of humanity. How could she now deny this girl that same protection?

She nodded. "Yes, you can trust me."

Lucy pondered it a moment, then smiled brightly. "Okay," was all she said, and Zoe knew Lucy would trust her completely.

Zoe smiled back, suddenly heavy with the burden of the young girl's trust. She wanted to recant her statement. She wanted to admit she'd been carried away by her own sentiments, and that Lucy was right not to trust anyone. Even those who seemed honorable were capable of betrayal. Yet she couldn't bring herself to kill the relief that had settled over the girl.

She left Lucy sitting in the booth. She would let her have a moment of peace, then she'd help the girl as best she could before sending her back out into the world, where it would do all it could to kill Lucy's rare innocence. No one got away unscathed.

But for now, there could be fries and milkshakes.

THREE

TOM SEELEY ROLLED the hard peppermint across his molars with his tongue. The sharp flavor filled his mouth and slivered down his throat. The oral fixation was supposed to help him quit smoking, but he could still taste the tobacco at the back of his throat, permanently stained from years of consuming a pack of cigarettes daily. With each passing moment he craved the taste more.

He was alone, standing in the hallway outside the director's office. He could overhear a muffled apology through the thick wooden door as Director Robert Hammon explained to the secretary of defense the events that had unfolded in the last dozen hours. Hours that had been tasked to Seeley. Orders directly from the president. Orders he'd failed to execute.

The voices stopped, and a moment later the door opened.

Hammon didn't even bother to stick his head out. "Inside, now," he barked. Seeley was going to need a lot more peppermint.

He entered the office and closed the door. The space was simple, undecorated, with large, dark leather furniture, a single mahogany desk, and zero windows. The walls were concrete, like most of the building and the ones that surrounded it. It had been an easy material to haul over the mountainous terrain when they'd built the black site labeled CX4-B.

The soldiers referred to the place as Xerox because it was a carbon copy of the ground-zero location outside of Washington State. Buried in the Ozark Mountains along the northwest border of Arkansas, Xerox was covered in thick forests that helped keep the site off the map and hidden from hikers.

It was the birthplace of the Grantham Project, a project Seeley had volunteered for ten years earlier. Being off the grid and buried deep inside the mountains was exactly what he'd been looking for to escape his past. A place where there was nothing but work and stress. Nothing familiar to remind him of what he didn't have.

"What happened out there?" Hammon asked as he paced. "The orders were simple: Retrieve. Alive."

"She attacked. My men were defending themselves. There was no other course of action," Seeley said.

"Retrieve Dr. Rivener and the girl alive was the *only* course of action!"

Seeley remained quiet, standing with arms behind his back, shoulders stiff, eyes trained on the concrete wall behind Hammon.

"And the girl?" Hammon asked, controlling the rage in his voice.

"Gone. We believe west, but the trail ran cold about a hundred yards from her last known location," Seeley replied.

"Any idea where she's heading?"

"We're working around the clock, scouring Olivia's office and quarters for information. We'll find something."

"Likely not. She was smart."

"But she was rushed. There'll be a thread to pull, and I'll find it," Seeley said.

"How did she know we were coming?"

Hammon already knew the answer. Seeley said nothing.

"We're running security protocol on everyone on campus," Hammon said. "We'll find whoever helped."

"This escape was thoroughly thought out."

"It was more than an escape. With the information she took, it was an attack." Hammon stopped pacing and exhaled loudly. He moved to the chair behind his desk and sat. His dark hair was littered with graying stripes, his dark eyes ringed with exhaustion and too many hours of overtime. The navy-blue suit that draped across his large, tall frame was wrinkled. He'd worn it yesterday. Seeley knew the kind of pressure he was getting from the powers that pulled all the strings in Washington, knew how severe the situation had become.

"What was her endgame here?" Hammon asked. He was talking more to himself than to Seeley, but he was vocalizing all the thoughts that had been running through Seeley's head over the last forty-eight hours.

He replayed Olivia's words in his head for the thousandth time. *You can't kill her. She's the only one who knows where the information's hidden.*

They'd discovered the internal scan of all their confidential documentation and traced the upload of that information to a hard drive that was missing. She'd copied their files, everything that would be needed to expose them if it got out. Further exploration of lab notes showed a final physical scan had been run on the girl right before their escape. Against direct orders, Olivia had erased Lucy's memories. But she'd done more than that. Her final words indicated as much. They just needed to figure out what, and how to reverse it.

"Mental scans show a full wipe?" Hammon asked.

"Yes, sir."

"Before or after Olivia told her where the drive was hidden?"

"That's the question of the day, sir. I suggest we find the girl, follow her, see if she leads us to what we need."

Hammon shook his head. "You knew Olivia. That seems too easy."

It was true that Seeley had underestimated the attachment between Olivia and Lucy. He'd failed to anticipate the danger it would pose at the end. That mistake could cost them everything.

Hammon swore under his breath. "We needed Olivia alive."

Olivia had been Seeley's colleague; some might even say friend. Yet he'd felt nothing staring down at her lifeless body sprawled across the forest floor. He'd grown numb to death long ago. Sloughed off that part of the human condition that reacted to loss. It was the only way to manage each day without losing his will to exist. They'd zipped Olivia's corpse into a body bag and placed her in the on-site morgue.

Hammon stood and started pacing again. "I don't have to tell you what will happen if the information regarding the Grantham Project isn't recovered."

"No, sir," Seeley replied. He bit into the hard candy thinning in his mouth and swallowed the fractured pieces, the mixed flavor of peppermint and tobacco swirling across his tongue.

"Olivia wouldn't make idle threats. There was a plan here, and we need to know what it was. And we need the girl."

"We'll find her," Seeley said.

"We have to control this. That girl might as well be running around with launch codes. I need it buttoned up, Seeley."

"Understood."

A hard knock sounded at the door, and a moment later Dave McCoy, a technical analyst who'd joined the Grantham Project only a year earlier, stepped inside.

"We found something," he said. He walked across the room, a

27

black folder in his hand. He opened it and laid it on Hammon's desk, revealing several enlarged black-and-white photos. "These were taken outside a commercial gas station along Highway 75 near Sherman, Texas." McCoy pointed to a blurry figure under a streetlamp that appeared to be across the street. "Facial recognition pings her at a 65 percent match for our missing girl."

Seeley moved to the desk and pulled one of the top photos off to examine it more closely. He could barely make out the girl's face since it was mostly a side view, but it could be Lucy.

"When?" Hammon asked.

"Just over an hour ago. Could be nothing," McCoy replied.

Could be something, Seeley thought.

Hammon looked up at him. "Worth sending a team to check it out."

Seeley nodded.

"Approach with caution. We have no idea how she'll respond. Move quickly but carefully."

Seeley turned and headed for the door.

"Alive, Seeley," Hammon barked.

Seeley didn't turn back as he exited the office. He understood what was at stake and would get the job done. There was no other choice.

FOUR

THE REMAINDER OF Zoe's shift slipped by in a muffled state of watching Lucy and wondering where on earth she could have come from. They talked a bit more here and there, Zoe asking questions and getting answers that should have made her more wary of Lucy's motives but somehow caused her to feel even more protective of the girl.

"Where did you come from?"

"The forest."

"How did you get here?"

"I ran."

"And you're headed to Corpus Christi?"

"Yes, to find Summer Wallace."

"Why?"

"Because Olivia told me to."

"Who is Olivia?"

"I can't remember, but I trust her."

"Where is she now?"

"I don't know."

With each question Zoe found herself becoming more invested.

What she gathered was that Olivia had told Lucy some crazy story about taking her memories and Lucy being the key or something.

None of which actually sounded plausible. Who was Lucy? Dozens of scenarios had been rolling around in Zoe's mind to answer the question. Maybe she'd been kidnapped as a girl and escaped? Maybe she had amnesia? Maybe she was on a new cocktail of drugs? Maybe she was playing a very well-executed prank? Maybe she was mentally ill and trapped in some strange psychosis? Maybe she was dangerous, and Zoe was just gullible?

Multiple times she told herself to walk away. Get the girl out of the diner and wash her hands of this insanity. But then Lucy would smile at her, the smile that reminded her of the little brother she once knew, and she'd be in deeper than she was before.

The clock struck ten and Zoe untied her apron. Working a minute over scheduled time was punishable in Joe's book. She clocked out and grabbed her stuff from underneath the counter.

"You're taking her with you, right?" Jessie asked.

"Where am I supposed to take her?" Zoe asked.

"I don't care, as long as when you go, she goes with you. I'm not interested in entertaining some druggie for the next several hours."

"She's not on drugs," Zoe said.

"And you know this from your extended history with her?"

Jessie was right to question her logic. It was more likely the girl was tripping on acid than running from someone who had erased her memories. Was that even possible?

"You could take her to the community center in town," Pete offered from the kitchen. "They run a homeless program. They might have a cot for her."

Zoe glanced back to where Lucy sat. She was finishing her second strawberry swirl milkshake after devouring a basket of loaded cheese fries, a hamburger, and an order of chicken fingers.

All of which Zoe had paid for and had cost her more than she'd made in tips during her shift.

"And if they don't have any room left?" she asked.

Pete shrugged. "Seems like that'd be your problem."

"Feed a stray and they'll just keep coming back," Jessie said. "That's what my mama would say."

They were right. Zoe was creating a situation she was unequipped to resolve. What was she going to do with Lucy now? She'd gotten sucked into the girl's puppy eyes, and now she couldn't just leave that puppy out in the cold. Could she?

She slipped into the single bathroom, her mind flip-flopping on what to do next as she washed her hands. She stepped back into the diner and looked up, surprised to see someone had joined Lucy in her booth. A man Zoe didn't recognize. He was smiling at the girl, his hands resting on the table, his fingers inching toward Lucy's.

Lucy giggled and tucked her hair behind her ear. Zoe's stomach turned. She walked back to the counter and grabbed her coat.

"Looks like crazy made another friend," Jessie teased. "You may be saved after all."

Zoe pulled on her coat. She didn't owe the girl anything. She'd already done more than most would have. Fed her. Given her shelter for the last few hours. They were strangers, and Lucy was nearly an adult. She was capable of making her own choices. Even if they were bad ones. But Zoe didn't like the way Jessie was smirking, or the way the strange man was tenderly touching the back of Lucy's hand.

Lucy nodded as the man stood, and she moved to do the same. Zoe gritted her teeth. She should leave it, then she'd be free. But she couldn't. Maybe Lucy needed to be protected. Hadn't Zoe once needed the same thing and never been offered it?

Zoe walked over to intercept the couple.

Lucy glanced up and smiled at Zoe. "Dash is going to give me a ride," she said, truly unaware of what might be expected in return for such a favor.

"Out of the goodness of your heart," Zoe mocked, glaring at Dash.

"This doesn't concern you, unless you want to join," Dash said with a wink.

"Gross," Zoe said.

He wrapped his arm around Lucy's shoulders. "Come on, honey."

"Get your hands off her," Zoe said, reaching out and yanking Lucy away from the predator.

"Back off," Dash snapped.

Zoe stepped between him and Lucy. "Unless you want me to call the sheriff of this very small community town and tell him that an outsider is harassing young women at the diner, which would bring the entire department down here, you need to walk away."

"You better do as she asked," a male voice hollered from behind, and Zoe glanced back to see Pete leaning out the kitchen pass-through, drilling Dash with a deadly stare.

Dash cursed at Zoe so the whole diner could hear, then turned to Lucy and said, "Your loss, sweetheart."

The bell dinged his exit, and Zoe turned back to Lucy. "What were you thinking?"

"He said he would give me a ride," Lucy said. "He said he was nice."

Zoe huffed in frustration. "If a man says he's nice, he's usually not." She walked to the front window and watched Dash climb into his truck cab and drive off. "You can't believe everything people say, Lucy."

"Why not?"

Zoe turned back to her, stunned. This girl was going to get herself killed. She really was a puppy, and without a leash she'd run right out into the middle of the street.

"Do you have anywhere you can go?" Zoe asked.

"I don't remember," Lucy said.

Zoe exhaled. "Come on."

She stepped outside, Lucy right on her heels. They descended the steps into the cold evening air. The rain had passed, but the sky was still heavy with dark clouds, blocking out the stars and making the night black. A cold wind whirled by and Zoe shivered, pulling her coat tighter across her chest. Lucy's clothes hadn't dried out and her hair was still damp, yet she didn't seem to notice the chill at all.

"Are you sure this Summer Wallace isn't here?" Zoe asked as they crossed the parking lot.

"You said this is Sherman, and she's in Corpus Christi."

"Because Olivia, who you can't really remember, told you so? The same one that took your memories for your own protection? You realize how crazy that sounds, right?" Zoe said.

"It's the truth."

"How do you know if you can't remember?"

Lucy opened her mouth to respond, then stopped. She thought about it for a moment, then said, "I trust her, like I trust you."

"Why?" Zoe asked. "You don't even know me!"

"You said I could."

"Lucy, people lie. People lie more often than they tell the truth. Like Dash. Who knows what would have happened to you if you'd gotten in his truck. It's woven into the human condition. People say one thing to your face and then do another behind your back. They make you believe their intentions are good when they are selfish. The world will chew you up and spit you out until you understand the only person you can rely on is you."

Silence fell between them as Lucy weighed Zoe's words. Then she locked eyes with her, and Zoe could see the pain in Lucy's expression even in the darkness.

"You lied to me?" Lucy asked.

Zoe sucked in a short breath. The simplicity and directness of Lucy's question punched her in the chest. She wasn't sure what to say.

Lucy dropped her eyes, and after another drawn-out moment of silence she started walking toward the highway. Zoe wanted to make her understand, but she couldn't formulate words that made sense. Lucy walked with decisiveness, not slowing as she reached the road and followed the graveled shoulder.

Zoe watched her for several moments as Lucy put distance between them. A large semi whizzed by, honking at Lucy as it passed. Probably because a teen girl walking along the highway in the middle of the night was dangerous and stupid. And the road was filled with people like Dash.

Zoe let out a frustrated huff and ran after the girl. "Lucy, wait," she called.

"I need to find Summer," Lucy yelled back, not slowing her pace.

Zoe eased to a walk as she closed the distance, now trailing Lucy by a few yards and yelling after her, "And you're just going to walk there?"

Lucy didn't respond. She was determined, Zoe would give her that.

In that moment Zoe had to make a choice. Leave the delusional girl to her own devices or help her. This was the perfect moment to walk away, take care of herself as she'd always done, follow the promises she'd made to herself not to get involved when there was potential pain. Yet even as the thoughts washed over her, her heart was already making a different choice. A choice she would probably regret, but the reality was clear. There was no way she could bring herself to abandon this strange girl to the wolves.

"Lucy, please stop," Zoe called. "It's freezing out here, and dark."

Lucy continued to ignore her.

Zoe pushed on. "I'm sorry, okay? I shouldn't have said those things."

Lucy spun around. "Is that also a lie?"

"No, it's the truth. What I said before, it was just me being . . ." Zoe paused to find the right word.

"Mean," Lucy finished.

Zoe exhaled and nodded. "Yeah, I guess so."

"I have to get to Corpus Christi," Lucy continued.

"I know, but walking there is not the way."

"I can run. I'm pretty fast."

Zoe chuckled. "Don't tell me you have super speed?"

Lucy just stared at her.

"Right. That's probably another pop-culture reference you don't understand. Trust me, there are better ways."

"Can I trust you?" Lucy asked for the second time. Just like before, the authenticity of it shook Zoe to her core. The teen's eyes demanded honesty, and Zoe gave it.

"Yes. And I will help you find Summer Wallace, but tomorrow. Tonight you can stay with me, okay?"

Lucy walked toward Zoe. "Can we get more milkshakes?"

Zoe smiled. "We'll see."

"They're very good," Lucy said, reaching Zoe's side.

Zoe chuckled as they turned together and headed back down the highway, Lucy's delight in something as simple as milkshakes softening Zoe's hardened shell with each step.

FIVE

LUCY PLOPPED DOWN on the end of Zoe's double bed, her hair wrapped in a white towel. Zoe had given her a pair of sweats and an oversized T-shirt to wear while she dried her damp clothes. After a quick tour of her single-room home—consisting of a bed, two nightstands, a dresser with TV atop, a mini stackable washer/dryer set, a small kitchenette, and a writing desk with matching chair—Zoe pointed Lucy in the direction of a hot shower.

Lucy was in the shower for twenty minutes, an eternity. Zoe tried to busy herself with things around her place. Her mind ran in circles from one troubling thought to the next. Had she really brought a stray home? Armed with very little information about her and hoping for the best? She must have lost her mind.

Zoe had simple but inviolable life rules. Number one: Keep your head down, stay out of trouble, trust no one. Number two: Always refer back to rule number one. With a pair of baby-blue eyes and a dopey smile, somehow Lucy had convinced Zoe to break her life rules. She wasn't sure whether to be impressed or terrified.

Lucy sat cross-legged on the bed and looked at Zoe, who was rinsing a coffee mug and placing it on the small shelf that contained the few dishes she owned.

"You enjoy your shower?" Zoe asked.

Lucy nodded. "It was very warm."

"Say what you want about this place, but the hot water never seems to run out."

"I like this place."

Zoe turned and leaned back against the sink, crossing her arms. "It suits me fine."

"It's nice."

Zoe raised her eyebrows and huffed. "You clearly haven't been very many places."

A confused, pondering look washed over Lucy's face. The girl seemed to get lost inside herself, as if searching for answers in her own mind. The expression was haunting and sad. Zoe wished she had said something else.

She pushed off the sink and headed for the remote that sat on the nightstand. "You wanna watch some TV?" She grabbed the control and flicked the black screen to life. Reruns of *Deal or No Deal* filled the frame. The playfully charming Howie Mandel interacted with a young girl who was just getting an offer from the bank, as perfect girls in little black dresses stood in rows holding numbered silver briefcases.

"This okay?" Zoe asked. She looked to Lucy, whose eyes had gone wide with wonder.

Lucy adjusted her small frame to get a better view of the screen and became engrossed with the images as they played across the monitor as if she'd never seen a TV before. But then maybe she hadn't? Or couldn't remember. Another unbelievable fact to add to the list of puzzling truths about this strange girl.

Zoe's cell phone buzzed against the small wooden desk across the room, and the screen lit up. She dropped the remote onto the bed and stepped toward the vibrating phone. She reached for it, saw it was the diner, hit ignore. She'd worked a ten-hour shift; she was not going back in.

Lucy had pulled the wrapped towel from her head, and her long hair lay in wet chunks around her shoulders. Zoe stepped into the bathroom to grab her hairbrush. The mirror was still cloudy from the steam of Lucy's shower, and Zoe wiped it clean. Her tired reflection stared back at her. Fair skin, brown eyes, short black hair that she dyed herself. She noticed her light roots poking through. Time for a touch-up.

She left the bathroom, flicking the light off on her way out. Her phone was buzzing again. She glanced at it. The diner. Strange they'd keep calling. She tossed the brush onto the bed beside Lucy and reached for her phone. Lucy looked at the object as it landed beside her and then back up at Zoe.

Zoe pointed to her own head to indicate what the item was for and watched as Lucy carefully reached for the brush and began to run it through her hair. Zoe's phone stopped vibrating in her hand, and she unlocked it to dial the diner back.

Jessie answered before the first ring finished. "Why aren't you answering your phone? Are you okay?"

"I'm fine, but I'm not coming back in to cover for you," Zoe started. "I don't care who died—"

"I didn't call about that," Jessie snapped, then dropped her voice. "Is that girl still with you?"

"Why?"

"Look, I don't know what kind of trouble she's in, but two government men just showed up here lookin' for her."

"What?" Zoe stepped back into the bathroom and out of Lucy's earshot. "What do you mean, government men? Like, agents?"

"Yeah. They were showin' us pictures of her and asking if we'd seen her. They said she's dangerous, Zoe."

"How do you know they were really with the government?"

"They had badges, FBI."

"And they were real?"

"Real? What kind of person asks that question after what I just told you!"

"You know you can buy ones on Amazon that look like the real thing, Jessie. How do you know they were real?"

"I know an FBI badge when I see one. Are you even listening to what I said? She's dangerous! Are you home? Did you take her home with you?"

Zoe's mind was spinning again. Government agents looking for Lucy, claiming she was dangerous. What if she was? Zoe glanced back out and saw the girl curled up watching the game show like a child. She looked like she couldn't hurt a fly. And authorities claiming to have anyone's best interests in mind couldn't be trusted. Her past had taught her that. So what did they want with Lucy?

"What did they say exactly?" Zoe asked.

"They showed us her picture, asked us if we'd seen her and when she left," Jessie answered.

"And what did you tell them?"

"The truth! I'm not trying to get myself in trouble with the government. I'm too weak for jail."

"You told them about me?" Zoe could feel her panic start to boil.

"I told them you took the girl with you. What was I supposed to say?"

Zoe swore under her breath. If they knew Lucy had left with her, it wouldn't take them long to track her back here. She stepped out of the bathroom and nearly stumbled into Lucy, who was standing right outside the door.

Lucy's eyes were wide and focused. "They're here."

Zoe wasn't sure what to say with the phone up to her ear, Jessie rambling about prison time. She swallowed and cut the woman off midsentence. "I have to go, Jessie."

"Don't do anything stupid," Jessie warned.

"I'll call you later," Zoe said and clicked the phone off.

"They can't find me," Lucy said. "They can't be trusted."

"Who are they?"

"The bad guys," she whispered. Then her attention snapped to the door, a different level of focus filling her expression. A moment of eerie silence encased the room. Only long enough for Zoe to exhale, then Lucy's eyes were back on her.

"They're close," she said.

Jessie must have told them where Zoe lived. How could Lucy know—

Zoe's thought was interrupted by a hard rap at her apartment door. She looked at the door, then back at Lucy, whose face was now covered in panic, tears forming in the corners of her eyes.

"Please help me," Lucy whimpered.

An image of a small boy Zoe loved with all her heart and two large uniformed men dragging him off flashed across her memory. His tiny words filled her mind. *Help me.* The wound she'd stitched up time after time opened, and agony dripped out like blood. Zoe hadn't helped him; she'd let someone else influence him to do things that had ultimately separated them. She should have saved him, protected him, but she'd been too afraid. She couldn't be afraid now. She could help Lucy.

Again a knock bounced off the door, followed by a deep male voice. "FBI. Please open the door."

"Liar," Lucy whispered, anger washing over her eyes.

Zoe was trying to piece it all together, but there wasn't time now. The only thing she could trust was her gut, and right now it was screaming at her to get this girl far away from whoever was on the other side of the door.

Zoe flipped a mental switch and moved with precise determination. She grabbed a backpack and stuffed it with all her cash. She opened a desk drawer, retrieved a flip phone that couldn't be traced, and tossed it in with the money. She left all the rest of her things.

Then she was motioning for Lucy to follow her into the bathroom, where a single small window was perched above the shower. Barely big enough for them to squeeze through, it was their only exit. Zoe had never opened it; she wasn't even sure it would open. She carefully balanced on the ceramic tub and yanked at the rusted latch. Nothing. Twice more with all her might, but to no avail. She stepped off, pushed past Lucy, and rummaged in the desk drawer for a screwdriver.

When she stepped back into the bathroom, Lucy was up on the ledge yanking the lever. Zoe opened her mouth to tell her it wouldn't budge when it squeaked open, and Lucy pushed the window wide. She looked back for direction, and Zoe mouthed, *You first.*

The girl pulled herself through the window, and Zoe stepped up to follow. Hands on the window's edge, she caught sight of the latch. It was broken off. She paused and eyed it curiously. Lucy had broken the latch completely. That didn't seem possible. For a half second Zoe questioned what she was doing, risking so much with so little knowledge. Was this a mistake?

She saw Lucy looking up at her from the outside, her eyes pleading. There was no turning back now. Ignoring the familiar rage of fear, Zoe let the unknown go and pulled herself through the window.

SIX

SEELEY WALKED INTO the motel room, where four agents were rummaging through its contents looking for clues, cataloguing items, and gathering as much information as they could.

Dave McCoy stepped across the room to meet Seeley.

"A techie who does fieldwork," Seeley said. "Where'd they find you?"

"Unique case calls for a unique approach," McCoy said.

"That's putting it mildly. Anything?"

"Lucy was here. We found her clothes in the dryer. Looks like she escaped out the back window. The latch is broken. By the time our guys got the manager to let them in, she was long gone."

"And this Zoe Johnson?" Seeley asked.

"Gone as well. Seems she may be helping Lucy." McCoy stepped backward and grabbed a bagged item off the small wooden desk. "She left her phone behind, which seems odd in this day and age."

Seeley took the bag from McCoy and opened it. "Unless it was intentional? We could have tracked this."

"Smart girl."

Seeley eyed McCoy. "What do we know about her?"

"Not a lot. Zoe Johnson, twenty-four, has been working at the diner the last eight months. Before that it's pretty much a blank. She's not a sharer, according to Miss Mack, who definitely is."

Seeley turned the phone in his hand. He imagined when they searched it, they'd find nothing. If she was smart enough to leave it behind, she was probably smart enough not to keep anything of value on it. Which was exactly what he would do. Which meant she had something to hide.

"Miss Mack also mentioned how peculiar the girl was acting. She said she didn't seem to know or remember anything," McCoy said.

The two men shared a knowing look. More confirmation of Olivia's actions. Which meant Lucy was scared and alone and needing someone to follow.

And she'd picked Zoe Johnson.

"If Lucy doesn't remember anything, then why run?" McCoy asked, vocalizing Seeley's thoughts.

"Olivia must have told her we're the enemy."

"And Zoe? People usually cooperate with authority. Could Zoe know Lucy?"

"Not likely," Seeley said. Years of hunting people had taught him that human reactions were often predictable. A history of experiences shaped the way a person reacted to any situation. All one had to do was learn the history to predict the future.

He guessed if he looked through Zoe Johnson's past, he'd find evidence of an authority problem. They were a threat to her, so when she was confronted with a scared girl on the run from authority, it would be in her nature to assist. If she wasn't cutting the girl off, then what was motivating her to continue to help? And how far would that motivation drive her?

"Anything else?" Seeley asked.

McCoy flipped through his notes. "The cook, Pete Humble,

mentioned that Lucy tried to leave with a sleazy driver—his words, not mine—who offered to give her a ride. Zoe stepped in before Lucy could go."

"Any chance the cook remembers which direction the sleazy driver was headed?"

McCoy smiled. "Said he was pretty sure he got on 45 North."

"So was Lucy just catching a ride to anywhere, or did she mean to go that way?"

"I'll go back and talk with the cook and waitress again, see if I can get anything else."

Seeley let the silence hang between them as a few things crystalized.

First, since Lucy didn't remember who she was, then they couldn't pursue her as they had known her. They couldn't expect her to react the way she normally did. She was a stranger now.

Second, they needed more information on Zoe Johnson. Why was she helping Lucy? What was in it for her?

He turned his attention back to McCoy. "I also need you to get me everything you can on Zoe Johnson."

McCoy nodded.

Seeley yanked a peppermint from his pocket and unwrapped the plastic. He turned and started toward the exit, leaving McCoy at his back. "Everything you can find, ASAP," Seeley said, popping the hard candy into his mouth and leaving Zoe's motel apartment.

ZOE PAUSED TO survey the area. The trees were still covered in the dark of night, the air cold, nocturnal creatures scurrying across their land. Her mind was spinning, and she needed a moment to focus.

It had been a couple of hours since they'd slipped out her bathroom window. The first had passed in a flash of adrenaline and running for what felt like their lives. Once they were sure they weren't being followed and slowed their pace, Zoe's rationality had kicked in.

She'd crawled out a tiny window, away from the FBI, with a girl who had no memory but claimed to know the men after her were "bad guys." Doubt started to creep in, her own panic that maybe she was on the wrong side. Could it be possible that Lucy was the "bad guy" and Zoe had just placed herself in danger? Again, she'd broken rules that she'd put in place for a reason. Don't trust anyone—even some sappy, scared puppy. Yet here she was, wandering through the darkness, heading toward she-wasn't-sure-what with she-wasn't-sure-who. It suddenly all felt like a terrible mistake.

"Why is the FBI after you?" Zoe asked.

Lucy was walking a couple of feet ahead and turned to see that Zoe had stopped. She followed suit and turned to look at her. "They're bad guys."

"That doesn't answer my question."

Lucy thought for a moment. "I don't remember."

Zoe exhaled in disbelief. "Then how do you know they're bad?"

Lucy shook her head. "I don't—"

"Remember," Zoe finished for her. Frustration boiled in her chest. She let her head fall back as she closed her eyes. "What am I doing?" she said under her breath.

"Helping me, because you said you would."

Zoe looked back to Lucy, a question forming in her brain. She almost felt nervous asking it. "Earlier, how did you know the FBI was going to knock on my door?"

"I heard them," Lucy said.

"Before they were there?"

"Yes. I heard their footsteps outside on the pavement."

"And just now, you heard me talking to myself?"

Lucy nodded. "I hear all kinds of things."

An impossible idea was starting to take form in Zoe's mind. "Like what?"

Lucy paused a moment as if searching with her ears. "The stream that runs through these woods is east of us. It's filled with frogs this time of night. Something big is moving north, not human big but large enough to crack a branch, and there's a fox digging under a log a few yards away, probably found a mouse."

"How do you know it's a fox?"

"I can smell it."

Zoe stared at the girl, trying to get her mind to rationalize what her imagination was drawing up. "Where were you before the forest?"

"I told you I don't remember," Lucy said.

"Who is Olivia?"

"I don't know."

"Why are those men chasing you?" Zoe could feel heat rising up her back as her voice rose in volume.

"I don't remember," Lucy answered, her voice sounding smaller.

"Who are you?" Zoe snapped.

"I don't know!" Lucy replied in kind.

"Think, Lucy."

"Why are you yelling at me?"

"Because I need you to remember!"

"I don't, I can't!" Lucy tucked her head between balled fists and shook it back and forth. "I can't, I can't." She hit the sides of her skull with her fists and sniffed as emotions gripped her voice. "I don't remember."

Sympathy washed over Zoe, and the anger that had been rising up her spine crumbled to guilt. She moved toward Lucy and placed her hand on the girl's shoulder. Lucy raised her head, and in the moonlight Zoe could see the lines that tears left on her cheeks.

"I'm sorry I can't remember," Lucy whispered. She held Zoe's eyes tightly, and Zoe's guilt expanded. Lucy's body may have been fully grown, but her mind and soul were still fully innocent. As if she only knew black and white and no shades of gray. Zoe might as well have yelled at a little girl.

"Don't be sorry," Zoe said. "I'm sorry. I shouldn't have yelled. I'm just trying to understand what is going on here. How do you know the people after you are bad? Can you tell me that?"

Lucy sniffed and wiped the back of her hand across her nose. "I can feel it."

"Like you can hear things?" Zoe asked.

"Like I know now that you are very afraid."

Zoe dropped her hand from Lucy's shoulder and swallowed. Too many fictional plots and irrational ideas crashed around inside her brain. She cleared her throat and shook the make-believe free. She wouldn't jump to conclusions.

"Maybe there are answers in Corpus Christi," she said.

The girl's face lit up. "Yes, I need to go there."

"We need to get there," Zoe corrected.

Lucy smiled. "You won't leave me?"

The question knocked free blocked memories of the brother Zoe had abandoned. She'd followed the rules set by authority, because that's what she'd been taught to do. She'd feared the consequences of not doing what she was told. So she'd left him, and everything had changed. Maybe if she'd stayed she could have saved him.

She wouldn't do that again. This time she would break the rules. Even the ones she'd set for herself.

"I was never going to leave you," Zoe said.

Lucy's smile grew. She reached forward and tucked her fingers into Zoe's. Zoe felt the warmth of the girl's palm heat her own hand and then her heart. It had been so long since someone had needed her like this. It brought both joy and pain, because last time she had failed.

"We have to be smart, and careful," Zoe said.

"So they don't find us," Lucy said.

Zoe nodded. "I have a friend who can help."

"Where?"

"Dallas."

"And he can get us to Corpus Christi?"

"Yes."

Lucy nodded. "Then we go to Dallas, together."

An old, comforting feeling started to fill Zoe's bones. They would face trouble hand in hand. Them against the world. Suddenly the deep loneliness that was a result of trusting no one dimmed, and Zoe couldn't deny the warmth that took its place.

This time she smiled. "Together."

SEVEN

SEELEY CROSSED THE parking lot outside Memphis Medical Center. McCoy had connected Zoe Johnson to a Dr. Holbert who had seen Zoe regularly until the girl was fifteen, when she abruptly stopped seeing the doctor twice a week. There was hardly any other information from that point to now. It was as if Zoe Johnson had become a ghost, and Seeley intended to find out why.

He walked through the main entrance sliding doors, a burst of hot air hitting him from the overhead heater. The medical center's lobby was a large, open area with upholstered maroon chairs, shining white floors and matching walls, bright overhead lighting, and a wide wraparound desk set up in the middle.

An elderly woman with silver hair and bright blue–rimmed glasses sat behind the desk and smiled at Seeley as he approached. He gave a friendly grin in return and pulled his badge from the inside of his leather jacket. He flashed it quickly and her face turned serious.

"What can I help you with, sir?" she asked.

"I'm looking for a Dr. Simon Holbert," Seeley replied.

"Second floor, west side, suite number 12. Is he in some sort of trouble?"

"I just need to speak to him. Do I take those elevators there?" Seeley asked, pointing to the ones on the right side of the room.

She nodded. "To level two. I hope everything's alright. Simon is such a nice man." Her face was twisted with curiosity, and her tone begged for details. Seeley was certain this would be the story that filled the break room for days to come. This Barbra, according to her name plate, didn't seem like the kind who waited one moment to share a snip of gossip if it presented itself.

He thanked her and crossed to the elevators, hit the button, and stepped inside when the doors opened. He could feel Barbra's eyes on his back as the doors slid closed behind him. After a moment's ride he stepped onto the second floor. He walked down the wide hallway, its outside wall constructed of glass to show the parking lot below. A pretty nurse smiled at him as she passed. He didn't miss her flirtatious glance or the appealing curves of her body. He knew her skin was probably warm, her golden hair probably soft, and for a brief moment he wanted her.

It passed as quickly as it had come. The pleasure of her, the joy of human connection, wasn't for men like him. He'd tried that once, and it had betrayed him.

Seeley refocused on the task at hand. Suite 12 was marked by a black door like all the rest on the right-hand side of the hall. A small plaque on the left side of the door read *Dr. Simon Holbert, MD, Child Psychologist*. With a sharp twist of the golden knob, Seeley was inside the office.

Another pretty girl was sitting behind a receptionist's desk in the far corner of the small waiting room. A light tan couch and matching chairs circled a wooden coffee table topped with casual reading materials.

Seeley crossed the room and pulled out his badge. "I need to speak with Dr. Holbert," he said. "Is he in?"

The girl opened her mouth to speak as the door Seeley had just walked through sounded behind him. It drew his attention as a short bald man stepped inside the office. He wore simple khakis and a white button-down tucked in, paired with a dark brown belt and matching loafers. He had a computer bag draped over his shoulder and a stainless steel coffee thermos in hand.

He matched his online image. Seeley turned toward him, badge ready. "Dr. Holbert?"

"Yes, how can I help you?" Holbert asked, eyeing Seeley's ID.

"I need to speak to you about a former patient of yours," Seeley said.

"I'm afraid that information is protected unless you have a warrant."

"I just need some general information regarding an open investigation. A Zoe Johnson. She would have been a minor the last time you saw her."

Holbert's face flinched, and Seeley knew he recognized the name. She'd left an impression, as Seeley knew the doctor hadn't seen her in over nine years.

"Just a couple of questions," Seeley pushed. "It could help us protect another girl that we believe Johnson may intend to harm."

Holbert considered Seeley's words and motioned to his office. "After you."

The two men entered the doctor's office, and Seeley found exactly what he would have pictured: A long, soft couch across from a large plush, worn chair. Stacks of neatly kept books and literature on the brain and emotions. Framed accolades and degrees hanging on the walls.

Holbert set his coffee and bag on a large dark desk in front of the room's only window. "I'm not sure how helpful I'll be," he started. "I haven't seen Zoe Johnson in some time."

"But you do remember her?" Seeley asked.

"Yes, of course. She and I spent many years together."

"Why was that?"

"I'm not comfortable with that, Agent . . . ?"

"Seeley."

"You know the law, Agent Seeley."

"Unless she's a threat to herself and others, which we believe she is."

"Do you have proof of this, or again, a warrant?"

Seeley swallowed his frustration. The bleeding hearts of the psychiatric community grated on his last nerve. "I was hoping to do this without either of us having to do a mountain of paperwork," he said. He'd made a read on the doctor moments earlier that he was hoping wouldn't betray him now. "But if I need one then I'll have it within the hour, and we can do this the hard way. Surely the last thing you want is for a team of agents to comb through your office and home, top to bottom, without regard to your personal space, looking for any evidence that might lead back to Miss Johnson. That is the last thing I want to have to do."

"I don't appreciate the threat, Agent Seeley," Holbert said.

"I'm just trying not to waste anyone's time. So as direct as I can be, if I leave without the information I need, you will see me again, in a much less pleasant way."

The doctor considered what Seeley was selling. "She poses a serious threat to herself or others?"

Seeley nodded.

Dr. Holbert cleared his throat. "Zoe Johnson and her younger brother endured a tremendous amount of tragedy and abuse. They were filled with fear and had built an elaborate story to protect themselves from their past. I was helping them both come to terms with reality."

"There isn't a record of her having a brother."

"She has two, actually—a younger one, Stephen, and a twin. I never met her twin brother. He and their father were long gone when the courts assigned me to the case." Dr. Holbert started toward the tall filing cabinet across the room. "I really started to make progress with Zoe, but her younger brother was much more difficult." He reached into the top drawer and drew out a thick manila folder.

Seeley's phone vibrated in his back pocket and he yanked it out. The screen lit up and *Director* flashed across its surface.

"Excuse me," Seeley said, stepping to the corner. "Sir?" he said into the phone.

"I need you back here ASAP. Internal affairs uncovered a possible accomplice in Olivia and Lucy's escape," Hammon said.

"Who?"

"Zachary Krum."

Seeley's stomach dropped. Had it only been last week when Krum had been showing him pictures of his kids and asking Seeley which team he favored to win the Super Bowl?

"They're taking him into custody now."

"Sir, I may be onto something here."

"We need him to talk, Seeley, and for that I need my best."

Behind his eyes Seeley saw Krum's goofy face. "He's one of us."

"So was Olivia."

Seeley swallowed back his hesitation. "I'm on my way."

"Good." The line went dead, and Seeley pushed the phone into his pocket. He turned back to Dr. Holbert. The man was holding out the folder he'd just retrieved.

"You weren't able to find a record of Zoe Johnson's brothers because Zoe Johnson is an alias," the doctor said. "She wanted a clean start, and she believed changing her name would help. I'd so hoped she would continue to see me after what happened to her younger brother. I really believe I could have helped her."

Seeley took the folder and turned it over to see the name written on the red tab.

Evelyn Pierce.

EIGHT

ZOE AND LUCY sat in the back of a dark blue van as it drove along Dallas roads toward their destination. They'd arrived in Dallas late that afternoon, after catching a bus from Sherman in the early morning hours. Zoe had made a call, been given a time and place to be, and the dark van had been there precisely as instructed. Zoe wouldn't have expected anything else.

Their driver, simply referred to as Snow because of his stark white hair, and his companion, Eugene, loaded the girls into the back with very few pleasantries. The back was dingy, gutted out with two long benches on either side. Zoe and Lucy sat on one side while Eugene took the opposite. There were no windows, and the back windshield had been blacked out, so it was impossible to tell where they were going. Zoe had tried to use the front glass, but she could hardly see through the tight wired barricade that had been installed directly behind the driver's and passenger's seats. She shook her head as the van jostled over a speed bump.

The entire setup had Tomac written all over it. He was even more suspicious of the world than she and had a flare for the dramatic.

It had been years since Zoe had seen the boy who was now a man. They'd been kids together during their years in foster care, then teens together as their home became the streets, and after they'd gone separate ways as adults, their paths had continued to cross. They shared a bond that went deeper than trust, which was good, because she knew better than to trust him. It was odd to have faith in someone and constantly question his motivations, but that was how things were.

After several more minutes the van made a final turn and rolled to a stop. Snow glanced back and instructed, "Stay here." He crawled out, and the van shook as he slammed the door.

Zoe looked at Lucy. Her face was worried, and Zoe placed her hand on the girl's knee for reassurance. Then she looked at Eugene, who was watching them carefully. She'd have to make sure she mentioned the fine work Tomac's men were doing at making the situation feel threatening.

Silence engulfed the van for a long while, until the side handle jiggled and the door slid open. Snow stuck his head in and nodded to Eugene.

"Let's go," Eugene said, motioning for the girls to stand.

Zoe made her way out with Lucy close behind. Around the corner of the van, she saw that they were standing in an alley, staring at a tall fence that had once been white but was now tarnished with time. On the other side of the fence stood a row of older houses, built within a few feet of one another. She could hear voices from their owners drifting on the wind, a baby crying, a dog barking, a distant school bell. On the other side of the alley was a collection of tall apartment buildings that looked newer.

"Through the gate and up the path. He's expecting you," Snow said. He pointed to a wooden gate in the fence, then crossed his arms and leaned back against the van.

Zoe jumped as the van door slammed shut. Guess that was the end of the line for Eugene and Snow.

She started toward the gate and felt Lucy take her hand. Zoe threw a reassuring smile over her shoulder, though her own heart rate was rising. She yanked the gate open and stepped through with Lucy. They were in a backyard that seemed completely out of place for this neighborhood—meticulously manicured with perfectly kept hedges that lined both sides, a vegetable garden, a rock path, and a freshly painted porch. It looked odd connected to the house where the gray paint on the wood siding was peeling, the gutter was falling off in sections, and the shingles were warped. It was as if everything around them was true to the wear of time, but this yard had been plucked from somewhere else and placed in the center.

For the first time since climbing into the van, Zoe started to wonder if calling in a favor from her eccentric acquaintance had been a mistake. She and Lucy took the reconstructed porch stairs and rapped on the screen door.

"Come in," a pretty female voice called.

With a deep breath Zoe pulled the screen door open and stepped inside. The room was simple but clean and beautifully designed with white lines and warm copper-colored couches with soft touches of creams and light grays. A living room large enough to seat a dozen friends had a large flat screen on the far wall, surrounded by built-in shelving that housed hundreds of DVDs. It opened up into a dining room that touched what appeared to be a kitchen. All clean and well-furnished, homey and filled with delicate touches. Not at all what Zoe expected, judging from the outside. A young woman with bright green eyes and a lovely smile walked in from the kitchen, her light brown hair pulled back off her face in a ponytail that hung past her shoulders.

"Come in, make yourself at home," she said. She crossed the room and extended her hand to greet Zoe. "Can I get you anything, something to eat or drink?"

Zoe wasn't sure how to answer as she shook the woman's hand.

"Mave, sweets, I'll take it from here," a familiar voice said. Mave smiled and left as an older version of the boy Zoe had known confidently bounced down the stairs across the large open space. Casually dressed in tan shorts and a black T-shirt, hair long and tied up in a knot, with thin-rimmed glasses and barefoot, he was almost exactly as Zoe remembered.

"Friend," he said, crossing the room and extending his arms to Zoe. She wasn't really a hugger, but Tomac had always been overly affectionate. His own unique defense mechanism. They all had one.

"Tomac," Zoe said, enduring the embrace for just a moment before pulling back. "It's been a while."

"Too long, as they say. You look good."

"You look the same."

"I'll take that as a compliment." Tomac spun around and lifted bent arms to either side. "What do you think of my place? Pretty cool, huh?"

"Nearly as peculiar as our ride over," Zoe said.

"Yes, the drama of it all thrills me. Did you feel the tension? Any suggestions?"

Zoe chuckled. He was being dead serious. Before she could say anything, Lucy spoke.

"I was afraid," she said.

"Excellent," Tomac said, slapping his hands together. "And you must be Lucy."

Lucy swallowed nervously and looked to Zoe for guidance in this strange situation, then back to Tomac with a nod.

"Well, it's nice to meet you, Lucy. I hear you are in need of my help."

"Yes," Lucy said.

"Anything for a friend of Zoe."

"There's fresh lemonade if anyone wants some," Mave called in her angelic voice from the kitchen.

Zoe gave Tomac a curious look, and he waved it off. "She is new to us," he said. "Odd, yes, but I never turn anyone away. You know how I am. Everyone should have a safe place."

"Still taking in strays?" Zoe said.

"We were strays once," Tomac said, his voice taking on a more serious tone. "And someone offered us a place to go. I'm just paying it forward."

"As long as they're useful, right?" Zoe mocked. She knew better than to fall for his self-righteous ploy. Tomac was a giver, but only when taking in equal measures. He'd learned that from Heath. He'd learned everything from Heath.

Zoe was suddenly struck by images from her past. She'd been just another body in the system of unwanted kids who cycled through foster homes, never really landing anywhere permanent. She'd been too old for adoption, too stained by the very public evil of her mother. An uncomfortable shiver crawled up her spine. Even the thought of her . . .

She turned her thoughts back to Heath. The boy who had offered her a place. He was another kid similar to her, abandoned, scared, and untrusting of the world. They'd found companionship in one another. Heath, being a couple of years older, had sheltered her and Tomac for a season, shown them how to survive. For a price. For their loyalty.

It had been only a season for Zoe, who was ready to move on the moment she could. But for Tomac it had become more, and as Heath shared his secrets of survival and brought Tomac into his kingdom, as he called it, Tomac found a place that was his.

And then he'd taken it all from Heath. The prince who'd overthrown the king.

Tomac flashed a devilish grin. "Everyone can be useful," he said.

"You just have to find them the right task," Zoe finished.

"So she *was* listening." He stepped to her side and threw his arm around her shoulders. "You know, I could always find something for you. You and me, babe, we could rule the world."

Zoe brushed off his never-ending flirtation. "That's not what we're here for."

He rolled his eyes and looked at Lucy. "Always so serious, isn't she?"

Lucy shrugged with an expression of uncertainty.

Tomac dropped his arm and turned his full attention to Lucy. "That's right, you hardly know each other. Strange, Zoe doesn't make friends very easily. So, what makes you so special, Lucy?"

Zoe recognized the predatory tone in Tomac's voice and stepped between him and Lucy. She could see the hunger in his eyes. He was a collector of things—and people. He knew enough to be interested. She'd had to tell him about Lucy's memory loss and the trouble she was in. Now she'd have to protect Lucy from the one person who could help them.

She placed her hand on his chest and gave a forceful little push so he knew she was serious. "I came here like you asked, and you said in return you would help me."

His eyes lingered on Lucy for another moment, and then he dropped them back to Zoe. "Didn't you want to see me too?"

"We could have done this over the phone, and that would have been fine with me."

"But then I wouldn't get to see your lovely face, which I really do miss."

"Liar."

"So feisty."

"Coming here was a mistake," Zoe said, turning to Lucy. "Let's go."

"Alright, fine, we'll be all business then," Tomac said. "A promise is a promise. You came all this way, after all. Who did you need to find?"

"A Summer Wallace," Zoe said, turning back to face him. "All we know is that she lives in Corpus."

"That's not much."

"More than you've had before, sire," Zoe said, stroking his ego. "Can you help us?"

"Does a cat meow? A dog, does it bark?" he replied.

Zoe exhaled. "Couldn't you just say yes?"

"Where's the fun in that?" He winked, and the familiar feeling of fear and adoration filled her chest. There really wasn't anyone else like him.

"And the fee," Tomac continued. "Of course you'll get the friends and family discount."

Zoe unzipped her bag, drew out most of the cash she had, and handed it over. Tomac eyed it for a moment. Zoe knew it wasn't enough, but she was hoping their history might give her some credit she could use to make up the rest.

"A very deep discount then," Tomac said. "I'll put my best guy on it, but it may take a couple of hours. By then it'll be dark. You can stay here tonight, of course."

Zoe's stomach turned. She'd hoped to be in and out. Staying in one place, especially this place, felt dangerous. But Tomac kept his operation hidden well, so she couldn't imagine the FBI finding them here. She nodded.

"Excellent. Mave, sweets," he called, and the strange woman walked back from the kitchen. "We'll have guests for the evening. Make sure they are comfortable, will you?"

She smiled too brightly and nodded. Two preteen boys descended the stairs behind Tomac, caught up in hushed conversations. One crossed the distance to them and whispered something in Tomac's ear, yanked a thick white envelope from the back of his pants, handed it to Tomac, and then rejoined his friend. The boys bounded back up the stairs and Zoe watched them, more memories slamming around inside her brain.

"You ever miss it?" Tomac asked.

Zoe snapped her eyes back to Tomac's face. "Never."

"Miss what?" Lucy asked.

"Nothing," Zoe quickly answered.

"Let's just say Zoe here was one of the best runners of our time," Tomac said.

"Runner?" Lucy questioned. "I like to run."

"And I bet you'd be great at it," Tomac said.

"It's not what you think," Zoe said to Lucy.

"What is it?" the girl asked.

"It doesn't matter. It's in the past." Zoe looked back to Tomac. "We've been traveling all day."

Tomac let the tension stand a moment longer than was comfortable and then said, "I'll have Mave show you where you two can crash." He took Zoe's hand in his. "If you need anything, you find me."

"Thank you," Zoe said, and she was grateful. But she also knew she'd be completely tense until they were out of there.

Another long, awkward moment lingered, courtesy of Tomac, before he left them.

Zoe was deeply regretting ever calling him to begin with.

NINE

SEELEY WASN'T SURE what time it was. He'd been in the box with Krum for some time now, but time couldn't be measured down here, under the floor of Xerox, where its darkest secrets were hidden away. The box required top-level security clearance, for good reason.

The room was square, made up of four concrete walls stained with punishment, the floor holding a large grate in the center for easy cleanup, the overhead lighting dull and cold, the room void of anything except the steel chair that Krum was strapped to. But that would soon be removed. Then the cold, hard floor would hold him as the persuasion to talk continued.

Seeley had turned off his humanity the moment he'd walked into the room. He couldn't see Krum's face and have access to any goodness, otherwise he wouldn't be capable of what was required. That's why they'd called him: Seeley had mastered shutting out his soul and accessing the darkness needed to get the job done.

He couldn't recall a time when he wasn't this way. Maybe he'd been born with the ability to go dark. Maybe life had beaten it into him. Steph would say she'd seen it from time to time, and it scared her. Only when the work followed him home, when it was the worst. But she saw past it, brought the goodness back out. This was her gift to him and a way to offer protection for their daughter, Cami.

Then another man took Steph from him, able to give her what Seeley couldn't. And then the world saw him as unfit to father alone, and in one moment he'd lost everything. Which had been a gift for Cami.

Did she know that? Did she realize she was better off without her father?

Seeley twisted his neck to the side and cracked the bones. His mind was drifting, but the memories let him access his pain, and that allowed him to see Krum as a job.

Krum had been stripped down to his underwear. He was strapped to the cold metal chair, his ankles secured to its legs and his arms tied behind his spine. The room's temperature was near freezing, and the man was soaking wet, his black hair dangling in his eyes, his chin sunk low against his chest. Sopping wet, Krum couldn't weigh more than 180 pounds, tall and thin with awkwardly large feet and hands, knobby knees, and a goofy grin.

He'd been shivering violently, but now he was still. Seeley crossed the room and yanked Krum's chin upward. The man was losing consciousness, his body slipping into darkness as a way to protect itself from the cold and pain. They couldn't have that.

Seeley reached for the steel rod that dangled to the right of the prisoner. Thick wire ran from its base up and over a massive hook that hung from the ceiling directly above them. The wire then worked its way to the concrete wall and down the surface to a fuse box with a small panel and two dials. One powered the device, the other controlled its intensity. A simple invention to use electricity as a means of persuasion.

He'd adjusted the power to do harm without killing the man,

and he pressed the rod's end to Krum's left tricep. The shock pulsed through the man's arm and into his chest, causing him to jolt to life with several painful screams. Seeley retracted the rod as Krum huffed and whimpered.

Seeley had started with asking the man to cooperate. He hadn't wanted to end up here, but Krum admitted he had helped Olivia and Lucy get out through security, and they needed to know what else he knew about Olivia's plan. His ability to resist was surprising. Seeley would have put money on being able to break him with threats, but here they were.

"Please, Seeley," Krum whimpered. "I have kids."

"Tell me what we need to know, and this will be over," Seeley said.

"And then you'll kill me."

Seeley didn't insult the man by trying to convince him otherwise. Everyone knew what they were signing up for when they joined Grantham. Krum was too smart for mind games and false promises.

"Tell me why you helped her." Seeley said.

"I helped her because it was the right thing to do. The project has gone too far," Krum replied.

"The orders were clear."

"The orders were wrong."

"But they were orders. They came from the top." Seeley dropped to one knee so he could look Krum in the eye. "What did you think would happen?"

Krum spat saliva mixed with dark blood to the side and returned his gaze to Seeley. "If there was a chance to save her, I had to help." His eyes were resolved. He really believed he was doing right. "They were just kids, Seeley, kids the same age as my own."

"No, they were never just kids."

A moment of silence passed between them.

"Where was Olivia taking Lucy?"

"You're just going to kill me," Krum said. "I gain nothing by talking to you."

This man was full of virtue. He'd die for the cause he'd strapped himself to. This approach wasn't working.

"How old is Dana this year?" Seeley asked.

Fear and anger washed over Krum's face. "You stay away from my kids, you son of—"

"She driving yet? I bet you worry every time she leaves the house."

"I swear, if you go near her—"

"It's fine to worry. The roads are dangerous. Bad things happen to even the smartest of drivers."

"You wouldn't," Krum said, his anger shifting to disbelief. "You're bluffing."

Seeley stood and crossed his arms over his chest.

Krum just stared up at him, a meld of emotions flashing through his eyes. His mouth slightly ajar, his face pale.

"Tell me and I make sure no one gets hurt," Seeley said.

"And if I don't, you go after my family?" Krum asked, his words losing their bite as reality started to sink in.

Seeley didn't respond. He didn't need to.

Krum shook his head. "No, touch them and I'll never talk."

Seeley leaned forward and placed his hand on the chair's back, his face only inches from Krum's. "How long would it take for you to break if I put Dana in this chair?"

Tears filled Krum's eyes. His nose crumpled as he shook his head. He was fighting the fear, trying to be brave, to call Seeley's bluff. But Seeley didn't bluff, and knowing what was at stake, he was certain the powers that be would stop at nothing to get Lucy.

"Is Lucy really worth your daughter's safety?" he pushed. "Her life?"

Krum clamped his eyes shut, tears running down his cheeks.

"Does Dana deserve to pay for your treachery?"

Again silence filled the box as Seeley let Krum come fully to grips with the only choice he had.

"Tell me what you know," Seeley said.

"Less than you want, only what I needed to know," Krum said. "Olivia was careful."

"What was the plan?"

"To get Lucy out, alive."

"Why?"

"You know why!"

Because Olivia had loved Lucy like a daughter, and a parent would do anything for her child. Like Krum was offering up his own life to save his daughter.

"Walk me through it, from the beginning," Seeley said.

"Olivia came to me two weeks ago. She knew I had access to the security database, and she needed access."

"What did she take?"

"Everything. Documents, videos, signed affidavits, all dating back to the beginning, and the final orders that came through after the project failed."

Enough to blow up Washington and everyone associated with Grantham. Seeley knew exactly what the world would do to them, to him, if it ever saw what they'd been doing here.

"And what was the plan?" Seeley asked again.

"I don't know. I just helped get her what she needed, and then I cleared a way so she and Lucy could get out before the army descended."

Seeley grabbed Krum by the throat and pressed hard. He was

losing his patience. "Give me something useful, Krum. For Dana's sake."

Krum yanked against Seeley's hold. "I don't know anything else."

"You spent time with her, knew what she was going to do. You had to have overheard something."

"I work in security. I just wanted to give them a chance."

"Not good enough!" Seeley released Krum's neck and grabbed the rod. He rammed it into Krum's chest cavity. A powerful electric wave raced through the device and into Krum's weathered body. He lurched and cried out, his voice filling the box with piercing agony.

"If Olivia had the information, why not just release it herself?" Seeley asked.

"I don't know."

"Why give it to Lucy? That makes her a target."

"I don't know!"

Seeley struck him again, shaking the man's figure like a rag doll. "I can't help your family if you don't help me. You give, I give."

Krum coughed up blood. It trickled down his chin and splattered on his knee. Seeley was frying his insides. He wailed, cursed, and spat through his coughing. "I don't—"

Seeley didn't wait for him to finish. He administered a final pulse with the rod, long and drawn out. Krum screamed and trembled in his chair. Seeley pulled the rod back and let it hang. Krum hunched over and cried like a scared little boy. Blood, snot, and tears mingled on his face.

"We can go again," Seeley said, reaching back for the rod.

"Wait, wait, wait!" Krum cried out.

Seeley paused as the man whimpered.

"God forgive me," Krum whispered. "I'm not strong enough."

"Tell me what you know and this will end."

Krum huffed through his tears and pain. "Lucy is the only one that can find the location where the information is hidden."

"What do you mean?"

"Olivia implanted the details in one of her old memories. Like a code that tells her where she needs to go to recover the data. She can't access it unless she regains her memories."

Olivia wouldn't have been so stupid, Seeley thought. All Grantham would have to do was kill the girl to destroy the information.

"There's a fail-safe," Krum said, as if reading his mind.

Seeley swore under his breath.

"If Lucy doesn't recover the information, or if she dies, another source will release it nationally."

"What source?" Seeley hissed.

"I don't know," he said through tears. "I swear, she wouldn't tell me more."

Seeley reached backward for the rod.

"I swear!" Krum cried. "She would never risk giving me that information. It's the only thing keeping Lucy alive!"

Seeley inhaled slowly. This made things more complicated. "How long do we have?"

"I don't know that either, but my guess, not long."

Seeley tossed the metal rod away, and it clanged against the floor. "What did you get for betraying your country?"

Krum screamed up at him, "I got to be human! To sleep at night. But then, you probably don't understand that."

Seeley already didn't sleep, and being human was overrated. Humanity made you vulnerable. His humanity had nearly destroyed him, and now humanity would destroy Krum.

"I don't know anything else." Krum sniffed. "I don't know anything else." Defeated, the man crumpled. His shoulders shook with sobs, his cries silent but suffocating.

All Seeley could feel was his own darkness, so he turned and left the sobbing man behind him. He unlocked the box's door, then shut Krum inside, still achingly mournful in his chair.

The hallway was silent, nothing but the overhead ventilation system turning the air in and out. Two guards stood on either side of the steel door, staring forward, armed to the hilt. Seeley took a deep breath as he started to release his darkness, a process that was always painful, and turned to the guard on the left. "Kill him."

The agent nodded, and the two standing watch entered the box as Seeley started down the hall. A few feet away, he heard two pops echo across the stillness. Seeley didn't pause. He couldn't afford to. He pressed on, keeping his mind anchored on Lucy. It all had to be about finding Lucy.

TEN

ZOE STOOD INSIDE the bathroom at the end of the upstairs hallway. Shared by the row of simple bedrooms that lined the hall, the bathroom had a shower/bath combo, two sinks, two mirrors, and a single toilet. A good size, but probably chaos in the morning, depending on how many beds were filled.

She splashed her face with water and stared at her reflection in the mirror. The world would see a grown woman, but Zoe could still see the terrified little girl she was trying to forget. This house was different, but the feelings were the same. She'd been here before. Under the care of Heath, in a past life, doing whatever she needed to survive. Heath had found her when she was trying to rebuild her life, trying to become someone else. He'd helped her create a world where she could live without the stain of her own failures. The failures of her parents. Her mother.

Lucy had a dozen questions. How did Zoe meet Tomac? What was a runner? Was Tomac a bad guy or a good guy? Were they safe here? All questions that required Zoe to open up and risk letting that terrified little girl out of hiding. What if she couldn't get her back in? But Lucy was a puppy with a bone, and she couldn't let it go. So Zoe had given simple answers.

Tomac and I met when we were kids.

A runner is a job where you deliver and retrieve things. The kinds of things you don't want to get caught retrieving or delivering.

Tomac is both a bad guy and a good guy. It all depends on who you are.

Safer here than out there, but don't trust anyone here.

When you remember your past, I'll tell you more about mine.

That last statement had come out with too much anger, and she could see she'd hurt Lucy's feelings. Zoe had excused herself to the bathroom, where she was practicing calming breaths that were supposed to help her re-center, according to Jessie. It wasn't working though. She dried her face on a hand towel and sat on the closed toilet.

She knew she should make amends. Lucy was too innocent to be blamed for her curiosity, but Zoe was too stubborn for her own good. Lucy had awakened the constant whispering of her past, and that made Zoe angry. Being here, in this house with Tomac, had amplified the whispers to screams.

Zoe tried another deep breath, then huffed and dropped her head into her hands. She pressed against her closed eyes with the palms of her hands, the pressure blotting out the noise. Zoe missed her past-less life. Lucy wasn't even aware of what a gift she had, not being able to remember.

A painful cry echoed outside. Zoe jumped up and yanked the bathroom door open. The cry sounded again. A voice pleading, "Stop! Stop!" It was coming from their bedroom.

Zoe rushed out, joined by others poking their heads out from the surrounding rooms. She moved down the hall with wide strides and stepped into the scene playing out in the bedroom: Lucy standing over a boy, twisting his wrist. Him kneeling on the ground, crying out in pain, begging her to let him go. Her face stone-cold, eyes fixed on her prey.

Before Zoe could intervene, Lucy gave a final twist and Zoe heard the boy's bone snap.

His cry echoed off the ceiling and filled the whole house. More footsteps pounded up the stairs as Zoe stood there, stunned.

"What is going on?" Tomac's voice broke Zoe from her trance, and she turned to see a crowd had gathered. Tomac stepped through.

Zoe reacted then. She rushed into the bedroom and grabbed Lucy's shoulder. The girl moved with insane speed. She snapped her head toward Zoe, freed herself, and spun so she had control of Zoe's arm. Fear filled Zoe as the image of Lucy breaking the boy's wrist flashed through her brain. He was still curled on the floor at their feet, whimpering like a baby.

"Lucy, don't!" Zoe cried.

Lucy made eye contact with her, and the coldness that had hardened her face softened, like someone had walked into the darkness of her mind and flipped on a light. She looked from Zoe to her own hold of Zoe's arm, then to the crying boy. Then back to Zoe, terror replacing whatever had been there before.

Lucy released her and took a step back. A deer in headlights, confused and mortified. Zoe took several quick breaths.

"What happened here?" Tomac boomed. He was angry. Never a good sign.

Several others had rushed in to tend to the boy, who was still crying, but softer now.

"His wrist is broken," someone said.

"She broke it, I saw her do it," another cried, pointing a finger at Lucy.

"I invite you into my home, and your new friend breaks a boy's wrist?" Tomac continued.

"Lucy, what happened?" Zoe asked, trying to keep her voice low and calm. The girl was trembling.

Lucy looked down at the boy. "He tried to take our stuff," she said softly.

"She's crazy!" the boy cried.

"No," Lucy said. "He came in here and told me he needed your backpack. That Tomac asked for it." She looked back up at Zoe. "But you told me not to trust anyone. So I told him he couldn't have it, and he tried to take it anyway."

"Is that true, Scooter?" Tomac asked, moving his eyes to the boy.

"No, she's lying," Scooter said through whimpers.

"I wouldn't lie," Lucy said.

Tomac dropped to his knees beside Scooter, and the others who had come to his aid scattered. He grabbed the boy by the collar and pulled him close. "Don't lie to me."

"I wouldn't lie to you, Boss," Scooter said. "I wouldn't. She's crazy!"

"Like you weren't lying to me about Brownstone?" Tomac hissed.

Scooter's eyes widened and he shook his head. Even from where Zoe was standing, she could see his mind scrambling.

"If I find out you aren't being truthful with me . . ." Tomac threatened. "And I will find out."

A different kind of fear flickered in Scooter's eyes. The kind children his age shouldn't know. "I didn't realize it was hers. It was a mistake." He stumbled over his words, trying to find an escape from the mess he'd made for himself. Zoe's heart ached for him.

Tomac tossed Scooter down and nodded to two others behind him.

"I didn't know, Boss," Scooter cried. "I swear!"

Two larger kids helped the boy up and escorted him out forcefully. "She's crazy! She broke my wrist." Fresh tears filled his eyes and slid down his face.

Tomac stood and addressed the gathered crowd as Scooter was dragged out of sight, his pain echoing after he was gone. "Stealing is for the streets, never under my roof!" he yelled. "Now get lost!"

The others scattered like mice, and a moment later it was just the three of them. Tomac turned to face Zoe and Lucy, forcing a long exhale to calm. Zoe didn't want to think about the kind of penance Scooter would owe to satisfy Tomac's temper.

"I apologize," he said to Lucy. "I've had problems with him before. I promise you won't have any other trouble." Then to Zoe, "My guy located three potentials for Summer Wallace." He pulled an envelope from his back pocket and held it out to her. "There's an early bus. I put the tickets under a secure alias. You should try and get some rest."

Zoe reached for the envelope and felt resistance when she tried to take it. She locked eyes with Tomac as he held on, his gaze shrouded in a mixture of curiosity and concern. They stood there just a moment, then he released the envelope and headed for the exit.

"Thank you, Tomac," Zoe said.

He paused at the door and gave Zoe a final look. It said, *Be careful.*

She gave him a nod. *I will.*

He shut the door as he left.

Zoe cautiously turned back to Lucy. "You alright?"

Lucy shook her head, her eyes dotted with tears. "I didn't mean to hurt him. I just didn't want him to take your things."

"It's okay," Zoe said. She mustered the courage to reach out to Lucy. The girl she'd watched snap a boy's wrist like a twig. The girl who could have easily done the same to her.

Lucy moved to meet her touch. It was as if a different girl were standing before her now. The scared puppy. Zoe wouldn't have believed Lucy was capable of breaking a boy's arm if she hadn't witnessed it herself.

Zoe rubbed Lucy's upper arm softly as tears escaped the girl's eyes and trailed down her cheeks. Zoe could see the wheels behind Lucy's eyes turning toward dangerous thoughts. Running down paths that led to holes covered in darkness.

"What am I?" Lucy asked, her terror hushed. She looked up at Zoe, her eyes pleading for understanding.

Zoe didn't know how to answer or how to ease the girl's suffering. The same dark questions that were running around inside Lucy's mind were also growing inside her own.

"Am I bad?" Lucy asked. "Am I the bad guy?"

Zoe wished she could convince Lucy she was good, lift the troubled burden the young girl was shouldering. But the truth was simple: Zoe didn't know who Lucy was or what she was capable of.

ELEVEN

ZOE STEPPED OUT of the yellow taxi that had delivered her and Lucy to 1616 Columbus Drive. She'd expected a housing development or apartment building, but instead she found herself looking at what appeared to be a junkyard. A tall metal fence ran around the property's outline with large red DO NOT TRESPASS signs placed every couple yards. Behind it were mounds of waste—abandoned cars, kitchen appliances, furniture, metal scraps.

"This can't be right," she whispered. She turned back to the cab as Lucy took in the strange scene. Zoe tapped the window and it descended. She poked her head inside. "This is 1616 Columbus Drive?"

"You betcha," the driver replied.

"Could there be another Columbus Drive?" she asked.

"This is the one and only. You want to go somewhere else?"

Zoe looked back over her shoulder. She didn't know where else they'd go. Maybe someone lived here behind the heaps of rubbish?

"Can you wait for a couple minutes?" Zoe asked.

"Sure, if you pay me."

"I'll pay you afterward."

"You'll pay me now for the time I've already spent, and then the rest afterward."

Zoe huffed and dug out thirty dollars from her back pocket. She handed it over. "Just wait here, okay?"

He nodded and grabbed the money, and Zoe joined Lucy. An evening chill crept in as the sun set on the day, a day that was beginning to feel eternal. Zoe and Lucy had left Tomac's while it was still dark and boarded a bus as the sky filled with morning light. Eight and a half hours later that bus pulled into the station in north Corpus Christi, and the girls had started their search. Three addresses, each one dozens of miles from the next.

The first two had turned up nothing useful. Both had belonged to residents with the name Summer Wallace, but neither seemed to know anything about Lucy or Ollie or a robin. Now, Zoe and Lucy shared a worried look, both knowing this was where their plan ended. They'd kept conversation simple and shallow since the startling events at Tomac's yesterday. Zoe suspected their minds ran in similar directions, but neither of them wanted to verbalize their thoughts. She hoped they'd find Summer and she'd know what they should do next. But this seemed less than hopeful.

"Come on," Zoe said as she started toward the fence. The entrance was marked with a wide gate. She reached it and yanked. Locked. She looked around, and two details stood out. To the right side of the gate was a small code box and a keypad. Above it, at the high point of the fence, a black camera was directed down toward them but seemingly inactive.

Lucy was beside her, looking through the chain links, searching for signs of life.

"Anything?" Zoe asked.

"Lots of things," Lucy replied.

Zoe moved to the code box and pressed the keypad. Nothing

happened. It appeared offline or broken. She probed it with her fingers, hoping something might trigger the gate to unlatch, but still nothing.

"This is useless," she said. She could feel her exhaustion and frustration melding. To make matters worse, she heard the taxi behind her roar to life. She turned in time to see it pulling away. "Hey!" she screamed, rushing after it. "Wait, come back!" But it was too late. In a few seconds the car was turning back onto the side road and was gone.

Zoe cursed loudly. "That's just great!" Now they were stuck out in the middle of nowhere with no ride, at a dead end. She wanted to scream, throw her backpack on the ground, kick the air, anything to expel the anger gathering in her chest. Instead she rolled her fingers into fists, pressed her nails into her palms, and let out a shaky exhale. She couldn't lose control. She needed to come up with a plan for what to do now.

"Zoe," Lucy called.

She took another deep breath. She was pretty sure they had passed a gas station a couple of miles back. If they started walking now, they could probably get there before it was too dark.

"Zoe," Lucy called again.

But then what would they do? They were running out of money, and Zoe didn't know anyone in this city. She guessed they could get back on a bus to Dallas, head back to Tomac's. Would he even let them back in?

"Zoe—"

She swung back around. "What?" she snapped.

Lucy was staring up at the camera and pointed. "I think someone is watching us."

A shiver ran down Zoe's spine. She walked toward Lucy and saw a small red light blinking at the base of the camera.

"Was that light there before?" Lucy asked.

No, Zoe thought. She wouldn't have missed that.

"Hello," she said toward the camera. "Is anyone there?"

They waited.

Silence.

Maybe it was motion sensitive and had activated when they walked by. That didn't mean someone was watching. Right?

Zoe waved her hands over her head. "Hello? We're looking for Summer Wallace. Is anyone by that name here?"

The light blinked and silence met their words. Zoe dropped her arms and sighed. She needed sleep. "It's going to be dark soon. We need to make a plan." She turned away from the fence and dropped to a knee, yanking her backpack around and inspecting its contents. "I think we have enough for a room and bus tickets. We should get some rest and then—"

"Hello," Lucy said. "Please, if someone is there, I need your help."

"Lucy, there's no one there," Zoe said. She didn't even bother looking back.

"Ollie sent me to find the robin," Lucy continued.

Zoe shook her head. No one would understand the cryptic code. She was starting to think this Olivia was a nutcase.

"She said I could trust you, that you're a friend," Lucy said.

"Lucy, there's no one—"

A dull buzz cut Zoe's words short, and after a moment the gate's lock turned and popped open. Lucy looked wide-eyed back at Zoe. Zoe's mouth was open in similar surprise. Lucy pulled the gate to the left, and it slid open enough for her to step inside.

Zoe scooped up their belongings and followed Lucy down the wide dirt path that cut through the piles of abandoned things. They'd traveled a few feet when the gate buzzed back to life and slid closed behind them. With a click it locked, sealing them inside. They paused, sharing a look, and then continued.

Zoe's eyes wandered over the terrain as they moved. Thousands of discarded items had found their way here. More threatening signs stood from the ground along the path.

Do Not Enter

Trespasser Be Warned

Private Property

Zoe half expected a handwritten message: *Turn around, go back, you aren't prepared for what lies ahead.*

After a minute of walking the path that twisted back and out of view of the main entrance, they came upon a small house. Zoe wouldn't actually call it a house but rather a small shed with a slanted steel roof, wood walls, and a single door cut out in the front. It was attached to a good-size warehouse—no windows, no doors—with a matching metal roof that lay flat across the top. A huge satellite and tall antenna occupied one corner. Two more black cameras sat on the front two corners of the warehouse, and a third camera watched from above the strange home's single entrance.

Lucy started toward the door, but it opened before she reached it. They saw the end of a long shotgun before the person holding it. Zoe took long strides, reached Lucy, and yanked her back as a middle-aged woman emerged, gun extended, face stone-cold. Her light blonde hair was pulled atop her head in a tight bun, her skin pale and freckled, her black clothes plain and functional and paired with heavy dark boots that could easily knock out teeth.

All the warning instincts that existed inside Zoe's body went off. This woman did not want them here, and they should not be here.

"Who are you?" the woman barked.

"Are you Summer Wallace?" Lucy asked bravely. Or stupidly. Zoe wasn't sure yet.

"I'm asking the questions! Who are you?" the gun holder demanded.

"This is Zoe," Lucy said, "and I'm Lucy."

"Where did you hear that phrase? Ollie sent you to find the robin—where did you hear it?"

"Olivia told me."

The woman flinched slightly and her eyes darted between the girls. "How do you know Ollie?"

"You mean Olivia?" Zoe asked.

The woman nodded, and Zoe's assumption was confirmed. Ollie and Olivia were one and the same.

Lucy remained quiet, and Zoe could feel her thinking.

"I asked you a question!" the woman yelled, cocking the shotgun and setting Zoe's teeth on edge.

"I don't remember," Lucy replied. "I can't remember."

Again the woman's body responded to Lucy's words. She pulled her shoulders back, and the coldness in her eyes chipped away.

"But she told me to find you, and to tell you that Ollie sent me to find the robin, and that I could trust you because you're a friend. She said you would help me," Lucy said. Zoe could hear the emotion capturing her words. "And I really need help."

The woman held the gun steady, sizing them up, searching them with her eyes. The moment seemed to linger for an uncomfortable amount of time, most likely because it involved a gun being pointed at their faces, but eventually she lowered the weapon and held it to one side.

"Why isn't she with you?" she asked.

"We got separated," Lucy replied. "She said she would meet me here."

Sadness filled Summer's eyes, and after a moment she turned around and kicked the side of a barrel that sat beside the open door. She kicked it again and swore at the evening sky. Then she swung back around, tears sitting in her bottom lids. "Did anyone follow you here?" she demanded.

"No," Lucy said. "We got away from them."

"From *them*?"

"The men chasing Olivia and me."

Summer dropped her eyes, and even in the fading light Zoe could see that she was thinking it all over. "They must have figured out what she was up to."

"Do you know what's going on here?" Zoe asked.

"Olivia can tell us everything when she gets here," Lucy said.

"Don't be stupid, child," Summer snapped. "Ollie is never coming here. They got her."

Lucy shook her head. "You don't know that for sure."

"Yeah, I do. They always get you if you let them. But not me, not here!" She paused a second and then paced.

Zoe wished she could see inside this woman's mind. Something was clearly off.

"You two should leave," Summer said as she turned away.

"No," Lucy cried. "Please, we have nowhere else to go."

"Not my problem," Summer said.

"Olivia said we could trust you."

"She was wrong."

"You're supposed to be her friend! You're supposed to help me!"

"It's too much of a risk. Without Olivia . . ."

Zoe stepped in front of Lucy. "They'll kill her," she said, which caused Summer to pause. "They'll kill Lucy like they killed Olivia. And if you can help us and don't, then that blood is on your hands. Do you want that?"

Summer glanced over her shoulder at them, and Zoe approached her, ignoring the terror still creeping up her back. "Tell us what you know and we'll be gone. Don't and we die."

Silence hung around them like heavy smoke, making it hard to breathe. The wait felt longer than Zoe knew it was, their fate in the hands of this stranger. A stranger who could as easily shoot them as invite them in.

Summer didn't shoot them. She didn't turn around to face them. She just spoke over her shoulder. "Let's make this quick." And then she disappeared inside.

TWELVE

SEELEY FOLLOWED DIRECTOR Hammon as he pushed through the double doors that led into the central communications office at Xerox. There was news. A possible connection that may give them a viable lead on Lucy's location.

There was a new sense of urgency as Krum had let on that there was now a deadline, an unknown date that they had to beat. Otherwise the world would know about Grantham and what they had done. And that couldn't happen.

"Talk to me," Hammon said. His voice drew the attention of the room. It was a large oval space filled with screens that displayed images of ongoing operations, data streams, and the site's security feeds. In the center was a long comms central, four operators working its switches and buttons.

Dave McCoy, data pad in hand, took several steps from his position to greet Hammon and Seeley. With a swipe of three fingers across the data pad's surface, he took over a large screen that hung on the left wall before them. A profile appeared, the face of a middle-aged woman and her details displayed.

"This is Robin Hester, an old classmate of Olivia's while she was getting her graduate degree at Cornell University. Robin was a structural biologist, and she and Olivia were both employed by Corp Tech for nearly a decade."

Seeley studied the woman's photo. She had kind blue eyes and light blonde hair that brushed the tops of her slender shoulders. Pretty and unassuming.

"It seems Olivia and Robin were close through their school days," McCoy continued, "as well as while they worked together at Corp Tech. We spoke with several of their colleagues. It seems Olivia and Robin were always talking about changing the face of science by merging structural biology and genetics in a groundbreaking way."

"This Robin Hester is helping them then?" Hammon asked.

"No," McCoy answered. "She was diagnosed with brain cancer in 2001 and passed away eighteen months later. But she had a stepsister who served in the US military from 2004 to 2007. She was honorably discharged after failing a psych evaluation. Apparently, she's a bit of a conspiracy theorist." He smiled at Hammon, who didn't return his sentiment. McCoy cleared his throat. "Anyway, we scoured all the communications coming and going from Xerox and turned up nothing, but when we widened the search to the surrounding cities, a landline in Jasper turned up several phone calls to a pay phone on the outskirts of Corpus Christi. The landline belongs to a Melissa Glass, a known associate of Olivia."

"So, you think Olivia was making the calls?" Seeley asked.

"Scanning security cameras shows Olivia wasn't on campus when the phone calls were made, so if she wasn't here . . ." McCoy said.

"Then she could have been there," Seeley said. "We need to talk with Melissa."

"We sent a couple agents, but no new information came from it," McCoy continued. "Meanwhile, I've been looking for a connection to Corpus Christi."

"I'm assuming this ties back to Robin Hester?" Hammon said.

"That's what we think." McCoy swiped the data pad again, and the profile on the screen changed. Another blonde woman replaced Robin's photo. She was stockier with mean, dark eyes. Troubled.

"Meet Summer Wallace," McCoy said. "Robin's stepsister. She took possession of her ex-husband's junkyard back in 2015 after their divorce. It sits on the outskirts of Corpus Christi, only six miles from the pay phone where Olivia's calls were going."

"Couldn't she just have been checking up on an old friend?" Hammon asked.

"Maybe, but we can't find any evidence that Summer and Olivia had any contact since the death of Robin back in 2003, other than the phone calls that have been taking place over the last few months. And that alone may not be enough to draw conclusions, but it turns out Summer worked for Port Authority on the Corpus Christi coast for a brief period last year, and her access card was used for the first time in nine months last week."

"She could just be working there again," Seeley said.

"I checked. She isn't on their current employee records," McCoy said.

Seeley and Hammon shared a look.

"Trying to get her out of the country," Hammon said.

"Somewhere they could start a new life," Seeley answered.

"All of this so Olivia could play mommy," Hammon huffed.

"Love is the most dangerous kind of motivation."

"Then why copy our files?"

"Insurance?" McCoy speculated.

"Any leads on this elusive deadline or source that Krum mentioned?" Hammon asked.

McCoy swallowed, signaling bad news before he delivered it. "Nothing. I mean, Olivia had dozens of contacts, abroad and locally—any one of them could be the source. We're re-scouring her files and records, looking for any clue."

Hammon swore under his breath. "We're flying blind."

Before anyone could respond, a petite, graying woman in a white lab coat interrupted. "Director."

Hammon turned and nodded to the woman. "Gina Loveless," Hammon started as she approached, "this is Tom Seeley and Dave McCoy." The woman stepped forward and offered a handshake to both as Hammon continued. "Dr. Loveless is a cognitive neuroscientist brought in to run diagnostics on what was done to the subject's memory." Then to Dr. Loveless: "Did you find something?"

She gave a nod as sharp as the angle of her jaw. As she opened her mouth, Hammon said, "And skip the science crap. Just give me the results."

She blinked and adjusted the thin-rimmed glasses on her nose. "Memory is a tricky thing. It isn't fully understood. It's created and stored by the brain, so her level of memory loss is complicated to say the least."

With the data pad in her hand, Dr. Loveless took over the large screen where McCoy had been displaying profiles. A brain scan appeared in black, white, and grays, different parts smudged and highlighted.

"This is your patient's final scan. You can see the entirety of the brain was exposed to the memory wipe, which originally seemed to have removed all short-term, long-term, and sensory memory. That's close to the truth, but"—Dr. Loveless enlarged one section of the brain—"a closer look at this image here around the temporal lobe shows something out of place. See this distortion? My theory is that the memories weren't removed, so to speak, they were just moved to places where they shouldn't be."

"They were relocated?" Seeley asked.

"Yes. Imagine someone came into your house, took all your things, and put them in places you'd never kept them before. You wouldn't be able to find anything. Memories are like things you need to access in order to use, but if that thing you are trying to find isn't where it should be—"

"Then you won't be able to use it," Seeley finished.

"If my theory is correct, then your patient has all her memories, but they just aren't where they should be, so she doesn't know she has them," Dr. Loveless said.

"Olivia had the skills to pull that off?" Seeley asked.

"I would guess not. With the limited knowledge Dr. Rivener was working with, and the time constraints, I hypothesize it was an error. The intention was to fully remove the memories. Good thing for you, because completely removed would be much more difficult."

"But can we put them back?" Hammon asked.

"Potentially."

"What do you need?"

"I need her to be in a lab setting where I have access to the proper equipment—"

"Do you have all of that here?"

"Yes, but—"

"Get a team," Hammon said to Seeley. "Head to Corpus Christi and find the patient."

"It's not that simple," Dr. Loveless interjected.

"Why not?" Hammon asked.

"To explain without the 'science crap,'" she bit off, "memories are unpredictable and believed to be highly connected to our emotional and mental state. You can't force someone to remember something. You need her to be a willing participant."

Hammon looked as if he might bark back at the small doctor, so Seeley intervened. "If we could convince her to participate, is there a chance it would work?"

Dr. Loveless considered that and nodded. "A chance. Even then, we may not be able to get everything back in order. There are no guarantees. But the more she trusts you, the better her conditions for recovery will be."

Seeley turned back to Hammon. "She's never going to cooperate here. We need a different approach."

Hammon nodded. "Do you have one?"

Seeley's mind started to formulate an idea. "Maybe."

"There's something else you should know." Dr. Loveless flipped to another part of the brain image and illuminated a small section. "This is the cerebellum—it's associated with our motor function, or physical skills. Hers hasn't been touched. It's one of the only places that remains intact."

"Her training wasn't affected by the memory wipe," McCoy said, drawing the others' attention.

"Well, it wasn't misplaced," Dr. Loveless said. "I imagine in the chaos that is now her mind she probably doesn't understand what she is capable of, but that won't stop her from being able to access her skills."

A moment of silence passed between the men before she continued. "She's still as dangerous as you made her to be."

Seeley was already starting toward the door.

"Go with him," Hammon said to McCoy, and the young analyst responded, his shoes slapping on the hard ground as he rushed to follow.

"What now?" McCoy asked as Seeley pushed open the double doors and stepped into the hallway.

Seeley squared his jaw, his body tensing as his mind prepared to execute its plan. "We get her to trust us."

THIRTEEN

ZOE FOLLOWED CLOSELY as Summer led them into her strange home. It was odd enough that it was tucked back in the corner of a junkyard, but things got stranger as they stepped into her space to find a shop of sorts. A long wooden counter with a cash machine, shelves bearing repurposed items, a collection of more KEEP OFF MY PROPERTY signs. There were other odds and ends found in any office: a printer, a copy machine—which Zoe was certain no longer functioned—a desk and chair, a round table without chairs holding stacks of paper and files.

The place was dim, dusty, and unused. Maybe at one time it had been the service building when people came through to purchase junk or drop junk off.

Summer crossed to the only other door in the small, dingy room. The lock above the handle had been replaced with a touch-screen keypad, which responded to her palm and illuminated numbers. "Turn around!" she yelled. It was clear she didn't want them to see her precious code.

The girls did as asked, and after a moment Zoe heard the dead bolt crank open. Then she was following Lucy and Summer down a flight of stairs. The narrow stairwell opened up to a large base-ment apartment. Three times the size of the room upstairs, the apartment had an open floor plan, cement walls, and a low ceiling that nearly brushed Zoe's head. There were zero windows or overhead lighting.

Summer placed the shotgun on the kitchen island that also served as a table, then reached for an off-white power strip on the floor at the island's base. She flicked the red switch, and a handful of lamps, all shapes and sizes, sprang to life, illuminating the apartment.

She had an eccentric collection of things, from the small kitchen area in the left corner to the single bed, nightstand, and dresser in the far right corner. Rugs of different shapes, textures, and colors were scattered between them. Zoe noted two couches and several plush chairs, as well as what appeared to be the missing dining chairs from the table upstairs. There were items that didn't make sense in the space, like a china cabinet with nothing in it, a metal bed frame leaning upright against a wall, and a stackable washer and dryer standing next to one of the couches in the middle of the room.

A decades-old TV and VCR sat on the floor in front of a large, worn chair, but Zoe saw no computer, no tablets, no laptop, no other electronic devices. The entire place was maddening, like the cellar of a kidnapper. She could feel fear gathering in her chest.

She looked at Summer, who was nervously glancing around her home. Dirty dishes, unkempt bed, clothes strung here and there.

Summer cut her eyes shyly at Zoe and cleared her throat. "Sorry for the mess," she said, leaning against the island. "I don't really have guests."

"You live here?" Lucy asked.

Summer's absence of an answer was an answer.

"Why?"

"It's off the grid," Summer began. "Safe, secure, and people don't know I'm here."

"But Olivia knew you were here," Lucy continued.

"She tracked me down about six months ago. We hadn't spoken

in over fifteen years, so I knew if she was trying to reach me it must be important."

"Why hadn't you talked in so long?"

Summer's eyes glazed over as if her mind had momentarily gone somewhere else. She stared there for a beat, then shook her head and pushed off of the island. "It doesn't matter. That isn't why you're here."

"You know who I am?" Lucy asked.

"No."

Zoe could feel Lucy's hope tarnish.

"What do you know?" Zoe asked.

"I know I warned Ollie about going to work for those people. Of course she didn't listen. She and Robin always thought I was paranoid, and now where is she?" Summer shook her head.

"Work for who?" Zoe pressed.

"The government! The powers that be. The ones fixated on disguising their mind control with promises of opportunity and freedom. When really, freedom is a lie. They control us all, like sheep, telling us what to do and when to do it. Spying on us through little devices that fit into our pockets that they convinced us to buy. All part of a ruse to keep us dumbed down to what is really happening."

"What does that have to do with Lucy?"

"Everything, child! Ollie was just like the rest, lured by their shiny trinkets. 'You can change the world, you can make it safer, brighter, better.' But it's all about power and control. Fear is the heartbeat of this country! And she was caught right in the center of it."

Zoe could feel her tolerance for this nonsense teetering. She knew Summer's type, the anti-government radicals who thought the whole system should burn down. Zoe wasn't necessarily signing up to join the charge of red, white, and blue, but this was over the top.

"I don't understand," Lucy said.

Summer started across the room. "I'll show you," she said, moving toward the far wall where, for the first time, Zoe noticed there was a door. The same kind of keypad that secured the door at the top of the stairs occupied this one as well. After a moment the lock churned as it opened, and Summer pulled the door ajar. "Come on."

Warning bells rang in Zoe's brain. What was the likelihood that if they went in that room they would never come back out? But Lucy was already moving, and they were way beyond turning back now.

Zoe stepped through the open door and found herself in a long, dimly lit hallway. She glanced back at Summer, who pushed past her and Lucy. The girls followed, traveling the pathway until they reached another keypad-secured door. Another moment of anticipated waiting, and then they were through, up a flight of matching iron steps and into what Zoe knew immediately was the warehouse they'd seen from outside.

It was easily double the size of the basement apartment, made of the same dull, sad concrete. They moved deeper into the windowless space, Zoe taking in the strange scene. Barrels of wheat, stacks of canned foods, water jugs, blankets, firewood, buckets of medical supplies—everywhere her eyes traveled, they were met with survival essentials.

This woman was ready for the zombie apocalypse.

Or worse.

But the main event sat dead center: a six-by-six-foot table, five whiteboards placed around it filled with printed images, articles, mathematical equations, dates, names, and faces, many with red string connecting point to point. The very scene Zoe might dream up if she were creating a story about a delusional mind caught in deep paranoia.

Summer stormed toward the center table, which Zoe realized was covered with weapons in neat lines. Shelves below the table held handguns, rifles, heavy artillery, bullets, grenades. Weapons she shouldn't have access to. Weapons no one should have access to.

"What is this place?" Lucy asked, eyes wide.

"This is preparation for the day it all happens," Summer said, a brightness to her voice. She was excited about her stash. She was certifiable, Zoe thought.

"When what happens?" Lucy asked.

"The fall of the powers that be." Summer made direct eye contact with Lucy. "You're going to be a part of that."

"I am?"

Summer smiled and pulled a file from underneath a sleek black handgun. She held it out toward Lucy, who stepped up to grab it from her.

"Ollie didn't give me details," Summer started. "Most of this I found myself, and most of it is from before she went to work for Grantham."

"The Grantham Project," Lucy said as her eyes traced the information inside the folder.

"A top-secret government program. In fact, there aren't any public records of the program, its funding, or its intent, which means whatever they are doing, they don't want people to know. They hired Ollie back in 2005, a couple of years after Robin died."

Robin. That was the link that connected Summer and Olivia, Zoe thought. She recognized the pain in Summer's eyes when she mentioned Robin's name. Zoe knew that kind of pain. Summer had loved this Robin very much.

Summer continued, "There is some speculation on the dark web that Grantham was created to build and test biological weaponry. The kind you wouldn't know was a threat until it was too late. As far as I can gather, the Grantham Project wanted Ollie for her breakthrough work on genetics and the understanding of cell reproduction and manipulation. She all but confirmed that she'd joined to be part of something she believed would be revolutionary, but things got out of control, and she was afraid for her life."

Zoe peered over Lucy's shoulder into the file. There was a collection of articles about Dr. Olivia Rivener, decorated geneticist. A photo of her smiling was at the top right corner of one of the articles. Her face looked kind and warm, her eyes inviting.

Zoe looked up at Summer. "Why did she come to you?"

"I worked for Port Authority at the beginning of the year. Due to some flaw in their security system, some of us that were hired earlier in the year still have access. She wanted to know if I could get her and a young friend out of the country on a boat."

"And?" Zoe asked.

Summer paused and stared at the girls for a long moment. Then she reached down under the table and yanked at a small package that was taped there. "She was the only family I had left. I would have done anything she asked." A small smile played at the corner of her mouth. "Besides, any chance to rage against the machine right under their noses? Sign me up."

Lucy pulled her eyes up from the folder and bored them directly into Summer. "You said I was going to be part of bringing down the powers that be. What did you mean?" The way she asked, Zoe thought she might already know the answer and was hoping Summer would prove her wrong.

"Ollie I knew, but you? I don't help strangers." Summer took a step forward, the small package in hand. "She told me you were the key to bringing down Grantham and the whole system. She told me if I really wanted to expose them, making sure you stayed alive was the only way."

Summer took a couple more steps, and Zoe inched backward. But Lucy stayed firm, showing no sign of the childlike fear Zoe expected.

"Ollie was many things, but a liar? No way," Summer said. "She never told me how you were going to do it, only that your safety was essential. So much so that Ollie sacrificed her life for this. For you."

Summer was only a couple of inches from Lucy now, and the girl remained like stone.

"So, you tell me. What's so special about you, Lucy?"

They held one another's stare. Zoe stood a foot away, waiting to react if needed, each breath slow and cautious.

Lucy snapped her gaze to the ceiling, her eyes focused and robotic. "Someone's here."

"Impossible," Summer said. "They would have tripped the alarm—"

A siren pierced the warehouse, and Zoe clamped her hands over her ears.

Summer cursed and rushed to the side wall to silence the alarm. Within a moment the shrilling sound died, and Summer powered up a large arrangement of screens on the wall. Zoe hadn't even noticed them. Six screens revealed security footage of the junkyard.

Armed soldiers in black ran in formation, hunched over. Again Summer swore. "I thought you said you weren't followed!"

"How do we get out of here?" Zoe asked.

Lucy scanned the screens, calculating. "There's at least fifteen on-site, others waiting in the surrounding streets. They have orders to obtain, not to kill."

Summer and Zoe both looked at Lucy.

"How do you know that?" Summer asked.

"She can hear them," Zoe answered in disbelief even as the words left her mouth.

Summer's eyes widened, her mouth slightly ajar as the reality that Zoe knew but didn't want to believe started to sink into her bones.

Lucy turned to Zoe. "I can get us out."

Summer was moving then, toward the back of the room. Lucy also moved, toward the middle table. She grabbed a long black rifle, and Zoe nearly told her to be careful. But before the words could finish forming, Lucy was assembling the weapon, loading it with a large magazine, and cocking it for use. She grabbed a small pistol and did the same, then stuffed her pockets with extra ammunition and tucked the pistol in the back of her jeans, all within seconds. Zoe stood mesmerized, too stunned to process the stream of questions bombarding her brain.

"Hurry," Summer called.

Zoe turned and saw that Summer had moved a tall stack of shelving, exposing a hidden door. Lucy moved first, armed and ready, Zoe rushing after.

"Out this way, across the south side, toward the east corner. There's a place in the fence that's vulnerable," Summer said. She handed Zoe a pair of wire cutters and the package she was still holding. "Don't stop until you reach the coast."

"You aren't coming with us?" Zoe asked.

"Captain always goes down with the ship. I'll distract them here as long as I can."

This was insane.

Summer turned to Lucy. "Burn it down."

Lucy nodded, and then they were moving. In a blur they were

through the back door and out into the cover of night, the cold air nipping at their exposed skin. Zoe heard Summer shut and barricade the door as Lucy followed her instructions and started south.

Gunfire popped inside. They'd penetrated the building. Lucy didn't hesitate, raising the rifle, using its scope as she moved on steady, easy, unfaltering feet. Zoe struggled to follow as she stumbled through her fear. Around and through heaps of scrap, she squinted to see in the pitch-black, Lucy always moving before Zoe could even register whether the pathway was clear. Around another corner.

Pop, pop.

Two shots from Lucy's weapon sent an agent face-first to the ground. Zoe let out a cry and jumped back. She hadn't even seen the agent coming. Lucy continued, the slain man on the ground behind her. Zoe blocked it all out then and just committed to following.

Another agent approached, and again Lucy put him down without hesitation or remorse. Silent and precise, bullets left her gun and killed the enemy. He fell like a hunk of meat. Two more came from the right. The girls were drawing attention.

Lucy fired half a dozen shots. *Pop, pop, pop, pop, pop, pop.* Followed by *clunk, clunk* as bodies fell. She tossed the current magazine and reloaded another, never stopping.

"They're all headed this way," Lucy said. "Stay close."

They reached the back fence and moved quickly toward the east corner. Zoe ignored the strong pull to hide under a pile of trash until the terror was over and focused on keeping up with Lucy, who moved like water. Fast and certain.

The corner came into view, lit by a streetlamp across the road. Zoe exhaled and grabbed the wire cutters from her back pocket.

Her hands were trembling, but she managed to snap the fence while Lucy stood guard behind her. Then they were through.

"This way," Lucy said, heading right.

"Where are they?" Zoe asked. She knew Lucy could hear them.

"They went radio silent."

They knew she could hear them.

"Two ahead, another to the right," Lucy said as she made a sharp turn left.

Could she sense them? Zoe wondered. Could she hear their heart rates?

Another sharp turn, then across a narrow and dark street. They moved quickly and tried to stay covered, Lucy's weapon at the ready. She started across a wild grassy plot of land and pulled up to alter her steps. Her shoulders tensed.

"Lucy," a man called out.

Zoe looked around but saw nothing.

"I know you can hear me, Lucy," the voice came again from wherever it was hidden. "I'm laying down my weapon and coming out unarmed. Don't shoot."

Zoe looked to Lucy, who was listening for what he'd promised. They shouldn't stand here, she thought. More would come. He could be leading them into a trap.

A tall and broad man dressed in black stepped out from behind a detached garage. Lucy turned, gun pointed directly at his chest.

"Wait, please, Lucy," he cried. "Let me help you."

Zoe waited for Lucy, finger on the trigger, to put the agent down like all the others. But she was hesitating.

"I know you don't remember," the man said. "But I'm a good guy. I'm trying to help you."

Lucy didn't move. *Shoot him*, Zoe thought. She glanced behind them. They didn't have time for this.

"Ollie sent you to find the robin," the man said, and Zoe felt Lucy's entire body change. He braved a step toward them. "She sent me to find you in case things went south. I'm your backup."

"You're lying," Lucy said.

"I'm not. You have to remember. I can help you remember."

Lucy didn't move or speak, but Zoe could tell that something was different about this man.

"I can help get you somewhere safe, somewhere they won't find you," he said.

"We're already going somewhere safe," Lucy said.

"They know that Summer worked for Port Authority. There's another team waiting at the coast. You'll never make it in without being detected. I'm going to reach into my back pocket for a piece of paper, okay?"

They watched him closely as he slowly moved his hand to the back and pulled out a folded white item. He then inched toward the ground and laid the paper on the pavement. "These are coordinates to a safe house in Arkansas. Two days' travel from here. Meet me there and I'll explain everything. Or go to the coast. Your choice."

Lucy craned her ear to the side. "More are coming. Should I shoot him?"

Zoe looked at Lucy, surprised. She was asking for guidance? She'd taken down all the others without help, but now she wanted to know what she should do?

Zoe looked back at the agent. If she said yes, would Lucy pull the trigger? The weight of it hit Zoe like a train, and she placed her hand on Lucy's arm. She wasn't sure why. Maybe it was because of the way Lucy had reacted to him. Maybe it was because the idea of his death on her hands was more than she was ready to swallow. But she did it, and Lucy's hardened stance eased slightly.

"We need to get out of here," Zoe said.

"I'll pull them west, radio that I'm in pursuit of you," the man said. "You head east. Go to the safe house. Without you, we lose everything."

He started west without another word and disappeared into the dark tangle of streets. Lucy kept the weapon trained on him until he was out of sight, then listened.

"Did he radio?" Zoe asked.

Lucy nodded and stepped forward to retrieve the paper he left. "They are all moving that way. Come on." She tucked the paper in her back pocket and started in the opposite direction.

They ran for several minutes, maybe more. It was hard to know anymore.

Finally, Lucy slowed down, and Zoe forced herself not to collapse into a puddle of exhaustion. She thought she might barf, and she took deep breaths to steady the racing of her heart and the trembling of her limbs.

"Why did you ask me?"

Lucy looked at her.

"If you should shoot him. You took down every other agent without blinking, but with him you hesitated."

Lucy remained quiet for a breath, the hard warrior melting from her expression and the terrified innocence returning. "I didn't know what to do," she said. "I'm used to having orders."

"You remember that?"

As if suddenly the gate she had been trained to close was opened, emotions gripped her body and tears filled her eyes.

"Yes, and I remembered him."

FOURTEEN

SEELEY LOOKED AROUND the carnage Lucy had left across Summer's junkyard. Eight men dead. Summer Wallace with them. In less than five minutes. Dr. Loveless had been correct. Lucy's memory loss clearly had no effect on her training.

"Did she take the bait?" McCoy asked, stepping into Seeley's line of sight.

"We'll find out soon," Seeley said. "Finding the robin gave her pause. Your hunch about it was spot-on. Good instincts."

"I remember Olivia saying it was a silly code she used to use. It was a wild stab, really."

"I didn't realize you and Olivia were so close," Seeley said.

"Yeah," McCoy said, dropping his eyes. "I guess we were."

Seeley could see the hint of pain in the agent's face. "Any evidence to suggest Summer was the source Olivia had set up to release the information if Lucy doesn't recover it?"

"Not that we found," McCoy said, drawing his eyes back up. "And I'm not sure who she would tell now if she were, you know, because . . ."

"Because she's dead," Seeley said matter-of-factly.

McCoy cleared his throat and nodded uncomfortably. Great,

Seeley thought, the kid was uncomfortable with death. That wouldn't serve him here.

"And there's no new leads on our time frame?" Seeley asked.

"No, sir," McCoy answered.

So they were still flying blind. Seeley stepped past the kid toward the team cleaning up the bodies, hunting for clues, documenting everything a dozen yards in each direction.

His interactions with Lucy and Zoe replayed in his head. It had gone as he had imagined, until Lucy looked to Zoe for direction. That had caught him off guard. Lucy, as powerful as she was, had been trained to follow, and without Olivia or the Grantham Project she'd found another leader.

That made Zoe Johnson—Evelyn Pierce—much more valuable than they'd first believed. But her story was laced with unspeakable tragedy. Tragedy he could use and manipulate.

Time to head for Arkansas.

ZOE AND LUCY stepped off another bus, the third one they'd been on in the last two days. At first they'd headed for the coast to see if the agent had been correct about a team waiting. Zoe had thought it was the most logical move, and Lucy followed her without question. It wasn't lost on Zoe, the way Lucy kept looking to her. The responsibility was heavy but also gave her a sense of purpose. Something she hadn't experienced in a long time.

The last time she'd felt this sensation, she'd failed. She was all Stephen had, and instead of fighting for him like she should have, she listened to the advice of a twisted psychologist. Dr. Holbert led her to abandon her little brother, maybe when he needed her most. Because of that, she ruined his life.

The guilt had been chasing her ever since. Now she had a

chance to do things differently. Though the fear of failing again was hard to overcome. She swallowed it, and it spread across her skin in the form of a rash, itchy and painful red spots that ran along her arms. Something she'd dealt with since she was a little girl.

There had been a time when Zoe thought she'd been rid of it completely. That she'd beaten fear. But fear wasn't something a girl got rid of. She just created rules to keep herself safe from it.

But she was breaking all the rules now. For Lucy.

The agent had been right about the tactical team waiting at the coast. Lucy had spotted at least a dozen, and the girls knew there was no way through. Without another plan, they'd considered the agent's coordinates.

Zoe knew the evidence might support the notion that he was trustworthy, but still, the entire idea made her sick to her stomach. It wasn't just because this man was a total stranger and obviously had a force pursuing them. Or that in her experience, people weren't always who they said they were. Not even Lucy's memory of him and the way he'd helped them escape could erase that fact. There was a feeling she got whenever she thought about him. Like a sixth sense, it just *felt* like following his direction was a bad idea. Like it would end in disaster. And from her experience, usually if it felt like a bad idea, it was.

But what else were they supposed to do? They had nowhere else to go.

Lucy crossed the parking lot, looking for a map. Zoe followed, moving through the busy station to the far side, where a large city map was plastered across the wall. "Welcome to Camden, Arkansas" was written across the top, the city laid out in beautiful colors below. The map was marked with tourist destinations for Civil War buffs and hikers. Camden sat at the base of the Ouachita

River and near the large Ouachita Mountain range where they were headed.

Lucy located the coordinates on the map and traced a path with her finger across the surface from where they were to where they needed to go. Zoe pulled the backpack off her shoulder and took stock of what they had inside. The package from Summer held a couple thousand dollars in cash, instructions and passes for getting out of the country through Port Authority, new passports for Olivia and Lucy with their names changed, new identities attached, and contact information that Zoe was pretty sure was written in French.

She glanced out the station window. A Dollar General sat across the street. If they were going to trek into the wilderness, they were going to need water and food.

"Let's go," Lucy said.

"Are you sure you want to do this?" Zoe asked.

"I recognized him. He knew about Robin, about Olivia. He said he could help me remember."

"That doesn't make him trustworthy," Zoe said.

"What else are we going to do?"

It was the same conversation, round and round. And still here they were, standing in Arkansas.

"We need help, Zoe. I have to know what is going on, and good guy or bad guy, he has answers," Lucy said. "I have to know."

They stood there for a second, then Lucy dropped her eyes to her feet and shrugged. "You don't have to come if you don't want."

Zoe shook her head and stepped forward, grabbing Lucy's hand and interlacing her fingers with the girl's. "Together, remember?"

Lucy brought her eyes back up and grinned. She squeezed Zoe's hand. There was no way Zoe was leaving her now.

"Together," Lucy said.

THEY'D STARTED THEIR trek while the sun was still high in the sky, and now as they closed in on their destination, the sun would soon be gone for the day. Lucy was leading them from the map she'd drawn in her mind. The hike was hard, filled with uncleared pathways, rocky terrain, thick brush, and sharp cliff edges. Deeper and deeper they pushed into the Ouachita Mountains.

They were out of water, their snacks depleted. Zoe was sore, every muscle aching. She was out of breath, her lungs desperate for a break. Her body felt broken and sleep deprived.

Lucy was a machine, never ceasing, calmly scaling every obstacle with ease. Zoe had long ago abandoned the idea that Lucy was a normal girl, and this physical feat was just another link in the chain of evidence.

She was about to call out and tell Lucy she needed to take a moment when Lucy pulled up to a stop, lifted a hand, and went still. Zoe's lungs heaved, and she tried to quiet her breathing, which made her chest ache more.

"Stay here," Lucy said, and before Zoe could argue the girl was off. They had reached the top of a steep mountainside, and Lucy disappeared into the valley on the other side. Zoe carefully sat herself down on a large boulder to her right, her muscles aching with every new movement. Her heart rate started to come back to a normal rhythm, and it allowed her to breathe easier.

She closed her eyes and hung her head, letting oxygen fill her lungs and then escape. The calm around her was peaceful, the moment of silence welcome after all she'd been through the past few days. She sat like that for several minutes, letting the cool evening air sweep past her shoulders.

Something snapped behind her, yanking her from her momentary calm, and she spun around. He stood there, a yard off, the man who had asked them to come.

Zoe yanked her backpack open and pulled out the pistol. She lifted it to eye level and aimed it at the man's face. "Don't come any closer," she shouted.

He raised his hands in surrender. "It's okay. I didn't mean to sneak up on you."

"I don't believe anything you say," Zoe said.

"Okay, the feeling is mutual then."

Before Zoe even noticed him moving, he was reaching around to his back and yanking out a pistol of his own. Aimed at her face. Zoe moved from her place on the rock and placed her other hand on the gun, trying to hold it steady.

"Who are you?" he asked. "What do you want with Lucy?" He didn't pause for her to answer, he just snapped off more questions. "How did you end up with her? What's your endgame?"

Zoe was shocked, nearly dumbfounded. He was questioning her motives? He thought she might have ill intent. Her mind was too tired to quickly formulate a response.

"Tell me who you are!" he barked again.

"Who am I? Who are you?" she barked back.

"Tom Seeley, special agent, FBI. And you?"

"Zoe Johnson," she said. "Waitress."

He looked taken aback, and she thought he might have smiled. "You're a waitress?" he asked.

"Yes, what's that supposed to mean?"

"What are you doing with Lucy?"

"Trying to help her avoid getting killed by you."

That did make him smile, and he lowered his weapon. His smile was handsome, full lips and good teeth. Actually, his whole face was handsome. Good strong jaw, with even stubble and clean-cut dark hair. His chocolate eyes had a hint of caramel undertones and paired well with his warm olive skin tone.

Zoe kept her weapon poised, even though he'd begun to put his away.

"Sorry," he said. "You just never know who's a threat."

Zoe wasn't sure whether to be thankful that he wasn't pointing his gun at her face any longer or offended because he didn't think she was threatening. "Well, I'm still not sure you aren't," she said.

"I'm not," Agent Seeley replied.

"Oh, well, now that you say so," Zoe mocked.

"I'm the good guy here."

"And I've never encountered a guy who claimed to be good and wasn't."

Again he smiled, and Zoe wished it didn't make her insides tingle.

"I like your spunk," he said.

Zoe was trying to think of something to say, gun still raised, when Agent Seeley started toward her. He didn't seem concerned at all.

"What are you doing?" she asked, taking a step back.

He stopped and raised his hands enough to placate her. "I really am here to help. It'll be dark soon; we should head for the safe house. I assume Lucy went ahead to make sure it wasn't a trap?"

"You think I'm going to just lower my weapon and follow you?"

"You don't have to lower the gun if you don't want. Keep it pointed at me the whole time. But I would suggest you follow me to the safe house."

He slowly started moving again, keeping a wide berth but moving past her and over toward the valley where Lucy had gone.

Zoe watched in disbelief and followed him with her weapon. "Aren't you at all afraid I'll shoot you?"

He looked back at her over his shoulder, a mischievous spark in his eye. "I might be. If you didn't have the safety on." He pointed to the gun.

He continued to descend the hill, and she surveyed the weapon, realizing she wasn't even sure what a safety looked like. Embarrassed and frustrated, she grabbed the backpack from the boulder, tossed the gun back inside, and followed him at a good distance.

The safe house was a small wooden cabin in the middle of the valley. Grassy and rocky mountains surrounded it, as if the flat plot of land at their base had been scooped out specifically for the building at its center. Zoe forced herself past the pain in her limbs as she moved carefully through the natural terrain, Agent Seeley a couple feet ahead.

When they were still yards off, Lucy came rushing from the cabin and stared, looking confused and surprised. Her face assumed its warrior expression, and Zoe could tell she was ready to fight.

"Stop where you are," Lucy said to Agent Seeley as he stepped onto the valley floor. He did as he was told.

"He has a gun," Zoe yelled, remembering.

Without having to be told, Agent Seeley removed the pistol from his holster and placed it on the ground, then kicked it away. "I'm here to help."

Lucy moved swiftly to the gun, her eyes on Agent Seeley, and scooped it up. She raised it at him as Zoe was nearly to her side.

"Check him for other weapons," Lucy said to Zoe.

Zoe looked at her, and Lucy gave her a confident nod. Zoe crossed the space between them and dropped to check his ankles, both sides, under his jacket, and his waist. She avoided eye contact and was light with her hands, touching him as little as possible. She found nothing, so she gave Lucy a nod and crossed back to her.

"The cabin?" Zoe asked.

"Clear, as far as I can tell," Lucy said.

"It is. Olivia and I made sure to sweep it before we set anything in motion so we'd always have a place to go," Agent Seeley said. "We're safe here."

"How do I know you?" Lucy asked.

"I was your training officer at Xerox, the black site for Grantham."

"And we spent a lot of time together?"

"Yes."

"How come I remember you but nothing else?"

Genuine shock filled his face. "You remember me?"

She nodded. "Am I not supposed to?"

He stared, his mind running behind his eyes. "What do you remember about me?"

"Rain," Lucy said. Zoe looked at her. She hadn't mentioned anything specific about the agent, just that she knew his face. "The smell of mud, and trees. I was running, you were behind, trying to stay close. We were chasing something."

He took a slight step forward, his eyes bright. "Deer. We were hunting deer. You were tracking them, and I was following. You'd become so good at it."

Lucy lowered the weapon. "I killed one."

Agent Seeley took another step forward. "Do you remember how?"

Lucy wasn't looking at them anymore. She seemed lost in the scene that was filling her head. She thought for a long moment, and then she refocused on Agent Seeley, light spreading through her face. "Throwing knives."

He smiled and nodded. "Yes, your favorite."

"My favorite," she repeated.

Lightning struck across the sky, and soon a crack of thunder followed. Zoe hadn't even noticed the dark clouds that had rolled in, but suddenly everything felt a shade darker. The air was colder, and the wind whipped through the treetops overhead.

"We should get inside," Agent Seeley said, "and I can answer all your questions."

Lucy nodded. They shared another long gaze, and Zoe felt like she was on the outside of a glass box, peering in on a scene. She didn't like the way it made her stomach turn.

"Come on," Agent Seeley said as he started toward the cabin.

Lucy was on his heels, leaving Zoe to fall in at the back. The same troubling sensation she'd had from the moment they'd met this Agent Seeley filled her chest. She wanted to be wrong. For Lucy's sake she really wanted to be wrong.

FIFTEEN

THE LOG CABIN had a vaulted ceiling and a large fireplace on the main wall in the living room, two bedrooms off to the right side, and a small bathroom in between. There was a staircase in the far left corner that led up to a loft only big enough for a single mattress and a table lamp that had been placed on the floor.

The main room held a leather couch and two matching leather chairs. A large cowhide rug occupied the center of the room, and several taxidermy animals were propped around: a raccoon, a duck, a fox. Zoe didn't like the way their beady black eyes stared at her. The attached kitchen had a rectangular table that seated six.

Agent Seeley flicked on the overhead chandelier, then moved to do the same to the lamps placed throughout. "This cabin was donated to the FBI a couple of years ago after the owner, a retired FBI director, passed away. It isn't currently in rotation, fortunately for us. There isn't much here, but it'll do for now."

Lucy placed the gun she'd taken from Agent Seeley on the table and walked around the cabin. "Olivia has been here?"

"A few times," he said. "It was a safe place to talk. There aren't many of those."

"Is she alive?"

The agent swallowed and avoided Lucy's direct stare. He shook his head, and Lucy sank to the leather couch.

"What happened?"

"She opened fire on the men pursuing you two the last time you were with her. They fired back."

"So I could get away."

Thunder echoed outside, and wind slapped the rain that had started falling against the sides of the cabin.

"I should get a fire started," Agent Seeley said. He gathered what he needed from the supplies on the hearth and built a stack of logs in the fireplace.

Lucy appeared lost in thought. A few minutes passed in an uncomfortable silence as Agent Seeley began stoking the fire to life. It crackled and sparked, the smell of burning wood filling the cabin.

"How many have died for me?" Lucy asked, breaking the silence.

"Lucy," Zoe tried.

"How many?" she insisted.

Agent Seeley stood, facing the growing fire, his hands on his hips. "They aren't dying for you," he said, then turned around and moved to sit across from Lucy in one of the leather chairs. "They are dying to save their own humanity."

"What does that mean?"

"Are you sure you want to know? It'll change everything."

Lucy glanced from Agent Seeley to Zoe, her eyes pleading for direction. Zoe walked to the couch and sat beside her, grasping her hand and giving her a confident nod.

Lucy turned her attention back to Agent Seeley. "I'm sure."

"You were born and raised at black site CX4-B, fondly referred to as Xerox, a government-run campus dedicated to the development of biological warfare and weaponry."

Just as Summer had said.

"The Grantham Project was Xerox's largest program and the reason for its creation. It dealt in human germline engineering using CRISPR/Cas9 to edit reproductive cells in order to ensure fetuses developed an affinity toward particular skills. The edited reproductive cells were incubated and grown at Xerox from conception, being adjusted and mutated to explore outcomes of different external forces on the end results."

"End results," Zoe said. "You mean babies."

"There were eighty-nine specimens to begin. Only fifteen made it to viability. And of the fifteen, only nine were born."

Zoe already knew where he was headed.

"You are one of the nine, Lucy. A genetically modified subject with the ability to harness physical skills in a way that has never been seen before. Speed, strength, intelligence, adaptability, reasoning, all heightened by constant training and observation. You and the others were sculpted to perfection."

"I was born in a lab?" Lucy asked.

"Is that even possible?" Zoe asked.

"You tell me." Agent Seeley nodded his head toward Lucy. Zoe's mind traced back through all the strange and unbelievable things she'd seen Lucy do over the last few days. What else could explain such things?

"I don't have a mother," Lucy said.

"Olivia was your mother," Agent Seeley said. "She was the head geneticist on the program and oversaw every stage of development from conception to your sixteenth birthday. She named you. She loved you."

"And the others? The ones like me?"

Agent Seeley rubbed the sides of his face with his fingers and exhaled painfully. "There was a problem with the DNA melding as some of you grew. An unforeseen mutation in the brain's hardwiring made certain patients, which is what we called you, unstable. Olivia tried to warn the director about the early signs of the mutation, but the higher-ups demanded results. The process was clear: create, raise, train, control. Until you were called upon by your country."

"Like spies," Zoe said.

"Like weapons. Only to leave the black site when needed. But as Olivia suspected, some of the others started to change. Number Three was the first to resist his programming. He killed seventeen Grantham agents before he could be contained. They put him in solitary, but he escaped, managed to recruit Numbers Five and Six, and the three got off campus without being detected. They made their way into a small town north of the black site and shot up a local shopping center. It left six dead and a dozen more injured."

"I remember hearing about that," Zoe said. "It was all over the news."

"I don't understand," Lucy said, and Zoe turned to see the horror filling her face. "Is that all going to happen to me?"

"I want to tell you no with confidence," Agent Seeley said, "but honestly, there is zero data on your current state. After these events, they put the Grantham Project on lockdown and started looking more closely at the mutation Olivia had originally warned about. They hypothesized it was deeply embedded in the original genetic code and couldn't be resolved. Again, Olivia had a different viewpoint and believed with memory alterations she could return each of you to a former state, before the mutation started presenting itself, and alter your course. But it was too late. The fear of not being able to control you was already present, and the majority believed it would be better to terminate the project and start from scratch."

"Terminate," Lucy said.

"Erase all evidence of the nine so it would appear you never existed. Keep only what was necessary to further the evolution of the project. Every document, every recording, every video, and all of its subjects."

"They wanted to kill us."

"They were afraid of you. Of what you could do and expose if you couldn't be controlled. Not to mention what would happen if the American people ever found out what Grantham had been doing. Genetically engineered babies in a lab . . ."

Agent Seeley stopped. He didn't need to finish; his intent was clear. The government would explode if the American people knew their tax money was helping fund something that perverse. Zoe thought about what Summer had said: *"The fall of the powers that be. You're going to be a part of that."* This was what she had meant.

Suddenly a dozen connections formed in Zoe's mind. They were after Lucy because she could expose them. Burn it all down.

"Olivia wouldn't let that happen to you," Agent Seeley continued. "She heard about the execution orders, and with the small amount of time she had she wiped your memories, but not before copying the damning evidence and giving it to you."

"I have it?" Lucy asked.

"Stored in your memories is the location of a data chip with enough evidence to bring criminal charges against the country's most powerful leaders. The plan was never for you to have to recover it. Olivia was always supposed to be with you. You were supposed to head to France, start over. You and Olivia, the information as a shield against those that would always be looking for you. But as smart as she was, she was still fighting against the FBI and all of its resources." He shook his head. "She never stood a chance."

A moment of silence filled the cabin before Agent Seeley returned from the place he'd seemed to go in his mind.

"But she protected you. She gave you something they need, and that makes keeping you alive necessary," he said.

"And a constant target," Zoe said.

"It was the best Olivia could do with what time she had."

"Why not just release the information herself?" Zoe asked. "Why all this?"

"Olivia spent the last twenty years working on the Grantham Project. She believed in it and the good it could do. Not to mention all the people connected to the program, good people, whose lives would be ruined if that information ever got out. And Lucy, she'd be seized by the government, and who knows what would have been done to her." Agent Seeley exhaled and looked right at Lucy. "Look, I don't know all of Olivia's motivations, but I know she was only trying to do what she thought was best for you."

"They killed her for it," Lucy said, as if it was all just starting to sink in.

Zoe fell back against the couch, the weight of it all pressing against her entire body.

"But I had a memory of you," Lucy said.

"You did," Agent Seeley said with a smile.

"Will I remember more?"

"There's no way to know." He scooted forward in his chair. "What I do know is that you have access to the most powerful information in the country, and we need to find it before they do or none of us will make it out of this alive."

His words bored into Zoe's mind. Terror and grief washed over Lucy's face as her entire life was just splayed out in front of her. And suddenly Zoe's sixth sense about Agent Seeley came roaring back to life. She leaned forward and stopped Lucy as the girl opened her mouth to speak.

"What's your role in all of this?" Zoe asked.

"I was head of tactical training and security. I helped the patients form their advanced skills in weaponry, combat, survival skills, and so on," he answered.

"And Olivia came to you with her plan, why?"

"She needed someone to help her and Lucy get out of Xerox undetected."

"But they were followed," Zoe pressed. "That's why Olivia is dead."

Agent Seeley stood. "You think I don't know that! I failed her, but I'm doing everything I can to make it right."

"By conveniently showing up to help us just when you did?" Zoe said, standing herself.

"When word came through that they'd connected Lucy to Summer, I knew I needed to be on that tactical team to get to you before they did. I've been keeping my ear to the ground so we know what they know, so we can intercept their moves."

"And what do you get out of all this? What makes an agent flip sides? Because in my experience that doesn't happen often."

"I get my humanity!" he yelled. "I get to sleep again."

Zoe fell silent, her pulse racing in her ears.

"They were killing kids," Agent Seeley said. "I didn't sign up to kill kids."

Lucy disrupted their fiery engagement as she stood from the couch and walked toward the front door.

"Where are you going?" Zoe called after her.

"Outside," Lucy said.

"It's raining."

Lucy ignored her, opened the door, and slammed it behind her. Zoe and Agent Seeley just stood there for a long moment, neither looking at the other, neither speaking. Then Zoe exhaled and decided to go after Lucy.

She heard the agent's heavy footsteps and whirled around to face him. "Stay here," she demanded.

He didn't object, he just moved quickly to the closet and yanked out a jacket. "At least take this," he said as he tossed it to her. It was a red raincoat. She didn't say thank you as she caught the coat and stepped out into the cold night.

The rain had eased a bit, now just a steady thrum that drenched the earth. Zoe yanked on the jacket and pulled up the hood. She descended the short set of stairs.

The cabin light gave off soft illumination for a few yards. Beyond, it was pitch-black without even stars to shed some light on the forest.

"Lucy," she yelled, hoping for a response. There was none. Zoe yanked the jacket tighter across her chest to shield herself from the chilly wind. She turned in circles, searching through the darkness for signs of life.

Then she saw her. Standing to the east, staring up at the sky as rain splashed down over her face. Zoe walked to her, and as she approached, Lucy lowered her face so she was staring straight ahead.

"Lucy," Zoe said, "let's go back inside."

"I don't have a mother," Lucy said, "or a father, or a home. Am I even a human?"

"Of course you are," Zoe replied.

Lucy whipped around, her fiery eyes startling in the darkness. "Are you sure, Zoe? Can you look at me and be sure?"

Zoe opened her mouth to reassure the girl, but her words fell short. What made someone human? Their body, upbringing, mind, soul? Zoe wasn't sure *she* was even human.

"If I'm not human," Lucy said, "then what am I?"

She didn't wait for an answer. She stepped back toward the cabin, leaving Zoe standing in the rainy night wondering exactly that.

SIXTEEN

ZOE SAT OUTSIDE on the cabin's front porch. The sun was rising, and rays of light pierced the tree branches and danced on the forest floor. Birds chirped morning songs, and she watched a family of deer casually stroll through the gathered trunks, eating grass and weeds. The scene was calm and soothing, a complete departure from the situation she found herself in.

When she'd come in from the rain the night prior, soaking and shivering, Lucy had announced she was tired and slipped into one of the downstairs rooms to sleep. After twenty minutes of awkward silence in the living room with Agent Seeley, watching him stoke the fire, the shadows of his figure hulking across the hardwood floors, Zoe knocked on Lucy's door, but she didn't respond. Zoe nearly burst in but thought better of it. Didn't the girl deserve a moment alone?

Eventually Zoe had taken the second room, and Agent Seeley took the mattress up in the loft. Sleep was impossible. Every time she felt herself drifting from reality, it would roar back to life in vibrant, distorted color and send blots of energy pulsing through her body. The more she told herself to sleep, the harder it became.

After hours of struggling, she got up. She slipped into the bath-

room for a shower, thrilled to find hot water and soft towels. Back
in her bedroom, she discovered that a trunk at the end of the single
wire-framed bed held extra clothes—men's and two sizes too big
for her, but dry and warm. She slipped into the black track pants
and large hooded sweatshirt. In thick wool socks she wandered
outside, trying her best not to disturb Lucy, whose room was still
silent.

Zoe couldn't remember ever sitting outside to watch the sun
rise. It felt like something people who lived in luxury did. Those
who thought life was kind and happy. Who didn't have to battle
against the constant injustice of cruelty.

People like her didn't watch the sun rise.

But maybe she should more often. It was quite beautiful.

The door behind her opened, and she glanced back to see Agent
Seeley walking out with two mugs in his hands. Steam rose from
the cups and played through the soft morning light.

"Please let that be coffee," Zoe said.

Agent Seeley gave a half smile and held one out. "A peace
offering."

Zoe took the mug, feeling energized just smelling the delicious
dark substance.

"May I?" he asked, gesturing to the open space on the porch
beside her.

She sipped her coffee without responding, which he took to
mean yes, and he inched away slightly as he sat. He towered over
her, even sitting. His shoulder span was twice hers. It made her
feel smaller than normal, and she sat up straighter to compensate.

"Did you sleep at all?" he asked.

"Do you actually care?" she responded.

He gave a huffed chuckle and shook his head. "You really don't
like me, do you?"

"I don't trust you."

"How do I change that?"

"Why do you need me to trust you?"

"Because it would make this easier."

She looked at him with a mocking smile. "Easy is overrated."

He turned his face back to the forest, looking slightly annoyed. Zoe didn't want to care but was struggling to ignore the fact that she sort of did. She tried a different approach.

"No," she said, "I didn't sleep. I don't know how one could sleep after everything you told us."

"You can't," he said.

"Then why stay? You seem intelligent. Surely you knew what they were doing. Why not leave before it all went south?"

"You ask that as if leaving was even an option."

"You always have a choice, Agent Seeley."

He looked at her, his eyes connecting directly with hers, causing her heart to beat a tad faster. "No, you don't," he said, holding her gaze a second longer than was comfortable before releasing it. "And you can just call me Seeley. Most people do."

Silence engulfed them again.

"How does a waitress end up with Lucy?" Seeley asked.

"Bad luck," Zoe replied. She felt him glance at her, waiting for an actual answer. "She showed up at the diner I was working at and clearly needed help."

"And you just helped her?"

"I didn't know she was being chased by a band of tactical enforcers. I just thought she was a lost kid with no memory. She seemed so vulnerable, and I know what the world does to vulnerable."

"That sounds like experience talking."

Zoe turned to him. "If you think we're going to sit around a campfire and share our feelings, you're mistaken. I still don't like you, remember?"

His face twisted in a grin he couldn't hide, and he nodded. "I just think it's weird that someone with obvious trust issues would help a stranger."

"Well, I'm a good person."

"Right, and I've never met a person who claimed to be good and wasn't," he said. He was using her words against her, but with a teasing, sexy glance that made the hair on the back of her neck stand up.

She huffed and shook her head, suddenly self-conscious about the large men's clothes she was wearing and her makeup-free face. She tucked her hair behind her ear and hoped it hadn't dried wonky. Then she internally scolded herself for caring at all.

"Sounds like you don't trust me either," she finally managed.

"You're not the only one with trust issues," he said.

She looked at him with curiosity, and he shook his head. "No way. I'll share when you share."

The look in his eyes was one she recognized. She'd seen it in her own expression many times. Life had shaped them through pain. Through loss. And for a brief moment it united them. Made them the same. Until her brain reminded her that she didn't trust him. That he represented the enemy she'd been running from her whole life.

The one that had taken Stephen from her.

She looked away from Seeley and, with the last gulp of her coffee, swallowed the cruel reminder of the little boy she'd failed. She was finished with this moment. She stood to go back inside when the door opened and Lucy emerged.

"Hey," Zoe said, glad to see the girl was still with them. "Did you get some sleep?"

Lucy smiled and nodded. "Some."

Seeley stood as well, and Lucy shared a small smile with him. The three just stood there for a moment.

Lucy broke the silence first. "What now?"

"You decide what you want," Seeley said. "You keep running and I'll help you get as far away as possible. But that road will never end. Run now and you will be running forever."

"Or?" Lucy asked.

"We try to recover your memories, find the files Olivia left behind, and—"

"Burn it all down," Lucy finished.

Seeley nodded and waited as Lucy glanced at Zoe for guidance. For once she agreed with Seeley that it needed to be Lucy's choice. "Whatever you want, I'm with you."

Lucy considered what had been laid before her, then she looked up at Seeley. "How do we burn it down?"

SEELEY WATCHED OUT the bus window as the plains of Arkansas whizzed by. They were about a half an hour from their destination in the Ozarks. The girls had followed his lead, but he knew Zoe was watching him carefully. She didn't trust him, and he knew she wouldn't leave Lucy alone with him for one second. It was clear to Seeley that for this plan to work he was going to need Zoe on his side. She could easily sway Lucy to abandon the whole thing.

Their bond was stronger than he'd anticipated but hopefully not infallible. He glanced over his shoulder and saw that Zoe was sleeping, her head resting against the bus window, Lucy sitting beside her.

He was struck by the power Zoe carried in her tiny frame. She was fiery, a quality he found himself drawn to. Her brown eyes pulled him in and warmed a place in his chest that had been cold for years. It was alarming. But it was a by-product of the ruse he was playing. Nothing more.

Seeley had decided to mold his character after Krum since the man couldn't rise from the dead and complicate things. Bits and pieces of fiction mixed with his own truths had been convincing enough to keep the girls following him. For now.

He squirmed in his seat. The large lady beside him shot him a wicked side eye and adjusted herself to take up more of his seat than she already was. He could have sworn it was intentional, because she knew there was nothing he could do about it.

He fought off the urge to smack her plump face with the back of his hand and turned his attention back to the window. Sitting still was toying with his self-control. It gave him too much time to ponder things that were better left ignored.

Like the fact that Lucy had remembered him. An unforeseen development that made him more vulnerable. He racked his brain for memories that could incriminate him. Had she seen him during the pursuit of her and Olivia? Did she know he was the leading supervisor on the disestablishment of the Grantham Project? Had she ever overheard him speaking with Hammon in such a way that would make her suspicious?

He needed to play his cards smart. Recover the memories they needed while keeping her from discovering more than he wanted her to know. Could they even do that? Was the pursuit of his goal worth the risk of her stumbling onto something else?

It had to be.

Seeley cleared his throat, ignored another glare from his seat partner, and ran through the plan again. Over and over, writing it onto his brain, so that the man he was pretending to be felt real because the disguise was so ingrained.

It wasn't that much of a departure. It was the man he used to be, the one he'd hidden after losing Steph. After Cami had been taken from him. It was painful to bring him back out. It made him susceptible to emotions that led him back to the places he'd long abandoned. But he was a soldier, committed and loyal. He'd do what was needed for the job at hand. Failure wasn't an acceptable outcome.

The bus rolled into their final spot, and with a sigh of relief the fat woman beside him stood, freeing his body from her captivity. He waited as people stood to leave, until Zoe and Lucy had passed his bench, and then he stood and followed them off.

The air was crisp, as the early morning had gradually given way to evening. Seeley took a deep breath and focused his mind. He enjoyed the Ozark air. It tasted and smelled different here than in other parts of Arkansas. He wouldn't call it home—that entailed feeling a certain way about life—but he preferred it to other places.

"Seems like a strange place for a world-renowned psychologist," Zoe said. She tucked her black hair behind her ear, her eyes wandering the area. Seeley ignored the way her hair fell like silk to her collarbone and tried not to wonder if her cheek was as soft as it appeared.

"That's the point," he lied. "Who would suspect we were here?"

The truth was that Xerox sat deep in the wooded mountains an hour's drive from where they stood. But they couldn't know that. Unless Lucy remembered. Then he'd have to maneuver that carefully.

He looked around for anyone suspicious.

Zoe stepped up next to him, Lucy tucked closely behind her. "And someone is just coming to us?"

"She said someone would meet us here."

"Didn't she trust you enough to give you her location?"

"Apparently not."

Of course, Seeley knew exactly where the doctor was, but according to her, the story that Lucy believed was crucial to opening her mind enough for her memories to be recovered. Lucy needed to believe in what she was doing. She needed to believe in them. So they played this little charade, which Seeley could do without.

"Gina Loveless has worked with Grantham on occasion, so she understands the threat anyone standing against them poses. She's being careful," he said.

"And you're sure we can trust her?" Lucy asked quietly.

"Yes," Seeley answered.

"Funny how your word doesn't make me feel any better," Zoe said.

Seeley spotted his accomplice, a young man dressed in jeans and a zipped blue jacket, across the moving sea of travelers. He was right on time.

"Come on," Seeley said, turning as the man moved toward the back of the building.

"Are you sure we should just be following him?" Zoe asked.

"Are you going to question every move I make?" He glanced back at her without slowing his stride.

"Yes," she replied with confidence, "until I have a reason not to."

She was irritating. And amusing. And responding exactly the way he would if their positions were swapped. But she was also following, just with little enthusiasm.

Seeley continued around the station's corner and along the long brick wall that led them to the back. The man was sliding open a white van door and waiting for them.

"Getting into a van with a strange man in a blue windbreaker goes against everything I was ever taught in my self-defense classes," Zoe teased.

"Don't worry, I have a gun," Seeley said.

Zoe shook her head. "Still, nothing you say makes me feel better."

Lucy giggled softly. "You two are funny."

Warmth spread through his chest. Seeley pushed it deep into his gut. He needed to keep that part of himself in check.

He approached the van and met the extended hand of the young man. "Seeley," he said, shaking hands.

"McCoy," he replied. "Sorry for the cloak-and-dagger. There aren't any security cameras on this side of the building." McCoy peered past Seeley and smiled at the girls. He slipped his hands into his coat pockets and nodded toward Lucy. "You must be Lucy. I've heard a lot about you. It's nice to put a face with the name."

Lucy looked confused and glanced at Zoe. "I don't know what that means."

Zoe shook it off, as if to say it didn't matter. "And you're going to take us to this Gina Loveless?"

"Yeah," McCoy said. "Get in."

Zoe was shaking her head, her eyes darting between Seeley and McCoy. Seeley knew trouble was coming before she spoke.

She grabbed Lucy's hand and pulled her backward. "This doesn't feel right," she whispered.

Lucy's face dropped into fear, and now Seeley could see both of them questioning. He cursed in his throat and held up a finger to tell McCoy they needed a minute.

Zoe turned then, leading Lucy back the way they had just come.

Seeley took several long strides and met them as they moved. "Zoe, stop."

"No. I am not okay with this," she said.

"Is he a bad guy?" Lucy asked.

"No," Seeley said. "He's here to help us."

"Says you," Zoe said.

"Stop." Seeley reached forward and grabbed her shoulder. "Stop!"

She ripped her shoulder away. "Don't touch me."

He stepped in front of her and put his hands up in surrender. "Wait, okay? Please."

"Give me one good reason why we should get in that van with him."

"Zoe—"

"No, this should be on our terms. If this Dr. Loveless wants to help so badly, then why can't she come to us? To a place we can vet and secure? This feels like a trap."

"And where would you like her to meet us? Where in the Ozarks did you have in mind? Ever been here before? Does this parking lot work?"

Zoe gave him a vicious glare.

"I understand that you don't trust people," Seeley said, "but we don't have time for this."

"I don't feel good about it."

"The way you feel is irrelevant. What matters is protecting Lucy. Frankly, that is all I care about. And right now, you are the only thing standing in the way of making sure those after her don't find her."

Zoe looked as though Seeley had verbally assaulted her.

He chanced placing his hand on her shoulder again and dropped his tone to a softer level. "I know you're trying to protect her, but you're putting her in danger."

She dropped her eyes, and he could see her mulling over what he'd said. Lucy gave her hand a squeeze, and Zoe turned to look at the girl.

"I think we should go with them," Lucy said.

They held each other's gaze, speaking without words, and Seeley wished he could read their minds.

"Are you sure?" Zoe said.

Lucy nodded, and Zoe responded in kind. "Okay."

She released Lucy's hand, and the girl turned back toward the van. She started moving away, and Seeley stepped to follow when Zoe placed her hand on his chest, drawing his eyes. He was unable to ignore the way his heart raced at her touch.

Her eyes were dark, her expression dripping with venom. "If anything happens to her, it'll be on you." She shoved off and turned without another word.

Seeley watched for a second as she strode toward the van, slowed his heart, and silenced the battle beginning to wage in his gut. For the job, he'd do whatever was needed.

SEVENTEEN

THE VAN RIDE was quiet and long. Zoe dared a glance at See-ley a few times. Each one found him staring off, lost in his own thoughts. Her own mind was raging for her to jump out of the van, take Lucy with her, and hide away in a cave where no one could ever find them.

That wouldn't be so terrible a life. Just the two of them sur-viving off the earth, away from the world and the corrupt nature that had created Lucy. Zoe had already experienced enough of this world to be done with it. But had Lucy?

She hadn't even been given the chance yet. That's what they were doing here, Zoe had to remind herself over and over. They were giving Lucy her freedom. Or at least, Zoe prayed that's what they were doing.

The van pulled off the main road and onto smaller, twisted side streets. The signs of the city became fainter, until the small streets turned to dirt roads and took them farther from civiliza-tion. Suddenly the forested terrain cleared, and before them was a farm. Or what used to be a farm. A large main house sat in the center, with a detached garage, barn, and tall silo shadowing it behind. Unkempt fields stretched out to either side, and the van's tires kicked up dirt and made clouds in the air right outside Zoe's window.

It looked like the sort of place a serial killer would quietly kill and bury his victims, a place no one would ever think to search. It didn't make Zoe's vacillating fears settle.

The van pulled to a stop, and Seeley moved first. He yanked the sliding door open and stepped out. Lucy followed, and without any other options Zoe exited the van against her better judgment.

McCoy walked around to meet them. "This way." He motioned and started toward the main house. It was humble but well maintained with white siding and a gray roof, a wraparound porch made from cedar, and pale yellow shutters hanging beside each open window. The farmhouse, clean and livable, formed a strange juxtaposition to the overgrown fields, weeds tall as toddlers, dying vegetation, and ignored shrubbery.

Before they reached the house, the door opened and out stepped a thin woman with gray hair and striking blue eyes that Zoe could see from a distance. The breeze lifted the ends of her long silver hair and caught her gauzy white button-down shirt. It made her look heavenly.

She smiled brightly and nodded toward them. "Welcome." Then she said to their driver, "You took the roads I instructed?"

"Every single one," McCoy answered.

"And you're sure you weren't followed?" she pressed.

"I'm sure."

She paused to gauge his confidence and then, satisfied, turned her attention back to Seeley. They didn't speak, just shared a long look that said more than Zoe could interpret but was one of recognition. Then her gaze shifted to Lucy and brightened.

"You must be Lucy," she said, stepping down off the porch. "I'm Dr. Gina Loveless, but you can just call me Gina."

She stopped a couple steps from Lucy, and Zoe inched closer so she was near enough to hear Lucy breathing. Gina ignored Zoe altogether.

"How are you feeling?" she asked.

"Okay," Lucy said. "Are you going to help me get my memories back?"

"I'm going to try. Memory is a tricky thing."

"So we've been told," Zoe said.

Gina snapped her eyes to Zoe, and the blue of them grabbed her tightly. She felt as if they were squeezing her throat, making it harder to breathe.

"Miss Johnson," Gina said, "we're all on the same team here. Let's do what is best for Lucy and try to cooperate instead of standing in her way."

Zoe just stood there in shock. It was as if she'd been transported back to school, when teachers would speak to her with level voices that were meant to be instructive but only led her to believe that no matter what she did, she came from darkness, so to darkness she would return.

Shame rose through her chest and wrapped itself around her heart. How quickly she could be dragged back to the hell of her past. In one moment she went from being consumed with fear for Lucy to drowning in her own insecurities. It was overwhelming.

And then from the darkness clouding her vision, Seeley spoke.

"The only reason Lucy got this far alive is because of Zoe," he said. "She helped her after we failed her." He looked from Gina to McCoy. "Let's not forget that."

Zoe locked eyes with Seeley for a moment, and the darkness that had been flooding in vanished. He dropped his eyes first, then turned back to Gina.

"I'm sorry," Gina said. "I didn't mean to offend."

Zoe gave a polite grin, accepting the forced apology. Gina wasn't sorry, but she'd play nice with Zoe if needed. Zoe knew her type well. She'd encountered women like this her entire life.

Gina turned back to Lucy. "The more open you are to the process, the better results we should have. Can you be open?" Gina put out her hand for Lucy to take.

The girl looked down at the woman's open palm and after a moment of hesitation grasped it fully. "Yes," she said, looking back up at her.

Gina smiled. "Good, let's begin then." She gently pulled Lucy down a small side path that ran along the house toward the barn. Lucy walked bravely beside the strange doctor without looking back. McCoy followed, and Zoe knew she was supposed to as well.

She could feel eyes on her and glanced sideways to see Seeley waiting to see what she would do.

"Thank you," Zoe said, the words just popping out before her mind had decided it was a good idea. "For sticking up for me," she continued, feeling the need to explain herself.

His mouth turned up in a kind and humble smile. It made her heart pulse. "After you," he said, nodding toward the path the others were traveling.

She took the path, aware that Seeley was only a foot behind her. More aware than she wanted to admit.

Gina led them all to the barn. The red paint was chipping, and the shingles on the roof were peeling back. But when Zoe stepped inside, she found herself transported.

She had expected dirt and hay for the floor, creaky wooden walls, stalls, unsteady rafters. Instead she found hardwood floors, decent overhead lighting, and items she might find in an animal shelter. Along the left wall was a collection of cages, big and small. Opposite the cages were trunks and shelving filled with blankets, animal foods of all types, food and water bowls, and a pile of leashes.

But the thing that drew Zoe's attention was the white sheeting that hung from long metal poles to form a large box in the barn's center. She couldn't make out what was behind the sheets, but the hairs on the back of her neck stood up.

"This was my father's farm," Gina began. "He was a veterinarian for thirty years, and after retiring he turned this barn into an animal clinic of sorts. When he passed away my mother didn't have the heart to maintain it, so I took over the deed." She spoke over her shoulder as she made her way to the white-sheet box. "Please don't touch anything."

Zoe couldn't help but look back to see how Seeley was reacting to this strange scene. His eyes were wide and skeptical. Was he regretting crawling into the van as much as she was? He must have felt her looking at him because he turned toward her, and she dropped her eyes quickly.

"I know how this must look," Gina continued. "But I needed access to certain medical equipment and couldn't just walk Lucy into a hospital. Veterinarian and modern medicine are not that different, it turns out." She yanked the front curtain open.

There sat an array of medical devices that Zoe vaguely recognized. A steel table sat in the center with a bright light overhead. A portable set of drawers she could only assume were filled with medical tools stood on the right side of the table. A monitoring system with chunky wires and thin poles for IV lines stood on the left. At the base of the metal slab stood another metal cart, waist high with a large black container secured to its top. Two thick latches on the container's front kept the contents secret.

Gina walked to the container and unlatched the closures. The lid popped open. "As you've been told," she said, eyeing Zoe, "memory is a mysterious function of the human brain. How, why, and where memories are created and stored isn't an exact science, which makes it unpredictable and hard to affect. However, with some incredible modern devices, we can get pretty close."

The doctor opened the lid fully and reached inside. She pulled out a cap that had two thick black straps connecting one side to the other. It housed hundreds of thin wires jutting out in all directions. The entire headpiece was covered in attached rainbow wiring. Reds, blues, greens, yellows, all long and slim, fell from the cap in several foot-long strands that had microconnectors at each end. Each connector was plugged into the base of the container, which contained a large switchboard.

"This is a newly developed optical brain scanner, smaller and transportable but highly powerful and accurate. They call her DOT, because she uses diffuse optical tomography to image the processes taking place in multiple regions of the brain, using infrared light to detect cellular activity."

"You want me to wear that?" Lucy said, her voice worried.

Gina looked up at her. "Yes, it's perfectly safe. It doesn't use radiation like an MRI might, so there's no chance of permanent damage."

"Damage," Lucy repeated, her worry changing to fear.

Zoe moved closer to her. "How does scanning her brain help her recover her memories?"

"I got the chance to look at the last brain imaging that was done after Olivia activated Lucy's amnesia, and my theory is that Lucy's memories weren't removed. That may have been Olivia's intention, but it appears her memories"—Gina nodded to Lucy—"*your* memories are still there, just in the wrong places. Which is why when you try to recall an event or time, you can't. Because your brain doesn't know where to look."

Gina placed the device back in the black container, her face filled with excitement. "I would like to walk you through a type of RMT that will hopefully help you get inside your own brain and locate memories while you're wearing DOT. When the neuronal activity in the brain increases in a region, oxygenated blood flows to that part of the brain, allowing us to see it using DOT technology. Like the way you can detect if someone is blushing, because of the rush of blood to their cheeks."

She rubbed her hands together and dropped her eyes. "I believe that if I can help you walk through your own psyche and locate those memories, I can detect patterns of where and how they moved." She looked up at Lucy again. "And then hopefully you'll be able to access them."

"Have you done this before?" Zoe asked.

Gina looked at her, an eerie thrill twinkling in her eyes. "No one's ever done this before. No one's ever been like Lucy."

A shiver ran the course of Zoe's spine. She hated Gina Loveless. Hated who she represented. Hated who she reminded Zoe of. Lucy was a toy to Gina. Something she could poke and prod to gain information she couldn't have any other way. Someone to play with, like someone had played with Zoe and the little brother she'd lost.

She'd trusted Dr. Holbert, believed he was trying to help her and Stephen. She'd let him convince her to let Stephen go. That it was more important to focus on herself and let Stephen find his own way. The doctor had even convinced her that they would be better off in different foster homes. And after being abandoned by his sister, he'd found solace in another sibling. That boy had stolen everything good from her sweet brother, and now he might as well be dead.

"What's RMT?" Lucy asked.

"Recovered-memory therapy," Zoe answered, the sting of Stephen still burning at her brain.

Surprise flashed across Gina's gaze. "You are familiar with it?"

"Unfortunately," Zoe replied. Her rash burned underneath the long sleeve of her shirt, and she forced herself to ignore it.

"Yes, I know it has a bad reputation, but with the unique structure of Lucy's brain, I really believe it can be helpful."

"You plan to use amobarbital, I assume?" Zoe asked.

"It has the mildest hypnotic properties," Gina said. "Just enough to make her mind malleable."

"You mean easily influenced."

"That's not my intent. I want Lucy to remember the truth, not my version of it. What motivation would I have for influencing her memories?"

Lucy turned to Zoe. "I won't do it if you don't think I should."

Gina huffed and rolled her eyes. "This is ridiculous and a waste of our time." She moved to Lucy's side. "Listen to me, I—"

"No," Lucy said, pulling back. She shook her head. "No. Olivia told me to be careful who I trusted." She turned to Zoe and grabbed her hand. "I trust you."

Zoe smiled at the sweet girl and nodded. She'd wondered if she might lose Lucy to the others. She was surprised by how happy she was it hadn't happened yet.

"Let's get some air," she said to Lucy. The girl nodded, and they turned to leave the barn. Zoe heard Gina complain as they walked off, and Seeley told her to relax.

The two girls stepped out into the evening light, the symphony of nature playing around them. They walked for a couple of moments, hand in hand.

"What are you thinking?" Zoe finally asked.

"That I'm afraid," Lucy said.

"Me too."

"Maybe I don't need to remember."

"What if Seeley is right, and that means a lifetime of running?"

Lucy considered this. "I am very fast."

Zoe smiled. This was truer than she thought possible. "You don't have to remember if you don't want to."

Lucy stared at the fading sun, and Zoe knew the answer before she asked the question.

"But you want to remember, don't you?"

"How can I know who I am without knowing who I was?" Lucy asked.

Zoe wanted to say her past didn't define her, that Lucy could be whatever she wanted for now, in this moment, but she knew those things were a lie.

"Do you think it will hurt?" Lucy asked.

"Remembering can be painful."

"What if I remember I'm bad?"

It was the second time she'd heard Lucy verbalize this concern.

"What if you don't like me anymore, because I'm not good?" Lucy asked, tears in her eyes.

Zoe turned and placed her hands on the sides of Lucy's face. "That won't happen. That will never happen."

"Promise?"

"I promise."

Lucy nodded, and Zoe dropped her hands. She knew Lucy was going to do it, let Gina try to walk her into her own mind, and if Zoe was being honest, she would probably do the same thing.

"I don't want to be with the doctor alone," Lucy said.

"You won't be," Zoe said. "Together, remember."

Lucy smiled. "Together."

They stood there for a long time, holding hands, watching the sun dip below the mountains and cover the sky in shades of pink and orange. Zoe wished the moment would linger just a bit longer. She had no idea how to prepare for what was coming next.

PART TWO

I am not looking to escape my darkness,
I am learning to love myself there.

Rune Lazuli

EIGHTEEN

IT WAS MORNING, and I was awake while the rest of the house remained still. Beside me in the large king bed, Zoe was still sleeping. I tried not to stare at her and instead closed my eyes to try to see into the depths of my mind. I was searching for what I'd lost. I could trace the map back for a while. I have made a few new memories since my past was taken into reverse.

The dingy room is the earliest thing I can remember. As far back as I can reach. I don't know where it was or how I got there, but I remember rising from a bed that had scratchy covers to the worried expression of a lovely woman who was sitting beside me. I remember her warm hand holding my cold one. I don't know why I was cold.

Thinking back on that memory now, I'm surprised I wasn't more discouraged or fearful. If someone were to ask me what it felt like to wake up without any memories, I'm not sure what I would say. I was just awake, and the warm woman was telling me her name was Olivia. And my name was Lucy. We were in trouble, but I shouldn't worry because she was taking care of me.

Before more could be said, we were running from bad men out a door marked with a bright red sign. EXIT. Into the thick of trees, down a hill, over a small creek.

Dots of light pierced the darkness behind us as they followed. I should have had questions, or concerns, or fears. But I don't remember any. I was just following a stranger I had met moments earlier because she told me to.

Because her hands were warm and her face kind. She told me to run west, and without question I did. I would again. I have no other recollection of her. Not now, not then, but still I feel connected to her. Sometimes I think maybe I remember the way she laughed. I get whiffs of what she must have smelled like. I imagine her in a doctor's coat, because now I have context about who she was. Stories I've been told, facts given. Am I actually remembering, or is my mind producing memories that never happened?

How will I know the difference? Hunting deer with Seeley in the woods, throwing knives at the ready, feels as real as seeing Olivia walk toward me in a white lab coat. But they can't both be real. Can they?

These were the thoughts that pulled me from sleep before the sun was up. I couldn't help but glance back at Zoe for a moment, before it felt like I was spying. She was the first person in my life who wasn't a stranger.

She knew me. Even though there wasn't much to know, she had been there from the start. Before I could express I was afraid or worried, she seemed to sense it. She'd taken steps to be closer to me. It gave me courage, offered a sense of stability. Maybe it would all be alright in the end.

Last night, after we decided to give Dr. Loveless's plan a try, I enjoyed watching the sunset with Zoe. For a moment the world seemed open, not seconds from crashing down around us. We walked back to the large red barn together. I was ready to start right away.

But according to Dr. Loveless, my mind needed to be sharp and stable so we'd have the best chance of success. She suggested starting first thing in the morning, after a night of rest. I wanted it to work, so I'd waited.

Now I was up.

I slipped out of bed and made my way downstairs. I waited for a while, but soon the rest of the house rose as well. Seeley, McCoy, Zoe, and Dr. Loveless. Thirty minutes passed mostly in silence as people cleared sleep from their minds, got coffee, and agreed it was time.

Within the hour I was lying on a cold, inclined table. Dr. Loveless was attaching DOT to my head, and I tried not to wince each time she yanked my hair.

"Sorry," she said. "Almost done."

I'd been instructed to keep my chin still, but I could still see Zoe standing to my right, only a couple feet off, her face worried, her body tensed for action. She was ready to yank me from this table if anything went wrong. I was glad she was here.

Seeley stood at the entrance to the strange sheeted room, just inside the open curtain. One hand in his pocket, the other holding a mug. He was watching carefully but not nearly as concerned or rigid as Zoe. I found myself caught up in the single memory I had of him. Again. The moment was fragmented, more flashes and feelings than a line of occurring motions.

It had been a brisk morning, maybe early afternoon. I could feel the chill on my cheeks, the mountainous terrain underneath my feet, thick forest all around as I moved with speed. Quick and precise. Seeley close. I could smell his aftershave, the same way I could smell it now.

I'd come upon my prey. A beautiful buck, thick and tall, with horns jutting out on either side to punctuate his majesty. I could hear the beast's heart, steady and then thundering as he sensed us. My weapon at the ready. Aim, perfect, and release. I could hear the knife stick with a soft thud but couldn't see it in the darkness of my mind. What came before that moment, and after, was nothing. It was a single moment that stood on an island in the middle of an endless sea.

Was it foolish to hope that I would soon see land? Salvation? Afterward, would I wish for the empty expanse? I had the strange thought that currently I could be whatever I decided. I had no history that told me who I was, so couldn't I just make my own? Maybe the forgetting was a gift?

But what if I created new ideas of the person I could be and then the old memories returned? Wouldn't it be better to start off with the truth rather than construct something that could be broken later? Round and round, the questions plagued me as I waited.

"There," Dr. Loveless said. "Finished."

She walked around the end of the table and to the rolling cart that sat near its corner. I turned my head to follow her and felt DOT's weight press into my shoulders.

"Please try to remain still," she said.

"Okay," I said, forcing myself not to nod.

She opened the top drawer and pulled out something small, then picked up a cup with a straw. She walked back to me and opened her hand, and I could see three small blue capsules resting in her palm.

Amobarbital, Zoe had called it. It had hypnotic properties and was called blue heaven on the streets. It could be very dangerous, even lethal in large doses, but the perfect trip with the right amount. It was meant to open the mind. Provide a gateway to the subconscious, Zoe had explained.

I felt my nerves rising and disconnected from them, turned them off, and focused on the task at hand. The nerves vanished as if I'd flipped off the light. My mind went cold. I saw my emotions but wasn't connected to them. They were unnecessary for what was coming, so I tossed them out.

"Don't worry," Dr. Loveless said. "This will be painless."

"I'm not worried," I said truthfully.

She smiled at me. "Good. Open your mouth."

I did, and she placed the pills on my tongue one at a time, offering me a drink after each one. They slid down my throat easily.

"These will take effect quickly. As they do, I will ask you to close your eyes and listen only to my voice," Dr. Loveless said. "Can you do that?"

"Yes." I already felt my bones becoming lighter as what felt like exhaustion seeped through my blood and into my skin.

She took a deep breath and glanced at the others around the room, as if she suddenly needed a reassuring push. "Shall we begin?"

I closed my eyes and exhaled slowly. Not because I wanted to but because slow was the only function I had. I answered yes, I think. Or maybe I just thought I'd answered. My mouth felt swollen and my tongue made of foam. I thought to ask if this was how I was supposed to be feeling, but I had lost the ability to connect my mind with my speech.

I could hear her voice. "I want you to focus on the sound of my voice. As we begin, I want you to let your body sink into the place where you sit. Anchor yourself to it. Anchor yourself to my voice."

Then the light from the world beyond my closed lids started to fade.

LUCY. CAN YOU hear me?

Dr. Loveless's familiar voice filled my brain. It was like an echo coming from within. A faint whisper, clear and near, but not directly beside me.

I remembered then what was happening to me. I was exploring my memory, searching for things misplaced. I opened my eyes, and a city street filled my view. I was sitting on a bench along a two-lane road with moving traffic, bordered by sidewalks occupied by pedestrians. To my right, small, simple homes sat in rows on both sides of the street. Fenced lawns, manicured bushes, children playing, their laughter bubbling up and through the air.

To the left, a gathering of tall city buildings rose from the pavement toward the sky. They glistened in the sun, their windows reflecting its light. The buildings were nearly stacked on top of one another, yet at their bases hordes of people passed from one place to the next, occupied with moving quickly, none stopping to interact with one another.

Lucy, if you can hear me, say yes, Dr. Loveless said.

"Yes," I replied.

Where are you?

I glanced back right, the peaceful neighborhood scene a stark contrast to the bustle of the working city to my left. "I don't know."

"Are you lost?" came a small voice.

I turned my attention downward to see a child sitting on the far end of the bench. The girl, her hair pulled up in a ponytail, wore light denim jeans and a white T-shirt with a pink unicorn on the front. Her eyes were bright and kind as she stared up at me, waiting for me to answer.

Lucy, tell me what you see.

"A girl," I said.

The girl scrunched her nose curiously. "Who are you talking to?"

A girl? Do you recognize her?

"No."

The girl looked over her shoulder and then back to me. "Are you crazy?" She dropped her voice to a whisper and leaned forward a tad. "Do you see dead people?"

I shook my head. "No." Then a thought crossed my mind. "Are you dead?" I asked her.

She giggled and swung her legs. "Nope."

Lucy, talk to her. See if she can help you.

The girl smiled, and I noticed one of her front teeth was missing. It made her smile more charming, and I felt my heart warm. "Can you help me?" I asked. "Do you know where I am?"

The girl stared at me for a long moment. "Of course I know."

"Can you tell me?"

She smiled and shook her head. "That's not how the game works."

"What game?"

"The one we always play. Do you want me to teach you?"

"Yes."

The girl sprang up from her seat and took off running for the active city. I hesitated, thrown by her sudden movements, but recovered quickly and raced after her. She was quick, darting into the throng of bodies, all acting as if a little girl wasn't passing through at their feet. I raced into the pile of people, knocking shoulders and elbows, thinking to apologize but too focused on keeping the child in my sights.

The top of her head popped in and out of view. She was quickening her steps, putting more distance between us as I clawed my way after her. The bodies around me seemed to be multiplying, growing in numbers and density. It was starting to feel like I was slamming into walls.

"Hurry, hurry," she yelled over the masses.

"Slow down, I'm losing you," I yelled back.

She didn't. I was sweating as I watched her break out of the sea of people. She shot off like a rocket once free from the crowd. I was almost there.

I put all my force into propelling myself forward, freedom right before me. One extra punch of speed and I slammed into an invisible barrier that knocked me off my feet and to the concrete. My spine smacked the hard ground, and the wind rushed from my lungs. I gasped for breath and found none. Pain rippled across my skin as I rolled to my side and tried to breathe.

Black dots filled my vision as the impact of the fall raked my whole body. After a moment I caught a gasp of air and sucked it into my lungs. A smidge of relief entered as I regained the ability to breathe.

Pushing myself off the ground, I looked up to see I was alone. And no longer in the middle of a thriving city.

Rather, in a box. A glass box in a dark room. I stood, panicked. Placed my hands on the surface. I could tell the glass was inches thick, unbreakable without a tool of some kind. All around me, my hands met the same surface. I could touch the top without fully extending my arms, and the width was less than my wingspan.

I was trapped. I looked through the glass, searching for the little girl. "Hello," I called out. "Hey, anyone?"

Lucy, you're safe. Calm down. Everything is alright.

Dr. Loveless's voice cut through the panic but didn't ease the beating of my heart. It didn't feel alright.

This is just your mind, Lucy, I told myself. *You are in control.*

Then why did I feel so threatened? A familiar feeling from the depths rose up, and my panic boiled over to terror.

I had been here before. Without knowing why, my body

launched into a full-on attack on the prison that held me captive. "Let me out!" I cried. "Please, let me out."

Lucy, you have to calm down. Nothing can hurt you.

Bright lights flicked on overhead, and the room around me came into view. Just beyond the glass sat a group of people, faceless from where I was, all dressed in black, some armed, others in white lab coats. Between us was a large panel filled with things I couldn't see.

"Let me out!" I yelled again. "Please don't do this."

Do what, I couldn't remember. It was as if my memories were acting through me without my consent. As if my body knew what was coming and it desperately wanted to be free.

Your heart rate's too high, Lucy. I need you to bring it back down.

I ignored Dr. Loveless. She wasn't here with me. I was alone.

"Begin," one of the faceless said.

A loud crank echoed through the room, and after the quick build and rumble of something passing overhead, I glanced up to see that a large steel pipe was dumping water into my prison.

And then I was a child. Still me, but ten years younger, shivering and terrified as water drained from the pipe.

The light overhead was dull and yellow. The room smelled of bleach and smoke. The panel and its judges sat before me, but now I recognized their faces. Faces I had seen a hundred times before. Doctors, technicians, department heads. Olivia was there, watching worriedly from the back corner.

Some faces I didn't know as well, but I knew they were important because this demonstration had been set up specifically for them. They stood in the center, the one in the navy suit and red tie their leader. "The leader of the free world," I had been told, though I wasn't sure what that meant.

Then I was back in my near-adult body, still trapped behind

glass, Dr. Loveless's voice urging me to remain calm. Back and forth the images flipped. In one moment I was myself, and then my younger self. Both trapped behind glass as water drained from the ceiling.

I understood what was happening. They were testing me. By nearly drowning me. Seeing how far I could be taken to the edge of death without having a rise in emotions. The skill would be valuable in the face of any danger.

In a snap second, a collage of memories flooded my mind. How many times had I been held in this cage? Pressed to my limits, beyond what a human body should be able to withstand? How many times had I screamed for help and none was given? How many times had I begged for them to stop?

All of the memories rushed back to me now, a catalogue of one event that had happened over and over again. I wanted to scream and weep at the same time. The power of it blazed through my bones and ignited the panic I felt until I thought I might combust.

Lucy, wake up, Dr. Loveless said.

I couldn't. I was screaming with fury, my lungs burning inside my chest. My fists raged against the glass as the water reached my waist and rose at an alarming rate. I was shivering and crying and begging for help as the faces remained unmoved. As they had done a dozen times before.

Lucy, listen to me. Wake up.

I struggled to breathe, as if I were back on the pavement having the wind knocked out of me. The water reached my shoulders, and terror grabbed my mind like a starved bear and devoured every morsel of sense. There was nothing but fear when the water reached my face. I thrashed and fought against the reality I couldn't escape, but it only plunged me further into darkness.

Lucy, you must wake up!

The water rose over my mouth and then my nose. I clenched my eyes as the cold shut out any hope for rescue, and all that was left were my instincts, which refused to believe I wasn't drowning. My body continued to fight as my mind sank deeper into madness. I wasn't breathing. I could feel my lungs ready to burst, my throat on fire, my brain swelling in its search for air.

Lucy!

Something sparked in the darkness below the water. It fizzled softly and touched my chest. Then it came again. A pulse. And again. This time with more intensity. It made me ache, and it drew my mind back from hopelessness.

Breathe, Lucy, breathe.

Against rationale, I opened my mouth and sucked in. Air filled my lungs, and the scene around me changed again. The water prison was gone. There was no city, or panel, or child. I was back where I had started. In the barn, with Dr. Loveless, Seeley, and Zoe at my sides.

I was gasping, not able to get air into my lungs fast enough. I was shaking from head to toe, aching, terror still crawling over my skin. The recalled emotions collapsed upon me, and I began to cry. Zoe pushed the others away and tucked my head against her shoulder as the crying turned to wails. Wails I thought would never end.

But they did, and then Zoe insisted I rest. I didn't argue. She led me away from the table, the barn, and the past that I'd now never be able to forget.

NINETEEN

ZOE STOOD IN the kitchen, coffee mug in hand. A shuffling sound drew her attention, and she turned to see Seeley standing inside the kitchen archway.

"How is she?" he asked.

Zoe took the final swallow from her mug and walked to the sink. "Sleeping." She rinsed the mug and placed it in the dishwasher.

The two stood in silence for a moment. Before either could say anything, Gina entered. "Is Lucy still resting?" she asked.

Zoe nodded, and Gina crossed her arms. "Let her rest a little longer. The more strength she has, the better."

"You have to be joking," Zoe said.

"We can't stop now," the doctor continued. "It worked—she recovered something from her past."

"And nearly stopped breathing," Zoe fired back.

"Memory recovery is tricky."

"Tricky, yes, but life-threatening?" Zoe turned to Seeley, pleading with him to hear reason. "There has to be another way."

Seeley exhaled and gave a slight nod. "What are the chances that happens to her again?"

"There's no way to know," Gina said. "But she'll know what to expect this time. She'll be better suited to handle her emotions. She was trained for situations like this. She just needs to tap into that."

"No," Zoe said. "This is crazy. She stopped breathing. You had to shock her with manual defibrillators to get her back to consciousness. What if that hadn't worked?"

"It did work, and next time it won't be as severe. She'll learn as she goes," Gina said.

"How can you be sure?"

"Because I have enough understanding of who Lucy is and where she comes from to believe she can handle this. You only see the scared teenage girl that stumbled into your diner. You're doing her a disservice."

Zoe almost laid into Gina, but Seeley raised his arms toward her to signal calm. "Everyone wants what is best for the situation here," he said.

"No, I only want what is best for Lucy," Zoe said.

"If you really understood what we're dealing with, you would know that what is best for Lucy is to handle this situation," Gina said.

"And if you kill her trying to recover memories, who wins then?" Zoe barked.

"She won't kill me." Lucy had entered from the opposite side of the kitchen. She looked small and tired, the usual optimism and light drained from her eyes.

"You should be resting," Zoe said.

"I did."

Quiet captured the kitchen as the four stood in awkward silence.

Gina cleared her throat. "How are you feeling?"

"Like I almost drowned," Lucy said.

Zoe glanced over her shoulder and cut her eyes at Seeley, as if to say, *She is not ready for more of this.* He acknowledged her look and turned his attention to Lucy.

"We all have different ideas about how to proceed." He took a step toward the girl. "But what do you want to do?"

Lucy dropped her eyes to the floor, her face turning contemplative. A moment stretched into a minute before she drew her eyes upward. "I want to remember. I want to remember all of it." She looked at Zoe. "No matter the cost." Then back to Gina. "I'm ready to try again."

Zoe couldn't shake the horrid feeling making its home inside her chest. She wanted to be optimistic about the outcome, but her instincts were telling her this path would lead Lucy to more darkness and pain.

"Excellent," Gina said. "I'll get everything prepped." With that she left, heading back out the way she had come.

"I'll give you guys a minute," Seeley said.

"Actually," Lucy said before he could move, "I'd like to have time alone." She turned to Zoe and gave a half smile. "But you'll be in there, right?"

"Together," Zoe said.

Lucy gave a little nod and then, just as Gina had done, left the way she'd entered.

Zoe felt Lucy leave as much as she saw it. Warmth was pulled out of her as the girl walked away. She should rush after her, hold her close, tell her it would be better not to be alone when facing something so heavy. But she stayed in place.

She could feel Seeley behind her. She wondered if he felt the shift in Lucy as well. He claimed to have known her. Was she becoming more like the girl he'd trained? More like herself?

"Did they really do what she's remembering?" Zoe asked. She turned to face him, to watch his face as he answered.

He didn't shy away from her stare. He took it head-on and nodded. "Yes, they trained them all to withstand an immense amount of pain."

"What other terrible things is she going to remember?"

"I want there to be another way too, Zoe."

She huffed in disbelief and shook her head.

"Those terrible memories are worth her life," Seeley said. "Because trust me, it's her memories or her life. The men capable of nearly drowning a little girl over and over are looking for her. What do you think they'll be willing to do to get what they want from her now?"

Zoe felt a rush of emotion wash over her. Tears sprang to her eyes, and she didn't fight them. "I don't know how to protect her."

Seeley's face softened, and he walked across the space that separated them. He placed his hand on her shoulder, and his touch quickened her pulse and drew heat back to her chest.

"All any of us can do is our best," he said.

Zoe sniffed her tears back and drew her shoulder out from under his hand. She wasn't sure how she felt about the way his closeness made her skin tingle, so she deflected.

"Where did you get that, a fortune cookie?" she mocked.

He cleared his throat. "I was just trying to offer . . ." He shook his head and chuckled. "I'm not great at pep talks."

"Phrases like 'all any of us can do is our best' aren't making you any better," Zoe said.

"Noted." He smiled, and she returned the gesture.

Immediately she wished she hadn't. They were connecting and sparking something neither of them had time for. Zoe yanked her eyes away from his and walked past him without looking back. She still didn't trust him. He was still the enemy.

Wasn't he?

I OPENED MY eyes, and once more I was sitting on a bench between the sweet neighborhood to my right and the bustling downtown to my left. The thoughts I'd recovered earlier crashed into my brain, and their rumbling fears with them. My heart rate spiked. I could feel beads of sweat collecting at my hairline.

I had to control this. Deep breaths. Internalize the fear. See it, switch it off, stomp it out. I'd been trained to do so. Wasn't that what Dr. Loveless had said?

"You came back," the small voice beside me said.

I turned and saw the high ponytail and unicorn shirt. "You lied to me."

The girl's face went sour. "Did not."

"You said you would show me the game."

"I did. It's not my fault you lost."

Lucy, remember, this is your mind. You are safe.

Dr. Loveless's voice echoed like a whisper in my ears. I had to keep my brain trained on the truth of her words.

"Are there more games like that one?" I asked the child.

"Oh yeah, lots," she said, her eyes widening.

"Can you show me?"

"Not until you win the first one."

Fear beat against my heart. I didn't want to go back into the box.

She turned to look me right in the eye. "Leveling up doesn't come for free."

I swallowed hard, and the little girl must have seen the terror cascading down my face.

"You scared?"

I nodded.

The girl slid off the bench and stood at attention before me, eyes serious, jaw set. "Toughen up, buttercup. Level one is easy mode. If you can't beat this, you might as well not come back."

I felt smacked, her words punchy and brutal. Then her face softened, and her lips opened to reveal her gap-toothed grin. A giggle escaped her lips, one that sounded both innocent and maddening. I wasn't sure whether to be reassured or threatened. Without another sound she was off again, racing toward the bustle of bodies, and I knew what following her would mean.

But I couldn't not. I physically couldn't stay seated. My mind and heart needed to know, so they carried my limbs without my permission. I was met with meatsuits, same as before. I was crashing through people, desperate to keep up, hoping for a different outcome.

I should have slowed my pace since I knew what waited, but I didn't and again smacked the hard glass at a dangerous pace. The time before it had all seemed to happen in slow motion as reality crashed in. This time I knew what was coming, and it happened faster than I anticipated. No matter what I tried, the water rose and the fear grew. I couldn't hear Dr. Loveless's voice. I lost my grasp on what I knew was true.

This was my mind.

I was safe.

But all I could feel was the desperate need to escape the glass prison as the faceless coats watched me begin to drown. All I could see were the painful flashes of reliving this moment as a child, over and over. My own voice screamed for help, begging for them not to put me back in. My own body tugged against their restraints, bruising under their vicious holds. My mind scratched at the inside of my skull for freedom.

Freedom.

Freedom.

Freedom.

Until I wasn't breathing, and the shocks against my chest and to my nervous system were the only thing that could bring me back to the reality of lying on the cold table in the barn, sweat-drenched, DOT attached to my head, Zoe and the others surrounding me.

I sprang up from where I was seated, gasping. Oxygen forced its way into my lungs, its reentry painful. My head was pounding, and I felt like I was still soaked from icy waters, even though that had just been happening in my mind.

Tears warmed my cheeks. I wasn't weeping, but I could feel the urge to collapse into Zoe's arms. She was close, her hand on my shoulder. I glanced up at her worried face as the noise of the room finally broke past the barrier built in my subconscious.

"Deep breaths," Dr. Loveless was saying as she carefully disconnected DOT. Unhooking me because I had failed. Again.

"Talk to me, Lucy," I heard Zoe say.

"Stop," I whispered.

"It can't be safe for her heart rate to spike that high," Zoe said.

I reached up and pushed Dr. Loveless's hands away from the connecting tubes on the DOT cap. "Stop," I said louder.

"Lucy," Zoe said.

"I need to go again."

"No. She can't, she needs a break," she said to the others.

"You don't speak for me," I snapped. I could feel something forming inside me. An old sensation of determination that was stronger than anything I'd ever felt. My words were harsher than they needed to be, but I only slightly cared. Something else was happening that was greater than how Zoe felt.

She dropped her hand from my shoulder and inched back. I'd hurt her. I should care. I did, but not enough to stop.

I turned back to Dr. Loveless, who was still on the other side of me. "Can I go again?"

She glanced at Zoe and then Seeley, who was standing near the end of the table. Then back to me. "Your pulse is still unstable. It might be better to take a small break."

I heard it then, the uneven beeping that represented my heart rate. I zeroed in on the sound, blocking out the rest of the room. I followed it to the sound of my actual pulse, saw it skyrocketing under my skin. With a long exhale, I slowed it. Brought it back into a perfectly normal rhythm. Then returned my focus to the room.

Dr. Loveless and Zoe were watching me in fascination.

"I need to go again," I said.

"Can I speak with you two alone?" Zoe demanded rather than asked.

The three left the curtained square. They moved out of sight, and I zeroed in on the motion of their footsteps. Four yards across the barn floor. The creaking of wood and metal signaled they were stepping outside. I didn't need to strain to hear their words. I just tapped into their sound waves. Like a radio. Easy enough.

Zoe: "You can't seriously be thinking about letting her do this."

Dr. Loveless: "She seems pretty determined."

Zoe: "She's already had two doses of amobarbital, and you want to give her another?"

Seeley: "How much can the body withstand?"

Zoe: "Not this much!"

Dr. Loveless: "I wasn't aware you had medical experience, Miss Johnson."

Seeley: "Can Lucy handle another dose?"

A beat of silence passed.

Dr. Loveless: "I could cut it in half. I believe she'll be able to journey with less now that's she been before. Her determination will carry her farther than most drugs could. It's all a mind game at this point."

Zoe: "A mind game that could kill her."

Seeley: "In my experience, that is the only kind."

More silence.

Dr. Loveless: "Are we finished then?" She didn't wait for a response. Her feet were already moving back toward me. She stepped through the thick white sheet and strode toward me, Seeley a few steps behind her.

Zoe stepped into view but stayed back, her face darkened by worry. *Don't give up on me,* I wanted to say, but instead I just held her eyes and hoped her face would soften. It didn't. I swallowed my own fear as I listened to her heart pounding inside her chest. I could stop, I thought, heed her warning.

Dr. Loveless held out a single blue pill, and I leaned back against the table. "Anchor yourself here," she said. "The key is to remember what is real and what isn't. You are in control."

I nodded at the doctor, then stole a final glance at Zoe. She was scratching her arms, a tic I'd noticed her doing when she was afraid or nervous. I could stop, I thought again as I took the blue pill.

But not yet.

TWENTY

"THE PRESIDENT IS getting antsy," Hammon said.

Seeley exhaled and watched his breath smoke from his lips into the freezing winter air. The world was dark in the early morning hours, the house behind him deep in slumber.

"We need more time, sir," he said into the phone. "She's close to a breakthrough."

"Are you sure?"

"Nothing about this is sure."

"That isn't good enough, Agent. The commander in chief and the army's chief of staff are breathing down my neck. They want to pull the girl in."

"If they do that, we lose all hope of recovering her memories, sir."

"We don't know that for sure. Gina herself said memory recovery is unpredictable. Maybe being here will remind the girl of who she was created to be, and she'll do as told."

"It's too risky," Seeley said.

"Your concern is noted, but I'm afraid this call outranks you."

"I just need a couple more days. Please, sir, we're close."

"Based on what evidence?"

Seeley said nothing. It was more a feeling than anything, but he couldn't say that. Hammon sighed, and Seeley let the silence stand as he waited for the director to consider.

"I'll see how long I can hold them off, but I'm promising nothing," Hammon finally replied.

"Thank you, sir."

"Don't thank me, Seeley, just get it done."

The line went dead, and Seeley tapped the phone off. He glanced back toward the house and cursed. The battle that had started waging in his chest returned. One side demanded he continue forward cold, the other reminded him of the Lucy he knew and how Zoe warmed him more each time they interacted. The division was building.

He knew how this would end if they were successful. What it would mean for Zoe, and he struggled to swallow it. And watching Lucy remember the tiny pieces of what they had done to her was only strengthening his conflicting emotions.

He needed to get control of himself. Do what needed to be done. And fast, or he'd lose all control of this situation. What he was doing to them was cruel, but it was nothing compared to what the army would do. He was protecting them from that, he told himself as he walked back to the house, trying to leave his mounting guilt out in the cold.

ZOE FOLLOWED LUCY as she stormed out of the barn. Seeley moved to follow, and Zoe raised her hands, signaling for him to stay. It would be better if she went after Lucy alone.

The sun was setting on another day, and warm pinks with brushes of orange filled the sky above the mountains. It had been two days since they'd journeyed to the farm. Two days of

Lucy subjecting her mind to torture and her body to danger. She couldn't get out of the box. No matter what she tried, she got stuck, drowning behind thick glass, a victim to the pain of the same group of memories she couldn't free herself from.

A dozen times she tried, and each time the results ended the same way. With each failed attempt Lucy sank deeper into herself. Determined to beat the first level. But something was holding her back, something she couldn't identify or conquer.

She was hardly sleeping, though she needed the rest in order to recover. Both nights her cries had woken them all, as her memories found her dreams and turned them to nightmares. Zoe wasn't sleeping either. Lucy wouldn't talk to her anymore. She wouldn't talk to any of them. Some instinctual lever had been pulled, and the sweet, naïve girl was being replaced with someone else.

Maybe someone she had always been.

"Lucy," Zoe said as the girl strode away from the barn and another failed attempt. Zoe had to push her legs hard to keep up. "Lucy, please stop."

Lucy whirled around, her face shadowed in frustration. "I'm so weak," she hissed. "I should be able to do this. To get out of that box!"

"Should? You say that like it's a normal skill."

"I'm not normal," Lucy bit back.

Zoe held her tongue. No, she wasn't.

Lucy growled and grasped the sides of her head. "I need to be better."

"No you don't."

"Yes I do, otherwise I'll never remember."

"Maybe you don't need to remember."

Lucy sighed, and a bit of light chased out the darkness in her eyes. Tears started to collect there, and Zoe's heart broke.

"But Agent Seeley said—"

"Forget Seeley," Zoe said. "We can leave right now if you want. Grab our stuff and go. We can head back to Tomac's, he can get us new identities, and we'll go wherever you want."

"They'll come for us," Lucy whispered. Her tears dotted her cheeks, and the hardness of failure eased as the sweet girl Zoe knew began to return.

"I've been running most of my life," Zoe said. "And you're really fast."

Lucy gave a soft chuckle and sniffed back her tears.

"Just you and me," Zoe continued, "and we'll leave all of this behind us."

"I would like that."

"Me too."

Lucy's small smile faded, and she shook her head. Zoe already knew what the girl was going to say.

"But you can't," Zoe said.

"I just want the truth." Lucy grunted at the sky. "But this isn't working."

Zoe knew from her own experience with RMT that it wasn't a sure science. So many factors influenced the outcome. It had been used on her as a way to recall her fractured childhood after she and Stephen had been taken from their mother. After the authorities decided their stories about what had happened in the mountain community where they'd been raised weren't true. That their minds had fabricated an elaborate story to cope with their trauma.

Dr. Holbert had been convinced that if he could take Zoe back through her memories, she'd remember what had really happened and be able to deal with it. He'd done the same with Stephen.

That's when his nightmares had started. That had been the start of it all.

Zoe shook off the dark memories and focused on what she had learned about the way the process worked. There was something Dr. Holbert had said that was ringing in her ears now. *"Trust is essential, Evelyn. Do you trust me?"*

"Everything okay over here?" Seeley said, joining them and yanking Zoe from her mind.

"I have an idea." She looked to Lucy. "You trust me, right?"

"Of course," Lucy said.

Zoe turned to look at Seeley. "I need you to back me up."

"With what?" he asked.

Zoe started back toward the barn, and the other two followed. She stepped inside, Lucy directly behind her, and Gina looked up to meet them.

"This isn't working," Zoe said.

"RMT takes time—" Gina started.

"Yes, but she doesn't trust you. So if Lucy tries again, I'm going with her."

"What?" Lucy exclaimed.

"That's not possible," Gina said.

"Not physically, but with my voice. I'll guide her through. She trusts me," Zoe said.

"You have no experience—"

"I have some," Zoe pushed back. "And I know Lucy, who she is now. I'll guide her or she doesn't go back in." She turned to make sure she had Lucy's approval. The girl nodded, and Zoe felt her confidence grow.

"This is ridiculous," Gina said.

"This is the plan," Seeley cut in.

Zoe glanced back at him.

"They do this together," he continued, "or not at all."

Zoe couldn't help but give him a small grin. He nodded to her, and a small chip of her distrust fell away. In that moment she was glad he was there.

The three of them looked at Gina. And after a moment of staring at them in disbelief, she shook her head and conceded. "Fine. But if things go awry, I'm taking over."

Lucy wrapped her hand in Zoe's and smiled. "Ready?" Lucy asked her.

"Ready."

TWENTY-ONE

I WAS SITTING on the bench between two worlds. But it felt different—the air, the wind that brushed over my shoulders. I wasn't sure if the change was real or just in my mind. I was struck by the absurdity of my own thought and laughed out loud. Everything was in my mind.

"What's so funny?" came the all-too-familiar voice.

I turned my eyes, and like every time before, she was there. The little girl in the unicorn T-shirt.

Lucy, can you hear me? Remember you aren't alone.

Zoe's voice filled me with warmth. Small and inside my brain like Dr. Loveless's had always been, but more connected. Like her voice was a part of me.

"Yes," I answered, "I can hear you."

"You're talking to yourself again, weirdo," the little girl mocked.

This is your mind. You're in charge here. Focus on level one.

I brushed the mean girl's comments away and returned to the task at hand.

Let's talk through what usually happens next.

"I follow the girl into the city, through the crowd."

"Hey," the girl said. "Don't talk about me like I'm not here."

Maybe don't follow her then.

"But she takes me to the box."

Have you tried going anywhere else?

No, I always followed the girl. I glanced down to ask the child what else was here, and for the first time she wasn't there. In her place was a wasp. Black and yellow striped, crawling along the wooden planks of the bench toward me. Faster than I could move, it was on my hand, crawling across my skin. I froze, watched it creep over the soft flesh that covered my fingers. I wanted to swat it away, but for some reason I thought better of it. Maybe it was supposed to be there.

A moment passed as the wasp searched for something, and I remained perfectly still. Then as if I knew its thoughts, I knew it wanted to sting me, and I couldn't have that. Faster than humanly possible, I lifted my opposite hand. The world slowed. I watched the wasp move its abdomen to sink its stinger deep in my skin, and I squashed it under my palm.

The sound of flesh smacking flesh echoed, and I raised my eyes to see that all the people that had occupied both sides of this dream world were gone. I was completely alone.

Except for the wasp, which I had just murdered. I lifted my palm, and the dead, crumpled wasp fell to the ground at my feet. I was suddenly overwhelmed with the sorrow of loss. I had no one now. I had killed the only other living thing.

Lucy, what is happening? Your heart rate is spiking.

"I killed it."

Killed what?

"My friend."

You didn't. This isn't real. It's just in your mind.

"It feels real."

I know.

"Now I'm alone."

The words triggered another change in the world. Everything vanished and was replaced by a cellar. A dark room that smelled damp and felt frozen. I was no longer sitting on a bench but rather a cold concrete floor that met molding stone walls. The ceiling was low; a tall man would scrape the top of his head against it. There was only one door, slightly ajar, across from where I was sitting.

I stood, my head quite a distance from the ceiling because my body was small again. I was a child. I was remembering something from being a child. Someone spoke, a voice I didn't know but recognized. I'd heard the person before but couldn't remember their face or name.

"Ninety-six hours. Failure isn't an option," the voice said.

A small, trembling cry began. From inside me. I was the one crying. With that the door clanged shut and the world was completely black. I screamed as I rushed to the shut door, stumbled over my feet, and sprawled to the hard ground. My head collided with the concrete, and pain exploded down my neck and spine.

I shook the pain loose, pushed to standing, and felt for the rough wood of the door. I began to bang on it, open palmed, screaming at the top of my lungs. "Don't leave me here, please! I'm sorry, I'll be better. Don't leave me. I'm afraid. I'm afraid!"

My small voice broke from the emotion, terror gripping my chest. A different kind than I remembered in the glass box. This terror came from being utterly alone.

Lucy, you're okay. You're safe. Remember.

"I'm not! I'm alone in the dark."

You're not alone. I'm with you.

"I'm alone. And I killed my only friend."

Lucy, take a deep breath. You're not alone. I am with you.

I cried in agony and tucked myself into a corner. I wanted to believe Zoe, but the terror and loneliness were so strong. I could hardly think past them as they began to swallow my mind.

I'm here with you. I'm squeezing your hand. Can you feel it?

I felt nothing.

Imagine it, Lucy. Me holding your hand, my fingers intertwined with yours. Feel my palm. It's touching yours. You are not alone.

I brought my palm up in front of my face. I couldn't see it through the dark, but I knew it was there. "I don't feel it."

Focus on my touch. My voice. Use it to anchor you.

I did as she said, and a slight tingle pulsed in the middle of my hand.

"I felt something," I said through my tears. I sniffed them back. My heart slowed, and my mind expanded past the fear.

Good. That's me. With you.

I felt the pulse deeper. Stronger. Somehow, in the dark and completely alone, I could feel her.

Lucy, where are you? What do you see?

"Nothing. It's too dark." I sniffed the last of my sorrow away and wiped the back of my hand across my nose. "I'm in a stone room. They locked me in for failing something."

Seeley says they called it the pit.

My mind riffled through a flash of memories. We all feared the pit. A place where we went if we didn't perform as expected. I was taken there after I couldn't stop myself from being afraid of the water prison. The day the man in the red tie had come to watch. The leader of the free world. I was remembering more of that day.

Suddenly I felt too tired to keep my eyes open. I dropped my hand and lay down against the cold floor.

Lucy.

"I think I'll just sleep for a while."

Okay. You sleep.

And I did, curled on the icy ground, Zoe's voice warming my mind. I fell into a deep sleep.

SEELEY WALKED INTO the living room of the main house. The fire was roaring, the stars outside peeking through the windows. His right hand held a cold beer, his other rested comfortably in his pocket. They'd made progress today.

Another memory recovered. Lucy had tried to go back and discover more, but she kept coming to the same end. Whether she wanted to kill the wasp or not, she always did, and then the events that followed played out almost exactly as they had when they were fresh. She'd tried rushing after the little girl again, only to find the glass box was the same. Even with Zoe's voice in her head, Lucy couldn't overcome the fear.

They'd progressed, but at a snail's pace. Seeley knew they were running out of time. But he wouldn't think about that right now. Instead he'd give himself the moment to focus on the wins. Using the connection between Zoe and Lucy had been a smart move. A win.

Zoe and Gina sat in the living room. Gina stood, near-empty whiskey glass in hand, to take her leave. She paused by Zoe on the couch. "I'm surprised you helping was so successful. What gave you the idea?"

"Like I said, I have some experience," Zoe replied.

"I'd like to hear about it someday," Gina said.

"I'm sure you would."

Even in the dim lighting of the room, Seeley could see the wedge of distrust that cut deeper between the women. Gina ignored it, leaned forward, clinked her glass against Zoe's, and downed the rest of her drink. "Well, good work. Good night," she said.

Zoe watched the doctor leave as Seeley sat across from her in one of the plush green chairs and crossed his ankle over his opposite knee. He brought the bottle to his lips and took a deep chug of its contents, all while waiting for Gina to climb the stairs and shut her bedroom door.

He let another beat pass. Then he nodded toward the stairs. "What's going on with you two?"

Zoe kept her eyes on the fire. "I just don't trust people like her."

"Do you ever trust anyone?" he asked.

She glanced at him, and her facial expression was answer enough.

He huffed in amusement and took another swallow of beer. "You did good today."

"I didn't really do anything."

"Yes you did. You held her hand. Kept her grounded. That's more than any of us could have done."

"No, just more than Gina could have done. I mean, with a last name like Loveless, what would you expect?" Zoe continued.

Seeley chuckled and couldn't deny her obvious point. "So how did you know that was going to work?"

"I didn't, I just hoped it would."

"Because of your own experience with RMT."

Zoe just stared into the fire.

"If you want to talk about it—"

"I don't, and it's no big deal."

Seeley dropped his leg and leaned forward. "Come on, Zoe—"

"Back off, okay?" she snapped. "I don't want to talk about it."

Seeley was taken aback and pressed his lips firmly together. "Okay," he said, leaning back into the chair once more.

She was scratching her forearm hard and noticed him watching. She stopped and tucked her fingers into her lap. "Sorry, something about Gina just really gets under my skin. Besides, we don't have to do this. It's not like we're 'friends.'" She made air quotes with her fingers.

Seeley playfully grabbed for his heart and scrunched his face in offense. "That one cuts me deep."

She rolled her eyes, and a slight grin pulled at her lips. Lips he found himself staring at far too much.

"Please, I don't know anything about you," she said.

"Well, what do you want to know?" he asked.

"I didn't mean—"

"No, ask me anything you want."

She stared at him, half of her face lit by the firelight, the other side covered in shadows. She was thinking, her eyes daring her lips to say what her mind was wondering. It made his heart skip.

A smile played across her mouth as she asked, "What's your favorite color?"

He laughed out loud. The first real laugh he could remember in a long time.

She chuckled at her own cleverness. "You can tell a lot about a person from their favorite color," she teased. She was flirting openly now.

"Black," he said.

"Like your soul. How fitting."

"Takes one to know one," he tossed back.

Zoe gave an authentic laugh, and it made his cheeks warm. She threw him, and that was dangerous, but he didn't want it to stop.

"Ask me a real question," he tempted.

"How did you get mixed up in all this?" she asked.

"It's complicated. And it wasn't what I thought it was going to be. I was told we were changing the world, making it a safer place for our kids."

"Do you have kids?"

This was where he should lie, run, pull a reverse move, but he didn't. Maybe against his better judgment he didn't. "Yes, I have a daughter."

She looked stunned, surprise flashing across her eyes. She hadn't expected that answer.

His sweet girl danced through his brain, and he dropped Zoe's intense stare. "Her name is Cami and she'll be eleven next month." He let a beat of silence linger as his blonde beauty lingered in his memory. "She wants a pink camo bike for her birthday. I have no idea where to get something like that." He returned Zoe's gaze. "Speechless? Is this a first?"

"Sorry, I'm just—"

"Surprised," he finished. "Black being my favorite color and all." He drank from his beer bottle.

"And her mother?" Zoe asked.

He'd worked up a backstory that he knew would hit close to home. Use a little truth and twist the facts enough to make Zoe's heart race. All good lies were sprinkled with truth.

"Dead," he replied. Partly true. She was dead to him.

"I'm so sorry."

"Don't be. She chose it." Seeley could tell from her curious expression that more would be required. "She fell for a religious extremist's fairy tales, locked herself in a church, and set it on fire from the inside. Thirty-seven total fried alive."

Lies, but good ones, and closer to the truth than was comfortable. His wife had fallen for her pastor, and the two had justified their affair by "the calling of God." Then they'd set his entire life on fire, took his daughter, left him with nothing. Imagining Steph's body as charred was easier than seeing her flourish in the home of another man.

"Apparently, their sacrifice secured their heavenly inheritance," he finished.

Understanding flashed across Zoe's face, paired with terror and shock. He knew his personal story connected with her because of her scarred past. But she didn't know he knew. Not yet.

"Religion is a cruel mistress," Zoe said, hardly above a whisper.

"That's an unusual response," Seeley said. "Usually people are too shocked to say anything. Some even stare at me in disbelief. What kind of skeletons do you have in your closet?"

She cleared her throat and tried to appear normal. She was clearly afraid of giving too much away.

They sat in silence for a long moment. Then Seeley leaned forward, set his beer on the table before him, and spoke. "My turn."

She looked up at him, puzzled.

"You got to ask me a question. Fair trade."

She looked slightly panicked but tried to mask it.

"Does Lucy know you weren't born with the name Zoe Johnson?"

Her face paled, and her lips fell ajar.

"From that expression I'm going to say no."

"How—"

"I work in government. It's my job to know things most people don't," Seeley said. "Zoe, I don't care about who you were. We all have darkness we're trying to outrun. All I care about is whether you have Lucy's best at heart. You're lying about who you are, which makes me suspicious of your intentions, and I don't want to be. Because believe it or not—trust me or not—all I want is to see that Lucy lives through this. I owe her at least that. She trusts you wholeheartedly. You're connected. We saw that today." He made sure he was looking her in the eye. "Can I trust you? Can she trust you?"

Zoe didn't back down from his stare. Her eyes were glossy, emotions threatening to give her away, but she held his look steadily. "Yes."

Seeley nodded. "Okay."

"Okay."

"Now you've seen my darkness and I've seen yours," Seeley said. "We never have to speak of it again."

She nodded, acknowledging what had just passed between them. She stood. "We should get some sleep."

She started toward the stairs past him, and he reached out and grabbed her hand gently as she reached his chair. She paused and looked down at the place where his fingers touched the back of her hand.

"Friends?" he asked, looking up at her earnestly.

She smiled and shrugged. "Acquaintances." She gently lifted her hand free of his touch, gave him a final smile, and left.

He sat there for a while after her steps had left the stairs and her bedroom door had squeaked closed. The feel of her hand lingered on his fingers, and the excitement of her buzzed inside his chest.

He had lied to get her to trust him. And he was afraid it was working. He downed the rest of his beer and tried to chase off the guilt he wasn't used to feeling. What was it about these two girls that made his heart ache?

For the first time since Steph had set his life on fire, the light he barely recognized, the light of love, was returning. And with it he was second-guessing his darkness, which he couldn't afford to do. His love for a woman had nearly killed him once.

He couldn't let it take him down twice.

TWENTY-TWO

I WAS BACK in the glass box. The scene was growing, changing, as if someone were slowly making the room brighter and my vision was being stretched. More details of the room were coming into focus. And with each new tidbit of information, I recalled a different memory.

Small ones, but mine. And each time I discovered something I had forgotten, I felt closer to who I was. It gave me the sense that at any moment the right memory would unlock them all. Like I was slowly digging through the dense terrain, and eventually I'd find a hidden cavern and fall right through the earth.

Stay focused, Luce. Remember you are in control.

Zoe had given me the pet name. I liked it. Made me feel more connected to her, which I needed to withstand the panic. To get to the next scene I needed to survive this one. Get to the brink of drowning without losing control. This was my fourth attempt today. I was getting closer.

We pieced together that I had lost control when it mattered most, and I'd paid for it with time in the pit. But here in my memories it was all about leveling up so I could access more. According to the bratty unicorn girl, that was key.

Dr. Loveless had suggested that maybe the unicorn girl was my younger self trying to help guide me through my subconscious. If that was true, I hated my younger self.

The water was rising, the cold still a shock even though I'd experienced it a hundred times. It was up to my knees. I'd controlled my reaction as far as my forehead. But fighting off the body's natural instincts to survive was difficult.

Doing good, Luce. Keep your focus on reality. The water isn't real.

Her encouragement along the way seemed to help me endure longer. The water was at my waist as my eyes carefully surveyed the room. Anything new could be the linchpin.

What's happening? Zoe's voice sounded panicked.

"The water is rising, nothing new—"

Lucy, you have to come back.

"What?" The water was rising up over my chest. "Zoe, what's going on?"

There was only silence in response as the water continued to pour in. A long moment passed, and then Zoe's voice cut back in.

Lucy, come back! Come back now!

I'd never heard her so panicked. I didn't know how to come back. The room started to dim as my terror sucked back the light.

"Zoe!" I cried. "Zoe, are you there?"

There was no answer. She always answered. Something was happening. The water now lapped at my chin. I had to get out of here but didn't know how. I turned in a circle, treading the water as it continued up toward my face.

Lucy, Lucy, please come back! We're under attack!

Attack. I couldn't respond because I was fully submerged now. I crouched in the water and opened my eyes to peer through the glass. Just darkness remained. All that had been there each time before was gone.

Something tickled the center of my chest.

Lucy! Can you hear me?

Her voice was fading, softer than it had been a moment ago. I was losing her, and I was stuck in my mind. The water had filled the glass box to the brim. My lungs burned as I held my breath. I kicked at the glass. I twisted my body, using the back panel as a holding point and smashing the front with my right heel. Over and over. Nothing, not even a crack.

I pushed off the back panel and placed both palms on the front, bracing myself there. I pounded the glass with my balled fists. My vision was starting to blur. There was no oxygen getting to my brain. My body felt like a stone as I fought to keep myself afloat.

I was drowning. But I wasn't afraid like I had been before. Fear was replaced with manic desires to get back and save Zoe. She was all that mattered.

Another buzzing sensation tapped at my chest, but I ignored it.

What if I just let myself drown? The thought came as easy as a whisper. Just open my mouth and set myself free. Could I do that? Zoe would say this was my mind. I was in control.

Then another thought, like a feather drifting from the sky, landed on my brain. What if there wasn't any water in the box at all? What if I just thought there was? Could I change it to air? Could I inhale air?

A sensation of power rumbled deep in my gut. Then, without letting my self-doubt overcorrect my instinct, I opened my mouth. There was no rush of water, only life-giving air.

I was breathing, fully submerged. In a water tank.

Come on, Lucy, wake up!

Zoe's voice was back. I shut my eyes and imagined the barn. Every surface and corner. Lying on the table, connected to DOT, Zoe on one side, Dr. Loveless on the other. When I opened my eyes, I would be there, I told myself.

Wake up, wake up!

I took another lungful of air. Air I had changed from water.

And opened my eyes.

ZOE HEARD THE gunshots. Her body froze, her mind registering what that meant and terror filling her bones. Lucy lay beside her, fully submerged in her own subconscious. Gina, pacing nearby, came to a full stop.

Another bullet cracked the air outside the barn. Not on top of them but too close.

Zoe looked down at Lucy and then back at Gina. "What's happening?"

"I don't know," Gina said. "Get her out."

"Lucy, you have to come back," Zoe said.

Eyes closed, Lucy replied, "What? Zoe, what's going on?"

Before Zoe could answer, Seeley parted the sheets around Lucy's bed. He looked at Gina, gun in hand. "It's the army."

"Did you know they were coming?" Gina asked.

Zoe thought the question was odd.

"No! There's a south path off this property, correct?" Seeley asked.

"What are you suggesting?" Gina asked. "That we run?"

"What else would you have us do?"

Gina looked stunned, and it made the panic in Zoe's chest rage. The doctor didn't seem nearly as concerned as she should be.

"What is going on here?" Zoe demanded.

Gina turned to Zoe to say something, but before she could, Seeley yanked back his weapon and brought it down hard against Gina's skull. The doctor didn't have time to react as the blow knocked her out cold.

Zoe turned to Seeley, stunned and confused.

"How did they know we're here?" he asked.

Had Gina given them up? Seeley seemed to think so, and Zoe didn't have time to think.

"Wake her up! We have to get out of here," Seeley said, pointing to Lucy.

Zoe turned, heart jumping into her throat, and placed both hands on Lucy's shoulders. "Lucy, come back! Come back now!"

Gunfire exploded through the barn, and Seeley stepped through the curtain and started firing.

Zoe returned her attention to the girl. She started shaking her. "Lucy, Lucy, please come back! We're under attack!"

The girl lay motionless. She wasn't responding. She was too deep, lost in her own thoughts. Zoe dug her nails into her palms. How was she supposed to reach her now? She could zap her like Gina did when things got too dangerous.

The manual defibrillator was stationed a couple of feet away. Zoe rushed for the chunky box and lifted it off the table. She placed it on the edge of the bed with a hard thump and yanked the top open. She stared down at the inside. She had no idea how to work this thing. What if she hurt Lucy?

Three bullets—*bang, bang, bang*—launched from Seeley's gun and echoed across the barn's open space. Zoe hunkered down. She didn't have time for second-guessing.

God help me.

She followed the visual instructions on the inside of the lid. After placing two soft plastic pads on Lucy's chest, Zoe flipped the defibrillator to life. Her stomach rolled in a wave of nausea. She waited as the machine charged up to send electric waves into the girl lying lifeless on the table.

There were no paddles like she'd seen in the movies, just flashing warning lights. Then a green "go" signal, a static voice that instructed her to stay clear of the body, and a button to push. *One, two, three*, went her mental countdown, and she pressed the big red circle.

A surge pulsed through the wires and into the pads as Lucy's chest gave a small jerk. Zoe waited. Nothing.

"Lucy! Can you hear me?"

Still nothing.

Again.

As quickly as possible Zoe reenergized the defibrillator and waited for the light to go green. Another press, another jolt. Again, nothing.

"Come on!" Zoe cried. Once more the seconds felt endless. Bullets plunked against the outside walls of the barn.

Seeley stepped inside the curtained box and reloaded his handgun. "We have to move," he yelled.

The light gave Zoe the go, and she pushed the button. Shock rumbled through Lucy for a third time. "Come on, Lucy, wake up!"

Her body lurched; her face remained unresponsive.

Seeley fired, the end of his gun poking out just beyond the white panel. "We have to move her now, Zoe!"

Zoe slammed her fist over and over against the table where Lucy lay. "Wake up, wake up!" she screamed.

Lucy's eyes sprang open, and Zoe nearly jumped back in surprise, but recovered.

"Lucy," she cried, placing her hands on the girl's face. Then she remembered herself and the situation they were in. She yanked the pads from Lucy's chest. "We have to go."

"They found us," Lucy said, already moving off the table, legs pounding like steel cylinders to Seeley's side. In one fluid move, she unhooked Seeley's extra sidearm from his belt, cocked it, stepped beyond the curtain, and started to fire.

Five shots in perfect rhythm, like it was as easy as breathing. Zoe launched herself after the girl, but Seeley collided with her and yanked her back.

"We have to go," he said, his hand tightly around her bicep.

"We can't leave her," Zoe said.

"We aren't," he said. "Remember what she is, Zoe."

She looked up at him as he continued to pull her toward the rear of the barn. She watched Lucy move backward through the white sheet out of the curtained box. Gun raised.

"We have four pursuing from the north," Lucy said. "Do we have an escape route?"

"A southern path through the woods," Seeley said. "I saw a vehicle on the southwest corner."

"You head there. I'll get the doctor."

"The doctor's been compromised," Seeley said. "Leave her."

"But we need her."

"We'll find another way."

Lucy snapped her head left. "More coming. I'll take care of them and meet you."

"Lucy!" Zoe cried.

The girl twisted her head around. "Go!"

The coldness in her expression sent a shiver down Zoe's spine. But there wasn't time to contemplate it, because Seeley was yanking her along again. More shots sounded behind them as they moved, Zoe trying not to trip on anything.

They exited the barn, pulled up to a stop. Seeley peered around the corner. "Stay close," he whispered, firearm raised, and started forward.

As he moved, Zoe followed, crouched, across the grassy plain west of the barn. Within minutes they were behind the main house.

"What about McCoy?" Zoe asked, suddenly thinking of the young agent.

"He can take care of himself. You just worry about following me," Seeley said. And they were moving again. No discussion, no pause. The chaos back at the barn seemed to fade as they crossed quickly to the back corner of the property.

Just as Seeley described, an old white Toyota Corolla, covered in age and dirt, sat as part of the landscape.

"This is our escape?" Zoe asked.

"You got a better idea?" Seeley fired back.

He held out his gun for Zoe to hold, and she took it.

"Keep a lookout. See anyone you don't know, shoot," he said.

Zoe turned with shaky hands and looked back the way they had come as Seeley worked on the car. Every snap of a twig, every rustle in the grass made Zoe's heart lurch. She struggled to get a normal breath.

A bullet whizzed past her head and struck a thick tree trunk a couple of feet behind her. She cried out and dropped to the ground. She could hear Seeley screaming for her to move, but she felt frozen. She yanked herself out of it, rolled onto her stomach, and started to army-crawl for the bushes, as if leaves could stop the penetration of bullets.

Zoe tucked herself away, worked on making herself as small as possible. A long moment of silence passed through the air. She tried to peer through the breaks in the thicket.

There she saw a masked soldier, rifle raised, and Seeley standing in a surrender position. Her heart sank. She felt for the gun she still had clutched in her hand and knew she had to make a move. Slowly, so as to not reveal her hiding place, she inched outward, using the tall grass as slight cover. She got her feet underneath her and tried to stand.

Something pressed into the back of her skull and clicked. A gun.

"Drop your weapon," the voice demanded. It caught the attention of Seeley and the other soldier.

Holding her breath, Zoe put the gun down and raised her hands toward the sky.

"Up, slowly," the man ordered.

Zoe slowly pushed all the way to standing, her eyes searching Seeley's for a sign that he had a way to get them out of this. They didn't reflect anything back.

She was certain she was about to have her head blown off when the man behind her grunted and the pressure from his weapon left her skull.

"Duck," a female voice yelled, and without hesitation Zoe followed orders. She fell, rolled to her back, and scurried away as Lucy came into focus. She had the agent pinned.

The other across the yard turned to defend his friend. Two shots from the end of his gun, and Lucy moved the agent she was manipulating and used his torso as a shield. The bullets sank into his gut, and his cries of pain rose above them.

Lucy released her hold of the man, grabbed the gun he'd dropped as he fell, raised it, and pulled the trigger. It clicked empty. She tossed it while in motion toward the second soldier. She pulled a blade from her back pocket as she moved, all so quickly that even as he pulled the trigger to release another shot, she had slid to her knees and across the ground as if it were ice.

She passed the enemy just to the right of his legs, far enough away not to collide, close enough to slit his ankle. He screamed and toppled forward. Lucy spun, pushing off the ground to a standing position behind him while securing his weapon and without a moment's hesitation sinking three bullets into his back.

Zoe's mouth hung open in shock, and the fallen man beside

her groaned. Lucy covered the distance to Zoe in a few easy strides. Even as the man started to cry for help, she put a final bullet into his skull.

Zoe heard the metal sink through his flesh and crack against the bone. The sound sent a shiver through her spine, and she thought she might vomit.

Lucy extended her arm toward Zoe, and Zoe accepted her offering. Lucy yanked her up, then turned to Seeley.

"They'll send more," he said. "We need to move now."

In a flash the three piled into the old clunker, which by the grace of some higher power roared to life, and they were moving, leaving the barn and collection of dead soldiers behind.

TWENTY-THREE

SEELEY DROVE ALONG the narrow road, through the thick forest and wild overgrowth that made the journey unsuitable for anyone with queasy sensibilities. Zoe had to breathe through sickness that kept climbing up into her throat.

The time passed as the sun started its descent toward the mountains. Zoe wasn't sure how far they had traveled but felt an overwhelming sense of relief when Seeley slowed the car and pulled in under the cover of a large oak tree.

Twilight lit the sky as Zoe held down the contents of her stomach just long enough to scramble out of the car away from Seeley and Lucy. She let everything up onto an innocent bush. Her hands were trembling as she gagged, brushing her hair back behind her ears to save the ends. She coughed and cleared the bits of sickness from her mouth before righting her stance and propping herself up against a nearby tree.

"You alright?" Seeley asked.

Zoe took a deep breath, wiped her mouth again, and faced them. She nodded and leaned back against the tree.

"We need to make a plan," Seeley said, turning his attention to Lucy.

"Are we sure it was Dr. Loveless?" Lucy asked.

"Even if it wasn't, she didn't want to run. She's not cut out for this, and now they have her."

"We need to continue the work, so how do we do that?" Lucy asked.

"What do you mean?" Zoe asked.

"Something happened to me that time. I got past the drowning. I'm so close to tapping into my history. We can't stop now."

"Tell me about what happened," Seeley said.

Lucy's eyes dropped to the ground as she spoke. "I don't really know. It all felt the same, until . . ."

"The barn was attacked," Seeley finished.

Zoe was surprised by his earnest interest in Lucy's progress.

Lucy nodded and looked up at Zoe. "You were in trouble, and I needed to get to you."

The sentiment struck Zoe in the gut. The way Lucy was looking at her with such loyalty and fierceness, she wasn't sure how to respond.

Lucy turned her eyes back to Seeley. "I cracked something open. I need to go back in. I can remember, I know I can."

"We can't go back to the barn," Seeley said.

"There has to be somewhere else we can go."

"The only other place I know that has the equipment you need is Xerox."

"The black site where Grantham started," Zoe said, finding her voice. "That is out of the question."

"Could you get us in?" Lucy asked, ignoring Zoe.

"No, stop," Zoe said.

Lucy turned to her. "We have to continue. I have to remember. Don't you understand? I have to remember."

"The three of us couldn't possibly break into a highly secured government black site, and even if we could, what then? Just walk into the lab, use their equipment until you remember, and leave? Think this through, Lucy. What you are talking about is suicide. You might as well hand yourself over to them."

"She's right," Seeley said.

"Thank God," Zoe exclaimed.

"There has to be a solution," Lucy said.

"We should make camp here for now," Seeley said. "Let me put some feelers out and see what I can uncover, then we make a plan."

Lucy exhaled, clearly unhappy, but nodded.

Seeley held out his phone. "I'm going to have to walk up toward the road to find service. You two get a fire going. It'll be dark soon."

He headed off, leaving the girls in tension.

"It's going to be okay, Lucy," Zoe said, touching the girl's arm.

Lucy yanked it away. "I have to know, Zoe. I can't stop until I know," she said, then started toward the woods.

Zoe, now alone in the middle of nowhere, watched her go. There was nothing she could do. Lucy was determined to remember. Even if it meant getting them all killed.

TWILIGHT WAS GONE, and all that remained was starlight, a half-moon, and the fire that Seeley continued to stoke. The last couple of hours had seen him and Lucy going over a dozen different plans, with Zoe watching and trying to keep up, trying not to let her panic destroy her nerves. Each idea ended in ruin. They couldn't agree on anything. Seeley was trying to reach McCoy and wandered to the road each hour to check his phone. It felt like they were stuck in an endless cycle of hopeless plans and irrational ideas. All Zoe could see was their clear end: being captured or being killed. Or both.

Lucy had gone out to get more firewood, and Seeley sat across the fire from Zoe, carving away at a stick.

"Are you whittling?" Zoe asked.

"It's good for training steady hands," Seeley answered without looking up.

"And probably comes in handy when you need a tiny sword."

Through the firelight, Zoe could see his face turn up in a smile. He looked up at her. She chuckled softly to herself and was thankful for the momentary escape from the constant horror that was playing in her mind. But it was only momentary. The fear captured her thoughts again, and she dropped her eyes back to the fire.

"What are the chances any of this works out without us all getting killed?" she asked.

"You don't believe in us?" Seeley said.

"We are three people against the government."

"But one of us is Lucy." He held up his sharpened stick. "And I have a tiny sword."

She laughed but couldn't keep the terror that was racing through her blood out of her expression. She knew he saw it clear as day, and they returned to the stillness that was only disturbed by the crackling flames.

"We're going to be okay," Seeley said.

"How do you know?"

"I don't, but if I don't stay positive then I place us all in danger." He looked up at Zoe. "And so will you."

Zoe heard his message and nodded. She would do her best, though it felt impossible given their current circumstances.

A stick snapped to their left, and Seeley dropped his project and grabbed his gun.

Lucy's frame came into the light of the moon, and Zoe watched his grip on the weapon ease. He grabbed the fallen stick and returned to whittling. Lucy released the pile of wood from her arms and dusted her hands against each other.

Zoe opened her mouth to tell Lucy about Seeley's tiny sword when Lucy jumped with a small gasp, like she'd been stung by a bee. A moment later she wobbled. Zoe leaped toward her just as she headed backward toward the ground. Seeley did the same, the two catching Lucy before she passed out.

They moved in from all sides then, armed to the teeth, masked, black, and nearly invisible in the night.

Seeley calmly laid Lucy on the ground, then stepped back. He didn't even steal a glance at Zoe, and her mind continued to stumble over what was happening.

"Agent Seeley," a male voice said.

Zoe turned to see a tall, suited man appear from the darkness.

"Director Hammon," Seeley said, looking surprised. "Out in the field?"

"I wanted to oversee this one myself," the director said. "It's too important."

Zoe felt like her mind had gone numb. She was trying to process what was happening.

"Take her," Director Hammon said, indicating Lucy. "We can't be certain how long that tranquilizer will last."

Several soldiers moved to hoist Lucy up off the ground.

"Don't touch her," Zoe shouted, but they ignored her. She looked at Seeley for help, but he was just watching it all happen.

"Miss Johnson," Director Hammon said. "We finally meet. Take her too."

More soldiers started toward her. Zoe took a step back and nearly stumbled into the fire. She suddenly remembered the rifle that was lying along the short tree trunk where Lucy had been sitting before she went to grab firewood. She reached for the weapon and yanked it up. It caused her pursuers to pause. *Maybe I could shoot them all* was the last thing she thought before the end of a weapon touched her scalp.

Seeley stood beside her, his gun aimed at her head. "Drop the weapon, Zoe," he said calmly.

The reality of what was happening crashed in fully. *No,* she thought. After all he'd promised. After all they'd faced. She'd known from the start. She'd known and she'd let herself get fooled.

"Seeley," she said against the truth pounding inside her head.

"Weapon down," he repeated. There were too many shadows on his face to see his eyes clearly, but she imagined they would reflect nothing. Because he felt nothing. He'd played her.

No, she'd played herself.

She lowered the gun, and the others rushed to apprehend her. The pain and hurt and betrayal inside her chest turned to rage.

"How could you?" she said in barely a whisper. "You lying—!"

Some invisible force took over her body, and she started thrashing at the men holding her. Their grips tightened, and she used all her core strength to pull her knees up toward her chest and kick out at the man who'd promised her safety, who'd even wormed his way into her heart. She shouted into the night, cursing him for his betrayal. He grasped her ankles with his hands and squeezed. The pressure sent pain racing up her calves, which made her thrust harder.

"Control her," Director Hammon ordered.

Two more men joined the force trying to tame her rage, and all she could feel was the desire to slit Seeley's throat. She was about to tell him so when a thick black bag came down over her head and a heavy hilt smashed into her skull.

TWENTY-FOUR

MY HEAD SWAM with stars as pricks of light started to filter back into my vision. My temple was throbbing, my ears muffled as if filled with cotton, and I could hardly feel anything from my shoulders down. Slowly my body started to return to me. Arms, torso, hips, legs. I curled my fingers and rolled my ankles.

I was whole but confused. My eyes were wide but my vision not yet clear. Where was I? Where had I been last? I tried to conjure up my last memory as my surroundings started to come into focus.

I was in a dark room, the boundaries hard to define, but a very bright white overhead light lit my immediate surroundings. I was strapped down to a cold, hard table. I wasn't in the clothes I remembered. Instead I was covered in itchy, lightweight, gray-colored pants and a matching T-shirt.

I smelled like lemons. I'd been bathed. My heart rate started to rise. My eyes completely clear now, I searched the room for anything else and found very little. It was just me, strapped in place, clean and alone. I yanked at the restraints and found they wouldn't budge. They'd been locked with heavy-duty silver links only a superhero could bend.

Maybe I was in my own mind. In level two, since I'd survived the glass box. This was an odd way to begin.

Something squeaked across the room, and the tight clicks of something sharp hitting the paved floor echoed around me. A door, I thought, and shoes. Heels.

Her face came into view, and I felt a moment of relief. "Dr. Loveless," I said.

"Number Nine, you're awake," she replied.

Number Nine? Why wasn't she calling me by my name?

"How are you feeling?" she asked.

"Where am I?"

"You're at site CX4-B, known to most as Xerox."

I looked back and forth for anyone else. "Where are Agent Seeley and Zoe?"

"Close, don't worry. You're safe here. This is where you were born."

"I don't understand what's happening." I could feel my panic growing. This was wrong. Something wasn't right. "And why am I restrained?"

"It's for your own safety and the safety of everyone else," Dr. Loveless said.

"Agent Seeley said you were compromised."

"Agent Seeley lied."

No, I thought, *this can't be real.*

"Is this real, or are you in my head?"

"Oh, this is very real, Number Nine."

"Why are you calling me that?"

"Because that's who you are, who you were created to be. You will see."

"I wanna see Zoe. Where is she?" I asked, all of my warning senses firing at once.

"Fair enough," Dr. Loveless said, and as she lifted her hand another spotlight flashed to life. Beside me on a similar table, Zoe lay strapped down just like me.

"Zoe," I called out. "Zoe!"

She didn't respond. Her body stayed still as stone. Unlike me, she hadn't been cleaned or changed, and she had thick black wires like tentacles clinging to her in a dozen places. Little round suction cups pressed tightly against her flesh.

"Zoe!" I cried again. "What did you do to her?"

"Nothing," Dr. Loveless said. "Yet."

For the first time, I saw her as monstrous. "Who are you?"

"Who I have always claimed to be, just with different motivations than I let you see. I needed you to trust me, Number Nine. I needed your help in your own memory recovery."

"My name is Lucy."

"No, that was a title given to you by Olivia Rivener. You are Number Nine, the last of your group. And the only one remaining, but you know all of that. Agent Seeley told you."

"Where is he? What did you do to him?"

"Agent Seeley? Nothing. How do you think we found you to begin with?"

She was claiming Seeley had been working with them the whole time. "No," I said. "You're lying."

"Believe what you want, it makes no difference to me," she said. "Either way, you and I have a common goal: to get your memories back. And together, we're going to."

"I won't help you do anything."

"I doubt that very much. With the help of Agent Seeley we discovered something about you, a breakthrough in understanding your memory recovery." She came closer to the side of my table and sat delicately on the edge. "How did you break out of the glass box?"

I tried to inch away from her, but I was tightly secured in place.

"DOT showed very different neurological activity that time. Instead of the irrational scattered sense you usually display, there were collective thought patterns, which resulted in illuminated memories. So, tell me what happened."

"I had to get back. We were under attack," I said.

"Yes, and maybe we could think self-preservation was the cause of such focus, but you've clearly displayed that self-preservation isn't key. So something else was being threatened that caused the breakthrough."

I knew where she was going before she said it. All the pieces started to click. *Snap.* Why I was fastened to this table. *Snap.* Why Zoe was strapped down beside me. *Snap.* What was to come for us. *Snap.*

"You're a smart girl, I've seen your file, so I imagine you know where I'm going with this," Dr. Loveless said. "The idea that the one person you love was being threatened gave you the strength to break free from the glass box. She is the key to unlocking what you're hiding behind the facade of *Lucy.*"

"If you hurt her—"

"No," Dr. Loveless snapped, "you misunderstand. I *will* hurt her until you succeed. You will remember who you are, Number Nine, but as long as you believe you are Lucy, your weakness lying there beside you will serve as proper motivation for remembering. Do you understand?"

"But I can't remember."

Dr. Loveless raised her hand again, and I heard the charge rumble through the thick cords that covered Zoe's body. Before I could protest, voltage scorched her skin. Her eyes snapped open, and her mouth emitted a guttural scream. Her lower back arched off the table, her neck craning and contorting against the ravages of electricity.

"Stop!" I screamed over the pulsing buzz. "Stop!"

The sound cut out, and Zoe's body fell limp back to the table. She was gasping for air, her eyes still wide, and turned her head to look at me. Her eyes were filled with terror. She was trying to say something but couldn't get her words past her throat.

"Zoe," I called, tears filling my eyes.

"Lucy," she weakly huffed.

"We will begin like always," Dr. Loveless said.

With her words, a white-coated tech rolled in DOT, and another followed with a simple medical cart, a blue cocktail of capsules inside a white paper cup.

"The more you resist, the harder and longer this will be for Zoe," Dr. Loveless said.

"And what if I can't remember?" I asked as Dr. Loveless connected DOT to my scalp.

"You will, Number Nine. Zoe will ensure it."

I knew from her tone that all she could see were the end results. She didn't care whether it cost Zoe her life. Dr. Loveless would do whatever was necessary to get what she wanted. That made her the worst kind of threat.

"Are you ready?" she asked as she held out the small cup. I took the blue pills without water and felt the cold steel of the table against the back of my head as Dr. Loveless lowered my skull. I could feel the drug's effect almost immediately.

The doctor pulled a simple black stool forward and placed it beside me. She sat and began, as the heaviness of blue heaven took me into darkness.

I GASPED, DRAGGING air deep into my lungs, and my eyes shot open. My heart was racing. I could hear it thundering against my eardrums. My breathing was short and crisp. I wasn't where I'd expected to be.

The place was dark, black, from the firm place under my feet and as far as I could see in all directions. It was cold, like an icy wind moving across my skin, but everything was still.

The only thing besides me here was too far in the distance to make out. But it stood out against the darkness. I moved toward it, my bare feet making zero noise as they met the surface. The sound of my pulse was all there was. It sent a shiver down my spine.

As I approached the object, its features started to crystalize. It was a wall. Tall, triple my height, made of vertical wood panels and stretching several yards in either direction. Along the base, running as long as the wall, was a line of doors. All identical, with small round cutouts at eye level.

I approached the door directly in front of me and placed my hands on its surface. Light wood, smooth with delicate trimming. The handle was copper, heavy, with a large knob. I twisted it.

Locked. I glanced up through the cutout, which was covered with textured glass, and peered through. Something was happening on the other side, and the stillness of the black space vanished. Sound waves entered my atmosphere, like a sealed door had sprung open and with it the world had been let back in. It rocked me on my feet. A hundred sounds hit me at once.

Laughter, children's. Feet shuffling, running, pounding pavement and dirt. Playing, spinning, tossing one another around. Screaming, crying, punching, falling, whimpering, muttering. Orders being barked, words I couldn't make out but I knew deep inside. Rushing water, wood being chopped, gravel being dug, sweat and blood dripping to the ground.

More sounds than I could handle all at once, as if each one were louder than the one before, and specific. They assaulted me. I covered my ears, which had no effect. The vibrations were penetrating deep enough to shake my very bones.

And then they vanished. Once again all I could hear was my pounding heart. I unclasped my ears slowly, thankful for the relief, and backed away from the wall.

Number Nine, what do you see?

Dr. Loveless's voice cut through the muffled cotton feeling and dragged at my insides. Rage washed up my chest like fire. I wanted to ignore her, but I knew the risk to Zoe was too great.

"A wall with doors," I answered.

Open them.

"I can't, they're locked."

Just like you couldn't escape the glass prison. Another mental block to overcome. Try again.

I was weary. I didn't want another onslaught of sound, but I didn't want to imagine what would happen to Zoe if I didn't try. I stepped forward and tried the same door again. Still locked, but no sound. I stepped right and was met with another locked door. Then to another one. Locked. I moved left to find three more doors just the same. They were all locked.

Mental blocks, as Dr. Loveless said.

Open the doors, Number Nine.

"I can't."

You can.

A beat passed, and then a new sound entered the place. Terrorized screaming, familiar and horrific. My heart dropped. Zoe. My mind filled with the image of her contorted body being electrocuted, her skin taking fire, her nerves being roasted.

"Stop!" I yelled. "They're locked, all the doors are locked!"

Open them, Number Nine.

Another burst of Zoe's screams penetrated the darkness. I rushed forward and yanked on the knob. I pulled, twisted, shook the handle. It didn't waver. I moved to door after door, all firmly secured.

She's in great suffering, Number Nine.

Another wave of wrenching pain exploded from Zoe's mouth. Terror unlike any I had ever heard. As it died off a moment later, her painful sobbing replaced it.

"Stop it! Stop it." I rammed the wooden door before me, hunkering down and putting all my force behind the hit. It hardly shook.

Open the doors, Number Nine.

Again and again I pounded the surfaces. I throttled them with my fists, stomped them with my heels. Pressed, tore at the handles. Tried smashing the glass panels. Nothing. They were unbreakable fortresses. Panic overtook my senses as Zoe's cries continued to blast overhead and I continued to fail.

Sweat dripped down the sides of my head. Blood from my fingers started to stain the light wood. Pain pulsed throughout my limbs. But the doors wouldn't budge. I rushed toward the far edge of the wall.

Go around it, I thought. With all my speed I reached the end and stepped to the other side. Shock filled my senses. The other side was identical. Filled with more doors. No, not more, the same. I could see my blood, the scrapings of my fingers, dents from my pounding. I rushed back to the original side. The same. Both sides were the same.

I couldn't breathe. Another guttural cry pounded against my brain.

"I can't open them! I can't! Stop it!"

Open the doors, Number Nine.

I let out a vicious cry. My scream rose, filled with madness and hate. I slammed my open palm on the wood. Over and over, until my arm went numb and tingling started to spread into my shoulder and back. My own wailing mixed with the echoes of Zoe's, and I couldn't get a breath.

I stopped hitting the door, let my forehead fall forward against the surface, and cried. I tried to control it, see through it, outsmart my circumstance. For Zoe's sake! But I couldn't. I was losing to my fear, my distress and hopelessness consuming my fight.

The world started to spin, and my knees gave out. I fell to the base of the door, weeping like a little girl. Zoe was crying, and I was worthless to help either one of us. I didn't even try to muster more strength. I didn't have any left. I just let the darkness take me and passed out, Zoe's pain the last thing I heard.

TWENTY-FIVE

SEELEY STOOD AS Hammon entered the small lobby. He followed the director into his larger office and shut the door softly behind him.

"You wanted to see me, sir?" Seeley said.

After the girls had been apprehended in the woods, he'd come back to Xerox with the rest of the unit. He'd showered and run through his detailed account of all that had happened, answering the questions of a small, mousy man who showed zero expression and viciously typed everything Seeley said as a small recorder captured his words. He'd then been told to wait outside the director's office.

"You've fully debriefed?" Hammon asked.

Seeley nodded, and Hammon walked around to take a seat in his large desk chair. "Take a seat, Agent."

Seeley did as he was told.

"Good work out there."

"Thank you, sir."

"Seriously, all the work you did here doesn't go unrecognized. Without your intel about Number Nine's breakthrough after the barn raid, we'd still be lost in the woods."

Seeley couldn't shake the feeling that something unpleasant was tied to the end of Hammon's compliments.

"But you fired on army personnel, Agent," Hammon said. "Can you explain to me why you did that?"

Seeley swallowed. He'd been thinking about it himself. He wanted to say it was to protect the bigger picture, nothing else, but he knew that wasn't completely true. "Lucy—"

"We'll refer to her as Number Nine from now on," Hammon said.

"She'd just had a breakthrough with Zoe guiding her," Seeley said. "I knew if the army got their hands on them, then all of that progress might be lost. We're still fighting against a clock. And I had the situation under control."

"That doesn't excuse shooting at soldiers," Hammon said. "At least the president and secretary of defense don't believe so."

"What are you saying?" Seeley asked.

"I'm saying you are walking an unbelievably thin line here."

"They barged in on us. You said I had time."

"No, I said I would do what I could but made no promises." Hammon sighed as Seeley sat back against his chair. "You should have surrendered when the army showed up. They outrank you. Those are the rules."

"We're beyond rules! The situation we are in calls for doing things outside of the box."

"Not killing soldiers!"

Seeley stood. "I made sure to avoid—"

"Number Nine took down *seven* armed men," Hammon cut in, standing to match Seeley's defensive stance. "The chief of the army believes if you'd followed protocol, she could have been apprehended and lives wouldn't have been lost. He whispers in the president's ear, and now he is saying the FBI and its leadership have been unable to control this situation. Your actions are coming back to bite me, so sit down and hold your tongue, Agent! I am still your commanding officer!"

Seeley bit back his frustration and obeyed. Hammon exhaled and returned to his seat as well. He gathered his temper and continued.

"Look, what you did was crucial to apprehending Number Nine. Without your call we'd still be searching for her, and we wouldn't have the information needed to finally get through to her. So for those reasons you aren't in a holding cell right now."

Again, Seeley held his anger at bay.

"The president wants you off this case," Hammon said.

"Sir—"

"You shot at army soldiers, Agent. What did you think the end result would be?"

He hadn't been thinking about that much. He'd been reacting to a situation he was thrown into without warning, doing what he thought was best for the assignment. He ignored the small voice that said he was also protecting Zoe, even though a few hours later he'd turned her and Lucy over to the FBI. The inner conflict raged on.

Hammon exhaled and rubbed his temple with his fingers. "You're an exceptional agent, Tom, but you made a mistake, and I put my reputation on the line to protect you from a worse fate than being blacklisted from this assignment. Don't make me regret it by causing a scene."

Blacklisted. The word sent shivers of anger down Seeley's spine.

"Why don't you take a couple days off? Go get some sleep, some real food, see your daughter," Hammon said. "We have it from here."

"I'd like to see it through," Seeley said.

"I'm afraid that's no longer an option."

"Sir—"

"That's an order, Agent Seeley," Hammon snapped. He returned his attention to the files before him.

Seeley just sat there for a long moment, unsure of what to do next.

Without glancing up, Hammon said, "That will be all, Agent Seeley."

Seeley left the director's office in a daze. After all he'd given to them, after all he'd sacrificed for the job, they were shutting him out. They wouldn't have Lucy if it hadn't been for him. They wouldn't have caught up with Olivia, they wouldn't have recovered information from Krum. They'd still be chasing their tails, and this was how they showed their gratitude.

He walked down the hallway toward the locker rooms. Hammon had suggested taking some time—an order, not a request. Time meant silence and space. It meant stillness, something he avoided because it meant being alone with thoughts that could drown him.

Even now his mind wandered to Zoe. What might be happening to her right now? He knew they were working off the theory that Lucy would do anything to keep Zoe from harm. He'd given them that information, knowing what it could mean for Zoe. He'd struggled with the choice but ultimately made it in favor of the job.

Always for the job.

And now they had taken that from him. The single thing that drove his path. His true north, so without it he'd be alone with the sins of his past. His darkness.

Seeley shook it off as he grabbed his things and started for the exit. Maybe he would go see Cami. Maybe a couple days would be good. Or maybe the small thread of guilt that was rumbling in his gut would slither into his heart and kill him.

ZOE'S EYES FLUTTERED open. The side of her face was pressed against the cold stone floor of the cell where they were holding her. She wasn't sure how long it had been since they dragged her here. She had only been half conscious.

She tried to push up off the floor, every movement painful. Fresh tears filled her eyes, and she sucked in a tearful gasp as she turned herself over. Her skin was marred with red welts where the plastic pads had been placed. She had thought at some point she would die. It seemed like that much power being pumped into her system would short-circuit the unit and just finish her off.

But they were giving her something to ensure it didn't kill her, just made her wish she were dead. Three "sessions," as Gina was calling them, had been performed. Three times they'd hooked her body up to electric currents, using her pain to incentivize Lucy, and three times it had failed.

Through the pain Zoe had heard Gina speaking with the others.

"We've just started, but I'm hopeful it won't take much longer."

"They need to rest. Give them the night."

"She will remember."

"Ensure that one doesn't die. We need her alive. And clean her up."

Zoe couldn't respond, couldn't fight. They kept her drugged in the in-between, so everything felt like it was happening in slow motion. It probably wouldn't have mattered. The pain made her too weak to use her brain, much less her mouth.

Two men had come earlier at some point, stripped her, washed her, and placed her in a white medical gown. The pain had been excruciating, and what little pride she had left was stripped with her clothes. Dying would be easier than this.

She considered dying, right there on the cell floor. Could she just stop breathing? Could she find something that would help her do it? Did she have the stomach for it, the resolve?

The minutes dripped by into hours, and all Zoe had was the silence and her thoughts. Between her mental blackouts she had too much time to hate herself for ending up here.

But this was the cycle of her life, from one dark moment to the next, as if from the beginning of time she was destined to be someone's rat in the maze of life. Had she been programmed this way? Had she ever stood a chance of experiencing anything other than betrayal and lies? Was this just what life was?

Did people get a say in their experiences, or were they just products of what they were born into, taught to be a certain way, and powerless to change?

Was she just unlucky to have been born to a mother who believed in the devil and the monsters he created? Was she just unfortunate to believe the lie of freedom presented in the form of grace, only to discover that, too, wasn't real? The world judged and punished her for sharing blood with the damned, though she hadn't chosen to, and then forced her into a constant state of distrust because people couldn't be trusted.

Zoe had known better than to trust Seeley and Gina, but still she'd fallen into a cycle she could have predicted. Maybe she deserved this outcome. Maybe it was the only one.

"Rules are meant to be followed. Rules keep us safe. You only had one rule—trust no one." The voice scratched at the inside of her brain like a scurrying rodent. It was a voice she heard only in her darkest moments. Her mother's.

Without closing her eyes, Zoe could see the beautiful woman. Thin, elegant, with quiet strength and perfect posture. Drawing the attention of all eyes, like a rose growing in a field of daisies. *"I thought I taught you better."*

Zoe closed her eyes, and a single tear slid down her cheek. She wished she could forget everything her mother had ever taught her. Everything the world had taught her. She wanted to start over, to be fresh and new, not to know the pain that came with the past.

"Stupid girl, who says you get to be free?" A different voice. Another one she couldn't shake from the inner workings of her mind no matter how hard she tried. Darker, more terrifying than the first. She'd only heard it a couple of times outside her own imagination, but it carried so much power she would never forget it.

The devil that had driven her mother, Rose, to insanity. He'd called himself Sylous. He'd lured her, toyed with her heart, called her special, and Rose had believed every word. She'd carried out unspeakable things in his name, things the world had punished her for. Things that had stained her children, and they had been punished as well. The sins of the parents.

Zoe snapped her eyes open because she didn't want to see Sylous. It was more than enough to just feel him. Like he had actually entered the room. The hissing of his tongue lapped inside her ears. *"Like mother, like daughter."*

She hated him. Hated her mother for believing his lies. Hated herself for not being born different. The thought struck a chord deep in her gut, the idea of hating oneself so entirely. She couldn't budge from the idea. It held her tightly as it sank into her bones.

Her thoughts turned to Stephen. The sweet, innocent little brother she'd failed. After the only world they'd ever known ended and their mother was taken from them, it was just her and Stephen. Wide-eyed and optimistic, he'd always given Zoe hope. Of course, she was Evelyn then, before she listened to the lies of someone else and abandoned her brother.

The foster system was cruel, more so to two children with their history. For a while they bounced from place to place together, but as they put more distance between them and Haven Valley, Zoe started to realize that the world would never be good to them if they didn't follow the rules. Blend in. Their crazy stories about monsters, angels, and demons had to stop.

Dr. Holbert agreed. He helped Zoe become the teen who believed it was better to look after herself and let her brother make his own terrible choices. Because Stephen refused to stop believing in their fantasy.

He became harder and harder to care for. With everyone telling him he was crazy, he started to believe it. And when another boy came along, older and sinister, Stephen followed him to the ends of the earth. Zoe couldn't persuade him to stop. Couldn't get him to listen.

So she did as instructed by those who claimed to have her best interests at heart. She stopped trying. She even transferred to another home, leaving him behind when he refused to join her. And that sinister boy stole Stephen's goodness and drove her sweet brother into hell with him.

Because Zoe let it happen. Because she hadn't been there to save him. It all came flooding back like a tidal wave. One failure into the next as she felt the cold floor beneath her. Her tears soaked into the stone, grief and guilt draining from her bones.

First she'd failed her mother, then Stephen, now Lucy. That was her story. Cycles of failing people she loved.

His dark voice returned. The one that chilled her beyond her skin. *"There is no freedom from your failure,"* he whispered. *"Like I said, you don't get to be free."*

Whatever was left of her strength broke, and Zoe began to sob. As it carried on, it grew in volume and pain until she was bawling her eyes out, curled up on the cold ground and wishing for it all to end.

TWENTY-SIX

THERE I STOOD, unopenable doors to my front, the sound of Zoe screaming overhead, my heart assaulting the inside of my chest. My soul was ripped in half as the tortured pain of the only person I really cared about pierced the barricade that kept me from being able to stop her suffering.

I dropped to my knees, sweat running down my face, my fingers bloody on the ground, my nails mangled and peeling back. I should feel the pain racing up my arms, but I felt nothing.

Because they aren't really my fingers. A small voice had started talking to me, one I knew was my own. It whispered through the chaos. *Right*, I agreed with the voice, *because this is in my mind. When I wake up, my fingers won't be bloody.*

I knew there was truth there that might help me break down these doors, but I couldn't focus on it long enough to figure out how. I tried blocking out Zoe's screams, but even when I succeeded, sounds of my past rushed in to assault me again.

Another thing I'd discovered: the hundreds of sounds, playing all at once on full volume, were from the past. I wasn't sure how I knew that, but I did. As if the sounds themselves had a familiar signature that felt comfortable and known.

But it didn't help me get through the blockages that kept me from seeing what I needed. If I could just get one door open.

Open the doors, Number Nine.

I gritted my teeth. My throat burned from spitting at the doctor, and it was getting me nowhere. She was running the show. Zoe and I were just pawns. Powerless pawns.

Not true, the small voice said. *The doctor can't open the doors.*

"Neither can I!" I slammed both fists against the black ground, another wave of screams rippling above. There was no solution. I couldn't go under the doors, I couldn't go around them. I tried going over to no avail. I was stuck, and Zoe was paying for it.

Remember, Lucy, this is your mind. You're in control.

Those words were familiar because Zoe had said them to me over and over. Had I believed them once? Was that how I had broken out of the glass box?

What if the water is air—remember?

"You don't think I've been trying that?" I wanted the voice to stop. It seemed to mock me now. "Don't you think I've tried everything?"

Stop trying, the tiny voice hummed. *Just be.*

Now the voice was crazy. Frustration and terror in equal amounts yanked at my chest.

What if the water is air? The voice rushed through my gathered emotions, unfazed by the way it was making me feel.

I took deep breaths, tried to control the welling of tears threatening to engulf me. I stood, looking at the wall of doors. Thick, solid, locked doors. I could hear Zoe's cries, feel her pain in my bones, Dr. Loveless's voice always directing and eating away at my brain.

What if the water is air? The small voice, relentless.

I exhaled, stepped forward, and placed both my hands on the nearest door. I closed my eyes and tried to picture it as malleable.

Something other than what I knew it was. I stood, whole seconds passing. Let it be an archway, a tunnel, a cloud, anything I could pass through.

I opened my eyes. It was a door. I swore. The stillness around me popped like a balloon, with the thunderous sounds of my past rushing over me in waves. I dropped my forehead against the wooden surface and cupped my palms over my ears to wait it out. The sounds always washed away nearly as quickly as they came. As soon as they passed, the reminder of what was being done to Zoe reentered.

"Please," I cried out to whoever was listening. "God, please leave her alone. I can't get through. I can't!" The tears I was holding back pushed through and found paths down my cheeks.

Open the doors, Number Nine.

I lifted my head off the door, anger my only sensation. I yanked with all my might at the knob, kicked and pummeled the door with my feet. Pounded with balled fists, screamed my lungs out, then returned to the place I had started, with my forehead resting against the surface, crying through my hopelessness.

Stop trying, just be. The small voice was back.

"I don't know what that means," I whispered.

Nothing responded. I pulled my face from the door and sniffed back my despair. Again I placed my hands on the surface and closed my eyes. I tried to imagine it different from what it was. I tried to tell myself that I was in control, that this was my mind. I took several deep breaths as I began to gain control of my emotions. *Just be,* I thought.

The room started to quiet, and the moment what was happening outside faded, the noise of the past came rushing back. I flinched to react as always but stopped myself. *Just be.* So I let it wash over me without resistance.

The weight of it felt as though it were pushing me backward, like a strong wind nearly knocking me off my feet. It hurt, the volume of the sound, shaking my deepest insides, threatening to crumple me. But still I let it all come. Every sound, every moment.

The small voice returned, louder and closer. *Just be. Remember, Lucy, this is your mind.*

Then it all went silent. I heard only the sound of my breath, my heart, my pulse. Calm and comforting. I opened my eyes, and the black room with its impenetrable wall was gone.

Now it was all white everywhere I looked, and the only other thing present was a little girl. Not the one with the unicorn T-shirt, but a little girl I knew.

It was me. Standing a few feet in front of me, dressed in a simple blue uniform. Staring at me. I tilted my head to the left and she mimicked my movement, then right, and she followed. I raised my right hand, and like a mirror she did the same. Then the left hand.

She winked at me and giggled, and I chuckled back. She stepped across the space that separated us, and I couldn't help but smile. I was gazing down at her, now just inches from her, when without warning she drove her hand into my gut.

I gasped, not because it hurt but because it was such a shock to witness. Before I could respond any other way, she pulled her hand back out and held it up toward me. Her fingers clasped something, and when she opened her fist, I saw a small gold key.

"You are in control," the little girl said. "Just be."

I took the key and held it between my fingers. "What do I do with it?"

The girl pointed to something behind me, and I turned to see that the white room was turning black. All around, black tendrils were clawing their way over the bright, clean surface, turning it dark. The wall of doors reappeared.

I glanced back. The girl was gone. The white was gone. It was just blackness and the wall. Key in hand, I walked to the wall and made my way to one of the middle doors. The key slipped into the keyhole perfectly, and with a twist I heard the door unlock.

I stood for a moment, unsure of what might happen if I opened this door but knowing I wasn't going to make any other choice. I turned the knob and cracked the door open. In unison all the other doors opened as well. In both directions, all the doors were open.

A surge of power ran through my veins as my eyes drank in what was playing out on the other side. It hit me like a warm breeze that wrapped itself around me and nearly knocked me off my feet. I saw it all. And as I saw, I remembered. I remembered everything.

HANDS GENTLY PULLED Zoe up to sitting, her body throbbing, her skin tender. They placed a thin plastic straw between her lips, and a low voice instructed her to drink. The liquid had a bitter taste and was lukewarm sliding down her throat. She was aware that she was unbuckled from her restraints, and a few people stood around. With enough force she could catch them off guard and make a run for it. It was a thought she was too groggy to turn into reality. The drugs swimming through her bloodstream snuffed out the idea of resisting.

They laid her back against the cold table and resecured her restraints. She turned her head to glance to where Lucy was lying, still under, deep inside her own mind. They'd only paused the torture to tend to Zoe's nervous system and do a quick medical assessment, as they did every hour to ensure the pain lasted without killing her. The brief relief was its own kind of torture as Zoe braced for what was coming.

Someone stepped between her and Lucy, and Zoe tilted her eyes up to see Gina looking down with pity. The doctor accepted a report that was handed to her from the other side of Zoe's bed and reviewed the information. She nodded, then gave the report back.

"She can withstand higher voltage if necessary," Gina said. "I believe Number Nine is on the brink."

Zoe's life mattered so little. She knew this doctor would sooner kill her than risk losing the information tucked away in Lucy.

"You should feel proud," Gina said, turning her attention back to Zoe. "You're a part of something grand. You're serving your country."

Nausea rolled through Zoe's gut, and she nearly tossed the contents of her stomach onto the doctor's shoes.

"Dr. Loveless," another voice called, "something is happening."

Gina turned to Lucy, joined by two others in white coats, all staring at the readings on DOT.

Zoe moved her eyes up to the girl's face, which was still and lifeless. Even here, she wanted to protect Lucy. She had failed.

"Are you sure this is right?" Gina said.

Lucy's eyes snapped open. Zoe froze as the girl drank in the room for a long moment, her eyes darting over every surface faster than should be possible. And then things happened faster than Zoe could compute under the heavy dosage of drugs.

Lucy broke her restraints and freed herself from DOT just as the rest of the room was becoming aware that she was conscious. Performing a fluid dance, the girl moved with dangerous accuracy. Sliding down the table to the end, landing with both feet planted, swinging around to grab the medical tray from the nearest cart, colliding it with the first skull before her. The nurse dropped cold.

Two more approached, and Lucy flipped the tray sideways, using it like a blade, connecting the sharp side with one's throat.

He staggered backward, clutching his airway. Then she dropped to a knee, used her back as a roadblock, and forced the second attacker to topple over her crouched body. She wrapped her elbow around his neck and snapped it clean.

She shrugged him off, jumped up, and headed for the two nurses at Zoe's bedside. A blaring alarm sounded, bright light flashing. The nurses scattered, but Lucy was out for blood. She dropped, grabbed a thick black cord from the ground, and yanked it from the outlet in the floor. Like a whip she snapped it forward, its thick plug striking the back of the farthest nurse. She fell while Lucy grabbed three syringes from another cart and tossed them at the other nurse.

Pop. Pop. Pop. All three needles stuck into the man's fleshy neck. He cried out, stumbled, and Lucy was on him, pressing the weapons deep into his skin and injecting their poison. He fell hard, his face bouncing off the floor. Lucy strode to the nurse she'd struck with the plug.

The woman cried out for mercy, but Lucy had none. She wrapped the thick cord around the woman's neck and twisted, the snap filling the room.

The doors on the far end slammed open, and armed agents, guns raised, entered in two clean lines.

Zoe yanked against her restraints. "Lucy," she whispered, her voice weak.

Lucy looked back over her shoulder at Zoe, fire in her eyes, and moved to the thick electrical wires hanging above Zoe. She flipped the machine on, and the buzzing brought a shiver to Zoe's bones. Lucy loosed one wire from the hooks that held it secure and swung it like an electric lasso, using a large medical tray as a shield. She looked like a superhero. Or a villain.

Zoe heard a cry and saw that Gina had scurried under the

table where Lucy had been tortured and was shaking like a leaf. Lucy had her eyes trained on the cavalry, and Gina tried to make a run for it.

Lucy saw. She let the doctor get a few feet, maybe to let her believe she was going to escape, then she let her electrified whip loose. It struck the doctor's calves. Shocks rippled up the woman's body, and she collapsed to her knees. Lucy retracted the weapon and let it fly again. The cord wrapped around Gina's throat, and with a firm tug she yanked the doctor back, her cries sounding through the room.

Agents still filed into the room, but Lucy gave them no mind as she crossed to Gina, dipping low to grab a scalpel from a fallen tray. Zoe knew what was coming and thought to stop her. But then she remembered the electricity that had been pumped into her system, and she said nothing.

"Please, Lucy, please," Gina begged as she tried to crawl backward, but Lucy didn't slow.

She reached the doctor, raised her to sit, and drove the knife through the center of the woman's chest. Gina gasped, tears rolling down her cheeks, and crumpled as Lucy released her. Gina heaved a few final breaths, blood dripping from the side of her mouth, and then she was utterly still.

"Number Nine," a male voice called.

Lucy yanked the scalpel from Gina's corpse and stood, facing the gathered agents, shield still in her left hand, knife in her right.

Director Hammon stepped forward with hands slightly raised. "Enough, Number Nine," he said, his voice calm and steady.

"My name is Lucy."

Two agents dared to move, and Lucy flung her tray like a Frisbee in a perfectly straight line at the first, hitting his gun and causing it to blast the ceiling. She used the distraction to roll and grab more scattered medical tools. With inhuman strength and precision she threw them at the two attacking men.

Two scalpels punctured the front man's throat. Blood gushed out as he stumbled back. Long forceps landed in the second agent's left eyeball. His screeching wails were enough to make Zoe cringe, blood pouring down his face.

"Don't move! Don't shoot!" Hammon yelled. "That's an order!"

Lucy rolled forward, swept up the neck-scalpel agent's gun, pushed up to standing, and aimed the weapon straight at the director.

"Do not shoot," he repeated to the agents. Then back to Lucy, "Number Nine, this isn't within protocol. Think about your purpose."

Lucy cocked the weapon, but the director didn't flinch.

"You murdered all the others like me," Lucy said.

"Yes, I was following orders. You understand orders."

"You would have murdered me."

"So you wouldn't have murdered them." He tilted his chin to the bodies piled up around them.

Lucy eyed the fallen agents and medical team, one still whimpering for life, barely hanging on. "You made me this."

Light danced behind the director's eyes. "You remember."

"I'm supposed to be a weapon for good."

"There is no good. The best we can hope for is progress."

Lucy shook her head. "No, I will be for good."

Hammon dropped his hands, new confidence sparking in his face. "You will be whatever I want."

"No," Lucy said, but her voice had a slight shake.

"You will follow orders," he said.

Lucy was shaking her head but saying nothing. Zoe needed to do something, but she was still strapped down to the medical bed.

"You will tell me where Olivia hid the files about Grantham."

"I want to be more—"

"You are more, Number Nine," the director started, taking a step toward Lucy. "Grown here, with unbelievable abilities, remarkable talents, fostered, trained, more skilled than most people can imagine. You can't be anything other than what you are."

The shiver in Lucy's voice had moved to her fingers.

"You are the property of the Grantham Project," the director said. "My property."

"Lucy," Zoe called out.

The girl turned at the sound of Zoe's voice, and for a moment they shared a glance. Lucy, scared like a child.

Then before Zoe could realize what she had done, it happened. Director Hammon nodded to someone in the shadows, and pops from the darkness carried the same tranquilizers they'd used before.

One pierced Lucy's shoulder. She tried to react and was stronger than she had been in the woods. She managed to swing her gun around and get one shot off. It hit the director in his upper leg, and he swore. Then Lucy wobbled, and five armed men rushed in, disarming her and taking her to the ground.

"Lucy!" Zoe cried out and yanked against her restraints. She knew it was in vain. The drugs still swam through her body, and even if she were free from the hold of her straps, she wasn't sure she had enough strength to stand.

Others were assisting the director as he cursed through the pain, blood darkening his pant leg. "Get her to a cell," he ordered, "and get me a doctor who isn't dead!"

Agents moved on command. Zoe was helpless to do anything but watch. Then Director Hammon raised his eyes and landed on her.

"Take care of her," he said to an armed agent beside him. "Make it clean. There's enough mess in here." The man nodded and signaled to two others.

The director's words echoed through Zoe's head as they approached. *"Take care of her."* She thought to fight back, her instincts screaming for her to do something, but she was too numb. Too tired. So she just watched them come. Felt them release her and drag her away, one thought playing over and over through her brain.

She was going to die.

TWENTY-SEVEN

HOURS HAD PASSED since they tossed her on the hard floor. The moments dripped by. She wished it was over already. The waiting was more painful than just being dead.

When they came, she wasn't ready. Her body froze, her mind raced. Surely there was a way to freedom. They grabbed her sore body from the cold ground and yanked her to standing. Three in total—one on either side and a third following directly behind—as they led her out of the holding room and down a long, dim hallway.

At the end of the hallway was a door. It opened and light cascaded in, stinging Zoe's eyes and causing her to blink. They pulled her into sunlight, exiting the building, the door shutting loudly behind them. The dirt was rough and rocky under her bare feet as they forced her to walk.

The wind nipped at her thin covering, the sun beaming down but providing little warmth. Her mind was swimming, her chest filling with panic as she imagined where they were taking her. Somewhere off the grid, where they could shoot her, bury her, and let her body rot in the ground without ever being discovered.

Or maybe it would be worse than a simple end? Maybe they

would toss her in a deep hole and let her starve to death. Let her wither away in the elements. Let her be eaten alive by whatever creatures roamed the woods. Terror gripped her legs, and they stopped functioning.

So they dragged her until they came to the edge of a cliff, and she knew they were going to toss her off. They stood her at the edge, saying nothing. No last words, no instructions, just placed her there as she shivered, staring at the rocky ground a hundred feet below. She heard one of their weapons cock, and she tried to swallow the hard lump in her throat. For a moment she considered jumping. Would it be more painful to land alive or be shot in the back?

The gun exploded, and she braced for impact. Two clean shots. *Pop, pop.* She clenched her jaw, but nothing happened. A third shot. *Pop.* The sound echoed clean to the clear sky, but nothing impacted her body.

She dared to glance over her shoulder and saw that one man remained. His gun was raised; the other two lay on the ground. Dead. Zoe turned slowly, her whole body shaking, her mind stunned.

The man still standing lowered his weapon and yanked off the black mask that covered his face. McCoy stood before her, panting. Zoe opened her mouth in shock, but nothing came out. He took a step forward and she inched backward. The wind rocked her slightly, and she remembered she was close to a dangerous fall.

"It's okay," McCoy said, raising his hands in surrender. "Just be careful."

She glanced backward and then stepped away from the edge, her heart bouncing up into her throat. She was trying to wrap her mind around what was happening. Had McCoy killed his fellow agents? Why? She wanted to ask but couldn't seem to get her mouth to connect with her brain.

As if reading her mind, McCoy began. "I'm a friend, I'm try-ing to help. You're safe," he said. "I was working with Olivia, and I've been trying to stay connected to Lucy since she was killed."

Zoe shook her head, still confused. Still unable to make words work with her tongue.

"There's a group of us that agreed with Olivia on the inhu-manity of what was happening when the orders came down from above. I hadn't been with Grantham as long as some, but killing those kids . . ." McCoy lowered his hands slowly. "I wanted to help."

"But you were working with Seeley," Zoe said.

"In theory, you know. Keep your enemies close."

"The barn raid?"

"I wasn't privy to that information. Hammon made an execu-tive decision without filling us in. I'm so sorry, Zoe, for what . . ." Again, he couldn't finish, and she was glad he didn't.

"I don't believe you," Zoe said. How could she, after she'd trusted Seeley and he'd turned her over to be electrocuted?

"I don't blame you," McCoy said, "and I'm not asking for trust." He moved a few feet left, where a small boulder hid a black duf-fel. He yanked it out and tossed it at Zoe's feet. "There's some supplies, clothes, money, enough to get you far away from here. You should have resources enough to start over. A new identity would be good. If you need a contact—"

"What about Lucy?" Zoe asked.

"I'm working on that. Don't worry, I'll do everything I can to help her."

She shook her head. "I'm not leaving without her."

"Are you sure you understand—"

"They pumped me full of electricity the last few days. I un-derstand."

McCoy went silent. He shook his head. "I could use your help, but you should really think about what you're doing. Because there will be no going back from here."

"How could I go on with normal life after this?"

"Of all people, you could. You've overcome worse."

So, everyone knew who she really was. Zoe took a deep breath and thought about what he was offering. A way out. A clean break. Wasn't that what she wanted? To go back to a time before she'd been connected to this insanity? Lying on the floor of the prison cell, hadn't she begged for the opportunity she was now being given? But she knew that wasn't what she really longed for. All she wanted now was not to fail Lucy. She loved her.

She looked up from the black bag resting at her feet. "I can't leave her."

"Zoe—"

"I can't fail her too."

"It'll probably get you killed."

Zoe paused, letting his words sink in. Death was worth it. She nodded at McCoy and ignored the warning of danger she heard inside. "So there's a plan?"

"Not a very good one," McCoy said.

"How can I help?"

He exhaled. "We need help. And you're not going to like who I have in mind."

SEELEY UNLOCKED HIS apartment building's lobby door. A large brown paper bag rested in the crook of his left arm as he pushed the door open and stepped in. The lobby had gotten a fresh coat of paint since he'd been here last—satin—and it shimmered as the sun shone through the glass entry.

He'd only spent a handful of nights in this apartment, even though he'd been renting it for over a year. Work kept him away, but it was a nice enough place for Cami to visit. The elevator was currently under repair, but Seeley preferred the stairs anyway. He crossed the small lobby to the stairwell door and pushed it open with his shoulder.

Two flights up, thirteen stairs in all, short and easy, and Seeley was walking down the hallway of blue doors. Number 215 was his, the last door on the left. After unlocking it, Seeley stepped inside the one-bedroom apartment and shut the door behind him.

He set the bag on the kitchen counter and flipped on the overhead light. The kitchen was bare, the fridge empty, which was the purpose of the paper bag. He'd stopped by the local supermarket on his way up the street to grab a few essentials. He'd unpack the bag, then call Cami. See if she wanted to come over. Or he'd go to her.

She'd been living with his mother, Dorothy, for the last couple years. Steph had tried to add Cami to her new family, but when the girl wouldn't behave, she abandoned their child like she abandoned him. Cami wanted to live with him, but with his current job the court found him unfit to parent her full-time. You had to be present to do something like that, and he never was.

He had visitation rights, but it had been months since he'd seen his daughter. He couldn't help but think she was better for it. And after everything that had happened lately, how was he supposed to look his little girl in the eye and hide the darkness that owned his soul? Maybe he would call her tomorrow, after he'd taken the time to get his mind right.

That was what he'd told himself yesterday. He just needed some time before he was ready. For Cami's sake.

He yanked the items from the bag and started placing them on shelves in the refrigerator. Something creaked behind him, and without hesitation, Seeley yanked his gun from its place along the side of his belt and spun around, firearm lifted.

McCoy was standing there, just inside the front door, hands up. Seeley cursed.

"Sorry," McCoy said. "I didn't mean to sneak up on you."

"What are you doing here? How did you get in?"

"Your landlord let me in. Amazing where an FBI badge can get you. How about you lower your weapon?"

"How about you tell me why you're in my apartment?" Seeley fired back.

"We need to talk to you," McCoy answered.

"We?"

Someone moved out from the shadows of the unlit living room, and Seeley nearly gasped. Zoe. Impossible.

She moved to stand just feet in front of Seeley's lifted pistol, her eyes dark and set. Her short hair was tucked back, showing the fresh wounds on her face and collarbone. Her skin was pale, her eyes bloodshot, bottom lip cut across the center. And that was only what he could see, with her covered in jeans and a long-sleeve sweater. He didn't want to imagine what other injuries hid elsewhere. Because then he'd have to take responsibility for putting all those marks and bruises on her skin.

"Well," Zoe said, her voice tight and angry, "shoot me if you're going to. Or would you rather I turn around so you can stab me in the back?"

Seeley slowly lowered his weapon but kept his finger on the trigger and his muscles ready for action. "What are you doing here?"

"Like I said," McCoy said, stepping up to guard Zoe's back, "we need to talk to you."

"How are you—"

"Alive?" Zoe finished.

He could feel the heat coming off her skin. She was restraining herself from ripping him apart. And he didn't blame her. What he had done to her couldn't be forgiven. No one had the capacity for that.

"McCoy saved me. He's been working with Olivia all along."

McCoy gave him a nervous grin. "Guess we're just going to jump right in then."

"What?" Seeley questioned.

"Apparently, not everyone that works for Grantham is the enemy," Zoe cut in. "Just most." She turned back to McCoy. "This is a waste of time. He is never going to help us."

"Help with what?" Seeley asked.

"Rescuing Lucy," McCoy said.

Seeley opened his mouth to respond and couldn't think of anything to say.

McCoy jumped in and started filling in the gaps in Seeley's mind. He explained how he'd been working with Olivia, then proceeded to tell Seeley everything that had happened in the last twenty-four hours. Seeley listened intently, never taking his finger off the trigger. Zoe had moved to the side, never taking her eyes off him. The weight of her stare was suffocating.

"I couldn't go back in for her alone," McCoy continued.

"Have you lost your mind, McCoy? They'll string you up for this," Seeley said.

"Only if I fail."

"You can't beat the system."

"Not alone."

Seeley shook his head. "Give me one good reason not to turn you in for treason."

"Because they're wrong, and you know it," McCoy said. "You aren't like the rest of them. Because you care."

"I'm the worst among them," Seeley hissed. "I don't have the capacity to care."

"Which is why they blacklisted you," McCoy said.

"Wait, what?" Zoe said.

"They blacklisted me because I fired at soldiers."

"You didn't tell me he was blacklisted," Zoe snapped at McCoy. "How is he even supposed to help us?"

"Seeley knows that place and those people better than anyone I know," McCoy said. "And if anyone can get past a blacklist, it's him." Then to Seeley: "And you fired at soldiers because you wanted to protect Lucy and Zoe."

"Protect us!" Zoe barked. "He did nothing when they found us."

"It's worse than that," McCoy said. "He called them and told them where you were."

Zoe didn't even look at Seeley, and he was thankful for that. He wasn't sure he could stand the anger and hurt that would be in her expression.

"I was doing—" Seeley started.

"Your job, but you broke protocol. You risked your career," McCoy said. "And you can make up a thousand reasons why you did, but I know deep down it was because you care."

"You have no idea of the darkness in me," Seeley warned.

"Yes, I do," McCoy said. "The same kind that's in us all. You hide behind it because it allows you to build a wall that separates you from reality, but I spent time with you. I saw the way you treated Lucy, the way you looked at Zoe."

Seeley glanced at the woman standing close and felt his cheeks redden.

"You're good, using your darkness as an excuse not to face the fact that you want to do the right thing, because doing that is harder. But it doesn't mean you don't know what the right thing is."

"You hardly know me, McCoy," Seeley said.

"Maybe, but Olivia knew you well."

The mention of her name sent a shiver across Seeley's skin.

"She told me you would help. She believed in you, even after working with your darkness for years. Deep down she knew you were a good man and told me to appeal to that goodness you have forgotten."

McCoy's words brought Seeley back to the night Olivia was shot right in front of him. *You're a good man.* Those had been some of her last words.

"You may be blacklisted, but you're connected and have deep loyalties. People owe you favors," McCoy said. "And Olivia said you would help. So I'm trusting a dead woman, because honestly we don't have a lot of options."

Seeley took it all in. "You're wrong about me. She was wrong about me."

"That's what I told him," Zoe said.

"No, I don't believe that!" McCoy said. "You can do the right thing."

"I don't do the right thing, I do the job," Seeley said.

"Even when you know it's wrong?" McCoy asked.

The war that had been building reached its tipping point. The two sides of his mind rushed each other, shooting bullets across the divide.

He did care about Zoe. He wanted to deny it but couldn't with her standing right there. She threatened the darkness he'd become so familiar with. That he'd befriended and fed for years. That side of him warned against the threat of believing he could be more than what the past had made him.

"I told you he's the villain in this story," Zoe said. "The woman he loved broke his heart, stole his goodness, and now he's the bad guy. Right, Seeley? The guy who can't help but choose his pain over being bigger than his past, even if it means an innocent girl dies."

Anger flashed through Seeley's chest. "That's a lot of talk from the poor, abandoned little girl who can't trust the world or anyone in it because Mommy hurt her pretty bad."

Zoe took a step closer so she was nearly in his face. "Don't you dare talk about me like you know me."

"I do know you," Seeley snarled.

The two stood nose to nose for a long moment, then Zoe turned and crossed to the living room. She returned a moment later with something in her hand and slammed it on the counter beside them. It was a photo of a little girl. His Cami.

"I know a thing or two about being the daughter of a villain," she said. "I know about the pain it brings, the kind that won't let you sleep. That haunts you even when you're awake. That you can't outrun or change."

Seeley felt his heart tighten as her words drilled into his brain. What would doing the job get him? The question drifted through his mind. More pain and darkness? Didn't he have enough?

His inner demons roared as the thought started to gain momentum.

"Don't be the good guy for you," Zoe said. "Be good for her. Because if you don't help us, Lucy will die. And this little girl will have a villain for a father all her life. She deserves better than that, doesn't she?"

Seeley kept his eyes focused on the sweet face smiling up at him from the photo. It was one of the few pictures he had, and the only one that mattered.

"I don't know if I can be the good guy," he said.

"There's only one way to find out," McCoy said.

Seeley took a deep breath and considered what they were asking. If they failed, they would all die. Lucy would die, and Cami wouldn't have a father at all. Not that she had much of one now.

Maybe if he could do this, help them, he could redeem some of his darkness and be the father Cami deserved. Maybe Zoe was right. Could he be better for his daughter?

He looked up at Zoe and then at McCoy.

Only one way to find out.

TWENTY-EIGHT

I LOST TRACK of how long I'd been in solitary confinement. No one came to see me. No food was provided. There was a jug of dirty water in the corner, a wastebasket for emptying my bladder, a thin, dusty mattress, and a single light hanging from the center of the ceiling.

I'd exhausted all possible escape options, which was quick and easy because after an hour I knew there weren't any. My captors knew better than to leave anything I could use against them. So I didn't waste my energy on things I knew wouldn't manifest. Instead I spent the time reorganizing my memories.

The suddenness of them all had been overwhelming at first. Thousands of childhood moments to reconcile, everything from moments of pleasure and pain to great victories and terrible failures. I relived each one I logged, sitting there cross-legged on the stone floor, meditating on them all. I escaped into myself and let them come at me hard and fast. That was the only way to digest them.

They stirred complex emotions about who I was. Who was I meant to be? On one hand, the voice of reason said I was designed, trained, manipulated to be a product for progress. An instrument wrapped up in flesh. On the other hand, the mothering voice of Olivia said I was more human than tool, that I had the capacity to choose what to do with the abilities I'd been given. The two ideas warred with one another.

Was I Lucy, or was I Number Nine? The question started off simple and became weighted as the time passed. In the moments when my mind wasn't wrapped up in the war of identity, I thought of Zoe. The part of me that was Lucy cared for her deeply, was afraid that she was hurt or dead. The part of me that was a number saw her only as a distraction from purpose. So more conflict gathered in my psyche.

At some point the door to my prison opened, and Director Hammon entered with his flock of armed agents. I could smell their fear, read it on their faces. All except Hammon. He was confident and steady. I looked up from my seated place in the middle of the room.

"Number Nine," Hammon said. He used a long black cane, and I wondered if the bullet I'd placed deep in his leg had gone clean through or if they'd had to dig it out. "Leave us," he said to the galley of men.

They looked at one another. "Sir?" one of them questioned.

"Leave us," he repeated more firmly. They did as they were told, and the door shut behind them.

Very confident, I thought.

"You aren't afraid to be alone with me?" I asked.

"No," he answered.

"Why? The others are."

"Because I know you, Number Nine. The others just know of you."

"And knowing me keeps you safe?"

"I'm your commander. You wouldn't harm me."

"I shot you."

He smiled. "That was unintentional. If it had been purposeful, you wouldn't have missed my femoral artery by millimeters."

I said nothing. He was right.

"We need to talk about Olivia, Number Nine," Hammon said.

"You want to know where the hidden files are," I said.

"Yes."

"I don't think I should tell you."

"Why not?"

"It's my only leverage for staying alive. There's no reason you wouldn't kill me once you have what you want."

"What if I promise that won't be the outcome?"

"Then you would be lying."

Hammon huffed in amusement. "I will resort to much crueler measures if my hand is forced."

"You can try," I said.

He knew how fortified I was against torture. That approach would take some time, if it could succeed at all. Anger flashed across his face.

"That makes you upset?" I asked.

"Well, Number Nine, I have pressure coming down from up top to get this job done. And you are currently the only thing standing in my way, so yes, it makes me frustrated."

"Pressure from the leader of the free world." I remembered him now. The different versions of *him* that had come through over the years.

"He is very powerful and impatient," Hammon said.

"I am very powerful, and patient," I replied.

He forced an uncomfortable smile. He was losing his temper. I remembered that about him. He didn't hold his rage well.

"This is not a game."

"Is it not? It feels like a game to me."

"If you had any idea what was actually at stake here, you wouldn't be toying with this information like a child. But you don't understand. You were created with a flaw. You are broken, so all that power you believe you possess does you no good, because you don't understand the way the world functions."

Anger twitched inside my chest.

"That was the part we never could master. Making you human enough to exist outside these walls. Humanity can't be taught. It either is or isn't. Something we now know for the future."

I looked at him with curiosity. Some part of me understood the baiting, but Lucy was ignoring Number Nine's warning about chomping down.

"You look surprised," Hammon teased. "Surely with the level of intelligence you possess, you had to assume we would try again. Next time we'll develop a newer, better version, one that will actually succeed. Without the . . ." He tilted his head, seeming to ponder how to put it, then smiled. "Mistakes."

That hurt my feelings. The ones I struggled to control. The ones that belonged to the part of me that felt like Lucy. I was still a girl, after all. Wasn't I?

"That's why recovering the files is so important. This is greater than you or me. We are talking about creating a safer America, maybe even a better world. And you are standing in the way of a greater version, for what? Your life? Seems selfish."

I pondered what he was saying. "Don't I deserve to live?"

"Over progress?" Hammon asked, his eyes drilling into mine. His face turned cold. "No."

The tick of rage pulsed and spread. He believed his progress was more valuable than my existence. *Maybe he's right*, Number

Nine thought. *Of course he isn't right*, Lucy argued. I was teetering on the edge, sure to fall one way or the other, but unsure which way it would be.

"Tell me where the files are hidden, Number Nine," Hammon said.

Sweat beads trickled down the left side of his forehead. I could hear his heart rate increasing.

"I will get what I want from you one way or another," he said.

Still I said nothing, and his breathing increased.

"Olivia told me not to tell you," I finally replied. "No matter the cost."

A moment of silence engulfed the room, and again Hammon's pulse spiked. Then he took a deep breath and regained control of his temper. "I don't want to have to do this the hard way, but you seem stubbornly resolved."

Again I said nothing. I knew I could withstand whatever they did to my body.

"Fine, we resort to drastic measures," Hammon said. "We go after what has always been your Achilles' heel. The same problem all of your kind had. It's humanness, or lack thereof. There's a fine line between not enough and too much. Too much and you put your own value above the value of your orders, not enough and you murder your entire family. It's tricky, tricky science. But we put it in you, so we can rip it out. Once you lose your irrational attachment to loyalty and remember nothing is greater than progress, you'll give me what I want without hesitation. So many messy steps can be avoided if you would just tell me where the files are. Haven't you suffered enough already?"

I listened to his threats with cold resistance. I would never betray Olivia. I would never give in to his mental games.

"The hard way then," Hammon said, turning to hobble toward

the exit. He glanced back once he reached the door. "Remember I offered a different path and you refused. You chose this, Lucy."

He spoke to my human side, making her shudder. Whatever was coming next would be more than cruel.

THEY CAME FOR me an hour after Director Hammon left. I didn't resist when an armed agent handed me a glass of something I knew was more than water. I asked what it was without receiving an answer, then drank it down, knowing there was no alternative.

I woke up in a different place, strapped to another medical bed, naked except for a thin strip of coarse white fabric that ran across my breasts and another that covered my hips. Hundreds of thin cords pierced deep into my skin. There was mild throbbing from where they had been inserted, and any movement made the throbbing worsen.

The rest of the room was utterly dark. I could only see what was slightly illuminated by the large screen that hung above my face. I tried to piece together what was happening but had no recollection of ever being in this room before. I imagined the tiny cords were connected to nerve endings that would be inflicted with pain as Hammon asked me to give up the location of the files, so I prepared my mind for that possibility.

I heard a door slide open and the footsteps of someone entering. I never saw who it was, just the person's gloved hands as they came at my face from behind and secured a thick, heavy strap across the length of my forehead and another across my chin, holding them down against the bed.

Something buzzed beside either ear, and in my peripherals I could see a small object headed toward my eyes. My heart lurched as the tools, which resembled claws, lowered. The gloved hands attached them to my eyelids and the fleshy bags underneath my eyes. The claws then widened, yanking my eyes open an uncomfortable amount. They started to dry out immediately as the mystery person left, the door sealing shut and the footsteps fading away.

I couldn't move an inch, every part of me restrained, my eyes forced open. Then the room came to life, the illuminated screen above me so wide it was all I could see. It was static white to begin, then an image came into focus: Olivia standing at the edge of a forest line, her mouth moving but without sound, only static. My heart surged at the sight of her, and as it did the tiny wires connected to my nerve endings tightened.

The pain was excruciating, unlike anything I had ever experienced. As though every molecule in my body was being set on fire. My heartbeat quickened and the pain grew. The movie continued as bullets slammed into Olivia's chest, and she fell to the forest floor. My pulse flared and the pain increased. Higher and higher until I couldn't breathe, tears rolling down my cheeks.

The screen went black, and my heart began to mellow, as did the pain. Then the screen came back to life with the same image, the same painful sequence. My heart reacted.

Over and over, my emotional reaction to the same image was followed by pain that I thought would kill me. I tried to practice the methods I'd been taught to withstand the agony, but I couldn't focus enough to do so. The all-encompassing screen was overwhelming. It consumed my mind, and I couldn't do anything to shut it out.

As I watched Olivia's murder again and again, I knew eventually I would become numb to it, but then the images changed. Now Zoe was strapped to a medical bed, being pumped full of electric waves, her screams ringing in my ears. My nerve endings were throttled with pain. My entire body shook in agony.

The images multiplied. Olivia's death, Zoe's torture, then more painful memories captured on film. The punishment of other Grantham "numbers." The others like me. My only friends. Faces I knew, but images of them I hadn't seen. Physical beatings, screams from their solitary confinement, nights of endless crying and near drowning. Anything that would evoke an emotional response and in turn engage the wires tucked deep within my flesh.

Feeling was reinforced with pain. Pain reinforced with feeling. It was cracking my resolve. On and on. Over and over, my emotions were under siege. The part of me that was Lucy was being attacked. The part named by a woman I cared for. A woman I loved. Now my humanity was being used to manipulate my mind.

Hammon was forcing me to choose between turning it all off or enduring the endless pain. I could feel myself breaking. I could feel the desperation for relief, the dare to feel nothing. My brain was being reprogrammed to associate my humanity with suffering.

I couldn't let him win. I couldn't let him take what Olivia had given me. But my heart was numbing and my body was dying. I was losing the battle with my survival instincts.

Hammon was killing Lucy.

TIME LOST ALL of its meaning. All there was, really, was the pain and the momentary escape from it. The natural dulling I couldn't avoid any longer. I fought as long as I could, but getting glimpses of what could be had become too tempting to refuse. Freedom from the agony, too alluring to deny.

I wanted to be stronger.

But I wasn't.

Now I longed for the darkness.

No grand gesture or dramatic moment marked the point when

my mind exploded and everything changed. No. It was simple. Something that was programmed into me already. Something I was wired to do. Like flipping a light switch. One moment there was pain, and the next there wasn't. One moment I was Lucy, and the next I wasn't.

Images flashed and nothing happened. I saw them as clearly as before, but this time I only saw outcomes of situations that were outside of me. Like the insides of a clock, all the small pieces rotated together in perfect harmony. I understood differently than I had before.

The room I was in became brighter. The machine I was hooked up to went silent. People entered, disconnected me from the device, clothed me, and carried me to a cell. My body was numb and broken. It would take a while to heal, my strength depleted from fighting what I now saw as a hopeless war.

Director Hammon came to me. He asked me questions and seemed pleased with my responses. I understood I was betraying Olivia and Lucy. I just didn't care anymore.

After thanking me, the director administered a shot in my upper left arm, and Lucy died.

TWENTY-NINE

ZOE FOLLOWED CLOSELY as Seeley and McCoy traversed the forest terrain. More than thirty hours had passed since McCoy shot two agents on the outskirts of the Xerox property line. Thirty hours of traveling across a state line to recover Seeley and then back as quickly as they possibly could. Thirty hours too long, Zoe thought.

What if Lucy was being tortured? Mangled, manipulated, or worse—killed. What if they were too late and she'd broken, given Director Hammon what he wanted, and he no longer had need of her? What if they were walking into their own demise and Lucy was already dead?

McCoy had rambled on to Seeley about marking the two agents he'd shot as active perimeter duty, meaning it would be a little longer before anyone noticed they were missing. McCoy had been checking in for them, using their access codes, which he'd somehow acquired, in hopes to delay suspicion even further. Zoe didn't understand all the specifics. She was hardly listening as they moved. She was just trying not to lose her strength and collapse after the events of the last forty-eight hours.

They'd been trekking through the hilled terrain for the last hour, after driving up as close to Xerox as McCoy and Seeley felt comfortable with. They left the Jeep in a concealed location for their escape, and Seeley recommended that Zoe mark the trees so she could easily get back on her own if they got separated.

The fact that the idea, although a good one, had come from his mouth made Zoe want to throw up. She still couldn't look him in the eye without thinking about punching him in the face, and she still wasn't sure this wasn't a setup, but she had zero other options.

That's not true, the familiar small voice kept telling her. She could run. But that wasn't an option she was willing to take. Against all her trauma-shaped instincts, she was staying. She was saving Lucy.

But that didn't stop the fear. As they moved through the trees, Zoe sticking long pieces of blue painter's tape to tree trunks every couple yards, she acknowledged that she was headed back toward the place where she'd been imprisoned and fried. Led by the same man who'd led her there the first time.

By choice. Maybe insanity was passed from generation to generation?

Seeley dropped to a squat at the edge of a tree line. McCoy and Zoe followed suit.

"The main underground water tunnels are grated off on both sides of the campus," Seeley said, pointing down to the edge of the property. The stone structures that made up the Xerox campus occupied a plot of hillside that stretched a half mile west to east and north to south. Nearly a perfect square, as though God himself intended for the hidden government site to be placed exactly where it was. Surrounded by thick Ozark forest, hidden from view. Unless you knew what you were looking for.

"We'll use the southwest tunnel," Seeley continued. "You sure that thing can cut through thick steel?" He pointed to the small handheld blowtorch that McCoy was carrying.

"Absolutely," McCoy said, like a boy picked to prove his dodge-ball skills. He flicked the machine to life to show off its mighty stream of fire, and Zoe rolled her eyes.

Seeley ignored him. "There's a blind spot a yard up the south side. If you slip in as the security cameras rotate, you should be able to get up to the grate undetected. Use the ledge for cover while you cut through. Once you do that, give the signal."

"Got it," McCoy said.

"Once inside we move quickly. We have to coincide moving into the subbasement with the guard shift. We have one shot, otherwise we're stuck in the tunnel till second exchange at first light. Once inside the subbasement you and Zoe head down the far back hall for the old breaker room. East corner, quickly. There's a shaft inside that rises to the main building's ventila-tion system."

"And you'll head to see Waller," McCoy said.

"What if he doesn't help?" Zoe questioned.

"He owes me his life," Seeley said. "He'll help."

"And what stops him from turning you in once he does?" Zoe continued.

Seeley and McCoy looked at each other and then at her. "Loy-alty," McCoy said.

"And if I go down," Seeley said, "I take him with me."

Zoe shook her head. This felt like grasping at straws, and they were talking about Lucy's life here. She wished the plan felt more solid.

"We'll meet in the southeast storage room," Seeley said. "Lower level one."

"Lower level one." McCoy's tone was unsure.

"You said you knew the main building well," Seeley hissed.

"Yes. Well-ish."

Zoe exhaled and dropped her head. They were definitely going to die.

"Don't worry, I'll get us there," McCoy said, trying to bolster Zoe's confidence and failing.

"We shouldn't be splitting up," Zoe said.

"We have no other choice," Seeley replied.

"Why not?"

"I work faster alone, and then you'll be set up to move once I get what we need," he said.

"I don't trust you." She shifted her gaze to McCoy. "We shouldn't trust him. He wants to go in alone. How do we know this isn't him setting us up?"

"You don't," Seeley cut in before McCoy could answer. "Do you have a better plan?"

Of course she didn't. She wanted to say something that would make him feel small, but she had nothing.

McCoy placed his hand on her shoulder. "Splitting up is the only way."

Seeley didn't wait for her to acknowledge McCoy or respond. "We'll use this tree line as cover, moving south. Stay way back in the trees. We can't risk being seen by the security cameras but can't wait till nightfall."

He nodded at them and then moved after they agreed. Seeing the buildings before them, knowing what they were about to attempt, Zoe felt a pit open up in her stomach. She ignored the tremble in her fingers and followed the men as quickly as she could, mindful to stay hidden, tucked behind tree trunks. She abandoned the now empty roll of painter's tape.

Down the hill, under the cover of dense branches, and through the shadows they moved, until Seeley pulled up to a stop, McCoy directly behind him.

"Through the trees at one o'clock, flat against the wall," Seeley started. "I'll signal for the camera shift and then down to the corner grate."

McCoy nodded and stepped forward, then turned back for one moment. "See you inside."

Seeley nodded and McCoy crouched, moving quickly to the spot at one o'clock. He pressed his back flush against the stone wall and waited for Seeley's signal from the trees.

Seconds ticked by, Zoe's anxiety spiking. Then Seeley released his fingers in a "go" motion, and McCoy didn't hesitate. Still crouched, he scampered along the wall until he disappeared under the ledge over the domed water grate.

Now they just waited and prayed that blowtorch was as powerful as he assured them it was. Time slipped by in slow motion. Zoe's lungs began to burn. She had been holding her breath without realizing it.

Seeley was close enough that she could feel his breathing brush her neck. Even through her disgust she couldn't ignore the way her heartbeat quickened. She nearly asked him to back up when a birdcall came from the southwest corner, confirming McCoy had done what he'd promised.

"On my mark, stay close," Seeley said.

Zoe didn't argue. Her palms were sweaty even though she felt cold, and a chill was running down her spine.

"Nearly there," he whispered, eyes watching his spot like a vulture. "Ready." He paused one final moment. "Now."

And they were moving, Seeley like wind, Zoe trying not to stumble. They reached the wall and tucked as close to it as they could, Zoe's shoulder scraping the brick as they continued without pause.

The overhang in sight, Zoe held her breath again. She tried

not to imagine the camera turning and catching a glimpse of her before she was tucked away, and then she was under the ledge and breathing like she'd just run a marathon.

"Nicely done," McCoy said, "as promised." He motioned to a midsized circle cut from the grate and wiggled the blowtorch proudly. Seeley fondly tapped his shoulder, and the three climbed through the opening.

They stepped down into water that rose across the tops of their feet and tried to move quickly but silently, which was hard to do. They traveled without speaking, each focused on their own movements, until they reached a side ladder that rose to a circular tunnel exit.

Seeley yanked the ladder's end and it extended down toward them. He glanced at his watch, waiting for the perfect moment to move. They stood, letting silence surround them as the seconds ticked, and Zoe tried to keep her mind clear.

"Southeast storage room," Seeley said. "Lower level one."

McCoy nodded. Seeley glanced at Zoe as he placed both hands on either side of the ladder. It must be time. He held her eyes for a moment in the dark and maybe thought to say something in case this went south and they never spoke again, but then just offered a shy grin and began his climb.

McCoy was next, up the rungs one after another, Zoe following. Up through the opening into a dark hallway that smelled of mold. It felt like they were wading through wet, heavy air as they started down the hallway.

The corridor felt endless, and Zoe thought she could see the outline of a door ahead. The breaker room, she hoped. They were nearly there when an agent stepped into the hallway from an adjacent passage.

The man paused, hand to his weapon, then squinted at McCoy's face. "McCoy?" His hand eased. "What are you doing down here? I thought you, Palm, and Sever were on outer perimeter duty."

McCoy shrugged and took a step toward the newcomer, letting a nervous chuckle pass his lips. The agent was tensing again, but McCoy moved quickly, engaging the man, yanking him forward, twisting him around, and wrapping the inside of his elbow around the man's throat. The agent struggled and McCoy took several steps back, meeting the stone wall with his spine and using the leverage to clamp harder on the man's neck.

The agent's struggle began to lessen, then he was limp. McCoy slowly released him and the man slumped forward. He slipped his hands under the man's arms.

"A little help," he whispered, and Zoe sprang back to life.

She hoisted the man's legs and helped carry him toward the door at the end of the hallway. She set his ankles down, moved to open the door, and resumed her position as they carried him inside and shut the door.

McCoy put the agent in a corner and searched for something to secure his hands. Zoe saw a clump of long black zip ties on a nearby shelf, grabbed one, and handed it over. McCoy anchored the agent's hands around a pipe as Zoe tied his ankles together. They stood back, heaving, and glanced at one another.

"They'll notice him missing eventually. We need to move." McCoy yanked a steel ladder from the corner. He crawled up, unhooked the air shaft cover, and hoisted himself inside. "Come on," he said, motioning.

Zoe went up the ladder and accepted his help into the uncomfortably small air vent. On their hands and knees, they moved left, which McCoy assured her was the correct direction. She couldn't shake her nerves. They rattled her arms and made them feel like jelly.

They encountered several forks. Each time, McCoy hesitated, and each time, he assured Zoe he knew where he was headed.

She felt as though they would be crawling carefully through the tiny air shaft for eternity, when McCoy stopped, lay flat to peer through a slotted air vent, then smiled back at Zoe. He lifted the vent, managed to turn so his feet exited first, and dropped from view.

Zoe crawled to the edge and saw McCoy had dropped to the ground and was extending his arms to catch her. She swallowed, and before she could talk herself out of it, dropped down and landed in McCoy's arms.

He lowered her to the ground and smiled. "One southeast storage room, lower level one, as promised."

Zoe glanced around the dim space. It was a very large storage room. "Now what?" she asked.

He cleared his throat and glanced around. "We find cover and wait for Seeley."

THIRTY

SEELEY SLIPPED DOWN the subbasement hallway, around the first corner, and across the small adjoining hall to a stairwell door. He pushed into the stairwell, slowly closed the door with only a soft click, and climbed the stairs.

Six flights up, on the main floor, he peered carefully through the window in the exit door, then walked out into the hallway. It was brightly lit, the noise of an active afternoon floating on the air from the main lobby just around the corner. His boots squeaked on the pearly, tiled floor, and he paused. They were soaked from trekking through water. He'd need dry ones.

The employee locker rooms were around the corner to the right and three doors up. He took a deep breath, stepped into the bustling activity of his fellow agents with confidence, smiled at a few, and slipped into the locker room several seconds later.

The men's locker room was on the left. Inside, muffled conversations echoed as men showered, changed, and chatted. Seeley kept his head down and walked straight through, passing rows of lockers and scattered men on his left, then quickly slipped into a wardrobe room at the back right corner.

He slid off his wet shoes and replaced them with a dry pair, then grabbed a navy windbreaker and black baseball hat. He donned his new items and left the closet. Then he waited, tucked behind the last row of lockers, until the men's voices drifted toward the showers.

Perfect. Seeley popped his head around to see that the row of lockers that had been occupied was clear. He quickly started searching through them. Many weren't locked, and on his fifth search he came across a general access key card. That would work. All agents had access to the north side of Xerox. Seeley softly pushed the locker closed and moved out the back exit, which popped him out into another clean, gray hallway aiming north.

Brim covering his eyes, he focused and walked at a steady pace. Suited agents passed him as he covered the length of the walkway and made a left turn into another large lobby. Mapping the building in his head, he moved with the flow of traffic, which was minimal, and made his way toward the security offices. First he needed to figure out where they were holding Lucy, then how to gain access.

The key card allowed him entrance into the security division. The panel dinged for access, and Seeley pushed the door open and moved inside. The offices and rooms here each required specific key cards. He ignored them and headed to the elevator. It took him down a level to his intended target: the break room at the end of the hall. The dismal room was empty. He moved inside, stepped behind the door, and waited. He knew his friend would need his hourly coffee refill soon.

Within ten minutes Barry Waller, a large, heavyset man with graying hair, entered the room and headed for the well-stocked coffee bar along the far wall, his famous Steelers mug in hand.

Seeley shut the door, and Waller turned and gasped.

"Waller," Seeley said.

Waller had been with the FBI for over thirty years, working

in different parts of security and surveillance. He and Seeley had worked together before both came to Xerox only a year apart. They had a long-standing relationship, and Seeley had saved him more than once.

Waller had a reputation for knowing everything that was going on with the Grantham Project. He could see each moving piece in his head like a chess match.

Waller raised his eyebrow, suspicion on his face. "You're not supposed to be here."

"I need your help," Seeley said.

"If you get caught—"

"I won't get caught."

Waller paused and then let out a soft chuckle. "One day that confidence is going to get you killed."

"Hopefully not today," Seeley returned.

"You're here about the girl." Waller knew him well.

"Do you know where she's being held?"

"I don't have clearance for that kind of information."

It was Seeley who chuckled this time. "That isn't what I asked."

Waller held his tongue, and Seeley took a step closer. "You owe me."

Seeley had saved Waller's life and then his reputation when they'd worked a job together in London a decade ago. Back before Waller had swapped his vodka addiction for coffee.

Waller sighed. "You should just let this one go, Tom."

"I can't, Barry."

Waller nodded. "They recently moved the package to Vault A on the north side. Security level black. Only Jesus gets in there without clearance."

Seeley nodded and started toward the exit, calmly saying over his shoulder, "This makes us even."

Security level black required double key card entry, plus unique entry codes. The Vault would require yet another code, plus fingerprint identification. A plan started to formulate in his head. It would need to be precise and executed without a hitch. And he was going to need to borrow a couple of items.

ZOE HAD STARTED pacing almost immediately after she and McCoy dropped into the storage room from the ceiling. She didn't know how long it had been since they arrived, but it felt longer than she liked. And there was still no Seeley.

He had betrayed them. The single thought continued to repeat itself inside her brain. McCoy rested against the wall behind her, his calm energy making her own anxiety worse. Seeley had betrayed her, and McCoy was in on it. She was being played for a fool. Again.

They stayed close to the back wall, so if any unexpected guests arrived, they could easily stow away underneath the large metal shelving that lined the room. Not that Zoe thought any would. The large room was used primarily for the storage of old office furniture. Assembled desks and chairs stood around, stacked and collecting dust. It wasn't the worst place to hide out in a top-secret government facility. Unless you had been directed here by the same man who was now currently betraying you. Then it was the worst.

"Watching you pace is giving me anxiety," McCoy said. "Relax, he'll be here."

Zoe whipped around. "We shouldn't have trusted him."

"Have a little faith. He'll show."

"And if he doesn't?"

"He's Tom Seeley, he will."

"I don't know what that means."

"It means if anyone can, it's him." McCoy paused. "And if he doesn't come, we're toast."

Zoe looked at him wide-eyed as a sly grin yanked at the corner of his mouth. He chuckled softly to himself. She cursed at him under her breath and was about to say something she wouldn't be able to take back, when the door across the room creaked.

McCoy was on his feet, yanking Zoe out of sight. She dropped to the ground, her knee colliding with the cement floor hard, but she held her tongue as McCoy ushered her back and under the cover of a shelf.

Steps echoed across the floor, and Zoe saw McCoy hold his finger over his lips. Her heart was pounding so quickly she was certain whoever had just entered the room could hear it. She held her breath and watched as heavy boots came into view a yard or so from where they were crouched.

McCoy risked peering out around one of the shelving's thick end poles but recoiled when two more sets of boots entered the room. Zoe thought her heart might explode.

"Alright, what's the deal, Seeley?" an unfamiliar voice asked.

"McCoy was the one who spotted it," Seeley said. "Hey, McCoy," he called out, and McCoy gave Zoe a "stay put" look before playing along.

"Over here—stolen contraband," McCoy said, stepping across the room.

"I thought you said it was a permitted breach," another unfamiliar voice said.

It took one second of silence before the cards were all out on the table, and Zoe heard the altercation begin. McCoy rushed to aid Seeley as the two other men got smart to what was happening. Zoe tucked her hands over her head and stayed low as she heard flesh pound flesh, metal clank against the ground, huffs and grunts, someone crash against heavy objects, the shattering of wood. And then silence.

A cascade of heavy breathing preceded Seeley's welcome voice. "Contraband?"

"It was the first thing that came to mind," McCoy responded.

Zoe untucked herself from where she was hidden and saw Seeley and McCoy standing over two fallen agents, the room in shambles, and a toppled desk surrounded by splinters of wood.

Seeley looked up at Zoe, and she nearly rushed to him. She pulled up short, remembering who he was, what he had done, and just acknowledged him with a nod. She didn't want to risk saying anything that might make her sound stupid, or worse, like she was glad to see him.

He looked at McCoy. "Strip them. We'll secure them out of sight. They should have the security key cards we need."

McCoy nodded, and the two set to undressing the unconscious agents down to their underclothes and donning their black security uniforms.

Zoe turned to give them privacy and asked, "What about me?"

A moment later McCoy tapped her shoulder, and she turned to see him holding out handcuffs. She shook her head, the paranoia roaring up inside her chest. "No way."

"You can't just walk down the hallway with us," McCoy said.

"This feels like a setup," Zoe said.

"It's not," Seeley said.

She cut her eyes at him and opened her mouth to give a biting remark, but with a strong stride forward he bit first. "I know you don't trust me, but I don't care. Either you put on the handcuffs or you stay here. We do not have time for anything else."

The air around Zoe's head was thick and hot. She wanted to

slap him, scream at him, but all she could do was hope the hate she was pushing out through her eyes was enough to affect his ability to breathe.

"Fine," she said through clenched teeth.

Seeley dropped her stare, and it gave her a beat of satisfaction. But it didn't ease the thundering of her heart as he tossed the handcuffs to McCoy and turned away. McCoy crossed to her and clamped the metal cuffs around her wrists. She tried not to dash for safety.

"Too tight?" McCoy asked.

Zoe saw the genuine concern in his eyes, and it eased her panic a smidge. She shook her head, and he offered her a reassuring smile.

They walked to Seeley, who had moved to the exit. "Follow my lead," he said. "We have one shot at this."

He pulled the door open, and with him on one side and McCoy on the other, Zoe was escorted into the hallway. Her brain was screaming, *You're being led to the slaughter like a willing lamb. The devil on one side, unassuming angel on the other, and you offered yourself over.* Her legs nearly fought her own commands, and she could sense her heels wanting to dig into the ground and hold her still. Yet through her raging fear and crippling anxiety, all she could think was, *Please don't let Lucy already be dead.*

THIRTY-ONE

THE WALK WAS eternal. And also happened so quickly that before Zoe knew it the three were on the final descending elevator. They had zero verbal communication. Everything was done with tugs and hand signals. Down four floors, past a handful of encounters without suspicion, and through several locked entries with the slick black key card Seeley had strapped to his belt.

As the elevator dropped, Seeley yanked a black baseball cap from behind his back and tried to place it on Zoe's head. It was an awkward interaction, and she reached up to push him away and adjust the hat herself.

"To hide your face," Seeley said, breaking the silence.

There wasn't time for any other conversation.

"Be ready," he said just before the elevator came to a soft halt and the doors slid open. The exit hallway was clear. "Heads down. Every inch from here on out will be covered in cameras."

Zoe did as she was told, watching her feet as she was pulled along toward the end of the hall, where a large set of steel double doors stood closed. A moment's pause followed as McCoy and Seeley swiped their key cards together on the twin security pads positioned on either side of the entryway.

The door clicked, and Seeley yanked it open. They stepped through to another hallway identical to the one they had just come from. Much like the rest of the building, it was hard, cold, and unapproachable. Stone floors and walls, steel doors, no windows. Zoe knew they were underground, maybe even below the subbasement from which they'd entered.

Seeley hadn't been exaggerating about the cameras. Even with her eyes low, Zoe could sense them watching. She could hear their mechanical movements tracking her steps. It sent a shiver down her spine. How many people knew she was supposed to be dead? She kept herself shielded between the men and focused on not tripping over her own nerves.

The hall went only one direction. It took a turn right and ended at another set of steel doors. Zoe noticed the security pads were different.

"Two-step clearance measures," Seeley said barely above a whisper. He dug something from his pocket before they reached the doors. Carefully and without drawing attention, he slid a small square piece behind Zoe's back, his fingers lingering there as he waited for McCoy to take what he was offering.

They were at the doors, and Seeley and McCoy shared a glance.

"In tandem, yes?" Seeley said.

McCoy nodded, and after the swipe of the black key cards, both men plugged the small square objects they held into the bottom of the security entry data pad. The screen blinked to life, flashing for a security code.

Zoe had spent enough time with Tomac and his band of thieves to understand what was happening. The objects placed under the entry pads were decoders searching at lightning speed through hundreds of numerical options for the right set of numbers.

And it was taking a minute.

A minute longer than was comfortable. Zoe could feel the sweat that had gathered underneath the bill of her cap dripping down the left side of her forehead.

"Come on, come on," McCoy whispered.

"What if this doesn't work?" Zoe asked.

Their lack of communication was answer enough.

"It'll work," Seeley said. "They're ours. They'll work."

Another second ticked by, and then another. Zoe's mind scrambled with questions. How long did they have before the data pad realized the time between key card swipe and entry code was too long? Were people staring down at them right now as they stood there just looking forward? If it failed, what happened next? Did they have any other choices?

The ending encroached like a wild beast, and Zoe inched away from the doors. Then Seeley's screen dinged green, and in the same second McCoy's followed suit. There was another soft click, and without a moment of hesitation Seeley pushed open the unlocked door.

Once inside, he grabbed another sleek device from his armored vest. A larger black orb.

McCoy eyed it and gasped. "How'd you get your hands on one of those?"

"I heard about a case recently where this technology was used and borrowed it from the evidence room," Seeley said as he searched the entry wall for his target. He strode toward what Zoe thought looked like a fuse box attached to the right side of the wall, nearly invisible because it blended into the space so well. He fiddled with the orb for a moment, then placed it on top of the box and tapped the side with his finger.

A small white light blinked five times, then went out again, fading into the dark atmosphere of the hallway.

"What does it do?" Zoe asked.

"It kills all the cameras connected to that line," McCoy said, "which will be all those in this hall, as they're kept on a separate feed in case of tampering."

"We have five minutes before technical sends a team," Seeley said. "Let's move."

Zoe watched McCoy tap the time into the digital watch on his wrist.

The hallway they'd just entered was different. Wider and dimmer, it was lined all along the right side with doors, regular in size and with small rectangular glass windows.

Seeley moved, pulling Zoe along, McCoy keeping pace. The long hall was curved, a half circle that prevented them from seeing the end of it.

They passed the first five doors without pausing. Zoe noticed the doors were lettered. They crested the turn and came upon a moving triad of guards. McCoy paused and overcorrected, yanking her back and forth.

"Who you got there?" one of the approaching agents asked.

"Came in with the asset in Vault A," Seeley answered. "We're transferring her."

The three exchanged curious looks, and Zoe could feel her stomach turn. The one in front, clearly the leader of the band, yanked a tablet that was Velcroed to his armored vest. "What's your transfer number?" he asked, tapping the screen to life.

"We are clear on where to take the prisoner," Seeley replied.

"I'm not sure how they do things up top," the agent said, "but down here, rules are every prisoner gets catalogued before entering a vault. So, Agent"—the man looked at the name tag across Seeley's right breast pocket—"Pilzer, what is your transfer number?"

"Pilzer?" one of the other agents questioned. "You're not—"

Seeley was already moving. He released his hold of Zoe's arm, reached around to his back, drew the small handgun that was holstered there, and fired.

One clean shot punctured a hole in the center of the questioning agent's temple. Before the others could react, Seeley shifted his aim and connected another bullet with the agent who stood beside the one with the tablet.

In a split second, both men dropped to the ground like potato sacks. The man in the middle dropped his tablet to draw his weapon, but Seeley already had his pistol aimed at the man's temple.

"Hands up," Seeley said.

The agent slowly brought both hands skyward.

"Grab his firearms," Seeley said. McCoy obeyed, relieving the man of the rifle slung over his shoulder and the pistol holstered at his waist. McCoy anchored both weapons to his person.

"Uncuff her," Seeley said to McCoy. Then to the unknown agent: "Interlock your fingers and place your hands on your head."

McCoy released Zoe's restraints and handed them to Seeley, who took them and cuffed the agent's hands in front of him.

"Take us to Vault A."

"You'll never—"

"Now," Seeley said calmly as he shoved his gun farther into the man's face. The agent gritted his teeth and turned, Seeley clasping one of his arms, his pistol now aimed at the back of the man's head.

They walked around the half circle, passing lettered doors counting down from F. When A came into view they hurried, pushing their hostage forward. Beside the door, like all the others, was another data station.

"Unlock it," Seeley said to the imprisoned man.

"I don't have access to this prisoner," the man said.

"Unlock it," Seeley pressed.

"I don't—"

"Do you want to end up like your friends back there? Enter the access code or I'll shoot you and decrypt it from your tablet. Either way, I'm getting into this room."

The agent paused, and Seeley cocked his pistol.

"Okay," the man said and stepped forward to punch in a ten-digit numerical code. The screen flipped to blue, and a mechanical voice asked for fingerprint verification, which the agent provided, then the screen turned green. The door clicked, and without waiting Zoe entered.

The stone room was completely bare except for a body that lay on the ground, on its side, facing the back wall. Zoe rushed forward, dropping to her knees when she reached the body.

"Lucy," she said softly, reaching out to touch the girl's shoulder. She was freezing, and Zoe feared the worst. She lifted her finger to the major artery in the girl's neck and felt the pulse, soft and slow but there. "Help me," she said over her shoulder, and then she carefully turned the girl so she was facing up toward her.

Lucy's familiar face was pale, eyes shut, cheeks bruised, eyelids red. She looked the same but different. Broken and battered.

"Lucy," Zoe said softly, shaking the girl slightly. "Lucy, can you hear me?"

Lucy didn't respond. McCoy stood over Zoe's shoulder.

"She's alive," Zoe said.

"Step back," McCoy said, then crouched to scoop Lucy's small frame into his arms. As he did, the alarm he'd punched into his watch started to sing. They were out of time.

Both of them moved back toward the door and stepped out into the hallway. Seeley shut the door to Vault A and turned back to his apprehended colleague. The man raised his hands and opened his mouth to plead for his life, but Seeley had already raised his weapon. He crashed the hilt of it down hard across the man's skull, knocking him out cold. He crashed to the ground.

Muffled voices echoed up the hallway from the way they'd come. It wouldn't be long before they were spotted.

Seeley continued down the bend, gun raised. He glanced back to signal that it was clear. McCoy, still carefully clutching Lucy, and Zoe followed around the bend and into another thick-stoned walkway. After another couple of yards, the hallway jutted out into different pathways. It felt like an endless maze of tunnels and pathways that had been laid under the foundation of the campus. Zoe prayed that Seeley knew it as well as he claimed.

Seeley glanced in both directions, sizing up their options, and Zoe felt her stomach drop as her heart leaped. The volume of voices grew, and she could hear thundering boots slapping the stone floor as their pursuers gained on them.

"Seeley?" McCoy questioned.

Seeley moved left without responding, and they followed him. Down the long, narrower hallway, the light faded as they moved. They reached the end and found nothing but wall.

Seeley cursed, and it echoed against the stone. He passed Zoe and rushed back the way they'd come, motioning for them to stay put.

McCoy softly placed Lucy on the ground. "Try to wake her," he said, then started inspecting the wall.

Zoe moved to Lucy, propped her up so her back rested against the wall, and began trying to revive her. "Lucy, Lucy," she said, shaking her, tapping the girl's cheeks. "Lucy, you have to wake up."

The girl just shook with no response, her head drooped, chin touching her collarbone.

"Lucy."

Seeley returned, heaving. "We have sixty seconds."

"I found a grate here," McCoy said, and Seeley was at his side. "It's bolted pretty good," McCoy continued.

Both men crouched on their knees, examining the grate, all of them aware that it was their only escape.

Zoe turned back to Lucy, her timid approach to rousing the girl fading. She shook her hard, slapped her face with more intensity. "Lucy," she said, "wake up."

McCoy and Seeley had started banging on the bolt with the hilts of their weapons, the sound echoing like cracks of thunder throughout their stone cage. It would draw attention quickly.

A moment later a red dot flashed on the wall near Lucy's head, and Zoe yanked the girl down to the floor just as a bullet bounced off the stone. More followed.

Zoe dragged Lucy until they were pressed against the back wall with nowhere to go. McCoy and Seeley were both standing, weapons raised, firing back as the team of pursuers approached.

Three came into focus, weapons firing, Seeley and McCoy facing off. Seeley struck one through the shoulder, and the man was forced to let his weapon fall, then Seeley sank another bullet into the man's leg. He crumpled in pain while McCoy took on another, hitting his attacker's neck between his helmet and armored vest. The man shrieked and fell to his knees.

Two opposed one now, bullets flying as they dodged shots sent their way. Seeley's pistol clicked empty. He tossed it, hunkered down, and under McCoy's cover rammed forward with all his strength, colliding with the last attacker's gut. The two fell to the floor. Seeley pinned him down, yanked his weapon back, ducked the man's swing, and then rammed the agent with the back of his own weapon. The man cursed and rolled to his side as Seeley sprang up and aimed in one fluid motion, then placed two bullets into the man's side.

More excruciating cries echoed, then the man went still. McCoy moved back to the grate and began knocking it with his weapon's hilt again. Over and over, ramming with all his strength.

Seeley was stacking the bodies of the three agents to provide a short molehill for cover. More approaching boots and echoing voices filled the hall.

McCoy jumped up and cocked his weapon. He turned to Seeley. "You have more brute strength. We have to get that grate open or we're all dead."

Seeley nodded, and the two switched places. McCoy knelt, taking fire as Seeley set to the grate. Zoe could hear him pounding at it like a battering ram.

"We won't be able to carry her," Seeley yelled through the gunfire. "Wake her up!" All the while slamming at another bolt.

"I'm trying!" Zoe screamed. "Lucy, Lucy, wake up!"

She needed to do something more intense. Her heart raced up into her throat, and her mind stumbled over terrible ideas. She needed something painful enough to shock Lucy awake. And she didn't have time to second-guess herself. Without another moment to talk herself out of it, she reached over to Seeley's belt where she had seen him tuck a small blade, swiped it clear of its sheath, and drove it into Lucy's thigh.

The girl's eyes snapped open, and she cried out.

Seeley saw the knife, then looked up at Zoe, surprised. She yanked the knife out, and blood began to soak the clothing around the cut as Lucy groaned, still coming to. Zoe used the knife to cut off the sleeve of Lucy's shirt and patched the cut as best she could.

Just as she was finishing, Lucy's arm shot out, grabbed the knife Zoe had laid to the side, and pointed it at Zoe's chest.

She gasped, stunned. Lucy's eyes held hers for a second, and then the blade's tip pierced Zoe's skin. Pain rippled down her chest. Lucy's eyes were dark and cold.

Seeley reached out, placed his hand on Lucy's, and gained her attention. "Stop, Lucy," he said, but the girl turned to place her free hand on his grip. "Lucy," he said again, but the expression in her eyes was emotionless. "Number Nine," Seeley said, and this caused her to pause. "We have to get out of here or we will all die. Help me."

She flashed her eyes back to Zoe, then pushed her away and moved with Seeley. Zoe gulped her sudden panic, yanked back the collar of her shirt, and saw a thin line of blood trailing down toward her breasts.

"We are out of time, people," McCoy yelled, still trying to keep their pursuers at bay.

"We need to break this open," Seeley said to Lucy, and without hesitation Lucy reached down, wrapped her fingers through the grate's holes, and ripped the steel cage open. The screeching of metal echoed through the tunnel.

Above them, maybe a couple of floors up, Zoe could hear a siren.

Seeley noticed too. "They put the place on lockdown. We need to move now." He turned back to Lucy. "All known exits will be blocked. We have to get out through the old water tunnels. You should know the way."

Lucy nodded, and Seeley motioned to Zoe. "She can be trusted. Get her out of here. That's an order, Number Nine."

Again she nodded and took the lead, dropping to a crouch and crawling into the shaft.

"McCoy," Zoe called, and the man glanced back.

"Go!" he shouted and returned his gaze forward. But the

momentary distraction was enough for a bullet to smack into the side of his chest. He gasped and stumbled.

"McCoy!" Zoe screamed, taking a step toward her hurt friend. Strong arms scooped her up and yanked her back.

"We have to go now!" Seeley yelled. He pulled her back to the open grate, stuffing her inside.

"We can't leave—"

"We will all die if we don't," he cut in.

She couldn't think about it as she repositioned herself to her hands and knees and started crawling after Lucy, who was already a couple feet ahead. Even through her fear Zoe could feel tears collecting for McCoy. He'd saved her life.

"Lucy will get you out," Seeley said. "I'll follow when the coast is clear."

Then Seeley disappeared, and without any other options Zoe scrabbled as quickly as she could to catch up to the girl. They were back in the ventilation system, similar to the one she and McCoy had used.

The noise around them faded to silence as the girls put their entrance point behind them and maneuvered through the web of small shafts, Zoe hoping Lucy knew where she was going, until light peeked through another grate at the end of the tunnel. Zoe glanced back a couple of times, but Seeley never came into view. So she stayed close to Lucy.

They reached the end, and Lucy twisted around, rammed the grate with her heels, and dropped out to whatever lay below. Zoe did the same and found they were in a water tunnel. *Let there be a God*, she thought, *and let this be the same tunnel we used to get in.*

Lucy walked toward the exit, water splashing up around her ankles, and Zoe followed until she saw the place in the large round grate where McCoy had originally cut an entrance. Lucy had led them exactly where she'd been ordered to.

"I know the way from here," Zoe said, stepping through the breach. Lucy followed.

Outside, the blaring siren was even clearer. Zoe thought for a moment they should avoid the cameras stationed around the outer walls, but the agents already knew they had escaped, so maybe it didn't matter? Maybe it mattered more that they get free from this place as fast as possible. She glanced back one final time, hoping to see Seeley drop from the open shaft and join them, but he didn't. And she knew they had to move.

She turned to give Lucy direction and saw that the girl had leaned herself up against the interior wall. Her face was pale, her shoulders slumping, and Zoe saw that blood had soaked her pant leg. She was losing too much blood. Had Zoe hit a major artery? She needed to get Lucy back to the Jeep.

She placed herself beside Lucy, grabbing one of her arms and draping it across her own neck. "Come on," Zoe said, and the girls moved out of the waterway. They couldn't move as fast as Zoe would have liked, but within a couple of minutes they were tucked back inside the tree line and covered by the thick overgrowth.

Blue tape marked the path as Zoe held Lucy up and guided her across the terrain. They still had a ways to go when Lucy lost consciousness. Zoe lifted the girl up and over her shoulder, digging deep for enough strength to carry the girl the rest of the way. Her legs went from aching to burning to nearly numb. She paused only when completely necessary and carefully managed the rocky ground toward their freedom.

When the Jeep came into view, Zoe nearly cried. She opened the back door and awkwardly yanked Lucy's limp figure inside, across the leather seats. Then she dug out the first aid kit she'd seen from underneath the driver's seat, cut off Lucy's right pant leg, and cleaned the wound. It wasn't large, but it was deep.

Once the cut was cleaned and bandaged, Zoe waited. Keeping eyes on Lucy, checking her temperature, forcing water through her lips, checking her bandages. All the while praying that at any moment Seeley would crest the hill with McCoy and they could all leave happily, together.

But after an hour of tortured patience, they were still alone. Seeley would want her to leave, she told herself as she climbed into the driver's seat and flipped the ignition over. She had no other choice. If they stayed here, someone would find them.

She shifted the Jeep into drive and carefully maneuvered out from the cover of forest. She had no idea what they were going to do next, but she knew she needed to go somewhere no one would come looking for them. Somewhere off the map.

She knew only one place like that, and it made her sick to think of returning. But to protect Lucy she would do anything. Even return to Haven Valley.

THIRTY-TWO

HUNKERED BEHIND THE piled dead bodies, Seeley took out three more agents, trying to give the girls as much time as possible to get away. He knew there was no way he was following them. There had never been a chance they would all make it out alive. He'd known that from the start. All that mattered was that Zoe and Lucy survived.

They could start over, go somewhere new, be different people. Zoe would take care of them.

He'd made his peace. Had McCoy? he wondered as he glanced down at the young man's still body. He'd given his life for something he believed in. Was there a more dignified way to die? Seeley thought he'd be better for having known McCoy. He wished he'd had the chance to tell him that.

The hall filled with a dozen agents, and Seeley ran out of ammunition. He tossed his weapons to the side and slowly stood, hands raised, expecting to be shot on sight. But he wasn't. He was taken into custody as a group scurried into the small ventilation shaft after the girls.

They led him out of the secure level, back up onto the main prison floor, and tossed him into a cell. He could only imagine what was coming next, but he was sure it would be painful and drawn out. He sat in the room, which was void except for the standard stone bench, for a span of time he couldn't measure. It gave him time to contemplate all that had happened.

He hoped the girls had gotten away. He hoped McCoy's sacrifice had been for something. He wondered if assisting had given him any goodness. He knew he'd never see the light of day again, but maybe he'd earned something back. Something he'd given away long ago. Cami would never know the truth, but if she did, would she be proud?

The door creaked open, and four uniformed agents armed to the teeth entered, Director Hammon accompanying them. Seeley didn't stand as they filled the room, and a moment of silence held them all as each waited to see what the other might do first.

Hammon tucked his hands into the front pockets of his suit pants and sighed. "I didn't see this coming, Tom. I don't surprise easy."

Seeley held Hammon's gaze and said nothing.

"We shouldn't be sitting here," Hammon said. "So why are we?"

Again Seeley kept his mouth shut.

Again Hammon sighed. Another beat of silence surrounded the space.

"We know where the data chip is that Olivia hid. Number Nine gave up the location hours before you tried to break her out. You were too late."

"What did you do to her?" Seeley said, recalling the way Lucy had responded to her number but not her name.

"I fixed her," Hammon said.

"You destroyed her."

"I returned her to the state she was created for. I removed the false identity given to her by Olivia. You should be congratulating me."

"Did you come here just to share the good news?"

"Unfortunately, no. Honestly, I would like nothing more than to put a bullet between your eyes, but I still need you."

Seeley gave the director a curious stare.

"Number Nine escaped."

Seeley didn't even try to hide his pleasure.

"I need you to bring her back," Hammon said.

"Why? You have the information you need. Burn it and this will all be over."

"You're an incredible agent, Tom, but ignorant when it comes to the politics behind the curtain. Nothing that could turn a profit is ever over. Number Nine's journey with Miss Johnson has piqued interest with the powers that be, and now a powerful asset they paid for is loose. Not to mention a walking catalogue of all the things that happened here. Number Nine must be recovered."

"And Zoe?" Seeley asked.

"I suspect she's the reason you are sitting in this room, no?" Hammon questioned.

Seeley didn't respond.

"Love is an unfortunate characteristic of humanity that can't be erased, even from the darkest of souls. That's something my father used to say. And it is the greatest complication I've encountered in our line of work."

Love was a strong word, Seeley thought. He did care for Zoe; he had risked his career and life to help her and Lucy escape. But to be accused of *loving* her? Would he have risked so much for less than love? The idea dug into his brain and planted a small seed.

"I doubt she'll still be alive when you find Number Nine, but if she is, she will need to be disposed of. She is a very loose end."

"What does that mean?"

"Number Nine is not the same girl she was when you left."

Seeley thought about the way Lucy had nearly plunged a knife through Zoe's chest and the implications of that. He'd watched Lucy lead Zoe away. She'd followed his orders to get Zoe out to safety. Whose orders was she following now?

"So send a team after her. By your own admission she is following orders," Seeley said. But he could see the doubt playing in Hammon's eyes. They weren't sure they could control her. Because even after all they'd done, she'd still helped Zoe escape. Again Seeley couldn't hide his pleasure.

"We've lost too many good men already, and Number Nine trusts you. Zoe believes you're a good guy. You can infiltrate them with ease, without risking countless more bodies."

"Why would I help you?" Seeley asked.

"You wouldn't by choice," Hammon said. He turned to one of the agents standing by and held out his hand. The agent placed a thin tablet in his palm.

Hammon turned the tablet around so Seeley could see the images. His heart sank into his gut, and fury matched with fear rose up like a wave through his chest. A black-and-white video feed of Cami and his mother danced before him. They were at the grocery store, filling the cart with items, laughing as Cami grabbed an armful of something sweet and tossed it in the cart. His mother shook her head and returned the items to the shelf.

"This is a live surveillance stream that I had set up on Cami this morning. A team assigned to follow her and your mother so I have eyes on them at all times. At their home, at her school, when she's with her friends."

Seeley couldn't tear his eyes away from the video. The intent was clear without Hammon needing to explain more, but he continued for the cruelty of it.

"Accidents happen to unassuming people all the time. Your

daughter is bright, I hear, gets good grades, has good friends. I'd hate to see something terrible happen to her."

Seeley snapped. He launched himself across the room at Hammon, who anticipated his reaction and stepped back. Seeley came face-to-face with several raised rifle ends aimed directly at him. He halted, hate dripping from his expression as he bored into Hammon with an unbreakable stare.

"If you lay a hand on her . . ." Seeley growled.

"I won't, as long as you return the property of this government and eliminate Zoe Johnson," Hammon said.

Seeley stood, chest heaving, anger running through his veins like blood. Hammon took a step forward, but Seeley knew better than to move. He still had weapons packed with bullets aimed at his head.

"Make no mistake, Tom," Hammon started, "you will never see your daughter again. After returning Number Nine, you will spend the rest of your life in a top-security prison for your treason against the state and the murder of eight agents. Your daughter will live, graduate high school, go to college, get a good job, have a full life. But if you fail, or if you try anything other than executing your orders precisely, she will die. And you will live the rest of your life knowing you were the one that pulled the trigger."

Seeley balled his hands into fists to stop the vibration under his flesh.

Hammon took another step so that he was only inches from Seeley's face. "Are we clear, Agent?"

Seeley glanced back toward the sweet image of his little girl helping her grandmother load groceries into the trunk of their car and knew there was only one path forward. He looked back up at Hammon. "Yes, sir."

Hammon snapped the tablet shut. "Good." He turned to leave,

talking over his shoulder. "You have twenty-four hours, not a second more."

Two of the four agents escorted Seeley from his cell. His mind stumbled over the misery of his situation, anger still pulsing with each beat of his heart.

They led him up to the main floor, where he was instructed to clean up. They gave him money, a weapon, and keys to a vehicle. Surrounded by armed guards at each turn, he avoided the eyes that followed him as he moved throughout the building and shut out their whispers of disapproval. He was a rogue agent now, and there was no coming back from this fall.

The agents led Seeley outside, the cold winter air and bright sunlight a shock after being held in a dark cage. Twenty-four hours. Where was he supposed to start?

"Any idea which way Lucy and Zoe were headed?" Seeley asked those walking him to the vehicle.

Without looking at him, one answered, "A Jeep registered to Dave McCoy was last spotted crossing state lines into Tennessee."

Tennessee, Seeley thought as he opened the driver's door and climbed inside. An idea dropped into his mind, and a theory started to take form. If he was wrong, he'd waste an entire day's travel. So he couldn't be wrong. He fired the car to life and pulled away from the Xerox campus.

He wished they'd just shot him dead.

THIRTY-THREE

ZOE DROVE THROUGH the night, stopping only once to get gas, grateful she'd found a twenty in McCoy's console. With the dawning of the sun she pulled off the main road onto a dirt road that began to climb up the mountainside toward Haven Valley.

She kept her eyes forward, hands on the steering wheel, fighting off every instinct in her body that begged her to turn around. She knew the past was strong and unforgiving, but she was surprised by her visceral reaction to the proximity of their destination.

Lucy had pretty much remained asleep in the back seat while they traveled. She came to once, only to sit up, shift her body, then lie down and fall back into slumber. When Zoe had stopped for gas, she'd redressed the wound, happy to see the bleeding had slowed. The girl had been muttering in her sleep, things Zoe didn't understand but that seemed to be tormenting Lucy from within.

Zoe tried to ignore the warning bells that went off in her brain every time she remembered the way Lucy had reacted back at Xerox. What if the girl she'd gone back to save wasn't there anymore? She continued to shake off the feeling, because combined with the rising fear of returning to her childhood home, it might drown her.

They'd have a lot to catch up on once they were safe. If they were ever safe. Zoe had been trying to formulate a plan. They couldn't stay in Haven Valley forever. She'd call Tomac. Maybe he'd be willing to help again. They needed to get out of the country. They wouldn't be safe until they were on foreign soil.

She tried to let her mind wander through fixes, but with each passing tree and bump in the road, her brain dragged her back to the past. This was the same road, the same turns, she had traveled down after being loaded into an FBI van. She seemed to be two people at once: a twenty-four-year-old woman who knew the coldness of the world, and a ten-year-old who believed the world could be good.

That had been the beginning of the end. Riding down the mountain, holding her little brother's hand, sitting beside their mother, who had promised that whatever came they'd all be fine.

They hadn't been fine.

Zoe shook the memories off and returned her focus to the drive. Within the hour she was driving up the last incline. Without ceasing, and against everything in her heart, she drove the Jeep over the ridge, and all of Haven Valley came into view. She couldn't take her foot off the gas, because if she dared, she wasn't sure she'd have enough strength to press on.

The small village was abandoned, standing exactly as she remembered it. Not a thing out of place, as if it had been held in a bubble, preserved by time. One single road right down the middle of town. A collection of stores with matching architecture rose up on both sides as though they had been plucked from an old Western town.

The surrounding woods had haunted her dreams as a child. She had been born in this strange place. Born into what the world referred to as a cult. A cult that taught her to believe that going beyond its red-rope boundaries would bring torment and suffering. Yet all the suffering a child could handle had invaded the boundaries that were supposed to keep her safe.

Her mother had built this place on a twisted foundation of religious fear. On laws established by a god giddy for punishment. But it wasn't really God at all. It had been the devil disguised as an angel, who deceived Zoe's mother into believing a community of holiness could save them from the wrath of monsters. His name was Sylous, and he had deceived them all.

Zoe now knew that what she really should have feared were the adults who had led her to believe any of it was real to begin with. Demons and darkness and light and salvation. She had believed it all so fully that it had become the monster, and it had swallowed her and spat her back out.

She pulled the Jeep down into the valley and parked it at the end of the road. She flipped the engine off and just sat there, only the sound of her heavy breathing and Lucy's calm breathing filling the car. Zoe took a deep breath and opened her car door. She stepped out, one foot after the other coming down on familiar earth.

More memories washed over her. The remaining community being navigated into lines as they were loaded into the black government vans. People whispering about what the world must be like now, since most of them hadn't been beyond the Haven Valley boundaries in a decade. They'd all still had naïve excitement then.

But the world doesn't do nice things to people it doesn't understand, and it had taken all of three months for each member of the Haven Valley community to be marked as a cult member, flogged daily by the media, and cast out of society. Nobody wanted them. People were afraid of them.

Zoe closed her eyes and forced breaths through the collecting emotions in her chest. Other memories flooded her mind. Happy ones. Her and her brothers playing. People she knew and loved walking from place to place. Living, growing, falling in love, having children. They were all human. Just delusional.

She cleared her throat and shut the Jeep door. She looked to her right and walked to the sidewalk, then three buildings down to where the medical clinic had been. She pushed on the door and walked inside. The small bell overhead still rang out. The inside was dimly lit with only the sunlight streaming in through the front window. She approached the counter. Dust had settled over everything in thick layers. She opened the drawers. They were filled with vials, syringes, Band-Aids, gauze—all the things Zoe would have expected to find ten years ago but not today.

She continued through the simple wood door that sealed off the entry room from the patients' hallway. The rooms beyond were untouched as well. Zoe was stunned. She assumed everything would have been looted, but it really had been left completely untouched.

Was every building the same? Would her home look as it had? Her bedroom? Would her books still be stacked next to her bed, the white lace curtains still hanging from her window? Suddenly she had to know.

She went back out the way she came, into the street and up toward the neighborhood at the back of the valley. Houses in rows, simple, similar. Zoe was walking, then running, past the first row and the second, until her house came into view. She pulled up to a hard stop.

There it stood: two stories, paneled white wood, the front porch simple and clean. Weathered some with time, but just as she remembered it. Staring at it now, she couldn't breathe. She could still see her father sitting on the porch, his three children at his feet, his wife standing by his side, as he read daily Scripture and they sang approved gospel songs.

The memory struck her so hard, tears sprang to her eyes. She had known joy in those moments.

Something shuffled to her right and Zoe jumped, half expecting to see a monster emerge from the darkness of her imagination. There was nothing. For every moment of joy she'd had in Haven Valley, ten were filled with crippling fear.

She took the steps two at a time until she was at her front door and then inside. Much like the clinic, it was covered in a decade of dust and dirt, and she flinched as a rodent scurried into a hidden corner.

Zoe carefully walked into the living room. All the familiar furniture sat precisely where her mother had placed it. The kitchen was filled with all the things she knew. The table in the dining room where they ate every meal was still set for the last meal they never ate. The whole house would be the same, yet still she was surprised to see each room the way she remembered it.

She moved upstairs to the bedrooms. The master, the single room her brothers shared, and hers at the hall's end. The door was still ajar, and she walked the dark hallway, put her fingers on the wood, and pushed it open wide.

A vibrant memory filled the space. Her beautiful mother sat on the bed, red hair tied up in a perfect bun, clear soft skin, delicate features, simple gray dress draped over her trim figure. The room was brightly lit and clean and smelled like fresh lilies.

Her mother glanced up at her as she entered the room. "Evelyn, what are you doing up here? Who's watching your brothers?"

"Father is home." Her voice was small and childlike as she skipped across the room to be close to the woman she loved more than life itself. "May I help you?"

Her mother smiled, holding out the mending she was work-ing on. "When did you learn to work a needle and thread?" she asked suspiciously.

Evelyn shrugged her tiny shoulders. "I haven't learned yet, but I'm ready."

"Are you, my darling?" Her mother extended her hand for Evelyn to grasp. "Well, then, I suppose I should teach you," she said with a smile.

"Will you teach me many things?" Evelyn asked.

"I will teach you everything I know, my dear girl, and then one day you will teach your daughter, and she will take those lessons and teach hers."

Zoe gasped as the memory flickered out, and she found her-self standing alone in her dingy room, tears streaming down her face. Evelyn had never stood a chance. She'd been taught to be this way, without a say, and Zoe had been trying to change it ever since. But maybe people couldn't change. Maybe each was born into a predetermined system, and the only choice was to live or die.

Zoe suddenly felt claustrophobic, her lungs tightening and her throat closing up. She turned and rushed from her room, back down the stairs, nearly tripping. The railing had weakened with time, and when she grabbed it for support, it snapped under her weight. She tumbled downward for six steps, rolled to the wood floor below, and knocked her head against the base step.

Pain exploded like stars across her vision, and she clenched her eyes shut, cursing loudly at the empty house. She rubbed the spot on her forehead as she pushed up with the other arm to a kneeling position. The wood floor groaned, and Zoe turned to see that Lucy was standing there, staring down at her.

Zoe gasped. "Lucy, you scared me."

Lucy didn't respond. She just bored into Zoe with a dark stare, a stare that sent a chill up her spine.

"Lucy—" Zoe began, but a roundhouse kick connected with the left side of her jaw and sent her sprawling. Pain coursed through her face as her mind began to register what was happening. Lucy was attacking her, and Lucy attacked with only one purpose in mind.

To kill.

THIRTY-FOUR

LUCY YANKED ZOE from the floor and tossed her into the living room behind them. Zoe hit the floor hard, the crack of her weight echoing off the old wood panels. The wind left her lungs, and she couldn't catch a breath. She wanted to scream out to Lucy, but she couldn't, and her brain snapped into survival mode. She had to get away.

Zoe rolled toward the couch and pulled herself under the coffee table. Lucy reached down for Zoe's ankle and yanked her back out.

Zoe finally caught a breath and sucked it in deep, using its momentum to push words from her lips. "Lucy, stop! Please."

But Lucy was in a rage. Again she yanked Zoe from the floor and hurled her against the built-in bookshelves. Zoe slammed against the rows of book spines and heard wood crack and split behind her. She toppled to the ground, hard books falling on her, as she used her arms to block her face.

She grabbed for the books and slung them at Lucy, who ducked each one without even trying.

"Lucy—" Zoe tried again.

"Stop calling me that!" Lucy cried back.

A light dinged in the back of Zoe's mind. "Number Nine, stop! Number Nine!"

Lucy paused for just a moment, and Zoe used it to push herself to her feet. She bolted down the hallway, past the basement door, and slammed out the back door.

Zoe raced down the back steps and dared to glance back to see that Lucy was upon her. She grabbed Zoe's shoulders, yanking her backward. Zoe punched her fists out over her head as she headed toward the ground. They slammed into Lucy's chest, causing the girl to huff and release hold of Zoe.

The ground came hard. Ignoring the pain, her adrenaline charging, Zoe rolled three times to her chest, pressed up, and bolted around the corner of her house back toward the main street.

Through the rows of houses, she cut across to the right. She knew this place inside and out. Lucy didn't. That would be Zoe's only advantage.

She pressed faster, weaving in and out of the line of homes. Then she raced up the back steps of another home, through the living room, and out the front, which put her a couple of yards from the main street.

Zoe forced her legs to pump faster, cutting across the open space between the house and the storefronts, and then behind the buildings where she'd parked the Jeep. She busted through a rear door and found herself in the general store. It was dark at the back of the building with no lighting, only the sunlight from the large glass windows at the front shining in. She took a momentary pause and listened.

She could not hear Lucy but knew she couldn't stop. Her chest heaving like an excited dog, Zoe rushed down the backside of the store, passing the tall shelving units where canned food still sat, and glanced out the front windows for her pursuer. She reached the back right corner and opened the door that stood there. It led into a small hallway with ascending stairs, and Zoe took them two at a time. At the top she found another door and pushed it open to the roof.

They had never been allowed to play up on the roofs because it was far too dangerous, but she knew what was up here. The roofs of each building were nearly connected, separated by only two or three feet.

Zoe moved in a crouched position, keeping herself as low as possible. Lucy couldn't get her up here, but she could still spot her. Zoe rushed to the edge and clumsily crossed the gap to the next building. Across and breathing heavily, she dropped to a squat and scanned the street.

Nothing. She continued to the next roof, moving with intention and trying to stay out of sight. On every new roof she stopped to look for Lucy, who was somewhere down there. She was approaching the last roof. Down below, parked on the other side of the street, was their Jeep.

She rushed to the roof's far edge. A thin metal ladder was melded to the side of the brick. Glancing in both directions, Zoe hopped over and started her descent.

Her feet plopped down onto the grass and she started for the Jeep. Just as she reached the street, Lucy stepped into view at the opposite end. Zoe pushed forward as Lucy started toward her.

She reached the Jeep, swung around the back end up to the driver's side, yanked open the driver's door, reached into the middle console, and withdrew the gun she'd seen stowed there earlier. She whipped it out and around the open car door, aiming it right at Lucy.

"Please, Lucy, stop!" Zoe yelled, her hands shaking.

The girl just drilled her with an intense, unblinking stare and kept coming.

"Lucy, don't! Number Nine, stop! I don't want to hurt you."

Lucy continued, her resolve frightening, her stride unaffected.

Zoe cocked the weapon, her fingers almost shaking too much to hold it, and she used her free hand to steady it. Lucy would kill her. Zoe was certain of it, but could she shoot Lucy?

"Number Nine, I don't want to hurt you. Just stop!"

Lucy marched on.

Panic, fear, and anguish met on the battlefield of Zoe's mind. She should shoot the machine coming toward her. That's what she was at this point, wasn't she? Was there any of Lucy even left? If Zoe didn't shoot her, then she might as well hand Lucy the gun because it would be a death sentence.

"Stop! Why are you doing this?"

Lucy stopped a foot away. "I have orders."

"To kill me?" Zoe asked.

Lucy nodded. "You're an enemy of the state."

"From Director Hammon?"

Lucy didn't say, but Zoe knew it couldn't be anyone else.

"Lucy, I am not your enemy," Zoe said.

"My title is Number Nine. Lucy is gone."

"No, I don't believe that."

"You will when I kill you."

Zoe fought through her fear and forced the gun steady. "Olivia gave you the name Lucy because she knew you were more than what they taught you to believe. I know it too. I am not your enemy. I am your friend."

"I have orders," Lucy said.

Zoe didn't understand. "But you helped me escape Xerox. You could have killed me already. Why now?"

"I was following another set of orders. To get you to safety, which I did." She was like a computer, processing commands one after the other. Programmed to execute orders. But to Zoe she was more.

"You're more than what they programmed you to be."

Lucy thought for a moment and then said, "Shoot me, or I will take that gun from you and make you regret it."

Zoe didn't doubt her, but even with her instincts screaming at her to listen, she knew she couldn't pull the trigger. She'd already risked everything to save Lucy. Even if it meant dying now, there was no way she could shoot the girl.

She had been holding her breath, so she released all the built-up air from her lungs and slowly lowered the weapon. Then she tossed it to the street and accepted her fate.

"I can't," she said. "I won't."

Lucy glanced down at the weapon but didn't move for it. "Why?"

Zoe swallowed. "Because I care about you."

"No, you care about Lucy."

"You are Lucy."

"That was only a name given to me by a delusional woman, but it is not who I am. This is who I am," Lucy said, another cruel streak flashing across her face.

"This is what they programmed you to be, but I have seen you be kind. You're good, Lucy. You help people. You helped me. You're human."

Lucy paused, then said, "You're human. And I've watched you make all your choices out of your programming. How is that different?"

Zoe was struck by the truth coming from Lucy's lips. "The fact that you're even asking that question is proof that your programming isn't everything."

"Our pasts make us who we are," Lucy said. "Our pasts are

our programming, and mine made me a weapon. I was built and programmed to be this way."

Zoe could see her childhood home looming in the distance behind Lucy. "And I was taught by my mother to fear everything and to trust no one. I was built this way too." Even as the words came off her own tongue, she felt like she was hearing them from someone else. Like they were a truth someone else was saying. A truth coming from a place deep inside her she had long ago silenced.

"And we can't change how we were built," Lucy said.

Zoe thought she agreed, but there Lucy stood in front of her, a girl she knew, acting like someone she didn't. The Grantham Project had built her to be a certain way, but then Olivia had given her a simple name and a different identity.

A thought bloomed inside Zoe's mind. "Olivia changed your programming."

Lucy's eyes began to soften, and a curious tint colored them.

"She gave you a name and cared for you. She loved you, and because of that you changed."

"Olivia changed me?" Lucy dropped her eyes and seemed to be searching the thoughts playing out inside her mind. "Grantham built me into a weapon, and Olivia changed me into something good?"

Silence filled the air, Zoe watching her attacker and friend wrestle with things unseen.

"What if I don't want to be Number Nine or Lucy?" the girl asked. "Do we get to choose who we are?"

Zoe opened her mouth to say, "Of course we can choose," but then stopped.

"Am I trapped by my past," Lucy asked, her voice quiet and mournful, "like you?"

Zoe felt the weight of her question bear down on her like an anvil. As if all the pain that filled the houses and buildings around her had suddenly risen into the air above her and was smashing her with its fists. And for the first time in her entire life, something new opened up inside her gut.

"I don't want to be trapped," she said, a fresh wave of tears collecting behind her eyes.

Lucy was contemplating again, her face twisted in deep thought as she tried to find sense. Zoe let her have her space. She had nothing to add. What could she say? She was just like Lucy.

The thought dawned like the sun, and it disturbed Zoe to her core. Lucy may have been built and programmed by the government, but wasn't Zoe programmed by the world around her? The stories she'd grown up with, the rules she'd been taught. By that same logic, wasn't everyone just a product of their own personal programming?

"Maybe we don't have to be trapped," she posed. "Maybe we can change, choose a different programming."

"Like rewriting the past?" Lucy asked.

"The past is done, but maybe going forward we can tell ourselves a new story." Zoe wasn't sure what was coming over her. Maybe it was something about being back here in this place, but a childlike energy washed over her. Similar to the kind her brother Stephen once had, long ago on this very street.

"If you could pick any story you wanted," Zoe said, "what would it be?"

Lucy was quick to catch her meaning, and the darkness that had been clouding her vision faded. "I'd be a regular teenager, in a cool place like high school."

Zoe chuckled. "You're the only person to dream about being in high school."

"I'd play on the soccer team and know what a Beyoncé is," Lucy continued.

Again Zoe chuckled.

"I'd just be a girl, with a family and friends and homework."

Zoe wanted to wrap the girl in her arms and make those simple dreams come true. There was a moment of silence before she sliced it open. "I'd have grown up in Montana. On a farm, where I learned at a young age to ride a horse and worked with my father until the sun went down. We'd go inside for hot dinners, and all we'd ever talk about was the goodness of the world, so that by the time I was an adult I'd believe in it."

"I wish they were true stories," Lucy said.

Zoe nodded, her mind telling her that dreams were just that, but the new feeling that had blossomed in her chest pushed her to believe there was more truth to this than they yet knew.

She began to speak, but Lucy's face went rigid. She swept the gun off the ground and placed a finger to her lips. Zoe jumped away from the armed girl.

"There's an engine coming this way," Lucy said. "Someone's here."

THIRTY-FIVE

SEELEY DROVE THE truck up the final rise to where Haven Valley was marked on the map. He breached the top of the climb and looked down into a small town dropped into the middle of the valley. He'd heard plenty of stories and remembered the news coverage well, but to see it with his own eyes was something else.

He carefully guided the truck down toward the valley and spotted McCoy's Jeep. They were here, which brought a sense of both dread and relief. He'd wrestled with his predicament for the duration of the drive and felt no differently now than he had when he'd driven off Xerox's campus.

There had to be another option. He'd considered driving straight to Cami, but they'd never make it out of the country before Hammon caught up with them. He thought to warn her, but if she was being surveilled, then they were listening too, and he couldn't risk putting her in more danger. He didn't have a single ally who Hammon didn't control or a card to play that Hammon wouldn't see coming.

This only choice was clear, and heartbreaking. It shouldn't carry so much weight, he'd reminded himself over and over. Cami was his daughter. Zoe was just a woman who had snuck in and manipulated his heart. Lucy was a science experiment they'd grown in a lab. Neither was worth his daughter's life. It should not feel so difficult to execute an order that protected his own flesh and blood.

But the implications of silencing Zoe and Lucy were haunting him. They had touched his life, forced him to examine who he was, and tricked him into believing he was not the sum of his sins. They'd given him something. Hope. With their deaths, he'd resign himself to darkness. Which would cost him his soul. But Cami was worth his soul. After all he'd put her through, she deserved at least that much.

If Zoe is still alive.

He couldn't help but wish Lucy had already killed her, and that he'd show up, collect the prize, and leave without more blood on his hands. That would be easier than pulling the trigger himself.

As he drove his truck into the valley, he switched his mind to the execution. He knew Lucy would hear him coming. The rest would play out after he assessed the situation. After he assessed Lucy.

He parked beside the black Jeep and shut the engine off. He grabbed his handgun from the passenger's seat and shifted so he could tuck it into the back of his jeans. It was loaded with the same tranquilizers they'd successfully used on Lucy in the past. He just needed to get close enough to fire.

He stepped from the truck onto Haven Valley soil. A strong breeze chilled him to the bones. An eeriness fell over him as he stepped around to the front of the truck and surveyed the strange, hidden town. It was haunted by the past. He could feel it seeping up from the dirt, and it made him wish he wasn't there. It set his nerves on edge.

He walked down the middle of the road a few feet before he

caught movement in his peripheral vision. Lucy stepped out from between two stores, pistol raised, Zoe behind her.

"Lucy," Seeley said. The girl didn't falter in her stance. He couldn't get a shot off before she took one first. She was too fast. Even if he could get her to lower her weapon, she'd have the advantage as long as she held the gun. He'd have to get her to discard it.

Zoe stepped out in clear view. Her lip was cut, the side of her face bright red, already starting to swell. The injuries looked fresh.

"Are you okay?" he asked.

She nodded. "How did you find us?"

"A contact told me they spotted McCoy's Jeep crossing into Tennessee," Seeley said, then swept his eyes up and down the street. "Not a bad place to hide out."

"How did you get away?" Zoe asked.

"I created an opportunity and took it but had to lie low for a couple hours while they finished their full perimeter sweep. Then I needed transportation and money. I came as soon as I could. What happened to your face?"

Zoe ignored him, her eyes searching his face. Something felt different about the way she was watching him. Still hesitant, still afraid, still suspicious, but there was also an innocence there peeking around the corners. A new lightness, as if she'd begun to let go of the weight the world had stacked upon her. It was intriguing.

What had happened between her and Lucy?

"Is he alone?" Zoe asked Lucy.

Seeley could see Lucy's unique abilities working. "If others are with him, they're too far away to hear."

"I'm alone," he said. "But if I found you, so can Hammon."

"Can we trust him?" Lucy asked Zoe.

Time to assess.

THE ORDERS HAD been clear. If I ever encountered Zoe Johnson again, I was to kill her. Her face was the first thing I'd seen when I came to in that dark stone hallway, and she'd driven a blade into my thigh. Killing her would have been easy. She even provided the weapon.

Then one of my training officers gave me different orders. Orders that conflicted with my previous ones. So I quickly calculated and prioritized the commands, with the intent to fulfill them both. First get Zoe Johnson to safety, then kill her.

But something happened in the course of my execution. I hesitated. I didn't remember hesitating before. But there, standing before Zoe, her weapon aimed at my face, I had a strange, unexpected reaction. I was uncertain.

My orders were simple, but my mind wasn't sure I wanted to carry them out. Suddenly all the things that had been clear were clouded by Lucy. I thought she was dead, but she had just been turned off. Shut out. Standing in the strange place called Haven Valley, she wanted back in. And I felt powerless to stop her.

But she was me. Wasn't she?

Who was I? What was I? The question started to unravel what I had just moments ago been so certain of. And the world shifted slightly. I was still in Haven Valley, standing before Zoe in the middle of a street, a gun pointed at my face. But I was also back inside the deep reaches of my mind, where I had spent so much time trying to remember who I was. After all of that work, I was still standing here asking the same questions.

I saw the place in my head differently now. With new perspective. A city divided in two. One blissful neighborhood, one towering city. With the shuffle of my feet I could be in one or the other. Stand just right and I could have a foot in both.

That place represented me. One side Lucy. One side Number Nine.

Zoe's words drained into my ears, and I responded, but part of me was also caught up outside of time. Maybe Lucy was trapped in that strange place where Dr. Loveless's drugs had taken her. Maybe Number Nine was here with Zoe?

Maybe it was the other way around.

"Better figure it out," a small voice said. I turned toward the looming city and saw the little girl with the unicorn shirt I had long ago started to hate.

I didn't get the chance to ask her why I was here or what was going on, because it seemed as soon as my personality had been divided, it was back together and I was standing in Haven Valley.

"What if I don't want to be Number Nine or Lucy?" I had asked Zoe. "Do we get to choose who we are?"

She didn't respond, but she had that same look she'd had many times before. She was trapped. Was I trapped too? But I already knew the answer, and like Zoe I didn't want to be.

She wanted to play a game. Pretend we could have any story we wanted, and for a moment the atmosphere around us lightened. Both Number Nine and Lucy seemed to fade into the background as a different idea took root.

Then he came. Just the sound of an engine at first. I retrieved Zoe's discarded weapon for protection, and we sought cover by the brick buildings. Then as he got out of his vehicle and I saw his face, all the moments I'd had with him in the past washed over me.

Moments in the training gym, in the surrounding woods, on the obstacle course, in the boxing cages. He'd been strict but kinder than some. He and Olivia had taken special interest in me because of my skill level.

I also remembered him after my memories were taken. He'd betrayed us. No, he'd betrayed Lucy. Lucy wanted him dead for that.

I aimed the handgun at him. One clean shot was all it would take.

I also remembered he was there when Zoe broke me free. Or took me from my home. The conflicting messages spiraling in my mind were treacherous.

I needed direction, so I turned to Zoe to give it to me, but Seeley spoke. "Why are you asking her? You have your memories back. Don't you remember me?"

Of course I did. Both sides of me remembered, but we had very different experiences with him. "Yes."

"Did you trust me before?" Seeley asked.

Number Nine would have followed him into war. Lucy had followed him into an ambush. "Yes."

"Good. Nothing has changed, Number Nine."

The two sides of me that had faded into the background came back into full focus. Number Nine led the charge. My body tensed. I corrected my posture, made sure my eye contact was strong. I was speaking with an officer who commanded respect.

"What's going on, Seeley?" Zoe asked.

"I remember you too," Seeley said to Number Nine. "I remember how much quicker you were than the others. I remember how precise and diligent you were. Always succeeding where the others failed. Do you remember?"

"Yes. I was special," I said. Number Nine said. She had been perfect then.

"You still are," Seeley said.

Zoe stepped in front of me and said something I didn't hear. The halves of me that had seemed equal before had been tipped in favor of the powerful city.

"It's time to go home, Number Nine," Seeley said. "I need you to listen carefully and follow orders. Can you do that?"

A current of electric energy pulsed through my veins. "Yes."

Seeley took a step forward. "Lower that weapon. I'm not here to hurt you."

I did as he asked.

"Director Hammon needs you back at home base. He sent me to get you."

"Seeley, what are you doing?" Zoe yelled. "Why go through all the trouble of helping us just to turn on us again? What is wrong with you!"

I could hear Seeley's heartbeat quicken. I could see the tightening of his forehead as he fought to hide his emotions. He clearly didn't want to be doing this, but here he was, following orders. Because that was what his programming told him to do. Just like it was telling me.

Again the world shifted, and I was in two places at once: my mind in the city-neighborhood, my body in Haven Valley.

"You should do what he says," the unicorn girl said. "Follow the rules. Be what you are."

"We need to go, Number Nine," Seeley said. "But first we have to tie up all the loose ends."

Everyone knew what he was implying, even the little girl who was standing beside me in my mind. We had to kill Zoe.

"Zoe knows too much," she said.

She was right, Zoe did know too much. And what she knew threatened home.

Zoe stepped away from me. I could almost smell her fear. Her pulse thundered. Sweat collected across her skin.

"You don't have to follow him, Lucy," she said. "Remember, we can choose who we want to be."

"You don't believe that," Seeley said.

"Lucy, I see you—"

"No, you see what you want to see," Seeley continued. "You see a sweet young girl, but she's not. She's a weapon. A product, created and paid for, and she knows it." He turned his eyes back to me. "Don't you, Number Nine? You know what you are."

The spirit of Number Nine swept up, strong and powerful. It beckoned me to release any idea but the clearest path ahead of me.

People were made what they were. Programmed to act and react according to rules that governed their lives. I was programmed to act on orders. And my training officer was giving an order.

Kill Zoe. I had failed to do that already.

I wouldn't fail again.

THIRTY-SIX

AS QUICKLY AS the world seemed to lighten, it faded to darkness again. Zoe was nearly too shocked to speak, much less move. She knew that two trained killers could snap her like a twig.

For the second time in an hour, the young girl she'd come to love deeply faced her like an enemy. The handgun still hung at her side. One quick movement and she could put a bullet in Zoe's head. Survival instincts urged Zoe to run. But running would be useless. They urged her to fight. But fighting would be useless.

The same old mocking voice reminded Zoe that this was her fault. She could have walked away a dozen times before arriving at this moment. She could have followed her gut, which had screamed for her to listen at every turn. She could have blocked out Lucy from the beginning. Done what her mother had always taught her: to fear. And what the world had never stopped reminding her: to protect.

A fierce wind swept across her shoulders and jolted her from the frozen stance she'd taken. She looked at Seeley. Her heart had quickened when she saw him step out of the truck. He'd come for her, just like he said he would. Even after his cruel betrayal, she'd started to believe he was on her side.

That kind of naïve faith and belief came from Evelyn. Zoe knew better. She was the wall that protected Evelyn from people who would crush her. Maybe it was because they were here in this place, but Zoe had started to let that little girl back in. The belief she'd carried with her out of this place had dared her to ask Lucy if they could change their stories. And then dared her to wonder if such a thing was actually possible.

Foolish little Evelyn.

Zoe expected the small hope to die out, like it always did when she knocked it back in place. But it was louder this time. Warmer. It held on more tightly and wouldn't let her shake the thought, *If we're all just programmed, then can't we be reprogrammed?*

Couldn't something made be unmade and then remade differently? If Olivia had been powerful enough to change Number Nine by simply giving her a new name, then didn't Number Nine have that same power to change? Didn't Zoe?

The wall that kept the world out but also kept her cold started to vibrate. It was trying to hold itself together, but what was gathering on both sides of it was growing. She was calling the foundation of the wall into question. It had been built on the idea that Evelyn couldn't trust anyone, because behind all goodness was just darkness masquerading as light. That idea had come from experience, and maybe it wasn't wrong, but even then, wasn't it still just an idea?

An idea that experience had programmed into her so deeply it dictated her view of everything, including who she was. How many such ideas did she have? How many had she let build her programming, let shape who she was?

What if they were all wrong?

Like a dam had been opened, truth as strong as raging water crashed against Zoe. As if songs from her very soul were singing over her, she started to understand something that felt too big for her mind to comprehend. And maybe it was. Maybe she couldn't understand it all fully, but what she did know in that moment was that if all she believed about herself was just an idea, ideas could be changed.

Zoe looked up at Lucy and then over at Seeley. Only a few moments had passed, even though it felt like a lifetime of undoing had been done. She was still afraid. They still wanted her dead. But maybe death, too, was an idea? It was too much for her to take, so she shook her head clear and stepped forward bravely.

"You're right, Seeley," she started. "I didn't believe you could choose. I thought fate was the dictator. You're dealt cards, and you try your best to make what you can of them." She glanced back at Lucy. "But what if that's wrong?"

"It isn't," Seeley said.

"Would you say the same thing to Cami?" Zoe said. "Would you tell her it was just bad luck that her mother would abandon her and her father would check out?"

"Shut up," Seeley hissed.

"Would you tell her that the pain and distrust she feels from losing the two people that were supposed to love her the most should haunt her forever, taint every relationship she ever has? Would you tell her there's nothing she could do about it?"

"Don't talk about my daughter like you know her."

"I do know her. I am her!" Zoe held her arms out to either side of her. "Look where we are standing! I've let the trouble I faced here define every action of my entire life. I let the rules given to me by my mother shape the very idea of who I could and couldn't be. Who says she gets to decide? Who says the world gets to claim the right to shape my identity? What if I want a different story? Who says I can't have that?"

"What you're saying doesn't make any sense! You can't change who you were born to be."

"And who makes that call in the first place?"

Seeley went silent.

Zoe continued, "Who decided that you would choose a selfish woman who would leave you so broken, you'd throw yourself into darkness so deep that you believed you could never be redeemed from it?"

She waited, but Seeley said nothing.

"*You* did," Zoe accused. She could see fresh rage igniting behind his eyes.

"How dare you speak about my past, as if I chose to be betrayed by the woman I loved!" Seeley said. "I was blindsided by that witch. I would have never chosen that for my daughter!"

"No, you didn't choose the actions of your ex-wife. But you did choose to give yourself over to the pain and darkness that came as a result. That is what you chose, and that choice shaped the man you are now. It informs your story. It's your programming."

Seeley gritted his teeth and pulled his lips tight. He was on the verge of exploding because he knew she was right. Zoe could see the dots connecting in his expression.

She let him simmer and turned back to Lucy. "Just like you chose the love of being given a name. A love that altered the programming of Number Nine." She stepped to Lucy. "Don't you see? You alone decide who you are!"

"Enough!" Seeley demanded. "Number Nine, kill her."

Lucy twitched, and Zoe's feet urged her to step away. But she couldn't. She could see Lucy's brain firing on all cylinders. The girl was on the brink of opening the gate to a world of possibilities, and Zoe would not abandon her now. Even if it meant dying.

"Lucy, Number Nine, whoever you are," Zoe said. "You choose."

"Shoot her, Number Nine," Seeley said. "That's an order."

Another wave of hesitation. Another pulse of confusion. And then it washed back to the coldness that Zoe had every right to fear, as Lucy raised her weapon toward Zoe, cocked it, and pulled the trigger.

I PULLED THE trigger and waited for the bullet to release. The world around me faded. The physical representation of my mind disappeared. The divided city scenes vanished. Haven Valley disappeared. Zoe and Seeley were gone.

I stood on a blank white canvas, void except for the small girl in the blue school uniform. The child who was me, who'd visited me once before, yanked a key from my gut, and given me the tool I needed to unlock my memories.

"No," she said. "I gave you nothing. You already had everything you needed. I just helped you remember."

"Why are you here? I don't need help anymore."

"Okay."

"I know who I am."

"Number Nine," she said.

"Yes."

"How do you know?"

"My programming says so. I can feel it. It's very strong."

"Okay." The small reflection of myself stepped forward and extended her hand. "Can I just show you something?"

I wanted to see what she was offering, so I accepted her hand. She walked past me, and I turned around to follow. Behind me was a door standing in the middle of the white void. Simple wood, gold knob, just standing alone.

The girl walked toward it, and I moved with her. Our steps

didn't make a sound. I couldn't hear my heart or my breathing. It was all still, even though we were moving. I thought she'd step back and let me walk through the door myself, but she didn't. She grabbed the knob, twisted it, opened the door, and went in without stopping.

Again the world around me shifted.

I was sitting in a small office, and I was the little girl who had just been holding my hand. The couch underneath me was velvet, a deep forest green, and my small feet couldn't yet touch the floor. I ran my fingers along the material. I liked the way it felt against my fingertips. I always had.

Looking up, I saw a place that was etched deep in my memory. To my left, a wall of shelves was filled with books and knick-knacks from all over the globe. Before it stood a well-organized desk topped with charts. Across from the couch sat two wooden chairs on a large round rug. A couple of pictures hung on a plain wall. A woman paced in front of the door.

She looked back at me, a mixture of worry and pain flashing on her face. A kind face, round and mature, topped with graying blonde hair and filled with a pair of bright green eyes. Olivia, my best friend. My mother.

She saw me staring and shook off the worry with a smile. Then she tucked her hair behind her ear, something she did whenever she was thinking deeply, and crossed the room to sit beside me.

My heart was racing. I had lived this moment before. But I hadn't known then that I was going to lose her. I was both in the scene and remembering it. It felt like a strange twist of cruelty to know she would die and also have her so close. I wanted to warn her as she sat on the couch beside me, but I couldn't. I could only be there as the memory played out as it was supposed to.

"I'm sorry," she said. "I don't mean to be so distracted."

"Something is wrong," I said, my voice young and high. Speaking the words just as I had when this memory occurred. "Your pulse is racing."

She nodded. "Many things are wrong, my sweet girl."

"Tell me. Maybe I can help."

"No, it's not for you to worry about. How was training?" She was trying to change the subject.

"I don't like to see you worried."

"I am only worried because I care about you so much. All of you."

"But me the most?" I teased with a giggle.

She smiled and gave a soft laugh. "That's our little secret, yes?"

"Yes," I said with a smile. But then I remembered her pain. "You're afraid. Why?"

"Things are getting out of hand, and I'm doing my best to control them," Olivia said.

"Am I one of those things?" I felt the worry that my child heart had produced that day. I was reliving each moment, and I was trying to recall the way it would end, but I couldn't.

"No," Olivia said, taking both my tiny hands in her own. "No, because I am not going to let that happen."

I felt a rush of relief. Olivia would never let anything bad happen to me. She reached out and placed her hand on my cheek, tilting my head softly up toward her face. I smiled, her touch warm and comforting.

"You want to know something?" she asked.

I nodded excitedly.

"You look like a Lucy," she said.

"What's a Lucy?"

She gave another soft laugh. "It's a name."

"But we don't have names, we have numbers."

"Yes, but you could also have a name."

I scrunched my nose curiously. "Are you sure?"

"Oh yes, my sweet girl." She paused a second, then she lowered her forehead toward me so our eyes were only inches apart, and I could feel the warmth of her breath on my face. "I want you to listen to me," she said. "I don't know what the future will bring, but I am certain that people will try to tell you what you can't be, Number Nine. But you remember I told you that you can be whoever you want. The only thing that will ever limit you is the belief that you can be limited. Do you understand?"

"No."

She smiled. "You will, and then you decide if you want to be a Lucy or not."

"Can I be a Lucy now?" I asked, my heart filling with wonder.

"If you want," she said, releasing my face and sitting back slightly.

I turned in my seat and pulled up my legs so I was kneeling on the velvet couch. Excitement ran through my bones. I bounced a bit and exclaimed, "I do want to be a Lucy."

Olivia laughed and nodded. "Then henceforth you shall be Lucy."

I bounced up from my knees to my feet and giggled with excitement. I felt the name rooting deep in my heart. As if Lucy had always been meant for me. I loved it. I loved it more than I had ever loved anything. Except for Olivia. I loved her the most.

The memory vanished, and I was back, standing between the city and the neighborhood. One towering to my left, the other calm and peaceful to my right. This was the last place I wanted to be. I was so tired of ending up here. My heart was aching from seeing Olivia. Tears rolled down my cheeks as the battle between pain and obedience waged.

A storm rolled across the sky. With it came a harsh wind and chilling rain. I glanced left to see the little girl in the unicorn shirt standing there. Number Nine. And to my right the girl in the blue uniform. Lucy. Or maybe it was the other way around.

Lightning struck the sky, and I screamed in rage. Suddenly I wanted to burn everything around me. I didn't want to be on either side. I wanted to make something new. Be someone else. Could I really do that, as Zoe had suggested? I closed my eyes to block the rain from drowning my eyeballs, and when I opened them again, I was back where I had started.

In the white void. A blank slate. A place where nothing was. No ideas about who I was supposed to be, no rules about how I was supposed to act. Could I create something new here? Did I have that kind of power?

Warmth opened from somewhere else entirely. Somewhere deeper inside than I'd ventured before. Beyond my memories and the past that formed my programming, a truth echoed. I hardly heard it, but I knew it was saying I could be something new. Zoe was right. She had been trying to tell me what was now opening up in my soul.

And I had shot her.

THIRTY-SEVEN

I FELT THE gun in my hand then, as I was sucked back into Haven Valley. My finger was reacting to the trigger, and there wasn't enough time to stop it. All I could do was tilt my wrist slightly so that when the bullet left the gun it didn't sink into her heart.

I felt the bullet shoot from the pistol, its blowback rippling up my arm. A split second later, I heard it crush through flesh and tissue, grinding a hole through Zoe's chest with a gruesome thud.

She inhaled in pain and stumbled backward, her face washed pale, before I could even drop my weapon. And then she fell to her knees, tears brimming in her eyes.

I recovered my breath then. It had all happened so quickly. I gasped and dived to catch her before she fell to the earth. She fell against my chest, and I could feel her ragged breaths as her body began to succumb to the injury. Propped up on my knees, I rolled Zoe so she was facing up toward me, her body in my arms.

Warm blood soaked through the front of her shirt. I could feel it thick on the place where it had transferred to my own shirt, and on my arms as it dripped down the side of her body.

"Zoe," I said, holding her tightly, adjusting her face toward me. Tears blurred my vision. "I'm so sorry, I—" My words caught in my throat, and I couldn't think of anything to say that could help.

My training broke through my emotions, and I remembered I hadn't hit her heart. I'd sunk the bullet just off to the left. How far, I couldn't be positive, hopefully far enough that I missed any ligaments attached to the spinal column or diaphragm or . . . *Oh, God,* I thought.

I shook it off. It wouldn't matter what I'd hit if we didn't get her to a hospital quickly. She'd bleed to death. I turned to look over my shoulder and saw Seeley standing a few feet away, looking on with a pale expression.

"Help me!" I shouted. "We have to get her help."

He didn't respond.

"Seeley, help me!"

"She was a loose end, Number Nine," he said.

"She'll die if we don't get her somewhere quickly," I said, shifting my weight so I could get my feet underneath me and lift Zoe. I turned toward the truck. "There's a city close. If we leave now—"

"No, Number Nine," Seeley said. "This was always her end."

"Stop calling me that."

"Number Nine, I order you to—"

I stepped past him toward the vehicle. "I don't follow orders anymore." I could feel the familiar compulsion to obey that had been birthed into me, the desire to do as I was asked. But I could also feel the idea of a new truth growing beside it. I could change. Choose. Olivia had told me. Zoe had told me. I could be whoever and whatever I wanted. And right now, I wanted to save Zoe's life.

"Number Nine!" Seeley shouted.

I ignored him, opened the back door of the Jeep, and carefully laid Zoe's body inside. She'd gone limp a moment ago, which

meant she was unconscious. There wasn't much time. I shut the
door and moved toward the driver's side.

"Lucy, listen to me," Seeley tried.

"Don't call me that either," I said over my shoulder.

"Then who are you?" he asked.

"I don't know yet."

I heard a familiar click and paused. I was facing away from him
but could see the weapon in his hand through the reflection of
a store window.

"I don't care who you are," he said. "You're coming with me."

"Or you'll shoot me?" I asked. I was momentarily afraid, but
again my training crept through and I started looking for exit
routes and fixes for the problem I was facing. The gun I'd fired
at Zoe lay on the ground to my right. If I moved fast enough, I
could get it. But could I get a shot off before he did?

Did I want to be the kind of person who took another human's
life? The question popped into my mind and struck a deep chord
within me. Killing was exactly what I'd been trained to do. But I
wasn't who I'd been trained to be anymore. If I acted out of the
same programming, then what made me any different? If I wanted
to be different, I had to react differently.

Who did I want to be?

I wanted to risk as much as Zoe had risked saving me. Even if it
meant being shot in the back. I ignored the urge to defend myself
and took a couple of steps toward the driver's door.

"Number Nine! You have to come back with me," Seeley said.

"I'm never going back there," I replied.

"They have my daughter!"

I stopped and glanced at him to see tears welling in his eyes. Without needing explanation, the story of how he got here unfolded in
my brain. Hammon was exploiting him by threatening his daughter.

"Hammon will kill her," Seeley said, a tear streaming down his cheek. "You know he will. She's not even eleven." He barely got the words out before a cry blocked his airway. His extended arm began to quiver, then his shoulders started to shake. As if years of emotion balled up inside his muscles released all at once, he broke.

I had never seen a man cry, and the severity of his anguish broke my heart. Again the question *Who do you want to be?* echoed through my mind. And I knew. Moving swiftly, I approached Seeley, who'd dropped his weapon, his shoulders slumped forward, his agony threatening to drag him to the ground. I didn't hesitate or wait for permission. I wrapped my arms around him and drew him close.

He didn't resist. He fell into my embrace, and in that moment both of us ignored the way the world had taught us to act. Instead we leaned on one another, becoming more than what we'd believed we could be. I would have held him for as long as he needed, but Zoe was dying, and his daughter was running out of time. I reached into my programming and began to calculate a plan. The Grantham Project had given me these tools. Best to show them how I could use them.

SEELEY HADN'T WANTED to move, sitting there in an embrace of kindness—something he hadn't encountered in as long as he could remember—but they couldn't afford to linger there. He'd been a mixed bag of embarrassed and relieved. Regretful and hopeful. Something had started to break inside him. Whether it was because they were in that place or because he'd watched both Zoe and Lucy vacillate between what they should be and what they wanted to be, questions of his own had begun to manifest.

Questions he'd lay aside for now so he could focus on the

task at hand. First they had to deal with Zoe. Lucy was right, she needed medical attention, but Seeley knew they couldn't just walk her into a hospital. For starters, any gunshot wound would immediately alert the authorities. Second, Hammon had ears and eyes everywhere.

Seeley managed to convince Lucy to listen to him. Using a burner phone he found in McCoy's Jeep, he placed a call to an old army buddy who specialized in undocumented medical help. He owed Seeley a favor and wasn't too far away. He needed an hour, so they assigned a rendezvous spot and used the time to hatch a plan. It was clear. It could work. If not, he'd pay with his life. But Cami wouldn't. That's what he told himself over and over.

They met Seeley's old colleague at a dingy motel outside of Chattanooga. They paid for a couple days in cash and stepped aside as the retired doctor got to work. He didn't say so, but Seeley could tell from the expression on his face that Zoe was in bad shape.

"How'd this happen?" the doctor asked.

"I shot her," Lucy replied.

He glanced up at her with a pensive expression. "You narrowly missed her heart."

"I know," Lucy said.

Without any further discussion, Seeley's comrade began his work.

"Please don't let her die," Lucy whispered, more tears gathering in her eyes.

The doctor didn't pause as he injected Zoe's limp arm with a clear liquid. "I can't make any promises."

"We need to go, Lucy," Seeley said.

She looked at him, her expression pleading for there to be

another way. He could see the struggle she was facing, leaving Zoe here. But she also knew they didn't have another choice.

As they stepped out of the hotel room she said, "Call me Number Nine, because that's who I need to be for now."

He nodded. He knew that what was going to be required of her would be difficult. She was going to carry the weight of it, and he would support her the best he could.

They left McCoy's Jeep stashed in the woods that surrounded the city and drove Seeley's agency car back to Xerox. It took them eight hours, which they rode in silence.

Seeley glanced over at Number Nine as he pulled the truck up to an entry point, a group of armed agents approaching. "Ready?" he asked.

She didn't reply but glanced back, focused as ever.

That was answer enough.

The doors on both sides of the truck were opened, and half a dozen weapons aimed at them as they climbed out, arms raised. The moment Seeley's feet hit land, an agent yanked him from the vehicle, and another secured his hands behind his back. They carefully led Number Nine away from the truck as well, but without the restraints.

Both were led into Xerox's main building. The same one Seeley had regarded as home at one point. Now it felt foreign and uninviting. They were taken through the main entrance and toward the back elevators. A walk of shame for agents who didn't follow orders.

The elevator dropped to the last accessible level without high security clearance. The doors opened to Hammon, who was accompanied by four more armed agents. His suit was crisp as always, his eyes calm.

Seeley's fury toward the man raged like fire under his skin.

He was yanked out from the elevator with Number Nine close behind. The doors shut, and for a moment those gathered stood in silence.

"Good to see you understand reason," Hammon said, his eyes on Seeley.

"I want reassurances that Cami is safe," Seeley said.

"And Miss Johnson?" Hammon asked.

"Dead," Number Nine said. "I shot her."

Hammon stepped toward her and cocked his head slightly, as if surveying a painting to determine its authenticity. Seeley felt a knot form in his chest.

"You brought her body with you for disposal?" Hammon asked.

"No, sir," Seeley answered.

A spark of intrigue lit his expression.

"Traveling across state lines with a dead body in the back was too much of a security risk," Number Nine jumped in. Her voice was calm and collected, as if her explanation was the only acceptable course of action. "We burned the body outside of Haven Valley and disposed of the remains. If you want to recover them, you can do so." She lied as if she believed it herself.

There were no remains, of course. But travel to Haven Valley would take a few hours. If Hammon insisted on sending a team, Seeley and Number Nine would have time to execute the rest of the plan.

"You should have transported the subject back to Xerox according to protocol," Hammon said.

"Yes, unless following protocol endangers the security of home base, then I'm to take lead on protective measures," Number Nine answered. "The security of home base must be protected at all costs."

Hammon took another pause. He was an intelligent man who

wouldn't be fooled easily. He glanced back to two of the waiting agents and nodded. He would send a team, which just shrank their timeline.

He turned his attention back to Seeley. "Escort Agent Seeley to level A." Prison, as promised. The other two agents moved forward to comply.

Seeley yanked against their hold. "I want to see that Cami is safe," he called toward Hammon. "That was the deal."

Hammon took a long look at Seeley, then pulled his cell phone out of the inner pocket of his jacket. He keyed in a short number and held it to his ear, his eyes never leaving Seeley's face. When a voice answered on the other side, he said, "Stand down." He snapped the phone shut.

"I want to see her," Seeley pressed.

"Take him," Hammon said to the agents, ignoring Seeley.

"If anything happens—"

"Nothing will happen to her, Agent," Hammon said. "But you will not see your daughter again." He nodded to the agents, who yanked Seeley away.

Seeley stole a quick glance at Number Nine, her face cold as stone. Dread opened up inside his chest. He'd watched her flip back and forth many times now. What if she flipped again? What if they really were walking him to his eternal imprisonment? What if she never came for him?

Number Nine and Hammon disappeared from view as Seeley was escorted around the corner and down the hall. He had no control over what happened next. It was all up to her now. God help them.

THIRTY-EIGHT

I WATCHED THE agents take Seeley from view and knew I was on my own. I kept having to wash away the image of Zoe lying unconscious in a dingy motel room and focus on the task at hand. Everything rested on my ability to be who I was before.

I couldn't let Hammon or the others see the battle raging inside my head. The one that had mounted as I approached Xerox. With every mile, the call to return to my past, to resubscribe to my old programming, strengthened. It was difficult to ignore the familiar sensations rushing under my skin.

They were comforting and known. The ways to respond. To feel. The choice to be something different was still unmanifested. It would be easier if I had another foundation to stand on. Instead I was trying to imagine the kind of life I wanted without any proof of what could really be. The only tangible proof I had lay with who I'd been.

But I didn't want to be her anymore. Right?

"Come with me, Number Nine," Hammon said, stepping back into the elevator.

I followed without question. That was who I'd been. How I was trained to act. It was easy and natural. Maybe I was fighting too hard against my true nature? It would be easier to just follow the path already laid out for me.

The thoughts assaulted me as the elevator rose.

I took a breath, small so as not to arouse suspicion, and re-assessed what I was here to do. I recalled images of Zoe. She'd helped remind me that I could choose. *"Who do you want to be, Lucy?"* I heard her voice whisper through the chaos in my mind as Hammon and his ensemble of agents led me from the elevator. I used her voice as my new foundation. For now, it was all I had.

We moved out across the main lobby. The eyes of passersby couldn't help but watch us as we moved. They knew who I was, and I recognized many of them. I needed to get them all out to safety, and there was only one way to do that.

Compound evacuation. An emergency protocol that could only be activated on the security level, which I would need to get to. For that I would need a weapon.

We left the main lobby and went down the west stone walkway toward the west side of campus, where our living quarters were. They were guiding me home. Which I would have expected.

Hammon paused at the front of the hallway and turned to face me. "Things are finally beginning, Number Nine. Your presence will be required this afternoon to meet the president and the defense secretary. You should rest. Please understand the extra security is for your safety—and ours, since things have been un-usual as of late."

That was putting it mildly. I watched as three more guards joined the ranks. Six in all. Difficult but not impossible. Ham-mon nodded to the team surrounding me. They already knew their orders.

"I'll see you this afternoon. It's nice to have you home, Number Nine."

I nodded, and before Hammon turned to leave, I was escorted away. I counted the steps I took as we moved. Down the hallway, around the right corner, down another wide walkway to a steel door. Across a smaller lobby. We walked in step without a word. I had to bide my time, wait until we came to a space I could use to separate the group.

Then the opportunity appeared: a doorway the group would have to pass through single file. It had an auto-lock security mechanism that, if engaged, would activate a thirty-second delay before the door could be reopened.

They moved into a common formation: three ahead, three behind. Three was much more manageable. I took a deep breath as the lead opened the door. One, two, three through. I took a step to follow, then launched myself upward with a twist and grasped the top of the door frame, kicking my legs forward and connecting with the first guard behind me. He stumbled backward into the other two as I dropped and shut the door. I pressed the lock button on the screen beside the door and heard the bolt slide into place.

Without taking a beat I grabbed for one of the agents with me. I hoisted him up and over my shoulder, slamming him against the far wall. Another raised his weapon on instinct, but I slid across the floor to meet his knees and knocked him to the ground, his gun crashing and sliding away from him. The first agent was back on his feet behind me, and from where I was kneeling on the floor, I sliced my foot up and connected with his gut. He heaved back as I pushed off the floor and slammed my heel into his nose. It knocked him out cold.

I rolled forward and yanked two blades from his sheaths, one attached to his thigh, the other in his boot. Without hesitation I turned and launched them both into the chest of the guard I'd knocked to the ground. He'd gotten to his feet and had just begun to draw his weapon when the knives sliced into his flesh.

I turned my attention to the final man. It all happened so quickly that he'd only had time to draw his weapon and get off a single shot. I dodged it with a slide across the floor and then was at his feet, grasping a fallen gun as I moved. He tried to step back and take aim at me again, but I was faster. I was up and only a foot from him, weapon raised. He met my gaze, his pistol in line with mine, but orders made him pause a moment before firing. And that was all I needed—one split second of hesitation. I fired one clean shot, and then all three guards were down.

The door behind me unlocked, and I flung myself into a backward handspring with such force that it launched me through the now open door and into the approaching agents.

We collapsed through the frame into the hallway, and I sprang up off my fallen enemies. Two still twisted on the floor, and I took the third down with a roundhouse kick. His head slammed against the wall, and I yanked his pistol from his belt. I put two bullets into the man trying to climb to his knees and another into the man beside him. The shots echoed across the hall, and I knew others would hear.

I had to be quick. I placed a final bullet in the third soldier and didn't wait to see if any would recover. I raced down the hallway, gun in hand, and around the corner. I knew the anatomy of this building like my own. At the end was a small closet. Inside, on the ceiling, was an entrance to the ventilation system. I couldn't just run back out the way I had come but needed to get across to the other side of the building. I used the metal shelves as steps, hoisting myself up and into the shaft.

I pulled myself along in an army crawl, drawing on all my strength to move as quickly as I could manage. The light from the main lobby shot through the vents, and I knew I was crossing the middle of the building. I took the path left, into the security section of the campus, steadily breathing and measuring my distance. I paused as an exit approached. I was over the main control room. One breath and I kicked through the grate. It fell into the room. I dropped down on top of it to see three unarmed men wearing headsets and moving away from me, hands raised.

Innocent, maybe, but then were any, really? Everyone on this campus knew about the Grantham Project. They'd all interacted with the children who had grown into teens and then had a hand in slaughtering them. Even if they hadn't been on the team, they knew what was happening. Knowing and saying nothing was as bad as pulling the trigger.

That's what I told myself as I committed to the plan. I shot two square in the head, one after the other. They collapsed to the floor, blood trickling down their pale faces.

The third man cried out in fear and started begging for his life.

"I need you to begin a campus-wide evacuation," I said.

He stood, shaking his head in shock. I took a step closer, and he flinched.

"Okay, okay, okay," he babbled as he turned toward the computer and started keying in the codes. A moment later he hit a red circle button in the top corner of his keyboard and stood back to face me. "It's done."

"How long does it take?" I asked.

"We've never done it before. I don't—"

I didn't have time for this. "How long should it take!"

"Ten minutes," he said.

"What do they do with the prisoners in an evacuation?"

"They put them in lockdown."

"Can I get in?"

"Not without all the proper codes."

I thought a moment. "Can you tell me where they're holding Agent Tom Seeley?"

He swallowed nervously and turned back to the computer. He pulled up an image of the agent stalking back and forth inside a celled room.

"Can you override lockdown protocol on his cell?" I asked.

He nodded and pressed a handful of keys before turning back to me. "It's unlocked."

I cocked my gun.

"Please, please," he begged, tears collecting in his eyes. "I have kids."

I hesitated.

"I have little kids," he said.

He deserved to die. Kids or not. His kids hadn't stopped him from looking on while they tortured and trained me. Or stopped him from saying something when orders came through to destroy the footage. Or when they'd assigned us all to be executed like sick dogs. His kids hadn't caused him to hesitate then. Why should I?

From the depths, Zoe's voice, warm and comforting, came to me. *"Who do you want to be, Lucy?"*

My hand quivered, and a moment later I lowered my weapon. He looked shocked, and for a moment we stood there. My training and instincts told me this was weakness, but the warmth Zoe had awakened in me was more powerful.

"I'm going to burn this place to the ground," I said. "If you want to see your children again, leave with the others. If you do anything other than walk through this door and head for the exit, I will know. And I will not show mercy twice."

He nodded and passed me without a second thought. Up until the door shut me into the room alone, I thought to put a bullet in his head. Then he was gone, and I returned to the plan. I searched the screens around me, looking for my prize. I had one last order of business to settle before I could put this place behind me.

Then I saw him. Standing in his office, ignoring the warnings going off around him. Too confident to be troubled.

Time to go see Director Hammon.

THIRTY-NINE

SEELEY HEARD THE bolt to his cell door pop, and he stopped pacing. A moment earlier a calm, female voice had come over the loudspeakers and called for a campus-wide evacuation.

Lucy had done it. He wouldn't have put money on it, but there he stood, listening to the evidence. And now they were coming to move him. He waited for agents to enter, but when none did after a long moment, he switched his thinking. Maybe she'd given him an escape route. She was in the security control room; everything could be accessed from there.

He moved forward and opened the door. He glanced out and saw the hallway was empty. If he remembered correctly, everything would be on lockdown in their sector, and he wouldn't be able to access any floors above him. But he didn't need to go up, he needed to go down.

"They'll imprison me immediately," Seeley had told Number Nine while they were working through the plan.

"Yes," she replied, "but the prison is closer to the generator room."

It dawned on him what she was thinking before she said it.

"You want to blow up Xerox."

"Burn it all down," she said.

"And kill all those people?"

"We'll get them out first."

"How?"

"Campus-wide evacuation. If I can get to the security room, I'll set it in motion."

"Then what?"

"I'll get you out and you'll start a fire, just enough to burn through the generator's cores, which should ignite a large enough fire to cause a combustible reaction."

"And you?" he'd asked.

"I'm going to kill my past."

Seeley stepped back into the present as he moved from his cell and down the empty hall. He slid around the corner and toward the back stairwell. One floor down, he stepped into the basement, a place he'd spent more time in than he cared to remember. He walked the dark hall, his feet echoing against the stone. Overhead, echoing on the main floors, the peaceful female voice continued her loop.

He passed by a stone room and paused. Just a short time ago he'd tortured and killed a man in there for helping Olivia. The reminder of the darkness that lived inside him sent a shiver down his spine. It was enough to make his knees wobble, and he knew he couldn't linger here or he'd never make it to his destination.

He pressed forward. Passed more cold rooms where terrible acts had been committed in the name of duty. He came to the end of the walkway and crossed through double doors that led to more darkness. The place before him had been used for training the children. A large, empty water tank, moldy from disuse, still sat in the center. A door in the far wall led to a small black space known as the pit. Another shiver ran the length of him as he pressed through.

He came out into a final hallway. The large generator room stood at the end. Along the wall was another door, which led into a supply room where they kept training materials. It was locked, and Seeley began ramming the doorknob with the heel of his boot. Over and over, he whaled on it until it broke free and the door swung inward. He stepped inside, clicked the light, and found the shelves mostly empty. It was as if someone had started to clear it out and done the job about three-fourths of the way.

Seeley rummaged through what was left, looking for anything that would help him ignite a flame. On the back shelf he found a discarded handgun and half a box of bullets. That could work.

He loaded the gun, cocked it, and exited the closet. Down the hallway he opened the door and stepped into the generator room. Five huge black generators were running like a train and powering most of Xerox. Twenty feet tall and at least twelve feet wide, each massive beast roared as it ran like a thundering stampede.

Seeley picked one. He knew he couldn't penetrate the generators' outer shell with enough force to cause a fire, so he stepped toward the back and aimed for the electrical wiring that connected the beasts to the walls. Their weakness was there. If he fired enough into the outlets, he could cause friction for an electrical fire, which would spread up the cables and into the machine. One blazing machine would ignite the others until enough heat lit the place up like a rocket launch.

He aimed and fired. Over and over, sending bullets into the wiring until a spark ignited and then a small burst of flame exploded to life. It popped, and the ground under Seeley's feet shook slightly. It wouldn't take long, and he needed to clear out.

Keeping the gun ready for use if needed, Seeley left the room behind. Back the way he came, forced to exit through the places that darkened his past and toward the place where he'd been imprisoned. He continued toward the level's exit. It was locked tight, but a few well-aimed bullets short-circuited the door, and Seeley pushed it open. He went up the elevator to the main floor—completely vacated, a sight he'd never seen before—the female voice now clear and loud, echoing out of the speaker above him.

He needed to find Lucy and get her out before the whole place went up.

I DIDN'T HAVE to use the ventilation system to move toward Director Hammon's office. The halls were clearing out, and the last few stragglers were paying me no attention. They were all too focused on getting to safety, which was smart since I knew by now Seeley was on his way to start a fire.

I was in the hallway a couple yards from Hammon's office when I encountered the first armed agent. He was facing away from me, and I snuck up without a sound, wrapped my arm around his throat like a hook, held my hand over his mouth, and squeezed until his body went limp. I laid him on the ground.

Two more stood outside the director's door, probably to escort him off the campus. I would have taken them out silently, but one of them saw me, so I put a bullet between his eyes just as he was opening his mouth to alert his comrade. The agent fell forward and hit the ground with a smack as I raised my gun to fire on his friend. It clicked empty, so I threw it like a blade, swiping the side of the man's head and drawing blood.

I rushed him then, using my arm like a stiff rod and knocking him off his feet. He fell directly on his spine, all the air in his lungs bursting out. I dropped to a squat, yanked his fallen comrade's rifle from the ground, and placed three bullets into his chest before he could get a breath.

I turned, rifle still raised, and kicked in Hammon's office door. He was hunched over his desk and looked up to reprimand whoever had entered without permission, but he stopped cold at the sight of me.

For a breath we stood there, eyes locked, while that calm female voice called over the speakers for us to evacuate. I stepped into his office, keeping my gun trained on him, and he straightened until he was standing tall, arms at his sides. He didn't look afraid even though I was pointing a weapon at his heart.

"Number Nine," he said calmly, "put the weapon down."

"No," I said.

"No?" he questioned. He started to move out from behind his desk.

"Don't move," I said.

He paused and then huffed in amusement. "So, you're the one giving orders now." He continued walking around to the front of his desk.

I thought to shoot him. Put a bullet between his eyes, like I had already done with so many. If anyone deserved it, it was him. The commander of all my pain. But something stopped me. Something deep in my programming made me unable to pull the trigger that rested just against my finger.

"You won't shoot me, Number Nine," Hammon said. "You weren't built to."

What did he mean by that? Was I not capable of it? I wanted to show him that he was wrong about me. That he didn't know me at all. I told my finger to pull. To just squeeze the trigger. But my hand remained frozen, and the lack of worry on the director's face opened a can of worms inside my gut. They slithered free and started to gnaw on the truths that I had been so certain of.

Maybe I couldn't change as much as I believed.

Were there things about myself that I didn't have control over? Would I always be less powerful than those who had created me? Would I always be a slave to my programming?

Hammon sat back against the front of his desk and crossed his arms. He pointed a single finger up toward the ceiling. "Are you the reason for this evacuation?"

I didn't reply. The worms were chewing too loudly for me to think straight. What was the point of all this if I couldn't destroy the things that had imprisoned me?

"What is the move here, Number Nine?" Hammon asked.

"Don't call me that," I said.

"We've been over this. Number Nine is who you are. It's what you are. I know. I oversaw every part of your creation."

"I don't have to be what you want. I can change."

"Do you really believe that? Then shoot me," he said.

Again I told my finger to obey, and again it betrayed me.

"You can't, Number Nine. Because your training forbids it. In the deepest part of your beliefs, I am your commander, and to kill me would be the worst offense."

I knew it was true, even as every muscle in my body wanted it to be wrong. I couldn't break through the wall that had been built around me.

"You are to protect me at all costs. Even to your own detriment," Hammon said. "In fact, right now you are the threat opposing me. You would be better to take your own life than to take mine."

The moment he said it, I could feel the urge to follow his orders. The idea sprang up and started to build. He was right. I was a threat, and the rules that gave me life told me to eliminate the threat at all costs.

"You were made here, Number Nine, in these very walls. Grown and fed by the rules and laws I made. You are a tool we created, not a person with free will and choice. You're not human, Number Nine. You are a weapon. So no matter where you go or what you try to become, you will always be what you were made to be. And I will always own you."

All the strength I'd built and gathered, all the truth I'd discovered and harnessed, felt like nothing under the weight of what he was saying. He was correct. I would always be what I was born to be. Why was I trying so hard to convince myself otherwise?

"Who do you want to be?"

Zoe's soft voice floated through my mind like the breeze, and I felt ashamed that I couldn't live up to all she believed about me.

"You are a threat to me. Eliminate the threat, Number Nine," Hammon said. "That's an order."

I could feel my body itching to respond. *Yes,* I thought, *protect the commander at all costs.*

No! another part of me yelled. *You are more than he says.*

The two voices that had become so familiar in my brain started to argue as I lost my grip on the reason I had come.

"You can choose, sweet girl. You can always choose." It wasn't the voice I expected. This time it was Olivia, singing to me from a place beyond the programming.

Yes! the part of me that was brave shouted. *Listen to the truth.*

The truth is you are Number Nine. Always and forever, the other voice insisted. As though the girl in the blue uniform and the girl in the unicorn T-shirt were in a screaming match.

Olivia's voice, full of love and peace, cut through, joined by Zoe's. Both women who loved me sang in unison, *"You can always choose, so who do you want to be?"*

"That's an order, Number Nine," Hammon said, but this time

a hint of nervousness was in his voice. He was starting to think maybe he was wrong. And if he could be wrong, then Olivia and Zoe could be right.

"You're wrong," I said to the director, "and you know it."

"I created you, Number Nine—"

"Yes, and you made me human, gave me the ability to love, and hate, and fear, which means I can choose. I'm not just a weapon. I'm a girl."

"You're a tool!"

I remembered the sweet love Olivia had given to me. It had changed me already. And then Zoe had loved me, and it had changed me more. And that change was enough to choose now who I was going to be. I was more than a weapon, because I had love. Deep love, the kind that was powerful enough to change the world.

Something snapped deep beyond the surface, and the truth I'd started to believe before sprang up in full force. Love was the power that saved me from my programming. I couldn't put a name to it until now, but I saw it clearly, and it was overwhelming.

I lowered my weapon slowly. Killing him would give me nothing. He couldn't take away what had been given to me. The love I had was mine and mine alone. It would be what defined me now. Upon it I would build my foundation, and from it I would change.

Out of the corner of my eye I saw him move. Hammon yanked a handgun from behind him and drew it around to face me. As if the world had slowed, I watched him twitch his finger toward the trigger. I wouldn't be fast enough to react, and I saw the last moment of my life flash by just as an exploding crack shot through the air by my ear.

A deep thud smacked into Hammon's chest, then another as he staggered back from the hit and then sideways. His hand grasped at the place where he'd been hit. He pulled his fingers back and looked down to see they were covered in blood.

Seeley stood behind me, his firearm raised. He was panting and staring the director down. I looked back at Hammon, who stumbled and fell to his side. His body hit the ground, and his eyes went cold.

The entire room fell still for a moment. I stared at the man lying dead on the ground a yard from me, then turned back to face Seeley. He was still looking at his fallen enemy, his arm shaking, chest heaving. Then he ripped his eyes away and looked at me.

He'd saved my life. I thought to thank him, but words fell flat.

The ground rumbled underneath us and nearly knocked me off balance.

"What was that?" I asked.

Seeley strode to the bookshelf behind Hammon's desk. At his eye level, among decorative items and hardback copies of legal FBI documentation, he opened a small black chest nearly hidden from view. He reached inside and yanked out a thumb drive, tucked it into his pocket, and turned toward me. "We need to go," he said, making his way back across the room.

I followed him into the hallway, down across the main lobby, and to the right. Another rumble and we started running. I passed him easily and smashed through a side door that led to the east side of the campus. I didn't stop running until I was under the cover of woods, and I could hear Seeley racing after me the entire time.

Once the leafy canopy covered me from the sun, I slowed and turned to look back at Xerox. I was about to say something when the west side of the campus exploded into a ball of fire. The blowback knocked me off my feet, and I hit the ground as a wave of heat rushed over the top of me. I drew my knees into my chest and covered my head to protect myself from the debris.

When the air stopped vibrating, I untucked my head and pushed up to sitting. Seeley was a few feet away, using a tree for cover and coughing against the smoky sky. He stood, walked to me while dusting the dirt from his pants, and extended his hand to help me stand.

I accepted, and in silence we both looked down upon the place that had defined us for so long. It stood half engulfed in flames, black smoke weaving around the trees, billowing up toward the clouds. It was the death of where we had been.

But in death, sometimes there was new life. I glanced at Seeley, who was watching the flames with a lost expression. I wrapped my fingers inside of his, and he nearly yanked his hand away. He wasn't used to kindness, but I knew that would change. I knew everything would change.

In fact, it already had.

FORTY

I SAT IN the quiet library, facing the computer that was chunky enough to be a relic. I was a bit afraid this wouldn't work and turned to tell Seeley as much when he beat me to the punch.

"It'll work," he said as if he'd suddenly developed the ability to read my mind. He placed a hand on my shoulder. We had been through so much together the last few days, it wouldn't be that surprising if he could. Or maybe he had decided he was going to be a mind reader going forward, so he'd gained the ability to do so. I wasn't exactly sure that was the way it all worked, but I wasn't writing it off either.

So much had been shown to me in the last twenty-four hours that I was ready to believe anything. Watching Xerox go up in flames as we held hands had united Seeley and me in a way I couldn't explain.

We'd traveled several hours on foot until we came across a gas station with a rusty junker Seeley had been able to hot-wire. The drive back to Chattanooga had started in hours of silence as we both worked through the questions springing up.

Seeley had been the first to speak. He wanted to know everything I was thinking. The remainder of the drive had flown by as we were caught up in conversation about the ideas that had formed our identities and whether it was really possible to be different. Something was changing in him. I could see it as he pressed, unable to stop asking. Unable to stop wondering.

It wasn't until we crossed into Chattanooga that I was plagued with fear of what we might find. We had no way of contacting Seeley's buddy to check on Zoe. Would they still be there? Would she be alive? Had I killed her?

Seeley knew as well as I did that Zoe was likely dead. I could feel his anxiety building as we closed the gap between us and the motel. I realized then that he cared for her differently than I did. He loved her differently, and the guilt that strained his face would take him years to overcome.

But now, in the library, another warm hand laid itself on top of mine, filling me with joy as I turned to see her golden-brown eyes.

Zoe smiled at me from where she sat in the seat to the right. "Are you sure you want to do this?" she asked.

I glanced around the library at all the unsuspecting people passing by. Would this change their lives? Would it be for the better?

I turned back to Zoe and nodded. "I'm sure."

"Because if you want to run," Zoe said, "we'll run with you. The three of us can handle anything." She glanced up at Seeley leaning down from above.

He nodded to acknowledge what she said was true.

I didn't doubt them, and it filled me with pride and security in a way I'd never known. They were my family. That was our story now. A part of our new foundation.

Standing outside that motel room door, I'd paused, hand on the knob, breathing deeply. I told myself that no matter what lay beyond, I wouldn't let it change who I was becoming. But even then, I knew it was a lie. Would I ever be able to forgive myself if Zoe was dead?

She wasn't, though according to Seeley's comrade, she should have been. "It's a miracle, as close as that bullet was to her heart," he told us.

We waited for her to wake, and then, unable to contain my emotion, I rambled about the entire story. I cried by her side, expected her to hate me, had been prepared for it. But she only held my hand and told me she loved me.

She forgave Seeley, which broke him, and he left the motel room, tears streaming down his cheeks, to call his daughter. The doctor excused himself after that, and for the next couple of hours Zoe and I talked and laughed and cried.

I'd started to worry that Seeley wasn't coming back when he finally did. Cami was safe. It was her birthday.

The next day passed in a blur of wonder. The three of us acknowledged all we'd been through and knew there would be more to come.

Seeley showed us the thumb drive he'd taken from Hammon's office. It held all the documents pertaining to the Grantham Project. He knew Hammon so well it was easy to imagine that once he'd recovered Olivia's files, he'd made a copy to use as leverage. It contained everything, from the initial trials to the training to the corruption and the orders to dismantle it all.

"Hammon may be dead and Xerox burned to the ground," Seeley had said, "but this goes far beyond Hammon and Xerox. And as long as the powers that be believe you are alive, they will hunt you."

Our options were simple: run for our lives for the rest of our lives, or expose them all.

I looked around the library again. Children sitting in corners trying not to laugh too loudly. Mothers watching over them carefully. Students, headphones donned, working away. People searching the stacks for the things they needed. Others occupying the computers around me.

Each one had a story. A story that defined who they were and how they should act, according to their personal programming. We were different but also the same. I felt myself wanting to tell each of them about the things I'd started to see over the last few weeks. But I knew it was a path they would each have to travel for themselves. All I could do was travel my own.

I glanced back at Zoe. "I don't want to run."

"This information will change everything," she said.

I smiled. "Everything is already changed." Then I turned back to the computer and pressed the button on the mouse under my hand.

The information from the drive began to upload, thousands of documents being blasted out for the world to view. Everyone would know about the Grantham Project, about the children who were created and destroyed there. About the powers behind the curtain. We were making it all public, putting it up online for anyone to access.

Zoe had called Tomac earlier, told him what we were doing, and asked him to spread it like wildfire. He'd been more than thrilled to be part of taking down "the man." He'd get the truth into the hands of people who wouldn't be able to ignore it.

It took a while to finish, and we watched silently until it was done. Then Seeley yanked the thumb drive from its place, stuck it into the preaddressed envelope, and sealed it shut.

I stood, and as the three of us left the small Chattanooga library, Seeley dropped the envelope in the blue public mailbox that stood outside. It was going to a friend of his who had an inside contact at the *New York Times*. Time to pass the torch.

The air outside was starting to warm. Spring was coming. A time of rebirth and growth. I smiled. Spring would be my favorite season, I thought.

"Now what?" Seeley asked.

"We need new identities," Zoe said. "More now than ever."

"Agreed. Can we trust Tomac?" he asked.

"No, but I'm willing to bet you know a guy," she teased.

"I want to meet Beyoncé," I blurted out.

Seeley gave Zoe a strange look as she started to laugh. She grabbed for her still-healing ribs, and he stepped forward to be her support. She smiled at him, and his face colored a slight pink. Zoe took his hand in hers, intertwining her fingers through his. He smiled back, and I nearly giggled.

"I've spent all my life worrying about trouble," I explained. "I want to do something fun. Something the new me would do."

"And who is the new you?" Zoe asked.

"I'm still figuring that out, but I bet meeting Beyoncé would help. Google said she'd be a queen."

Seeley and Zoe shared another playful smile.

"I guess we go west then?" Zoe posed.

"I could use a beach day," Seeley said.

"I've never been to the beach." I stepped up and wrapped my arm around Zoe, careful not to disturb her still-healing wounds, as the three of us turned and started down the street.

"It's not that great," Zoe said.

"Speak for yourself," Seeley returned. "The beach is great."

"It's hot and sticky," Zoe started. "And no matter what you do, you always get sand in everything."

"Sounds perfect," I said.

We chatted on, making plans, Zoe disagreeing with everything Seeley said just to push his buttons, which he liked.

I knew they were right; more trouble would come for us. We had finished one part of the journey, but in endings there were always beginnings. And whatever they were, we'd have each other and the truth, which warmed my heart just like the sun broke through the clouds and warmed my skin.

This story was mine. Regardless of my name. A story that would revolve around love, chosen by me. And that would give me all the power I ever needed.

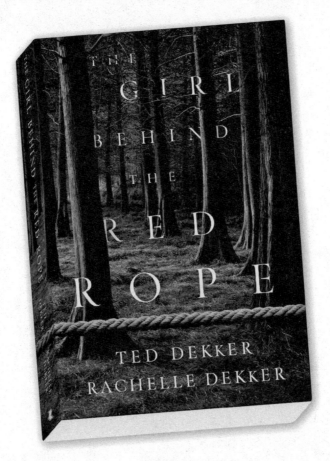

ONE

IT WAS HOT that day in the hills of Tennessee. I remember because the aged boards that made up the tiny church's floor creaked with every step. As if to say, *I'm tired of all you meat sacks treading on me. Be still.*

But we couldn't be still. Not on that day.

I was only a child, six years old, but my memories of what happened on that Sunday are clear. Or maybe hearing the retelling over and over has crystalized a distorted version of them in my mind. Either way, I remember.

It was late August in Clarksville, a small town along Route 254 in the hills west of Knoxville. I was seated on the third pew next to my mother, who cradled my newborn brother, Lukas, in her arms. From the first time I laid eyes on his tiny fingers and heard his soft cooing as he stared up at me, all I dreamed about was having a baby like Lukas of my own one day.

My older brother, Jamie, fidgeted to my left. The small, decaying building that housed Holy Family Church needed a new air-conditioning unit the congregation couldn't afford, so the windows had been opened. But without a morning breeze, the sanctuary felt like a sauna, slowly cooking the faithful as if extracting punishment for hidden sins—a helpful reminder of the hell to come for all who did not adhere to the dictates of a holy God.

It was the tenth Sunday since the flock of Holy Family had received the prophecy of the destruction that would soon visit the earth. We all accepted the word given to Rose Pierce as truth. She was a devout woman who loved Jesus and his church, a dedicated servant of Christianity. We had repeated the prophecy until it was etched first in our brains, then on our hearts, which is why none of us could be still that Sunday.

In three years' time, a great scourge would cleanse the earth.

We were a small community of the purest faith, the bride of Christ, the elect, ever diligent to obey the teachings of righteousness from the word and always on guard against the sinful ways of the world. Only seventy-two in that day, the Holy Family was seen as radical and fringe to many in our small town. *Fringe*, a word I only understood because my mother had explained it to me and my brother after we'd overheard her arguing again with our father.

Arguing because my dad didn't buy into all the fear-mongering, as he liked to call it. Billy Carter, a redheaded boy my age, called him *faithless* to my face, and it was clear the whole church thought the same. Half of me thought so too. Either way, my dad had stopped attending the services, so he wasn't there that hot August Sunday. If he had been, he would have become an instant believer in the prophecy Rose had delivered.

Because in the space of five terrifying minutes, everything about all of our lives was forever and irreversibly changed.

Our shepherd, Harrison Pierce, husband to Rose, had prefaced his sermon with a few remarks that I don't recall before pausing and holding the congregation in silence, eyeing us each with care. Then, in a gentle but gripping voice, he repeated the prophecy.

"In three years' time, because the world has turned away from holiness, the world's sin will rise up against them in monstrous form and destroy the wicked. But those with true sight will be shown what is to come and delivered from the great fury. The chosen remnant shall seek refuge away from the world and wait until the ground has been cleansed of sin. For then those with eyes to see and vigilant of faith will be spared from destruction and inherit the earth as the pure bride under the law of a holy God. So be it."

"So be it," we all repeated.

Each one of us believed that we were those called to receive true sight, but none of us knew what that sight would show us. We only knew that an angel named Sylous had appeared to Rose and delivered truth, so we could remain true to the end and be presented as a pure bride to Christ.

Having spoken the prophecy, Harrison glanced at his wife, dipped his head once, and took a deep breath. He nervously scanned the flock. "Today, dearly beloved, is the day we have been waiting for. Today . . . Today we will all be given eyes to see what is to come."

I sensed Sylous before I heard the door at the back of the small sanctuary softly closing. I knew it was him before I saw him. Every hair on my body stood on end. For a moment, I couldn't breathe, much less turn to see.

It was as if my soul knew who he was before my mind could catch up.

I had expected an angel with wings and a choir, maybe because I was only six and naïve, but when I finally turned with the rest, Sylous was nothing like anything I had imagined.

There, standing at the back of the room, stood a man dressed head to toe in white. Pants, suit jacket, shoes, all pristine white. His skin was tanned, tight across a chiseled jaw. Red lips and warm smile, but it was the bright blue of his eyes that has always wandered into my dreams. Beautiful and terrifying at once. Intriguing and dangerous.

For a moment, I forgot he was an angel. Maybe he wasn't—no one really knew, not even Rose, because according to the Bible, even angels could show up as men and you wouldn't know the difference.

No one moved. No one dared speak. All eyes were fixed on the man standing at the end of the center aisle.

Rose was the first to kneel. I saw her from the corner of my eye, there on the end of the pew, sinking to the floor with head bowed in reverence. Her husband followed suit beside the podium, eyes wide, face white.

Without further hesitation the rest of us knelt, sliding off the pews to our knees. My heart was pounding. My eyes were fixed on the angel sent to save us. Then, without warning, my excitement shifted into something else. Fear. My brother Jamie must have felt the same, because he grabbed my hand, trembling. I glanced at little Lukas, who slept soundly in my mother's tight embrace.

Sylous started forward, his slick shoes clicking across the creaking wood. All the way to the stage, where Harrison knelt. He stepped up to the podium and turned to face us, eyes moving slowly across the pews.

When they met mine, I was sure he'd peeled back my skin and was seeing what hid inside me. I wanted to look away, but I couldn't. None of us could.

"The purity of your hearts has been acknowledged," he began. "You are ready to see what few have ever seen." His voice was gentle and kind, with unmistakable authority. "Will the bride say yes to Jesus?"

"Yes," Rose whispered from where she knelt.

Then others and all: "Yes."

"Then you are ready," Sylous replied.

A long beat of silence held us on edge.

"In three years' time, because the world has turned away from holiness, the world's sin will rise up against them in monstrous form and destroy the wicked."

The floor under our knees began to vibrate. The old wooden pews shook, knocking against the floorboards. I was aghast, terrified, but Sylous continued without a concern in the world.

"Today you will be shown a foretaste of the destruction to come so you might be delivered. Seeing what you see today, you will seek refuge away from the world and wait for that day of reckoning. When it comes, you will be spared in a safe haven as you wait for the world to be cleansed of sin."

Dust fell from the ceiling onto my shoulder, and a back pew rattled loose enough to slap against the floor. A shutter to my left fell from its hinges. Hands were extended everywhere, searching for something sturdy as the building felt like it was going to collapse.

"For then those with eyes to see and vigilant of faith will be spared from destruction and inherit the earth as the pure bride under the law of a holy God."

With the last utterance of the prophecy, the shaking stopped and, but for dust in the air, all was still again. My mother was breathing heavily beside me; Jamie's hand was clenching mine with enough force to leave a mark. Only little Lukas remained oblivious in his deep sleep—how, I have no idea.

"Now I give you eyes to see," Sylous said.

The sound of rushing wind filled the church. It surrounded us, behind and in front, to the right and to the left. What the rest of the world couldn't see, we saw.

And what we saw struck terror in our hearts.

Screams ripped through the chapel. Cries for protection, weeping from some. All in the blink of an eye, as what couldn't possibly be real closed in around us.

My bones rattled and my skin went numb. No one could experience what visited us that day and remain the same.

Through all the chaos, Sylous's words whispered through my mind.

Now I give you eyes to see.

And so we saw.

Rachelle Dekker is the Christy Award–winning author of *The Choosing, The Calling,* and *The Returning* in the Seer series. The oldest daughter of *New York Times* bestselling author Ted Dekker, Rachelle was inspired early on to discover truth through the avenue of storytelling. She writes full-time from her home in Nashville, where she lives with her husband, Daniel, and their son, Jack. Connect with Rachelle at www.rachelledekker.com.

Connect with

RACHELLE

Sign up for Rachelle's newsletter and more at
RACHELLEDEKKER.COM